Cursed

Cursed

MARISSA MEYER

FEIWEL AND FRIENDS
New York

A Feiwel and Friends Book
An imprint of Macmillan Publishing Group, LLC
120 Broadway, New York, NY 10271 • fiercereads.com

Our books may be purchased in bulk for promotional, educational, or business use. Please contact
your local bookseller or the Macmillan Corporate and Premium Sales Department at (800) 221-7945
ext. 5442 or by email at MacmillanSpecialMarkets@macmillan.com.

Library of Congress Control Number: 2022907405

First edition, 2022
Book design by Michelle Gengaro-Kokmen
Feiwel and Friends logo designed by Filomena Tuosto
Printed in the United States of America

ISBN 978-1-250-61891-7 (hardcover)
ISBN 978-1-250-88762-7 (B&N edition)
1 3 5 7 9 10 8 6 4 2

This one's for the writers, the dreamers, the creators—
from one storyteller to another.

Be still now, and I will tell you a tale.

It begins deep within Verloren, the land of the lost. From the time the first humans were buried in damp, fertile earth or sent out to sea on burning pyres, their souls have been guided into Verloren by the eternal lantern of Velos, the god of wisdom and death. Taken to rest and to dream and—once a year, beneath the Mourning Moon—to return as spirits to the mortal realm and spend one night in the company of their loved ones left behind.

No, no, of course that does not happen anymore. This was a very long time ago. Hush, now, and listen.

Though Velos has always been the ruler of the underworld, there was a time when the god was not alone. Monsters roamed the dark kingdom, and spirits filled the caverns with laughter and song.

And then there were the demons. Wicked beings, the embodiment of all things foul and cruel, made of mortals' sin and shame. When humans passed through the gates into Verloren, these despairs drained out of them, step by step, staining the bridge that connected our world to the next and dripping into the river beneath. It was from these poisoned waters that the demons were born, flesh and beauty—crafted from the regrets and secrets and selfish deeds that mortals carried with them after death. Today, we call these demons the dark ones.

Their numbers swelled as centuries passed, and with time the dark ones grew restless. They yearned for independence. Thirsted for a life beyond the shimmering caves and misted swamps of Verloren. They went to Velos and asked to be allowed to travel forth into the mortal realm, to gaze upon the constellations of stars, to taste a salty wind on their tongues, to feel the press of warm sunlight on their ice-cold skin.

But Velos ignored such pleas, for even gods can be foolish.

Or perhaps it was not foolishness, but cruelty, for the god to keep the demons thus imprisoned, century after century. Or perhaps it was wise, for having been born of wickedness, the demons were capable of nothing but envy, brutality, and deception. Perhaps the god already knew the truth: There was no place for these creatures among humans, who—despite their many faults—had also shown that they could lead lives full of goodness and grace.

The dark ones stopped asking for freedom, and instead—clever things—they waited.

Hundreds of years they waited.

Watching and listening and planning.

Until one Mourning Moon, when the sky was so thick with clouds the moon's swell was shrouded from view. While Velos held their lantern aloft at the gates, showing the lost souls the way to return to the world above—the dark ones suddenly surged forward.

They cut through the throngs of waiting spirits. Slaughtered what beasts tried to stop them. They were prepared for the hellhounds, Velos's beloved servants, having cut strips of their own bodies' flesh to lure the hounds to their side. It worked. With the hounds placated and the god unprepared, the demons overtook the bridge.

In a desperate attempt to stop the horde, Velos shifted into their beastly form— the great black wolf that even today is said to guard Verloren's gates. The beast was as big as a house, with fur like ink, massive, protruding fangs, and twin stars like burning flames buried deep in each eye socket.

But the dark ones were not frightened.

The one who would become Erlkönig, the Alder King, lifted a bow that he himself had crafted from the bones of heroes and the ligaments of warriors. From his quiver, he took an arrow—its fletching made from the fingernails of dead children, its head cut from the hardened tears of their mothers.

The demon nocked the arrow into place, took his aim, and let it fly.

Straight into the heart of the god of death.

The wolf roared and stumbled from the bridge, down into the depths of the thrashing river below.

Where Velos fell, the arrow that had pierced their heart stuck deep into the riverbed, where it would take root. Where it would grow, pushing past the bridge and through the gates. A great alder tree that would never stop reaching for the sky.

Velos would not die that day, if gods can die at all. But while the god of death lay powerless in the river below, the dark ones stormed overhead, their king at the helm. They emerged into a pitch-black night. Torrents of rain splattered upon their glorious faces, while the Mourning Moon hid behind lightning and thunder, choosing not to bear witness to the horrors that had just been unleashed upon the mortal world.

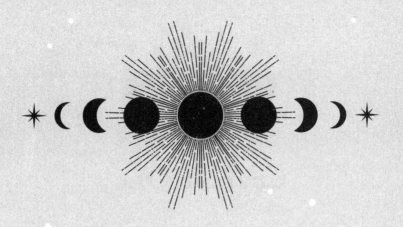

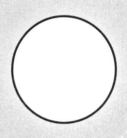

THE
SUMMER
SOLSTICE

Chapter One

Serilda stopped telling her tale, checking to see if the children had finally fallen asleep.

A moment passed, before Nickel opened bleary eyes. "Is the story over already?"

Serilda shifted toward him. "You should know by now," she whispered, pressing down a lock of his fluffy blond hair, "that the best stories are never truly over. I would argue that 'happily ever after' is one of my more popular lies."

He yawned. "Maybe. But it sure is a nice lie."

"It sure is," she agreed. "Now hush. It's time to go to sleep. I'll tell you more tomorrow."

He posed no argument, just rolled onto his side to make more space for little Gerdrut, who was sandwiched between Nickel and Hans, with Fricz and Anna splayed at awkward angles at the foot of the bed. The five children had taken to sleeping in Serilda's bed, even though they had been given their own cots in the servants' halls. She didn't mind. There was something about their cluster of tangled limbs and open mouths, blue-tinged eyelids and muttered complaints that someone was hogging the blankets that filled her heart with something close to contentment.

How she did love these children.

How she hated what had been done to them. How she tortured herself with guilt, knowing it was her fault. Her and her traitorous tongue and the stories she couldn't stop telling. The imagination that had carried her away on so many fancies ever since she could remember . . . yet had brought her nothing but trouble. A life full of misfortunes.

The worst misfortune of all—the lives taken from these five precious souls.

But they kept asking her to tell her tales, so what could she say? She could deny them nothing.

"Good night." She tugged the blankets up to Nickel's chin, covering the spot of blood that had leaked through his nightshirt over the hole in his chest, where the Erlking's night ravens had eaten his heart.

Leaning forward, she brushed a kiss to Nickel's temple. She had to bite back a grimace at the sensation of cool slipperiness on his skin. As though even the gentlest touch might crush his skull, as if he were as brittle as autumn leaves in a child's fist. Ghosts were not delicate beings—they were already dead, and not much more harm could come to them. But they were caught somewhere in between their mortal forms and decaying corpses, and as such, it was as though their figures could not decide where to end, what amount of space to occupy. To look at a ghost was a bit like looking at a mirage, their outlines shifting and blurring into the air. To touch one felt like the most unnatural thing in the world. A bit like touching a dead slug, one that had been left to rot in blistering-hot sun. But . . . colder.

Still, Serilda loved these five little ghosts with all her being, and even if her body was missing, trapped in a haunted castle, and she could no longer feel her heart beat, she would never let them know how much she wanted to pull away every time one of them wrapped her in a hug or slipped their dead little hand into hers.

Serilda waited until she was certain that Nickel was asleep and Gerdrut had started to snore, quite impressively for such a tiny thing. Then she eased herself off the bed and dimmed the lantern on the bedside table. She approached one of the leaded windows that overlooked the great lake surrounding the castle, where evening sunlight shimmered on the water.

Tomorrow was the summer solstice.

Tomorrow she would be wed.

A light tap at the door interrupted Serilda's thoughts before they could fall into despair. She paced across the carpet, keeping her footsteps light to avoid disturbing the children, and opened the door.

Manfred, the Erlking's coachman and the first ghost Serilda had ever met, stood on the other side. There was a time when Manfred had served the king and queen of Adalheid, but he had died in the massacre when the Erlking and his dark ones murdered all the inhabitants and claimed the castle for themselves. Manfred's death, like so many, had been brutal—in his case, a steel chisel through one eye. The chisel was stuck in his skull even now, the blood dripping slowly, eternally, from his eye socket. After all this time, Serilda had begun to get used to the sight, and she greeted Manfred with a smile.

"I wasn't expecting you this evening."

Manfred bowed. "His Grim has requested your presence."

Her smile fell fast. "Of course he has," she said, her tone sour. "The children have just fallen asleep. Give me a moment."

"Take your time. I don't mind making him wait."

Serilda nodded knowingly and shut the door. Manfred and the other ghosts might be serving the dark ones, but they loathed their masters. They tried to find small ways to annoy the Erlking and his court whenever they could. Small acts of rebellion, but rebellion all the same.

She retied her long hair into twin braids. It occurred to her that many girls, upon being summoned to the side of their husband-to-be, might pinch some color into their cheeks or place a dab of rose water along their collarbone. Whereas Serilda was tempted to sneak a dagger into her stocking on the chance she might have an opportunity to stick it into her betrothed's throat.

She cast one more glance at the children, noting how they did not exactly appear to be sleeping. They were too pale, their breathing too still. In rest, they looked utterly dead.

Until Gerdrut's head drooped to one side and she let out a sound like grinding millstones.

Serilda bit her lip against a laugh, remembering why she was doing this.

For them.

Only for them.

Turning away, she slipped out into the stairwell.

Serilda had memorized the route to the Erlking's chambers, but she was nevertheless grateful for Manfred's company as they made their way through the corridors, lit with torches and hung with eerie tapestries that depicted the most grotesque scenes of hunting hounds and ravaged prey. She was growing accustomed to the ominous, haunting shadows that filled the castle halls, but she doubted she would ever feel comfortable here. Not when any corner could reveal a dark one sneering at her or some other-worldly monster watching her with hungry eyes.

Soon she would be queen of this place, but she doubted even that would bring her much security. The ghouls and creatures that had been here long before her made it clear in their haughty expressions and snide remarks that they would sooner devour the skin from her bones than bow before a mortal queen.

She tried not to take it personally.

"Is everyone eager for the festivities to be over?" Serilda asked as she and Manfred wound their way through the labyrinthine halls.

Manfred responded in his usual monotone. "Not at all, my queen," he said. Opposite to the dark ones' indifference—perhaps, in part, *because* of it—the ghostly servants had adapted quite graciously to Serilda's rise in station. Many had already begun to use royal titles when they addressed her—*Majesty* and *Queen* and occasionally even *Your Radiance*. "My understanding is that many have seen the wedding preparations as an enjoyable distraction."

"Distraction from what?"

He glanced sideways at her with his good eye, a subtle smirk making his gray-speckled beard twitch. "Our lives," he said dryly. Then, with a shrug, he added, "Or lack thereof."

Serilda frowned. Though Manfred and many of the ghosts had been dead for centuries, it was obvious how their deaths remained open wounds. Literally, in many cases.

"Manfred," she said slowly, "do you remember serving the former royal family? The ones who lived here before the dark ones came?"

"I remember little of life in the castle before. But I do recall feeling"—he considered his words a long moment, and appeared oddly wistful when he finally said—"proud. Of my work. Though what I had to be proud of, I could not say."

Serilda offered him a soft smile, which quickly shuttered his expression back to stoicism. She was tempted to say more, to push him on this, to urge him to remember something, anything—but it was useless. All memories of the former royal family had been eradicated when the Erlking cursed the prince and his name, erasing the royal family from history.

She found, in trying to get to know the resident ghosts, that the closer someone had been to the royal family, the fewer memories they had of their lives before the massacre. A maid who scrubbed pots and pans in the scullery might remember her former life almost in its entirety, but someone who had regularly been in the presence of the king and queen, or prince and princess, would remember almost nothing.

No one else knew it, but their prince was still here among them. A forgotten prince.

These days, the people of Adalheid knew him as Vergoldetgeist. The Gilded Ghost.

Others called him poltergeist. Gold-spinner.

Serilda knew him simply as Gild. The boy who had gone along with her lies, spun straw into gold in order to save her life, again and again. Who had unwittingly crafted the golden chains that the Erlking planned to use to capture a god.

Even Gild's own memories had been stolen from him. He could

remember nothing. Not of his life. Not of his death. Nothing from the time before he was a cursed boy, a poltergeist trapped in this horrid place. The Erlking had even erased his name from all of history—from the books to the gravestones. Gild had not known he was a prince until Serilda told him the truth of what had happened to him and his family. Him, cursed. The others, dead. Murdered, all in an act of vengeance against the prince who had killed Erlkönig's great love—the huntress Perchta. To this day Gild acted skeptical whenever Serilda mentioned it.

But Serilda didn't care about any of that. Not his name. Not his legacy.

She cared that Gild was the father of her unborn child.

She cared that once, in a fit of desperation, she had promised this unborn child to him, in return for his help spinning straw into gold.

She cared that she was a little bit in love with him.

Maybe—more than a little bit.

"I imagine you were very important," she said as she and Manfred passed a series of parlors. "Higher ranking than a coachman, for sure. The king's valet, perhaps. Or a royal adviser. That's why you can't remember much. But I am sure that you have every reason to be proud."

Manfred remained quiet. She had told him, during their nightly walks, a little bit of the story of what had happened here. To the royal family. To *him* and all the people who had been unfortunate enough to be in this castle when the Erlking exacted his revenge. There was a time when she had told the story to Gild, believing it all to be a made-up fairy tale, but now she knew it was true. A gift from Wyrdith, her storytelling godparent, no doubt.

None of this castle's tragic past came as much of a surprise to those who had been forced into servitude to the dark ones for hundreds of years. They knew *something* horrible had happened to them. Many had the wounds to prove it. Some had fleeting memories of life before. They wore clothes befitting various roles in the castle, from chambermaids to pages to fancy courtiers, though former status meant nothing to the dark ones.

It was no far stretch to assume they had been serving royalty when the

Erlking took over and murdered them all, even if they could not recall their monarchs' faces or names or whether they had been respected and loved.

No one knew that Gild, the meddlesome poltergeist, was their forgotten prince. She dared not tell anyone the truth. She could not risk the Erlking finding out that she knew, and she couldn't trust anyone to stay silent. Much as she liked many of these spirits, their souls belonged to the Erlking. He might allow them some freedoms, but ultimately, they obeyed him.

They had no choice.

It was the same with the children left sleeping in her chambers. The Erlking pretended they were a gift for her. Attendants for his queen. But they were also his spies. Or they could be, if she gave the Erlking any reason to spy on her.

She couldn't trust anyone in this castle.

Anyone, except—

Ahead of them, a glint of gold caught her eye. A tiny thread looped around the base of a candle on one of the wall sconces. The tiniest detail, easily missed by anyone. By everyone.

But these past weeks, Serilda had grown accustomed to searching out tiny details.

She stood straighter. "Thank you, Manfred, but you needn't escort me the rest of the way. I can find it from here."

"I do not mind, my lady."

"I know you don't. But I have to learn my way around this maze eventually, don't I? And I could use a moment . . . to steel myself."

A touch of pity flashed over his features. "Of course, my lady," he said, bowing. "I will leave you be, then."

"Thank you, Manfred."

He walked away with the same unyielding posture and measured steps with which he always carried himself, and Serilda couldn't help but think of him as one of the few true gentlemen in this castle, surrounded by the demons and all their callous frivolity.

As soon as he'd turned the corner, Serilda let her shoulders relax. She reached for the candlestick and slipped the knot of golden thread up and over the flame. She wrapped it around her finger as she studied the hall.

Silence and shadows.

"Come on out, Gild," she said, smiling. "I know you're there."

Chapter Two

Summoned to the king's chambers yet again?"

The voice came from behind her, so close she imagined the tickle of warmth on the back of her neck. She did not startle. She was used to Gild's sudden appearances. His spirit had been cursed and bound to this castle like hers was, but he could move freely within its walls, able to vanish and reappear at will anywhere he liked. It was a marvelous magic trick, and he used it often—to pull pranks, to sneak up on people, to eavesdrop and spy. He especially loved to jump out and frighten the children, sometimes even passing right through them, since he could walk through ghosts. They pretended to be angry, despite their bewildered giggles.

He had been trying to teach Serilda the skill as well, but it was more difficult than he made it seem. So far she'd only managed it once, and though she'd tried to transport herself to the queen's boudoir, she'd ended up in the buttery instead, along with a vicious headache.

Despite Gild's closeness and the subtle dance of breath against her skin, there was an edge to his voice. An envy he had tried to keep from her since the king first announced their betrothal, but that became more apparent as the wedding approached.

Serilda hated lying to him about this. It was the most difficult lie she'd ever had to tell.

Gild knew that the Erlking wanted a mortal wife so that he could father a child. Gild assumed—and Serilda let him—that her frequent visits to the king were for this purpose, though the mere idea made her want to claw off her own skin.

What Gild didn't know, and she could never tell him, was that she was already with child. That she had been since the night Gild pressed his lips to hers, trailing kisses along her jaw, her throat, the swell of her breast. They had been intimate only once, and Serilda still shivered when she let herself remember his closeness, his touch, the way he'd whispered her name like poetry. That night, in their passion, they'd conceived a child.

But the next time she'd seen Gild, the Erlking had him strung up on the castle keep with golden chains—the same gold chains he himself had spun in an effort to save Serilda's life. As soon as the king learned of Serilda's condition, he'd concocted this scheme: to marry her and claim the child as his own. If she told anyone the truth, he would never free the souls of the children she loved to Verloren. They would be trapped here, enslaved to the dark ones, forever.

She couldn't let that happen, which meant she couldn't risk telling anyone.

Not even Gild.

Especially not Gild.

"Yes," she said, once she was sure her voice would not tremble. "I have been summoned to visit with the monster yet again." She turned and met Gild's eye. "Lucky me."

She made no effort to hide her disdain for her betrothed, not with Gild. This arrangement with the king was never her choice. It was not to be a marriage of love. She wasn't even sure it could be called a marriage of convenience, as it certainly wasn't convenient for *her*. This was the man who had abducted her mother when Serilda was just a toddler, left her father for dead, and murdered five innocent children just to spite her—and that barely touched upon his multitude of evils. Families torn apart, lives discarded at his whim, magical creatures hunted—some to extinction.

She could not keep Gild from being jealous. He believed the Erlking had claimed her hand in marriage and her body in his bed. She might not have been able to tell him the truth, but she would never allow him to think that she felt anything for the Erlking beyond revulsion.

She had to play along, had to keep up these lies, so she might eventually get what she wanted: freedom for the children's souls. The Erlking had promised to release their spirits—Hans, Nickel, Fricz, Anna, and Gerdrut. He would grant them peace.

In exchange, she would lie for him. She would say the child in her womb belonged to him. She would keep their secret.

But she would not feign love for a man she despised. There were some lies even she could not tolerate.

A shadow flashed across Gild's face and she could tell he felt properly chastised. His shoulders hunched. "I hope he—" he started, but paused, lips tight as though he'd bitten into a lemon. It took him a moment to try again. "I hope he's a . . . *gentleman.*"

Gentleman was spat out like a lemon seed, and for some reason, Serilda's heart softened. She knew he was trying to understand, to *accept*, as well as he could.

Swallowing hard, she settled a hand on his wrist.

"He does not hurt me," she said.

Which was true, in its way. He had never hurt her physically . . . excepting the time he'd cursed her by stabbing a gold-tipped arrow through her wrist. He hardly touched her when they were alone, in stark contrast to the gross affection he showed her in the presence of others. Serilda sometimes wondered what the court thought of the whole situation. Their king— beautiful, tranquil, dangerous—apparently pining for her. Mortal and plain by anyone's estimation, with strange golden wheels overlaid on the irises of her eyes. In the mortal realm, her eyes had marked her as someone to be avoided. She was strange. She was cursed. She would bring misfortune on anyone who got too close to her.

But the dark ones and their king did not harbor these superstitions. Perhaps because *they* were often the misfortunes that humans were so afraid of.

Maybe the demons assumed it was her anomalies that the king was attracted to.

The lines on Gild's brow eased, but only slightly. He gave a curt nod, and it hurt Serilda—an actual sharp pain beneath her ribs—that she could not say more.

True, the king did not hurt her. She would not be warming his bed, not tonight or any night. She would not be giving him a child, at least not in the way Gild suspected.

It isn't true, she wanted to whisper. To lean forward and nuzzle her cheek against his temple. To press him against the wall and mold her body to his. *I am not his. I will never be his.*

But I still want to be yours.

She said nothing, though, and released Gild's wrist before continuing her journey through the castle halls.

Toward her waiting groom.

Gild followed with soft footsteps, and she couldn't help being glad that he hadn't vanished. It was torture to be around Gild while she harbored these secrets, but it was far worse to be without him. At least when he was near, she could imagine that he felt this way, too. A shared agony. A mutual desperation. A longing for what they'd once had. What had felt, for an achingly brief moment, like it might become something more.

They came to a crossed path at the end of the hall, and she couldn't recall if she ought to turn left or right. She stood, struggling to remember, when Gild sighed quietly and gestured to the left.

She smiled at him, shy and grateful, but the misery on his face constricted her chest. There were gold specks in his eyes, catching on the firelight. His copper-red hair was unkempt, as if he'd spent the last week dragging his hands through it rather than a comb. The row of buttons on his linen shirt was uneven, a hole missed.

She didn't really decide to do it, so much as her hands were on the fabric of his shirt before she could stop them. Undoing the misplaced button.

Gild went statue-still beneath her touch.

Warmth flushed across Serilda's cheeks, even though it was a phantom blush. She had no heartbeat, no real blood pumping through her veins anymore, thanks to the curse that had separated her spirit from her mortal body. But she was well acquainted with embarrassment and, these days, even more with yearning.

The button popped free in her fingers, which had started to tremble. She smoothed out the material, aligning the two sides of his wide collar against his throat.

Gild inhaled sharply.

Her fingers stalled, lightly gripping each side of the collar, now revealing his bare throat, the dip of his clavicle, pale freckles at the top of his chest.

She could lean forward. Kiss him. Right there on that bared skin.

"Serilda . . ."

She glanced up. Countless thoughts were written in his eyes, echoing her own.

We can't.

We shouldn't.

I want this, too.

She pressed the pad of her thumb against those freckles.

Wishing.

Gild shut his eyes and tipped forward, pressing his forehead to hers.

Tensing, Serilda hastily did up the buttons. "I'm sorry," she breathed. "I know we can't . . . I know."

If anyone saw them . . . if there was even the slightest rumor that Serilda was unfaithful, bringing the parentage of her child into question, the Erlking would see her punished for it.

Which almost certainly meant that he would punish the children.

She pressed her fingers against Gild's chest one last time, before pulling away.

"I shouldn't keep him waiting," she whispered. "Much as I might wish to."

Gild swallowed. She traced the action with her gaze, the struggle within his throat, as if he were biting back words that wanted to choke him.

"I'll walk you the rest of the way."

"You don't have to."

He smiled—a little wistful, a little cheeky. "There are monsters in this castle, in case you hadn't heard. If something happened to you, I would never forgive myself."

"My protector," she said teasingly.

But his expression darkened. "I can't protect you when it really matters."

Her chest tightened. "Gild—"

"I'm sorry," he said hastily. "It won't matter. Once we find our bodies. Once we break this curse."

Serilda slipped a hand into his and squeezed his fingers tight. It was the one thing that gave either of them hope. The chance that they might find their bodies and snap the arrows in their wrists, breaking the curse that kept them tethered to this castle. That they might someday be free. "We will," she said. "We will break this curse, Gild."

His grip tightened briefly, but he was the first to pull away. "You should go," he said. "Before anyone sees us and tells the king that you've been cavorting with the poltergeist."

Chapter Three

The first thing Serilda thought when she had seen the king's chambers, some weeks before, was that he was a man who knew how to meet expectations.

There was no bed, which led Serilda to believe the dark ones never slept, though she'd never outright asked. There was, however, an array of exquisite furniture. High-backed chairs and elegant sofas, all upholstered in the finest of fabrics and trimmed in black rope and tassels. Tables inlaid with mother-of-pearl and ebony wood. Thick fur rugs that were so large she shuddered to think what creature they might have come from.

A cabinet of wonders against one wall held a curated collection of animal skulls, unusual weaponry, marble sculptures, hand-painted pottery, leather-bound books, grotesquely leering masks. There were the usual antlers and horns and taxidermy hung above tapestries, but here he also kept small, dainty creatures. Warblers so lifelike they seemed like they could start singing at any moment. Sprightly foxes that could have scampered right off the wall.

The opposite wall was hung with a lavish collection of maps. Some appeared ancient, drawn onto animal skins and parchment. Some featured places in the world that Serilda had never heard of, that she wasn't entirely sure were real, with flourishing depictions of the strangest of mythical beasts, their names written in neat penmanship and faint red lettering. *Inkanyamba*, a long serpent with a horselike head. The giant *Buto Ijo*, a fanged green troll.

Gumiho, a nine-tailed fox. Serilda loved to study the creatures, loved to trail her fingers over the words and sound out the unfamiliar names on her tongue. She couldn't help but wonder if they were real. If they lived somewhere far away. She'd seen enough creatures on the dark side of the veil, creatures she'd once thought were only in fairy tales, that she would believe just about anything.

All in all, the rooms were dark and a little gloomy, yes, but cozy in their own bizarre way. If there was a piece of wood, it was ornately carved and polished to a rich, glossy sheen. If there was a scrap of fabric, from the drapes to the cushions, it was black or deep jewel tones and of the very finest quality. If there was a candle, it was lit.

And there were *lots* of candles, so that the room gave the impression of a god's altar at a busy temple.

The thing that most held Serilda's attention in the Erlking's chambers was the tall floor clock that stood within an alcove near the hearth. It had a brass pendulum that was longer than Serilda was tall, and a face that tracked not only the time, but also the cycles of the moon and the yearly seasons. Four hands ticked slow and steady around the circle, each one carved from delicate bone. Serilda couldn't help watching it when she was in the room.

In part, perhaps, because she, too, was counting the minutes until she could leave.

When she arrived on the evening before the summer solstice, a table had been set by the balcony, containing a carafe of burgundy wine, a block of cheese next to a loaf of dark bread, and a bowl overflowing with crimson cherries and glossy apricots. She had once assumed that the dark ones, especially those who partook in the wild hunt, must hunger constantly for the meat of their prey. She imagined them dancing around great slabs roasted over fiery pits, flames hissing with the fat that dripped from the bones, crisp char edged along the haunches of wild boar and stag. And there *was* plenty of meat eaten in the castle, but its occupants had more refined tastes as well, and fresh fruit was in constant demand. Not unlike at home, when there was such a rush of delight when the orchards and fields grew colorful with plums, figs, and wild berries—such a luxury after a hard winter.

The Erlking stood at the window. In the distance, a waxing moon hung above the Rückgrat Mountains, its light shimmering across the black mirror surface of the lake.

Serilda claimed one of the upholstered seats at the table and helped herself to a cherry. The flesh burst in her mouth. Sweet and the tiniest bit sour. She didn't know how a proper queen was supposed to dispose of the pit, so she spat it into her fingers and dropped it into an empty wineglass before helping herself to another.

And a third.

She thought of what everyone else in this castle *thought* was happening in this room right now, and it made her want to laugh. If only they could see how their supposedly lovestruck king spent most of their evenings completely ignoring her.

Then she thought of Gild, and how what he *thought* was happening was probably tearing him apart, and she quickly sobered.

"How fares my progeny?"

She started. The king was still turned away from her, his raven-black hair trailing loose down his back.

Your progeny does not exist, she wanted to say. *This child is not yours. Will never be yours.*

Instead, she pressed a hand to her stomach. "I feel no different. If I'm being honest, I'm beginning to wonder what all the fuss is about." She spoke lightly, to disguise the very real concerns that had started to bubble up inside her. "I'm hungry all the time, but that's nothing new." She grabbed a nectarine and bit into it. When the juice dribbled down her chin, she wiped it away with her sleeve and kept eating, ignoring the king's disapproving gaze upon her.

If Erlkönig wanted a queen schooled in courtly etiquette, he'd chosen poorly.

"Is there a midwife in the castle?" she asked. "One of the ghosts, perhaps?

Surely the previous royal family employed one. I have so many questions. It would be nice to have someone to talk to."

"A midwife," the Erlking repeated, and Serilda could tell the idea had never occurred to him. "I will find out."

Serilda licked a drop of juice from her wrist before it could reach the cuff of her sleeve.

Snatching a napkin from the table, the king tossed it at her. "Try to improve your manners. You are going to be a queen, and my wife."

"*Your* choice, not mine." She ignored the napkin and took another bite of the nectarine. When she was finished, she grinned and dropped the stone of the fruit into her glass beside the cherry pits. She then used her velvet skirt to wipe the sticky residue from her fingers, one by one. "But if you're embarrassed by me, there is still time to change your mind."

His expression cooled, which was a feat, given its usual iciness. "At least I will not have long to tolerate you. Six months. Barely a blink."

She prickled at the implication. Surely he should at least try to hide his intention to kill her once she'd served her purpose?

Out of spite, she broke off a hunk of cheese and shoved it into her mouth, knowing full well it was the king's favorite. She was still chewing when she asked, "Will we share your chambers once the ceremony is done?"

The king scoffed. "Absolutely not. We will continue on as we've been until we can announce the pregnancy. There is no need for anything more."

Serilda exhaled. She'd been dreading that question for weeks, and she felt dizzy with the relief of knowing she would not have to sleep here, with him. They would just go on pretending.

For now, she could do that.

How long had she been there? She glanced at the clock. Barely ten minutes had passed. It felt like ages.

"I wonder if we should have held the wedding ceremony on the Lovers' Moon," he said. "Choosing the solstice had a poetry to it, but it seems my bride has grown impatient."

"It is not impatience that I feel."

"You have not dreamed of being a summer bride?"

She snorted. "I'm *not* a summer bride. I'm a summer sacrifice."

The Erlking laughed. It was a rare sound, and one that always gave Serilda a twinge of satisfaction, even though she didn't want it to.

The sad part was, she meant it.

This was not to be a wedding. This was to be a ritual sacrifice, and she was the lamb. When the time was right, he would slaughter her and take her child, who she somehow already loved with a ferocity unlike anything she'd ever known.

Serilda rubbed her fingers across the scar on her wrist. In truth, the sacrifice had already been made, from the moment the Erlking thrust a gold-tipped arrow through her wrist and put a curse upon her soul, splitting her spirit from her mortal body and tethering it to this haunted castle, trapping her here, on the dark side of the veil.

She had witnessed her body lying on the floor of the throne room, breathing, yet lifeless. Serilda didn't fully understand the magic. She could no longer feel her pulse or the steady drum of her heartbeat. She could hold her breath for an eternity, and yet she continued to breathe from habit, or comfort.

And then there was her unborn child, who she could only hope was all right. She felt none of the symptoms of pregnancy, the bouts of stomach sickness or the aches in her back and ankles that she remembered women in Märchenfeld complaining about. She did not know if the baby was *physically* inside of her, even now, or if it was growing in the corpselike version of her, hidden away in this castle.

She had to trust that the Erlking would not have done anything to harm the child, given his plans for it, and she very much hated having to put her trust in him.

Finally abandoning the window, the Erlking reached for his wineglass. He hesitated, his eyes lifting to hers.

"What?" she asked. "I didn't poison it." Then she gasped. "Though perhaps I should try that next time."

"I suggest wolfsbane, if you do. I've always found the aftertaste to be mildly sweet and quite satisfying." He lifted the glass to his lips, studying her while he took a sip. When he lowered the glass, he said, "You see yourself as a storyteller, if I'm not mistaken."

Serilda sat straighter, feeling a little vulnerable that the king might have noticed this quiet, hidden part of her. "I've been called worse."

"Then tell me a story."

She scowled. "I am not in the mood. And don't try to order me around. I am not one of your ghosts."

His lips curled, amused. "I only thought it would pass the time." His attention turned meaningfully to the clock, as if he'd noticed her watching it.

She huffed. "Actually, there is a story I heard long ago and I've always wondered if it was true. They say that the Lovers' Moon was named for you and Perchta."

The Erlking cocked his head at her, but did not reply.

"As the tale goes, it was beneath that moon that the two of you shared with each other your truest names, therefore tying your fates together for eternity. That is why some people share their secrets beneath the Lovers' Moon, because supposedly, the moonlight will protect them."

"Superstitious nonsense," he muttered. "Any idiot should know that if you wish to protect a secret, you should speak it to no one, no matter which moon you're under. But you mortals give such power to fairy tales. You believe fate is determined by old gods and superstitions. That every misfortune can be blamed on the moonlight, the stars, whatever ludicrous thing suits you in the moment. But there is no fate, no fortune. There are only the secrets we share and those we conceal. Our own choices, or the fear of making a choice."

Serilda stared at him. How many times had the villagers of Märchenfeld blamed their misfortunes on her?

Yet she couldn't ignore that she was the goddaughter of Wyrdith. She had been cursed by the god of stories and fortune, and to say that those things were of no importance didn't feel entirely true either.

Perhaps there was something in between.

A place for things that were out of control, things guided by destiny . . .

But also, for one's own choices.

Dread welled inside her. The tragedy was that she wanted to believe in choices. She wanted to believe that she could have control of her fate. But how could she? She was a prisoner of the Erlking. She had made choices and she had made mistakes. But in the end, her fate had been decided for her.

The irony. How Wyrdith must be laughing, wherever they were.

"So," she started uncertainly, "the story isn't true, then?"

He scoffed. "That Perchta and I shared names beneath the Lovers' Moon? Hardly."

"Shame. I thought it was romantic."

The Erlking shook his head as he refilled his wineglass. "We do not need fairy tales to distort our romance. Perchta and I . . . our love was destined from the beginning. I am incomplete without her by my side."

Serilda stilled, embarrassed by his candor.

It didn't help that she knew the Erlking intended to bring back Perchta. On the Endless Moon, that rare night when the winter solstice overlapped with the last full moon of the year, the Erlking and his wild hunt planned to capture one of the seven gods. And when the first rays of sunlight struck the realm, that god would be forced to grant a single wish.

The Erlking would use this wish to bring Perchta back from Verloren. The cruel huntress would once again walk the earth, and he would have Serilda's baby ready to hand over to her. The Erlking had kidnapped many children in attempts to please her, but never before had he given her a newborn babe.

The thought of it sickened Serilda. To him, the life growing inside her was a thing to be wrapped up and given away. A doll, a toy, a thing easily discarded.

And while she might not have met the huntress, from all accounts, Perchta was not the motherly sort, despite her yearning for a child of her own. They said she was ruthless and haughty and cruel. Whenever she tired of one of the children gifted to her, the Erlking would take him or her out into the woods, and he would return alone.

That was the way of the dark ones.

That was the mother her child was destined for.

That is, except for one little problem. A small caveat that the Erlking himself didn't yet know.

She had already promised this child to Gild. Her firstborn, in exchange for him spinning a roomful of straw into gold. The bargain was struck with magic. She did not think it could be broken.

But she wasn't about to tell that to the Erlking.

She would figure it out, she told herself. She still had six months to come up with a plan. To save her child. Herself. Gild. The children asleep in her room.

"How thoughtless of me," said the Erlking, startling her from her thoughts. He paced around the table until he was standing beside her chair, then dropped to one knee beside her. "To be pining for another when my bride sits before me. I hope you can forgive me, *my love.*"

"Of all the things you might apologize for," she drawled, "telling me that you are in love with a sadistic demon who died three hundred years ago would not even make the list."

His jaw twitched. "Keep that fire, little mortal," he said, taking her hand into his cool fingers and bending over it. "It makes it easier to dote on you."

He stood and grabbed an untouched nectarine from the table. He took a bite as he towered over her. Juice dripped down his chin as it had hers. He grinned smugly and used his sleeve to wipe it away. "Another ten minutes, I think, before you can see yourself out."

Picking up his wineglass, he turned his back on her, which was exactly the moment Serilda had been waiting for.

In one motion, she grabbed the silver-handled knife on the table and drove it into the Erlking's back, right between his shoulder blades. She felt the give of flesh. The crunch of vertebrae.

The king stilled.

For a long moment, Serilda wondered if maybe, just maybe . . . *this time . . .*

Then he took in a long breath and released it—a slow, drawn-out sigh.

"Please," he said, "remove the knife from my back. I would hate to ask Manfred to do it. *Again.*"

Serilda cursed beneath her breath and yanked the knife out. Rather than blood dripping from the wound, there was a wisp of black smoke that dissipated into the air.

She scowled. The first time she had stabbed him, she'd been sure he would fight back.

But he hadn't even tried.

That first knife had gone into his side, just beneath his ribs.

The next time she'd tried, it had been a knife to his stomach, or approximately where she thought his stomach should be.

The third time—she hit his heart, and she'd been so proud of herself for her exceptional aim, she'd squealed with delight.

The Erlking had merely rolled his eyes as he pulled the knife out and held it up to the light. Spotless, as if it hadn't just been buried in his chest up to its hilt.

Serilda dropped the knife onto the table. "The next will be to your head," she said, petulantly crossing her arms. "Maybe I'll take out one of your eyes, like one of your hunters took out Manfred's."

"If it makes your time here more tolerable," he said, taking a sip of his wine, "then do your best."

Chapter Four

Anna was supposed to be Serilda's lady-in-waiting, but as she was only eight years old and had the attention span of a housefly, she was not particularly adept at her role. Instead, on the day of the summer solstice, two ghost attendants wearing blood-drenched aprons arrived in Serilda's chambers to mold her into something resembling a queen. Or a bride.

Or rather . . . a demon huntress, as it turned out.

Serilda had been expecting a gown. Many of the dark ones enjoyed dressing themselves in luxurious fabrics, and she had imagined the king would procure some lavish spectacle of a dress for her to wear during the ceremony.

But no—when the maids swept in, they were not carrying silk and brocade and voluminous skirts. Rather, they brought her a leather tunic that laced up over a flaxen blouse. Riding breeches and arm braces, goatskin gloves and the softest boots she had ever worn. Most notably, they brought her a finely crafted crossbow—smaller than the Erlking's, but with bolts just as sharp. Serilda was afraid to touch the weapon for fear she would accidentally bump the trigger and send an arrow straight into someone's head. No one in this room needed any more open wounds than they already had.

"Lovely," said Serilda, who had tried repeatedly to persuade her groom to give her any details about the wedding ceremony, with no success. "Please tell me I'll have the pleasure of putting an arrow into my husband's heart by the end of the night."

The children laughed.

The servants exchanged uncertain looks, and one answered, "I do believe there is to be a ceremonial hunt, of sorts."

Serilda groaned. "I might have guessed."

Soon, she was seated at the vanity, her twin braids hastily undone and oil rubbed into her hands and cheeks, which made her smell a bit like the larder. All the while, Anna and Gerdrut practiced flips on the mattress, and Nickel and Hans played a game of dice they'd been taught by the stable boy, who was a few years Hans's senior and had taken an instant liking to them all.

Serilda peered into the looking glass that hung above her vanity. In the dim candlelight she could see the golden wheels on her black irises. When she had first met the Erlking, he had mistaken them for spinning wheels, which was why it was so easy for her to convince him that she was blessed by Hulda and could spin straw into gold. But no—she was marked with the wheel of fortune. She was the godchild of Wyrdith, god of stories and fortune and lies.

It should have been a blessing, given that her father had helped the god years ago on an Endless Moon. But in reality, her cursed tongue had brought mostly misfortunes upon her and the people she loved.

If she ever had cause to meet Wyrdith, she would smash that wheel of fortune over their ungrateful head.

A knock was followed by Fricz—her "messenger"—bursting into the room. "Is she ready?" he asked, directing his question to Anna at first, even though Anna was upside down in a handstand, her feet on one of the posters of the bed for balance. "Never mind," he said, turning toward Serilda and the attendants. He took in her hair, now done in an intricate single plait down her back, and the riding gear laid out on a tufted chair. "Best hurry, or the king might start murdering people out there."

"Who is he going to murder?" asked Anna, her pigtails trailing on the carpet. "Everyone here is already dead."

"Why is he upset?" asked Serilda. "I'm not late. Not yet."

"And it isn't like they can start without her," added Anna. She dropped her feet back to the floor and stood up.

"We are working as quickly as we can," said one of the attendants, dabbing something from a small pot onto Serilda's lips. "It would be easier without so many distractions." She sent an unsubtle glare at Anna and Gerdrut.

Fricz shrugged. "It's the poltergeist, I think."

Serilda stiffened. "What about the poltergeist?"

"He's gone missing. Some guards were sent to catch him this morning, meant to keep him chained up during the ceremony. You know, so he can't cause trouble like he does. But no one can find him. Some of the servants are saying he might try to interrupt the ceremony."

"I hope he does!" said Gerdrut, hopping up onto the bed, which was high enough that her legs dangled more than a foot off the floor.

"Remember when he replaced the taxidermy in the north wing with rag dolls and turnip heads?" asked Nickel, eyes shining. "It must have taken him ages to carve them all, but the look of surprise from the hunters was priceless."

The children started bantering stories between them, and Serilda couldn't force back her smile. In the time since the Erlking had killed them and abducted their souls, trapping them here in this castle, Gild and his antics had made quite the impression.

A small part of Serilda sparked with hope at the idea that Gild might stop the ceremony. Being rescued on this dreadful day sounded very appealing, even a little romantic.

That, and she hated to think of Gild being chained up again like one of the king's prized beasts. Serilda suspected the Erlking would have happily left him strung up on the keep for a century or two if he hadn't wanted the golden chains back to use on his hunts. That, and Gild had made such an obnoxious ruckus, hollering drinking ballads for hours, that even most of the dark ones agreed it was better to let him go free.

Serilda never wanted to see him tied up like that again.

And yet—she had a deal with the Erlking. Her compliance, and her child, in exchange for freeing the souls of these children she loved. Hans,

Nickel, Fricz, Anna, Gerdrut. Serilda had to marry the Erlking. Give him the child. It would destroy her when the time came, but it was her fault these darling children were here, and not home with their families, planning for their long, uncomplicated futures.

Biting her lip, she squeezed shut her eyes and sent a silent wish to Gild, wherever he was.

Don't ruin this. Not today.

"All finished," said the attendant, stepping back from Serilda's hair. "Let's get you dressed."

She was in a daze as she let the attendants guide her behind a screen and show her how all the pieces of armor fit together. Serilda was not comfortable in hunting gear, but as soon as she was bustled back out into the room, the children gathered around her, wide-eyed and impressed. Except Hans, who was the serious sort, and lately had sunk into a dour disposition that Serilda didn't know how to remedy. Not that she could blame him. He was old enough to know that no amount of enchantment in this haunted castle could make up for the lives that had been stolen from them.

"You look like a warrior!" said Gerdrut, ogling her, one of her front lower teeth missing. The first, and last, milk tooth she would ever lose.

Serilda couldn't help feeling a sense of satisfaction to be called a warrior, of all things. To be someone capable of more than spinning unhelpful tales.

"No," said Hans quietly. "She looks like a hunter."

They were just the right words to dampen the mood. The lights dimmed in the children's eyes, and Serilda felt her heart sink again into the dread that had plagued her ever since the Awakening Moon, the night that had sealed her fate.

She swallowed hard. "Nothing is going to change. It's only a silly ceremony."

"A silly ceremony," said Hans, "that will end with you being the Alder Queen."

"I will always just be Serilda to you," she said, tousling his hair—as much to make him squirm away in annoyance as anything.

"No, you won't be the Alder Queen," said Nickel. "Not to us. That makes it sound like you belong to him, and I won't accept that. We'll come up with something else."

"The Golden Queen!" said Gerdrut. Beaming, she reached for Serilda's hand. "You can make something from nothing. You can spin straw into gold."

Serilda's breath caught. As she couldn't have the children accidentally tell the Erlking the truth, she'd had to maintain the lie that she was a gold-spinner, even with them. But Gerdrut's comment reminded her of that day, many months ago, when they had gathered in the shelter of a pine tree, surrounded by banks of snow, and listened to Serilda tell them a tale of the wicked Erlking and the huntress Perchta. That day, Gerdrut had been the one to liken Serilda's storytelling to the magical gift of gold-spinning.

Looking back, Serilda could see that was the day everything in her life had changed. She pressed a kiss to the top of Gerdrut's curls, then drew the others tight against her. She ignored the shudder that scuttled across her skin at the feel of them all, their bodies like brittle leaves ready to crumble. She was grateful to have them close, dead or otherwise.

One of the attendants cleared her throat and pulled open the door. "Forgive me, my lady, but we should not keep His Grim waiting any longer."

Chapter Five

Serilda did not know what to expect from her nuptials. When she asked the Erlking, he told her there was nothing for her to do but be a happy bride. To which she responded that, since for her to be happy would not be possible, perhaps she would just sleep through it all and he could send someone to wake her when the feast started. She'd been trying to annoy him, but the Erlking had merely laughed.

Like she was *joking*.

She tried not to worry. It didn't matter if she had to say some absurd vows about love and eternity. It didn't matter if he gave her a ring or kissed her or did anything else to sell the spectacle. This marriage was a farce. Nothing was going to change.

He could claim her hand in marriage, but her heart would always be her own.

Well, except for the part where her heart was trapped inside her physical body and hidden away somewhere and she might never see it again until her baby was born and it was too late.

She was led over a high bridge that she had never crossed before to a portion of the outer wall she had never walked, a reminder that the castle was so vast, and so full of nooks and crannies, rooms and towers where her and Gild's bodies might be kept.

She walked down a set of steps, into a long narrow corridor. The day was sunny and warm, but even now these windowless halls held a chill. The leather of her hunting uniform made soft groaning noises with every step, and though a part of her felt ridiculous in armor and breeches, another part of her felt shockingly bold, almost brave. No one could touch her, and if they dared try, she had a loaded crossbow to ensure they'd regret it.

Her entourage paused at a doorway hung with a heavy velvet curtain. They held the drapes aside, ushering her through.

Serilda stepped out onto a stone balcony and her burgeoning confidence immediately began to crumble. Her muscles tightened.

The balcony stood two stories above the northeast gardens. She had spent little time on this side of the castle, where the grounds were largely utilitarian, housing the dovecote, the infirmary garden, the groundskeeper's cottage, a small orchard, and a vineyard.

Now a field of sorts had been set up below, fully fenced in by wooden posts. The grounds around the enclosure held the entirety of the Erlking's court. She saw Manfred, the coachman, his impaled eye dripping blood as he looked up at her with an expression that was just a touch sadder than his usual indifference. She spied the bruised stable boy, whose head was lowered, fingers fidgeting with the hem of his tunic. The headless woman had traded her usual riding gear for a simple gown and tied a scarf around her neck to hide the wound, though her blood had already seeped through the fabric.

And there were the dark ones, who were so breathtaking it almost hurt to look at them. But theirs was a hollow beauty, absent of compassion and joy. Most appeared bored, even irate, as they glowered up at her. She returned a smile.

Gild was nowhere to be seen. She wondered if the guards had managed to capture him after all. Perhaps he was even now bound up in golden chains. The thought made her ill.

She hoped he was all right, hidden away somewhere safe.

She hoped he wasn't planning something disastrous.

And then there was a tiny, ridiculous part of her that wished he were here. Not in the audience, watching this spectacle of a nightmare play out. But *here*. On this balcony. Taking her hand into his . . .

Foolish, foolish.

The balcony she stood on had been decorated for the ceremony. The stone rail was hung with a garland of roses the color of claret wine. The balusters ornamented with posies of sage and lamb's ear tied with black lace. Gold and black banners decorated the castle walls, and spicy incense burned below, trailing a heady perfume into the air. The overall effect was lush and decadent and might even have been thrilling to Serilda, if the groom hadn't been a cruel tyrant that murdered children and mythical creatures for sport.

The moment she thought it, she spotted the balcony directly opposite her, jutting out from the wall of the castle keep, lavishly decorated like her own. The curtains parted and the king stepped out. He was dressed in fine leather armor and tall black boots, just as he had been the first time she met him, on the night of the Snow Moon.

A hunter, and a king. The sight filled Serilda with equal parts awe and disgust.

"My bride," he said, his honeyed voice carrying across the silence that stretched between the keep and the castle wall. "You are as radiant as the solstice sun."

"Charming," she responded, unflattered, as she set the small crossbow on the rail. "In Märchenfeld, we have a tradition of shattering a bunch of clay dishes right before a wedding ceremony in order to frighten away wicked spirits. I would suggest we start with that, but we might lose half our guests."

"No dark one has ever been frightened off by broken platters and soup bowls. But the idea does amuse me." He flashed a simpering smile, one that might have tricked their onlookers into believing that he did so dote on his strange human bride. Was anyone fooled? Was this charade even necessary?

Surely no one believed there was any love between them. It would require an imagination far beyond her own, and that was asking a lot.

"Our customs," he continued, "are a little different."

"I gathered as much," said Serilda. "I've never been to a wedding where the bride and groom were first handed deadly weaponry."

"Then you have never lived," said the king, stroking the curve of his own crossbow. He looked down at the crowd below. "Welcome all. I am honored at your presence in witnessing the union between myself and the lady I have chosen for my eternal companion." He raised an arm. "Release the game."

Down below, a series of carts were pulled toward the large fenced area, each one loaded with crates. As the crates were opened, dozens of animals were released onto the course. Hares, pheasants, a couple of boars, and two small deer. Ducks, geese, and quail. A mountain goat, half a dozen sheep, even a peacock, who unfolded its fan of bright-colored tail feathers as soon as it was free of its cage. A dozen partridges spread their wings and flew up into the boughs of a fig tree, unbothered by the fence that kept the other animals caged.

Lastly, from the largest crate, emerged a single enormous stag with glorious antlers reaching toward the bright afternoon sky.

The animals scattered across the field, some hiding in what shelter they could find, others meandering about the yard, befuddled and frightened. There was a cacophony of squawks and honks and snuffles. The mountain goat claimed a corner of the yard for itself and was quick to lower its horns threateningly toward any creature that dared to approach it.

"Our custom is simple," said the Erlking. "You shall make a vow to me and take a shot. If your aim is true, then so shall be your words, and the vow will be considered unbreakable. When our vows are complete, then we shall all feast on our happy sacrifices." He swept his arm toward the animals.

A sour taste gathered on Serilda's tongue. She had eaten meat all her life, and she had no qualms about visiting the butcher in Märchenfeld or enjoying roasted pork during a feast or cooking up a hearty beef stew for her and

Papa. But she had never been hunting. Never been the one to shoot an arrow into an animal's heart or drag a knife across its throat.

But she supposed this was the way of life and death, predator and prey.

"My bride," said the Erlking. "You may have the honors of making the first vow."

She lifted an eyebrow. "With pleasure," she said. "There are so many things I might say to you."

Below, the dark ones tittered in a way that made her fingers tighten around the crossbow.

The king smiled back, but his gaze carried a warning. A reminder that they had an audience.

Nonsense with sauce. She had promised to carry on the lie that she bore his child. She had never promised to pretend to be in love with him.

"I vow," she started, "that so long as my spirit remains detached from my physical body and I am given no other choice in the matter, I shall remain *resentfully* by your side. Now, let's see." Surveying the animals, she chose a target that she knew she had little hope of hitting—a pudgy quail that was skittering back and forth across the yard.

Serilda took the crossbow into her hands, rather liking its heft and the sense of power it gave her. She took her gaze off the bird to look up at the Erlking—not intending it as a threat, but not able to keep away a flash of fantasy. What would happen if she shot this bolt straight into his head?

She would probably miss. Even if she didn't miss, it wouldn't kill him.

Though it *would* be satisfying.

As if he knew what she was thinking, the Erlking grinned at her.

Serilda scrunched her nose, turned her attention back to the quail, and took the shot.

The bolt struck the dirt. It wasn't even close.

Their audience laughed, but Serilda wasn't bothered. She hadn't really wanted to hit it.

"I vow to you," said the Erlking, drawing back the bolt on his own weapon, "that I shall never forget the many great sacrifices you have made in order to be a part of my court, to be my wife, to spend eternity at my side."

Serilda scowled. As if he hadn't taken everything from her. As if her sacrifices had been by choice.

The Erlking pulled the trigger. The bolt struck a wild boar straight through the side of its head. The death was so quick, it did not even squeal with pain.

Serilda shuddered.

It took her a moment to realize she was expected to make another vow.

She sighed. "I vow," she said, glaring at her groom, "to never again let you lead me before the entire court without first telling me what it is you expect of me. I've had no time to prepare for this ceremony, my lord."

She aimed for a turkey this time.

And missed, no closer than the first shot had been.

The Erlking shrugged. "I've been under the impression that you enjoy making things up as you go along." He held her gaze as he went on, "I vow to cherish you, body and soul. That my adoration and desire for you shall continue to grow with every passing moon."

A chill swept over Serilda.

The king sounded almost . . . sincere.

He waited, his gaze fixed intently upon her in a way that brought unwelcome heat rising to her cheeks.

She wanted to snarl in response. What game was he playing now?

Finally, he looked away. He had barely glanced down toward the yard before his finger squeezed the trigger. This time, he claimed a goat for their feast, as swiftly as he had the boar.

"So much for a true shot making for an unbreakable vow," she muttered, hoping the Erlking wouldn't see how he had unsettled her. "I vow that on the best days of our eternal marriage, I shall continue to find your presence almost tolerable."

This earned another round of laughter from their audience, and this time, it wasn't the mean laughter that had come from her failed shots.

Serilda did not bother to aim. What was the point?

Holding the Erlking's gaze, that tight smile on her lips, she pointed the crossbow toward the yard and fired.

A scream of pain echoed up from the yard. Startled, Serilda nearly dropped the weapon off the balcony.

She had struck the stag, but it was not a killing blow. The bolt had buried itself in the stag's abdomen, and it reared back on its hind legs, its enormous black eyes rolling in its head.

Serilda gasped. Nausea swirled inside her as the stag bucked and jolted, trying to free itself from the pain. "No . . . I'm sorry," she said breathlessly, tears gathering in her eyes.

Across the yard, the king clicked his tongue. "It is unmerciful, my queen, to leave an innocent creature to suffer."

Nostrils flaring, she glared up at him. She wanted to snarl and snap, to ask how many innocent *creatures* he had let suffer in all his years as the leader of the wild hunt. She could think of five such precious souls who were suffering still, not to mention the countless ghosts that wandered these castle halls, or her own father, who had been left to rot on the side of the road, only for his corpse to be reanimated as an insatiable nachzehrer.

Or her mother—her mother, who had been taken by the hunt and never seen again.

But she bit back her anger and resorted to pleading instead. "Please," she said, "put it out of its misery. I did not mean to . . ." Hot tears blurred her vision. "Please do not let the suffering go on."

The Erlking did not move.

She wanted to strangle him. But she wanted this to end more.

She swallowed back her bile. "Please. My . . . dear husband."

One corner of his mouth lifted, and she could sense his temptation to draw out this moment. To let her go on pleading.

But hardly a breath had passed her lips before she heard the *thunk* of his crossbow.

The bolt went into the stag's skull and it collapsed, lifeless.

Serilda wilted, relieved and yet horribly, horribly sad. And suddenly so very tired.

The feast would go on all the night, she had been told. But she did not know if she could even make it to sundown. All she wanted was to throw off this constraining hunting gear, crawl into her bed, and sleep until all memory of the solstice and this sham of a wedding had passed.

But there would be no such respite.

So instead, Serilda raised her chin and forced bitter words from her mouth. "Thank you, my lord. You are a merciful king."

He inclined his head toward her. "Make any wish of me you like, for surely I could deny you nothing, my love."

She couldn't help the ireful laugh that escaped her. Obviously, he was lying. He would never grant any wish that did not suit his own desires.

It was only with his next words that she realized he had not framed that promise under the guise of one of his vows.

"My final vow to you, my mortal queen," he said, voice carrying over a crowd that had grown eager with the death of the stag, "is that I shall never again take your presence for granted." His tone softened, and Serilda frowned. Never *again*? "I vow that every moment of your company shall be held as dear to me as god-spun gold, as precious as fleeting mortal lives. I vow that even with an eternity to have you by my side, I shall never tire of seeing your eyes cast in moonlight and your lips kissed by the sun. With you at my side, I can never feel lost, never feel loneliness, never feel the endless agony of a life without purpose. With you at my side, I am complete, and I dedicate all my life to loving and completing you."

At some point in his speech, Serilda's lips had parted. She stared at him, unblinking. Sure that if she had a heart in her chest, it would have stopped beating. A hush had fallen over the castle grounds. Even the squawking and braying of the animals had fallen eerily silent in the stillness of such a proclamation.

The Erlking regarded her, as if waiting. But what was she supposed to say to that? This was a mockery of love. He had no true feelings for her. She was merely a pawn to him. And yet, he sounded like he meant it, and Serilda—simple mortal girl that she was—could not help but feel light-headed to be the recipient of such poetry, spoken in that voice that sounded like a song even when he was making threats on her life.

"You . . . forgot to take a shot," she managed.

Eyes glinting, the Erlking raised his crossbow.

Aiming it straight at her.

Serilda's eyes widened. "What are you—?"

The loud *thunk* of the weapon. The whistle of the bolt.

Serilda screamed and ducked.

A bird squawked.

Something fell on the rail beside Serilda, mere inches from her elbow.

A puff of gray and brown feathers drifted past her face.

Serilda gaped at the dead partridge.

The king's laugh echoed off the castle walls. "We are wed! Chefs—prepare the feast!"

Chapter Six

Serilda had been instructed to wait in the corridor until she was summoned, so that she and her husband could enter the feast arm in arm—a spectacle to the last.

But she didn't mind waiting. She was in no hurry. With all the servants preparing for the night's celebrations, she was blessedly, unusually alone.

For the first time in weeks, Serilda felt like she could exhale.

It was done.

She was married.

She was the Alder Queen.

What she felt wasn't relief so much as resignation. More than seven weeks had passed since the Erlking announced that she would be his bride, and though she'd believed he meant it—along with all the other threats he made—she'd still retained a desperate hope that it might not come to pass. Something would stop the wedding or the Erlking would change his mind or . . . or *something*.

But now it was done.

She need not waste another minute hoping her fate might be avoided. Now she could turn to what she'd vowed to do: persuade the Erlking to give peace to the five children who had been brought here because of her.

And perhaps, also, find some way to save her unborn child.

And if she could manage it, it would be lovely to break the curses. Her curse. Gild's curse. The curse that had made the world forget the royal family that once lived here.

Somehow.

"My wife."

Serilda startled and looked up from the bench she'd been waiting on to see the king standing in the golden light of one of the hall's few windows. She often thought he seemed unreal in the daylight. The Alder King was the sort of being that ought to be cast always in shadow. Whose portrait could only be captured in charcoal and the blackest of inks. Whose countenance might inspire poetry, but it would be poetry filled with words like *melancholia* and *sepulchral* and *bereft.*

She stood. "My lord."

He held his elbow toward her. "The festivities await."

She eyed his arm, clad in a billowing black shirt. For a moment—the briefest of moments—she wanted to ask him about the vows. What had he meant by them? Had he meant them to be genuine, or were they merely a part of their farce?

Serilda shuddered. It was easier to pretend that his words of eternal devotion had not affected her in the slightest.

To admit otherwise would be insufferable.

And so, Serilda swallowed back her questions and tucked her fingers into the crook of her husband's arm.

They walked toward the stairs that would take them down into the gardens beside the main courtyard, where there was to be music and dancing and feasting—not only on the animals from the ceremony, but on countless dishes the cooks had been preparing all week.

But they had just turned into the narrow stairwell when they came to an abrupt stop.

A piece of rolled-up parchment dangled eye level to the king, tied with a velvet bow and hung from the doorway with a piece of twine.

Serilda blinked. "Did you not see this when you arrived?"

"It was not here," said the Erlking, snatching the parchment from the air. He undid the bow and dropped it to the floor as he unrolled the note. Serilda peered around him to read.

To Erlkönig, Thou Lucky Lord of the Castle,

In honor of traditions most ancient, I see that it is my sacred duty to follow the customs laid out by generations before. Surely, as a man of honor and duty yourself, you understand the importance of maintaining such a valued ritual within the court of Adalheid.

Thus, as we are all in agreement, I am writing you this note as a symbol of goodwill.

Let it be known that our new illustrious queen—may she reign with wisdom and grace—shall not be harmed in the course of this night.

But neither shall she be yours, until a full ransom is paid.

Such ransom I shall convey when I declare that you, Your Grim, have well and truly suffered from the absence of such a charming mortal as you have managed to secure for your wife.

I hope you were not needing her?

Very truly yours,
The Poltergeist

"Poltergeist," Serilda whispered, her lips barely forming the word.

With a snarl, the Erlking crumpled the note in his fist with such violence that Serilda jumped back from him, startled.

"What is that insolent wraith up to now?" he said, glaring around at the empty hall, his porcelain skin flushed a shade of amethyst. Though the Erlking knew Gild was the castle's true prince and heir, he always pretended that Gild was nothing more than a nuisance. Serilda assumed this was because the Erlking didn't want her or the ghostly court or even Gild himself to figure out his true identity. He didn't realize that Serilda had figured it out a while ago.

She glanced around, too, but Gild was nowhere to be seen. "What traditions?" she asked. "What rituals?"

"Nothing but nonsense," said the Erlking. Nostrils flaring, he held a hand toward her. "Come."

"I think not," came a voice from behind them, followed by a rope being tossed around Serilda, cinching her arms to her sides.

She gasped and glanced over her shoulder to see Gild, grinning wickedly with the end of the rope in his hands. "What are you—"

"Until the ransom is declared and paid, your lovely bride is officially . . . kidnapped."

The Erlking started to reach for one of the numerous weapons kept at his belt, but he was not fast enough.

Gild shoved Serilda toward the nearest window and pushed her up onto the windowsill. "Enjoy the party, Your Miserableness!" he shouted.

The lake glittered cerulean and gold before them—but they would crash upon the jagged rocks below the castle wall long before they hit the water.

Gild threw them both into the air.

Then Serilda was falling. Screaming. Wind in her hair and whipping at her cheeks.

But they did not crash upon the rocks.

Instead, she and Gild blinked out of existence mid-fall.

Serilda stumbled as her feet hit hard ground that had not been there before. Instead of vivid sunlight, she was surrounded by tall columns and a dais holding two majestic thrones, lit by a row of candelabras.

She would have fallen to her face had Gild not been gripping the rope. He hauled her up to standing and made quick work of untying her.

Then he let out a whoop of laughter. "His face! That was everything I'd hoped for!"

Serilda turned to him, bewildered and trembling. In the span of half a minute she'd gone from being led to her wedding feast on the arm of her wicked husband to being kidnapped and shoved through a window where she should have fallen to her death, to being magically transported into the castle's throne room.

"What did you do?" she asked, her voice still shaky. "And why? What are you—"

"I'll explain later," said Gild, yanking the ropes off her. "Come on, we need to keep moving. He'll know we were sent back to the throne room."

He grabbed her hand and raced for a narrow door tucked behind the dais, where presumably servants might have waited to heed the monarch's summoning. Beyond the door, a dim, narrow corridor stretched in the direction of the kitchens.

"Gild, stop," said Serilda, even as her feet hastened to keep up with him. "What are we doing?"

"Just a fun little wedding tradition," he said, coming to a stop as the corridor branched off into a T. He peered around both sides, before waving for Serilda to follow him. He turned right, hurrying down a hall, then up a flight of steps that ended in a closed door. Gild put his ear against the wood, listening.

"What wedding tradi—"

He shushed her, frantically waving his arms.

Serilda crossed her arms over her chest.

A moment passed, then Gild looked at her, eyes glinting, and nodded for her to go on.

This time, she whispered. "What wedding tradition?"

"You know," he said, "the one where the bride is kidnapped and spends all night hiding from the groom until he's forced to pay a ransom for her return."

She stared at him. *"What?"*

Gild cocked his head. "Don't they do that in Märchenfeld? It's great fun. You'll see."

She shook her head. "The Erlking will not think this is *great fun*, and you know it."

"You're right, he won't." Gild snickered. "But I will." His eyes widened and he held up a hand, urging her to be silent again.

They listened, and it took Serilda a moment to pick up on the footsteps. At first she thought they were coming from beyond the shut door, but no, they were coming from the corridor behind them.

Gild's eyes widened as he realized it at the same time.

He shoved the door open and took Serilda's hand again, pulling her through.

The door slammed in their wake.

"There!" someone yelled.

Serilda started running, Gild beside her.

It took a moment to get her bearings, but as they ducked in and out of parlors and studies and game rooms and libraries, all the while hearing the storming of dark ones in pursuit, Serilda found she didn't much care if she was lost. Or if she was kidnapped, for that matter.

Every time they barely evaded detection—

Every time Gild pulled her into an alcove and their pursuers unwittingly sped past—

Every time they simultaneously dove beneath a desk or behind a curtain, their bodies pressed as tightly together as they could, as they struggled to contain their panting breaths and the giggles that threatened to overtake them—

Serilda wished that she might never be found.

"I think we lost them," she said some twenty minutes later, as she and Gild pressed against the back wall of a tall cabinet filled with fur cloaks and moths. "For now."

Gild gave her hand a squeeze, a reminder that he had not let go. Not even when she tripped and had been sure the game was up. He'd just laughed and urged her on, overturning a couple of tables to slow their pursuers as they made their escape.

"We shouldn't have done this," said Serilda, catching her breath. "He will be angry. It was too big a risk."

"It will be fine. He can't exactly blame you for your own kidnapping, can he? Besides, he expected me to try something. It would have been more notable—and suspicious—if I'd behaved myself."

Serilda laughed. She could not see Gild in the darkness, but she could exactly picture his expression. Proud to the point of cockiness. She could practically *feel* him winking at her.

She wanted to argue, except he had a point. The king *had* expected him to try something.

"Consider this my wedding gift to you," he went on. "You can't tell me you'd rather be stuck in a stuffy old party with your dearly beloved and his sycophants."

Serilda slumped against the back of the cabinet, even though some paneling dug painfully into her shoulder blade. "You're right. I much prefer this company."

"And if he didn't want me to kidnap you, then he should have invited me to the feast. It was the least he could do."

"Gild, are you doing this because you felt left out?"

"Wouldn't you? I've been spying on the cooks for days. This feast is going to be incredible. How would you feel if you were the only one in the castle who didn't get to enjoy it?"

"They do like their grand celebrations, don't they?"

"And they've got surprisingly good taste. The best of everything. Straight down to the serving dishes. Stoneware from Ottelien. Blown glass from Verene. Even the soup ladles are fancy, with these intricate little carvings."

"They were probably hand-carved by Hulda," said Serilda. "I bet they've got magic properties, those soup ladles."

"Wouldn't doubt it. The cutlery was probably forged by Tyrr. The bread baskets woven by . . . Freydon?"

"Hmm, probably Hulda again."

"Being the god of labor sounds like a lot of work."

"To be fair, I suspect most everything in this castle probably belonged to your family once."

Gild hesitated. "Hadn't thought of that, but you're right. I must come from such tasteful folk."

They were met with a short silence, and Serilda wondered if he was still thinking about the feast, or the family he couldn't remember.

"I can't help but worry," she said, "about what he might do once he finds us."

"No need to worry, Your Luminance. I have everything under control."

Serilda frowned, doubtful.

"Don't give me that look," he said, and she laughed again. It was far too dark for him to see her. "Everything *is* under control."

Serilda scooted closer so that their shoulders were touching. "They are hunters, Gild. And we are trapped inside a castle on an island that we cannot escape. He will find us."

"The point isn't to evade him forever," said Gild, tilting his head to press his brow against hers. "Only until sundown."

"What happens at sundown?"

"The veil falls and the feast begins. But they can't start without the bride, which means he'll have to pay your ransom, which means bargaining with me. The poltergeist. He will be very embarrassed. And *that* is the point."

Serilda considered this. "All this, just to humiliate him?"

"You say that like it's a petty goal."

"Well . . . it is. A bit."

"I can't kill him," said Gild. "I can't defeat him. I can't keep him from marrying you. Let me have this, Serilda."

She wilted. "All right. Until sundown, then."

Sundown.

It wasn't that far away. An hour at most.

An hour.

What would they do for an hour?

She inhaled sharply, suddenly aware of just how confined this cabinet was. The heavy cloaks pressing against them. The wooden walls squeezing them in together. The length of his arm against hers. The warmth of his palm. The way her skin tingled with every accidental touch.

If they were accidental at all.

What *could* they do for an hour . . . ?

Gild cleared his throat and scooted an inch away from her, which was all the space he could move. "Those were, um—" he started, then cleared his throat a second time. "Some pretty intense vows, during the ceremony. Almost romantic, even."

It was as if he'd known exactly what to say to chill the feelings that had started to simmer inside her.

She released his hand and pulled back toward her corner of the cabinet.

"Just another one of his games," she said, wishing she weren't already so flustered, for her wavering voice did not make the statement sound particularly sincere. "He was mocking me."

"Yeah. Yeah. That really sounded like mockery."

"Gild, you know I don't love him. I could never love him. Or even *like* him. I would never choose him if I had a choice."

"Of course," he said. "Of course I know that."

But she wasn't sure if she believed him.

"He killed my father," she said, more forcefully now. "He killed—"

"Hush!"

"No, Gild, you have to—"

"Serilda!"

She froze, hearing it, too, now. Howling.

They had released the hellhounds.

"Great," whispered Serilda. "How long before they find us?" She hesitated, considering. "*Can* they find us? We're spirits. Can they still smell us?"

"Us, maybe not," said Gild. "But I bet they can smell that ridiculous costume you're wearing easily enough."

Serilda pressed a hand to the sides of her leather jerkin. She'd forgotten about the hunting gear. "You don't like it?"

Gild's response was a grunt, which she did not know how to interpret. "You know," he said, "this would be easier if you could just . . ."

Serilda heard a finger snap.

Then, silence.

"Gild?" She reached for him, but her hand met empty space, then the back of the wardrobe.

A creak of a door was followed by a flood of light. Serilda threw up her arm to protect her eyes.

"Come on," said Gild, reaching in and grabbing her arm. He tugged her out beside him. "Do you think you could try?"

"Try what?" she said, squinting as her eyes adjusted to the pink light filtering in through the windows. Twilight was approaching. "Doing your . . . thing?" She snapped her fingers in imitation.

"Exactly. You've got to learn sooner or later."

"Do I, though?"

"Just try it. Meet me in the gatehouse."

No sooner had he said it than he vanished.

Serilda glowered. "Show-off." But her words were met by another howl, much closer than before. "Fine. No harm in trying."

She squeezed her eyes shut and pictured the gatehouse above the draw-bridge as clearly as she could. Then she raised her hand and gave a snap of her fingers.

And waited.

There was a change in the air, she was sure of it. The light filtering through her eyelids was different, dimmer.

She opened first one eye, and then the other.

Definitely not the gatehouse. Instead, Serilda had transported herself to what had been guardrooms before, but were now mostly for storage and—from the looks of the plain straw cots laid out along the floor—for housing some of the ghosts.

She held still a long moment, listening. When she heard no hounds and no footsteps, she approached the door and opened it a crack, peeking out into a small dining room with a long, narrow table and benches.

A face appeared on the other side of the door, inches from her own.

Serilda gasped and slammed the door shut, hurling herself backward.

She collided with a body that surely hadn't been there before. Arms encircled her. She opened her mouth to scream.

"Shhh, it's me!"

The scream caught in her throat.

Yanking herself away, she spun to see Gild beaming at her. "Sorry," he said. "Didn't mean to scare you."

Pulse racing, she pointed at the closed door. "Was that you, too?"

"Yep. When you didn't show up at the gatehouse, I thought maybe I'd try here. Gatehouse, guardhouse—so similar, right? It happened to me when I was first figuring out how to do this, too. So, it's a start. And we were able to evade capture a while longer."

Catching her breath, Serilda strained to listen again. She thought maybe she heard voices, but they were distant and might have been coming from the far-off courtyard for all she knew.

The courtyard. Where the dark ones who weren't actively involved in hunting down the missing bride would now be gathered.

Where the servants would be gathered, finishing their preparations for the night.

Where the children would be waiting for her.

She swallowed. "Gild . . . I think it's been long enough. He will already be furious, and if he should lash out at the children . . ."

She met his gaze and watched as his easy grin slipped away, replaced with worry. "He'll be angry with me, not you. He wouldn't punish them for this."

"I hope not, but . . . I can't be sure. And neither can you."

He opened his mouth to speak, but hesitated.

"When he killed them," said Serilda, "it was to punish me. Because I tried to escape him. He took them instead." Tears began to gather in her eyes as soon as she said the words and the memory of that awful morning returned. At first she'd thought the hunt had taken the children as a threat, and that the Erlking would return them to their families once Serilda gave herself up.

But then she'd seen the bodies . . .

"It isn't your fault," said Gild. He slipped his arms around her, pulling her against his chest. "He's a monster. You didn't do anything wrong."

She sniffed into his shirt. "Maybe, but even so . . . they're my responsibility now. And if I anger him, I don't know what he'll do."

Gild squeezed her tighter, even as he let out a frustrated breath. "Damn bloodthirsty demon, always ruins everything."

She let out a strained laugh.

"All right. If you're that worried, I'll take you back."

With a nod, Serilda wiped the tears from her eyes. "I wish I could defy him like you, Gild. But I can't. I'm sorry."

"You don't have to apologize for anything." He cupped her face, rubbing his thumbs across her cheeks to catch the tears. "I'll defy him enough for the both of us."

She smiled through her watery eyes. "Now, *that* is a romantic vow."

Gild's face reddened behind his freckles and for a moment, just a moment, with the look he had fixed on her, she was certain he was going to kiss her. She leaned closer, eyes closing.

Gild sighed, an achingly sad sound. Lifting his chin, he kissed her brow instead. So soft she barely felt it.

"All right," he said. "Let's go claim that ransom."

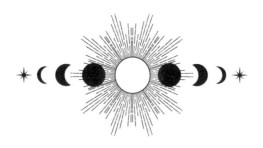

Chapter Seven

Serilda could smell the feast long before she and Gild reached the north side of the keep. Musicians played a pretty but somber tune that echoed through the castle halls. The sound of wavering waldzither strings mostly covered the chatter from the court. In her time in the castle, Serilda had come to think of the dark ones as quiet, dour sorts. They kept to themselves, carrying on conversations in hushed murmurs and slinking through the castle halls like silent shadows. They were ever-present, but their demeanor was that of disapproving glowers and curled lips.

It was always strange to her, then, when they came together for a celebration. Their fetes were not exactly like those in Märchenfeld, which were made up of bawdy songs around bonfires and raucous dances in the village square to music so vibrant no one was spared from tapping their toes in time. But even the dark ones, for all their gloomy dispositions, enjoyed their festivities and might be seen leading one another in intimate dances or calling for another cup of wine as the sun began to rise.

"Wait here," said Gild, when he and Serilda reached a large open window that looked down onto the gardens below.

It would not be long now before the veil separating their worlds dissolved with the fading rays of daylight. Already the sun had descended beyond the western wall, casting them in shadows that felt refreshing after the hot summer day. The gardens were lush this time of year. Clusters of cherries hung on trees like plump gems, and sprawling ground covers crept onto the cobbled pathways.

From this vantage, Serilda could see the servants bringing out last additions for the feast. It seemed every table that could be conjured up from the entire castle was here, now draped in embroidered linens and lit with towering candelabras.

Serilda's mouth began to water at the aroma of onion and garlic, ground mustard seed and rosemary. Fresh-baked breads were arranged into complicated knots, running down the center of each table like a braid, with butter dripping down the golden crust. Parts of the braided dough had been speckled with black and white seeds, some dusted with salty cheeses, and yet others topped with almonds and pistachios. Placed around the ropes of bread were plump summer fruits that shone like jewels. There were tomatoes and asparagus roasted with butter and herbs. Summer squashes stuffed with thin-sliced ham and golden raisins. Pork sausages still sizzling atop a bed of syrupy baked peaches. Roasted nuts beside jars of honey and preserves.

While waiting for the feast to begin, dozens of servants moved among the crowd carrying skins of ale and wine and berry liqueurs.

Two tufted chairs sat in the center of the activity, but only one was occupied. The Erlking sat angled upon his makeshift throne, one leg tossed over the chair's arm, his temple rested against the knuckles of his fist. Despite the casual posture, his face was set with grim annoyance.

"Enough!" he snapped suddenly, flicking his fingers toward the ghostly musicians, who immediately fell silent. "One would think you know nothing but funeral dirges." Something caught his attention and he lifted his chin. A moment later, Giselle—the master of the hounds—strode into view.

"Forgive me, my lord," she said with a bow. "The poltergeist continues to elude us."

The Erlking glowered. "We captured the tatzelwurm, yet we cannot find my queen, who is confined to this castle?"

"You are aware of the poltergeist's tricks," said Giselle. "I suspect your *queen* may be able to move among the castle halls as he does."

"I would mind your words," said the king, fingers dancing across the stock of his crossbow, "or it might seem as though you mean to blame this childish act on my bride, who is nothing more than a hapless pawn in one of the poltergeist's pranks."

Giselle bowed her head. "I meant no offense, I assure you."

The king grunted and gestured toward Manfred. "I will not allow the poltergeist's games to delay us any longer." He gestured toward the far wall, where a waxing moon had just risen into view in the starless sky. "Soon the veil will fall. Let us commence with the feast, with or without my bride."

"Now, now, such haste," rang out a new voice from the gardens.

Serilda blinked and spun around—but Gild was gone. She pulled back the curtain just enough to see the statue of the Erlking that stood in the castle garden, which Gild was now leaning against, arms folded and one foot propped up against the statue's crossbow.

"Those certainly do not strike me as the words of a man who has just vowed eternal devotion." Gild glanced around at the dark ones' annoyed expressions. His pranks had irked more of the demons than just the Erlking over the centuries. "And here I thought you were in love."

Though the Erlking had not moved from his draped position across his chair, his whole body had tensed. He and Gild studied each other, divided by a few rows of boxwoods and tables overflowing with enough food to feed all of Märchenfeld for the rest of the summer.

"You are not welcome here tonight," said the Erlking. He cut a glance toward Giselle, an unspoken command passing between them.

Serilda leaned forward. She did not know when the group of hunters had arrived on the edges of the garden, but she saw them now, stealthily moving through the trees, an occasional flash of gold among them.

She recalled Fricz's message. They had been searching for Gild before the ceremony, intending to tie him up with golden chains. They were ready for him now that he had finally revealed himself.

Gild laughed. "As if I've ever been welcome." He gestured toward the hunters in the shadows. "I see you back there. I won't be caught in one of those traps again."

With that, he disappeared.

Only to blink back into existence perched on the high back of the Erlking's throne.

But not perched particularly well. Losing his balance, Gild cried out and fell forward.

The Erlking made a move to dodge out of the way, but in the next moment, Gild tumbled right into his lap.

"Well, this is awkward—" started Gild, at the same moment the king let out an enraged roar. He grabbed Gild around the throat and stood, dragging Gild up to the tips of his toes. In the next moment, he had a dagger pressed against Gild's stomach.

"What do you want, poltergeist?" said the king.

Gild grabbed the king's hand, struggling against his hold, trying to free himself—

Then he went still.

Smiled.

Winked.

And vanished.

Serilda released the breath she hadn't realized she'd been holding.

"The ransom, obviously," said Gild, reappearing on the Erlking's throne, in a mockery of the king's indifferent posture. "And also, some of that ale might be nice. You have plenty of it." He crooked a finger toward a servant.

The servant cast a wide-eyed look at the Erlking, who gritted his teeth.

Gild sighed. "Fine. Just the ransom, then. As promised, I will release the bride in exchange for . . . Let's see. What *do* I want? I honestly haven't given that part any thought." His attention landed on one of the iron gates that led to the back gardens. "Ah. I will exchange the bride's freedom for the release of the animals in the menagerie!"

A loud *kachunk* echoed off the castle walls, and a crossbow bolt struck the back of the throne—right where Gild's chest was a moment before.

Serilda gasped. It happened so fast, she hadn't even seen the Erlking reach for his weapon. She didn't know how Gild managed to disappear in time.

"Well," said Gild, poking his head out from behind the throne and glaring at the crossbow bolt buried in the tufted brocade, "let's not overreact."

"I grow weary of this game," said the Erlking.

"Come now, it's all in good sport. Something to make the occasion more memorable. Besides, what's a few wild beasts when there's true love at stake? Don't tell me your vows were all a farce. They seemed so sincere." Gild threw his elbow on top of the chair's back, flashing another grin.

"I will pay no ransom," said the Erlking. "I will find my wife when it suits me to do so."

"Oh? You would allow her to miss out on this joyous merrymaking because your pride is too swollen to offer up a few little tokens proving your affection?"

"Little tokens?" The Erlking snarled. "String him up!"

The gold chains came from nowhere and everywhere. Serilda had been so distracted she had not seen the hunters approach.

But Gild must have, for once again, he eluded capture, vanishing the moment the chains swung toward him.

"Fine, fine!" yelled Gild, and it took Serilda and the onlookers a moment to find him, now perched upon one of the garden gates. "How about the dahut, then? Your bride in exchange for one lopsided mountain goat. Surely she's worth that much to you?"

The Erlking looked murderous, still clutching the crossbow, while the hunters awaited his command.

"You wouldn't want anyone to think that your affections for that funny little creature outweigh those for your beautiful bride, would you?" Gild prompted. "As I see it, you can keep failing to capture me, embarrassing as that's been so far, or . . . you can let me have this one small victory and you get to enjoy the rest of your party with your beautiful wife at your side. Can you really say it's a terrible deal?"

They stared at each other in a long, agonizing silence. Gild appeared unconcerned, though Serilda, in her alcove, was trembling. She wondered if Gild sometimes hoped that he might just manage to push the Erlking so far he would decide to be rid of this troublesome spirit once and for all. Perhaps that was the plan, she thought. To annoy the Erlking to the point where he broke Gild's curse himself and sent him on his merry way.

Or—more likely—killed him and let Velos claim his soul.

With the hatred so palpable between them, Serilda wondered that the Erlking had tolerated Gild for as long as he had.

They seemed at a stalemate, and the wedding guests were growing restless. Serilda could tell because many of the dark ones had begun turning their backs on the scene, and a number of the feldgeists, in the forms of cats and crows, had landed on a table and were busily tearing apart a haunch of deer.

Finally, Gild let out a pained groan. "You drive a tough bargain, do you know that? Fine. Forget the dahut. You can have her back for . . ." He cast his gaze around, until it landed on the burgeoning feast. *"That."*

"You are not invited to partake in my wedding feast," the Erlking said through his teeth.

Gild rolled his eyes. "Oh? And we used to be so close."

The Erlking lifted the crossbow again.

"That's sausage to me. I don't want to join you for your pretentious feast," said Gild with a heavy sigh. "I'll give back the bride for *that*. That soup ladle. Right there. The pretty wooden one with the . . . carvings. Are those elderberries?"

The Erlking's frown deepened.

"I mean it," said Gild. "Never had a soup ladle of my own before. And there's a rumor that the utensils here have magical properties. Is it true?"

"I should have skinned you alive when I had the chance."

"I'll take that as a yes. Also, after those vows you said today? You can't tell me she isn't worth it. Magic or not, it is just a ladle."

With those words, the sun descended beyond the horizon, and the veil fell. There was a shimmer in the air, and then the world became a little more vibrant. The cool breeze sweeter. Every sensation suddenly heightened, which was the only way Serilda knew that her existence beyond the veil was dull by comparison. One might grow used to the dreariness, the gray, the lifelessness in the shadows of Adalheid Castle . . . if only one weren't reminded every month what lingered just beyond the veil. What true living felt like.

Down below, the Erlking drew himself to his full height. "Fine. My bride in exchange for the . . . soup ladle."

Gild beamed. He vanished, and reappeared again by the table, grabbing the ladle in question from where it sat unused beside a pot of aromatic summer stew.

"Lovely doing business with—"

A shrill caw interrupted him. Serilda looked up to see a nachtkrapp circling the gardens. It made its plaintive cry again, then settled onto the back of the throne that was meant for Serilda. It cocked its head, one empty eye socket turned toward the king.

The Erlking's eyes narrowed. He glanced once at Gild and smirked.

"You will bring my bride to the courtyard," he ordered. "She and I have a guest to welcome."

Chapter Eight

Serilda did not wait for Gild. With the nachtkrapp's cry still shrill in her ears, she turned and raced through the castle. She was on the opposite side of the keep from the courtyard, but she knew her way well enough that she figured she had a better chance of reaching the entry hall on foot rather than trying to transport herself there and risk getting lost in the undercroft instead.

Gild found her as she was darting through one of the king's favorite halls, lined with the most horrific of tapestries. "There you are!" he cried. "I thought you were going to wait at that window!"

"What did he mean when he said we have a guest?" she panted. "Who would possibly come here on a solstice?"

"I don't know," he said, running to keep up with her. "Been mostly try-ing to find you, but I heard a ghost say something about a human girl."

Human girl. Human girl.

No one she knew would dare come to this castle when the veil was down. Would they?

They reached the entry hall and Gild grabbed her elbow, stopping her in her tracks.

"Serilda, I'm sorry."

She blinked. "For what?"

"About the prank. If he's in a worse mood than usual because of it."

Serilda glanced down at the carved wooden ladle gripped in his other hand. "It was fun while it lasted, wasn't it? But I must go be a queen now."

He stepped back and dropped into a flourishing bow. "Of course, Your Luminance."

Shaking her head, trying to still her racing thoughts, Serilda shoved open the castle doors and emerged into the warm night air.

Already the wedding guests were gathered near the gatehouse, the Erlking at their helm. Serilda heard the crank of the drawbridge as she went to stand beside her husband, pretending that nothing had been amiss. That she hadn't been kidnapped from her wedding festivities and exchanged for a kitchen utensil.

The king cast her a sideways look. "Welcome back," he drawled.

She pressed her lips into a thin smile. "What an exciting day it's been. Did I hear we have company?"

The drawbridge lowered with a heavy clunk. Beyond lay the long stone bridge to Adalheid, the city that had come to feel a bit like a home in the months prior to Serilda's curse. She felt an unexpected twinge of homesickness at seeing the half-timbered buildings along the lakeside, the plaster walls in cheerful colors illuminated by the moon.

Torches lit either side of the long bridge, casting their orange glow across the wooden planks, the cobblestones—and the small cloaked figure in the middle of the walk.

Serilda's brow pinched. She took an uncertain step forward.

The figure stepped forward, too, and peeled back the cloak's hood, revealing brown skin, round cheeks, and thick black hair tied into twin buns atop her head.

Leyna. The daughter of Adalheid's mayor, and one of the first souls who had welcomed Serilda to their town, who had even helped her try to solve the mystery of the haunted castle.

"Is that a mortal child?" mused the Erlking.

Serilda swallowed. "I know her, my lord. She is—was—a friend, of sorts. But she should not be here . . ." She trailed off.

Leyna should not be here. What was she thinking, coming to the castle on such a night? She should be back at the Wild Swan Inn, safely asleep in her bed.

"What luck, then," said the Erlking. "Perhaps she has come to offer her congratulations."

Serilda's frown deepened. There was no way for Leyna or anyone in Adalheid to know of the wedding. She figured they would have assumed that she was dead now, as she had disappeared into this castle nearly two months ago and not returned.

Straightening her spine, she stepped forward. "I will speak to her. See if there might be something that she—"

"Stop."

Serilda froze, more at the tension in the king's tone than because of his command.

She glanced back, and the Erlking dropped his gaze to her feet.

Serilda followed the look. Her toes were mere inches from the wooden planks of the drawbridge.

The invisible boundary of her cage.

"You should wait here, my turtledove," he said, reaching up to tuck a strand of Serilda's hair behind her ear. She grimaced. "I will greet our mortal guest."

"No. Don't. Please—leave her be."

Ignoring her, the Erlking drifted past, his boots soundless on the bridge, his figure cutting in and out of the torchlights like a wraith.

Leyna shrank away instinctively, but in the next moment straightened herself and faced the Erlking with a resolute set to her shoulders. She even dared to take some steps forward. Serilda could see now that she held a small basket in her hands.

When the Erlking was a few steps away, Leyna dipped into a stiff curtsy.

Serilda squeezed her hands into fists. She had to order her feet not to go a step farther, lest her curse transport her straight to the throne room. She could not risk vanishing into the castle now and wasting precious moments rushing back out here. But it was agony to stay put when her murderous, child-stealing husband was approaching one of the few people alive that she still cared about.

In the distance, she could see them conversing, but though she strained to hear, none of their words came to her. She glanced around and noticed Manfred not far away, that look of stoic indifference on his face. Beyond him, she spotted Hans and Nickel, and she could assume the other children were nearby. Hans was watching her, concerned. He had never met Leyna, but he must have been able to tell how upset Serilda was at her unexpected appearance.

Serilda swallowed hard and attempted to replace the horror in her expression with something like pleasant surprise. She looked back across the bridge and felt her gaze harden into brittle ice.

The Erlking had taken Leyna by the hand, an oddly paternal gesture, and was leading her toward the castle.

Leyna's eyes were round as full moons, and though she stood with her head high, she was trembling. Serilda wished she could smile encouragingly at her. But with every step drawing Leyna closer to this castle, this nightmare that lured in lost children and never let them go, thick bile was filling her mouth.

"Behold," said the Erlking, "this small mortal has chosen to meet us on this solstice night in order to deliver a special gift to none other than my new wife."

At this, Leyna stumbled a bit. "W-wife?" she stammered, her voice dry and quiet.

The Erlking beamed down at her, and if he intended any harm to the child, it was impossible to tell from his doting face.

Serilda had heard many tales of the Erlking taking children away from their homes, or enchanting them as they wandered through the forest; yet in all her imaginings she'd pictured these as traumatic events. He would grin evilly, the child would scream and try to get away, only to be chased down by his warrior horse and swept, kicking and flailing, up onto the saddle.

But that impression was almost erased by the gentleness with which the Erlking held Leyna's hand. Leyna, who was perhaps trusting to a fault. Serilda wanted to holler at her not to give in to the Erlking's charms. He was wicked, through and through. She had heard enough stories. Surely Leyna must know that.

"Indeed," said the king. "The Lady Serilda has only this afternoon taken the vows to become my queen."

Leyna blinked. She returned her searching attention to Serilda.

Serilda had no choice.

She pressed her lips tight and nodded.

To her horror, Leyna seemed to relax, a trusting lamb being led toward the waiting demons and ghouls. Though her fear was palpable, so was her wonder as she began to take it in. The castle in its true glory—no longer the ruins she had seen from the shore every day of her life. On the dark side of the veil, it was a masterpiece of architecture. Elegant towers, tall spires, stonework that shimmered beneath the silver moon, the stained-glass windows depicting the seven old gods glowing on the upper floor of the keep.

All the splendor was offset by the monsters lurking everywhere. The ghosts with their fatal wounds that never stopped bleeding. Goblins perched on the roofs of nearby stables, gnawing on chicken bones and watching the newcomer with glowing green eyes. At this very moment, a bazaloshtsh was screeching from the upper floor of one of the watchtowers, its foul cry sending goose bumps over Serilda's skin. She'd become rather used to the assortment of horrible creatures that lived within these walls, but she suspected it all was a shock to little Leyna, as it had been to her when she'd first arrived.

The Erlking paused once his and Leyna's feet touched the wooden planks of the drawbridge.

Leyna was studying the fine hunting gear Serilda wore. The girl appeared confused, perhaps slightly enraptured to be promenaded to the gates of the castle on the arm of none other than the Erlking himself.

She and Serilda stared at each other a long moment.

Then Leyna detached herself from the king and held up the basket. With a shy smile, she said, "Remember? I told you that if you died and became a ghost of the castle, I would bring you honey walnut cakes. Your favorite."

Only then did Serilda catch the familiar scent wafting from the basket, sweet and nutty.

A sob caught in her throat.

Throwing herself at the girl, Serilda scooped Leyna into her arms and lifted her off the ground.

Leyna squeaked and laughed. "I brought you something else, too," she said, as soon as Serilda had set her down. "A book of fairy tales that's been very popular at Madam Professor's library lately. Written by some famous Verenese scholar, I guess. Frieda says she can't hardly keep it on the shelves. She'll probably be mad when she finds out I took her last copy, but . . . I thought you would enjoy the stories."

With tears in her eyes, Serilda peered into the basket. The small cakes were wrapped in a linen towel, and a finely crafted book was nestled in beside them. "Thank you," she breathed. "To you and Frieda both, even if she didn't know you were bringing it. I can't tell you what it means to me . . . to see your face again. Have you been well? How is your mother?"

"Fine, fine," said Leyna, glancing uncomfortably at the Erlking, then around at the court of dark ones and ghosts. "She and Frieda started courting officially a few weeks ago, at long last. But it's been dull without you at the inn. We miss your stories." She gulped. "I thought for sure, if the Erlking kept you, he'd have made you the court's bard or something. And now you're telling me you've gone and married the villain? I thought you planned to kill him!"

At this, the Erlking barked a rare laugh, and the rest of the court followed suit.

"It's a very long story," said Serilda, squeezing Leyna's shoulders. "My goodness. Mortals really do feel lovely, don't they?"

Leyna frowned. "What do you mean?"

Serilda grinned, a moment's joy at seeing her old friend eclipsing her horror. The first night she'd met Gild, he had been speechless when he touched her. He'd never touched a mortal before; he'd known only the eerie wrongness of the ghosts. He hadn't imagined that a person could feel so soft, so warm.

After only a couple of months inside this castle, she understood now what he meant. Embracing Leyna was a bit like being wrapped in a soft-worn quilt on a winter's night.

"It doesn't matter," she said. "You should not be here, you foolish girl."

"I know." Leyna beamed impishly. "Mama will kill me when she finds out."

And though she was joking, the words opened up that same hollow dread in Serilda's gut.

Oh—she desperately hoped that Lorraine would have the opportunity to scold and rail and mete out as many repercussions as she could dream up for this blatant disregard for Adalheid's most important rule.

Never cross that bridge. Never go into the castle.

"In that case," said the Erlking, laying a hand on Serilda's elbow, "we will do everything we can to make your visit worthwhile."

He drew Serilda against him and lifted her hand to his mouth, kissing the base of her wrist, right beside the pale scar from his arrow.

She shivered. "Don't be silly. She has to go back, before she's missed." She took the basket from Leyna. "Thank you for this thoughtful gift. Please send my regards to—"

"Don't be rash, my love," interrupted the Erlking, plucking the basket out of Serilda's hand. "The child is our guest. She must stay and enjoy our hospitality." His grin grew sharp. "I will hear of nothing else. Boy!"

Serilda did not know who he was summoning until Fricz stepped forward and the king set the basket into his hands. "Take this to the queen's chambers."

Fricz instantly turned and trotted away, though his sour expression told Serilda he much rather would have stayed and seen what was to become of the courageous girl from Adalheid.

As soon as he had gone, the Erlking again took Leyna's arm and paraded both her and Serilda across the courtyard. "Let us celebrate."

Dark ones and monsters and ghosts followed them back toward the gardens. "What a lovely night you chose to visit us," the Erlking went on. "My wife has told me little of her acquaintances in Adalheid. I had not realized there was someone so special left behind."

Serilda's jaw clenched. She could easily imagine how the Erlking might use Leyna against her. He thought he had already taken away everyone she loved. Her mother, her father, her beloved schoolchildren, all killed on the hunt. There was a reason she had never mentioned Leyna to him, or Leyna's mother, or Frieda, the librarian.

"Are you truly *married*?" Leyna said in dismay. "To each other?"

Serilda smiled thinly, wishing she could explain everything.

"Truly," answered the king. "How would you describe our romance, my sweet? Something like a fairy tale?"

"Oh yes," said Serilda. "It's been precisely like one of those fairy stories in which the children get their hearts eaten by monsters and the heroine is trapped inside a dismal castle until the end of her years." She fluttered her lashes. "A fairy tale come true."

Leyna's brows pinched in confusion, but the king merely chuckled. "Those are my favorite tales, to be sure. Musicians!"

Serilda jumped, even though he hadn't shouted loudly. Her nerves were humming, her insides roiling. Would he let Leyna go?

Or would he keep her here—to punish Serilda, or as one more threat against her if she did not live up to their bargain? She wanted to grab Leyna and shove her back toward the barbican gates. Tell her to run. Run as fast as she could and never come back.

But to do it would be to risk the Erlking's wrath—against her. Against the children.

And so, feeling helpless, all she did was nod in appreciation as the ghost musicians struck up a waltz.

"Now we shall celebrate," said the Erlking. Releasing Leyna's arm, he flicked a wrist at the children who had followed. Hans immediately stepped forward. "Our guest requires a dancing partner."

Hans gaped. "I don't know how—"

Before he could finish, his body bent into a stiff bow, and then he was stepping forward and taking Leyna's hands. Leyna, under no such spell, tried to back away, her wide-eyed gaze drawn to the gaping wound in Hans's chest. But whether she was frightened or repulsed, she put up no resistance as Hans whisked her off around a large fountain, leading her as if he'd been taught by one of the great Verenese masters himself. It wasn't long before Leyna's surprised giggles floated above the trees.

With a snap of the king's fingers, a gaggle of ghosts followed after them, waltzing in majestic unison. Puppets on strings. Smiling through their teeth, their open wounds leaving drops of blood scattered across the torchlit paths.

"Who is the child?" asked the Erlking. He maintained his air of tranquil curiosity, though Serilda could see the way he was scrutinizing Leyna. Trying to determine how attached she was to Serilda, and Serilda to her. Whether or not the girl could be useful to him.

"Just a girl I met in Adalheid. Her mother owns the local inn. I was ordered to stay there for a time. By *you*, if you recall."

"I believe you mentioned that the innkeeper was accommodating."

"She was."

"The child must adore you, and I daresay, the feeling appears mutual." His teeth glinted. "Would you like to keep her? She could be my wedding gift to you."

She tried to hide her terror beneath a throaty scoff. "Gods alive, no. You have given me enough children. I'm beginning to feel more like a governess than a queen."

The king grinned, and she doubted very much that she had fooled him. "We should give her a tour of the grounds. Perhaps she would like to see the menagerie."

Serilda suspected that Leyna would very much like to see the menagerie: the wild hunt's collection of magical creatures. Leyna had been one of Serilda's most attentive listeners during her stay in Adalheid, when she would spend hours spinning stories beside the fire at the Wild Swan. Over time, she had amassed a reputation, and the townsfolk began to gather nightly to hear her stories, but it was Leyna who was always seated right beside her. Chin cupped and eyes bright, eager to hear more. More about witches and trolls and punishments doled out to naughty little children. More about knights and fairy folk and castles among the stars. Just *more*.

She had reminded Serilda a little of herself that way.

She started to shake her head—even considered pleading with the king to send Leyna back home. But she stopped herself. Her pleas would be in vain. He was toying with her, and to show distress would only please him more. She could not help feeling that this was a punishment for allowing herself to be kidnapped by the poltergeist and embarrassing the king on this most important occasion.

Besides. Leyna really *would* enjoy seeing the creatures.

She did her best not to look alarmed. "What a thoughtful idea, my lord."

Chapter Nine

Serilda had lost count of how many waltzes the children had endured. Fricz had returned some time ago, pouting to have missed the fun, even though his companions were clearly annoyed to be under the king's control when usually they were allowed a fair bit of freedom as Serilda's personal attendants. No one liked being ordered around, even if it was just being told to dance. Only Leyna seemed giddy and breathless as she was twirled around the gardens.

The musicians offered to play a song of her choosing, but they did not know any of the songs Leyna suggested—their knowledge of popular music being somewhat dated. Leyna finally assured them she was delighted with anything they cared to play.

A couple of hunters enchanted Leyna with a contest of knife throwing, which left Serilda practically gasping in terror for fear one of those daggers would plant itself into Leyna's heart at any moment. But the demons behaved themselves, making merriment without maiming or killing anyone for once.

Platters of spiced buns and fruit-filled pastries were brought around. Glasses of wine were continuously filled. The dancing went on and on and on.

It seemed ages before Leyna was brought back before Serilda and the king, her elbows linked between Hans and Gerdrut.

"Goodness," she said through a twinkling laugh. "We don't throw parties like this in Adalheid. Serilda—is the food safe to eat? I've been avoiding it, but I'm famished!"

Nearby, a silver-skinned man chuckled dryly. "The human child must think we live on poison and the blood of little girls."

Beside him, a woman cackled. "She is not entirely wrong."

Leyna shrank away. She must have forgotten that the dark ones were still the villains of too many warning tales to count. They were as ephemeral and pretty as they were vicious and frightening. They had mostly lingered in the background since her arrival, but now Serilda could see them creeping closer, their curiosity spurred on by the king's interest. Or perhaps they merely scented new prey.

Serilda wished her mind would stop conjuring things like that. It was making it very difficult to maintain a semblance of calm.

"I meant no offense," said Leyna, her mood deflating. "It's only . . . Serilda once told a story of an enchanted castle that was all manners of wonderful, but if one were to eat even one morsel of food they would"— she hesitated, glancing at Serilda as if checking to see if she had the details correct. As if the place might actually have existed and not been merely a silly story made up to entertain—"turn into a bird," she said. "And be forced to fetch seeds and nuts for the fairy queen until the day they died."

The dark ones let out peals of laughter.

Leyna pouted.

"What a darling child," said a woman with hair like burning embers. "We should keep her."

"I am considering it," said the Erlking, beaming, as if bringing Leyna here had been his idea to begin with. "Come, mortal girl. Would you care to see the menagerie?"

"Menagerie?" asked Leyna, eyes widening. "Of . . . animals?"

"Like none you have ever seen." The Erlking glanced at Serilda, a hint of smugness on his bruise-dark mouth. "Why don't you lead the way, my queen?"

Serilda gave a tight smile, a tighter curtsy. "With pleasure." Taking Leyna's hand, she headed down the path toward the far wall of the castle.

The Erlking signaled to the musicians to keep playing. "I trust the festivities will not suffer for our absence."

"Is it very far?" Leyna whispered, a hint of fear overtaking her. The gardens, though lit by torches interspersed throughout the trees, grew darker as they moved away from the keep with its glowing windows.

"It's all right," Serilda said, hoping it was not a lie. "The king is only trying to impress you."

Leyna tucked her head closer to Serilda and whispered, "When last I saw you on the Awakening Moon, you were downright murderous. You said he'd kidnapped a child from your village, and you were going to try to bring her back. Serilda—I thought for sure I would never see you again. Not alive, at least. But . . . you don't look exactly like the other ghosts that are here. And now you've gone ahead and married the Erlking?"

"It's complicated," said Serilda. "I wish I could explain everything to you, but know that I would have returned if I'd had any choice. Leyna— this place, it is dangerous. The dark ones can be charming, but don't be fooled. The first chance you have to leave, I want you to go and never come back. Do you understand me?"

Leyna peered up at her, a hint of stubborn refusal on her face, but Serilda gave her hand a tight squeeze. "Those children you danced with? They were from Märchenfeld, and he kidnapped and killed them all. They can never leave here, never go home to their families. I couldn't stand it if he hurt you, too. And think what that would do to your mother."

Leyna's frown eased into something like guilt. "I hadn't planned on coming into the castle. I was just going to leave the basket for you and run, but then the sun set and the gates opened and . . . and I really did wonder whether you were here. I wanted to see you again. I never imagined I would get to come inside and see . . ." She followed the line of the pathway as they came to another sharp-tipped gate, and froze. "What is *that*?"

"Which one?" Serilda asked as she escorted Leyna through the gate and across the lawn until they were standing before a row of gilt cages.

Leyna's eyes had caught on an enormous black bear with eyes that glowed like torchlight. The bear had been resting, though its burning eyes were open, watching them. In the shadows, it looked like a hulking black lump, furry and—when sleepy like this—almost harmless.

"It's a bärgeist," said Serilda. "I might not get too close. It can't escape its cage, but that won't keep it from trying to grab you through the bars. It would definitely like to eat you."

Leyna seemed in awe of the massive creature, but it wasn't long before her attention moved on to the next cage and a delighted gasp sent her rushing toward the bars. "Oh! What is this adorable thing? This one wouldn't eat me, would it?"

Serilda laughed. "No, it is not dangerous. It's called a dahut. Look at its legs—the ones on the left are shorter than the ones on the right. Easier to go up the mountains that way, but only in one direction."

The creature, which was similar to a typical mountain goat, bleated at them. Leyna swooned. "I want one!"

They made their way down the row, Serilda telling her what each creature was. A wolpertinger. A schnabelgeiss. A matagot. "And this over here," said Serilda, leading her to the next cage, where a small, hairy creature was prowling, "is a dreka—"

She was cut off by a scream.

Serilda spun toward the sound. Air rushed into her lungs.

The tatzelwurm—the most impressive beast in the menagerie—had wriggled its long tail out of its cage and wrapped it around Leyna's ankle, pulling her to the ground.

Leyna screamed again, her fingers leaving deep gouges in the dirt as she resisted being dragged across the grass. As soon as it had her close enough, the tatzelwurm stuck one of its claws through the bars and used it to puncture Leyna's skirt, pinning her to the ground. It was a serpentine creature with an enormous scaly tail, two forelegs with jagged claws, and a head that resembled a great mountain lynx, with slitted golden eyes and tall pointed ears.

Looming over Leyna, the monster opened its jaws, revealing a row of needle-sharp teeth.

Serilda lunged forward. She grasped Leyna's wrists and pulled. The fabric of Leyna's skirt tore, ripping a large pocket. Something fell out, clattering to the ground.

The tatzelwurm hissed and swiped out with its tail, knocking Serilda backward. She crashed into someone. Hands gripped her elbows to steady her—and for one frantic moment she thought it might be Gild there to help her—but it was the Erlking, his head cocked with curiosity.

"Stop that thing!" Serilda shrieked. "Help her!"

"Whatever for? If you do not wish to keep her, she will make a fine treat for our pet."

Serilda let out a disgruntled cry and shoved him away with all her strength. He only stumbled back a step, but it made her feel a little better anyhow. *So much for eternal devotion.*

She rushed forward again and grabbed Leyna just as the tatzelwurm's nose pressed against the bars, sniffing its prey. Its head was too big to get through, but its front claws swiped at the child. Leyna barely had time to duck back, but with her skirt freed and Serilda's help, she managed to scramble backward on the grass. She looked a mess—her dress filthy and torn and one of her pigtails coming loose from its ribbon.

But she was out of reach of the tatzelwurm.

Relieved, Serilda fell beside her and wrapped her arms around Leyna. The attack had happened fast, but they were both breathing hard. Though Serilda had no heart, she imagined she could feel it just the same, pounding inside her chest. "It's all right," she said, smoothing down Leyna's hair. "It can't get you from here."

She hadn't realized the tatzelwurm could get her at all. It had never occurred to her that the beast could extend its snakelike tail through the bars. She'd never seen it try. Always when she'd been near the creature, it had appeared docile and quiet, even despondent. Now its slitted eyes were wide with intent as it stared—not at Leyna, the snack that got away—but at the small trinket that had fallen from Leyna's pocket.

Something sparkled gold in the dim light. The tatzelwurm growled and clamped its claws over it.

No—not growled.

Serilda frowned. Was it . . . *purring*?

"Now, now," said the Erlking, sauntering closer. "That does not belong to you, little wurm."

The purr, or growl, or whatever it was, devolved into an angry hiss. Its eyes narrowed. It watched the king, as if daring him to take one step closer.

And the king did, until he was close enough that he could have reached into the cage and stroked the black tufts of hair at the tips of the tatzelwurm's ears.

"Go on," he said lowly. "Leave it."

The tatzelwurm hesitated a long moment. Calculating. Its shining nostrils flared with every breath. Serilda noticed a spot of green-tinged blood leaking from a wound in the tatzelwurm's side. An arrow could still be seen buried in its sinuous flesh, never removed or allowed to heal, though the creature had been captured months ago.

In a movement quick as a spark, the tatzelwurm released its treasure and reared back on its tail, then lurched forward and drove its claws out through the bars again. Straight for the Erlking's chest.

He swiveled to the side, catching the creature's foreleg in his hands. He pressed the limb up and back, snapping the bone around the cage's bar.

The howl was like nothing Serilda had ever heard before. She and Leyna both cowered against each other as the tatzelwurm's agony filled the gardens. Leyna buried her face into Serilda's neck. "I'm ready to go home now."

"I know," said Serilda, kissing the top of the girl's head. "Soon."

Serilda grimaced at the unearthly yowl, though the king seemed unaffected.

With no more concern than he would give to a moth with a crushed wing, he reached into the cage and picked up the trinket.

The beast did not try to attack again, even as the king turned his back. As its shriek died off into a pitiful wail, the tatzelwurm pulled its broken limb carefully back through the bars and half-limped, half-slithered to the cage's far corner before curling into a heap.

"How curious," said the Erlking, inspecting the object in his hand for a long moment, before he finally lifted it up for Serilda to see. She felt Leyna tense as they both took in the tiny figurine. It was shaped like a horse, and crafted entirely of finely spun golden thread.

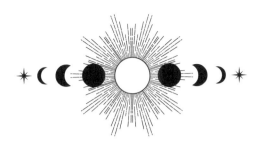

Chapter Ten

Serilda recognized the figurine. It was one of the gifts Gild had crafted in secret from the Erlking. She had helped him throw those trinkets over the castle wall on Eostrig's Day as a gift to the people of Adalheid. It was a bit of amusement for Gild, a way to keep busy, but also a way to feel connected to a world that had forgotten him, that he could never be a part of again. Because of these gifts, given once a year, he had earned a reputation among the townsfolk.

But the Erlking didn't know any of that, and he *couldn't* know any of that.

"Sweet child," said the Erlking, "where did you obtain such a precious treasure?"

Leyna peeled her face away from Serilda's throat, tears on her face. "V-Vergoldetgeist," she whispered.

Serilda went rigid. It was the name the people of Adalheid had given to their mysterious benefactor. Vergoldetgeist. The Gilded Ghost.

The king angled the figure back and forth so that it shone in the light from dozens of torches atop the castle wall. "This is unusual gold. God-blessed, if I am not mistaken. A very valuable commodity, rather . . . wasted on such a frivolous icon. Who is this . . . Vergoldetgeist?"

How the Erlking could tell that this was true gold, spun with the blessing of Hulda, Serilda had no idea. It might have been made by any talented goldsmith.

"Don't you—" Leyna started to answer, still shivering, but Serilda cleared her throat.

"Vergoldetgeist is what they call Adalheid's goldsmith," she said. "A very respected artisan with a shop on the main thoroughfare." She reached down and took Leyna's hands into hers. "Was it a gift from your mother? Did she purchase it there?"

Leyna stared at her for a beat, then nodded. "Y-yes. For my . . . birthday."

Serilda stifled a grimace. Leyna was a terrible liar, and her words carried too much hesitation.

If ever given the chance, she was going to have to teach her better.

"How quaint." The Erlking towered over the two and chuckled adoringly. "Unfortunately, I do despise a liar."

Leyna started to tremble again. Serilda wrapped her arms around the girl, determined to protect her, though she didn't know how she could.

"It has been an unusual solstice, and I suspect the hounds will be growing bored to have missed our chance at a hunt," he said. "You will make a fine enough toy for them. Not that I expect you to last that long."

"No!" Serilda cried. "Leave her alone! You will leave her alone!"

"My dove," said the Erlking, "surely you understand we cannot tolerate this child's disrespect."

She glowered at him, realizing how he had been toying with her and Leyna all night. He never intended to let the child go. Not if he could use her against Serilda.

But the sky overhead was growing lighter. Dawn was approaching. Blissful, hopeful dawn, which would drape the veil back over this horrid place and take Leyna out of the king's grasp.

"What do you want her to say?" snapped Serilda. She scrambled to her feet, keeping Leyna tucked against her side. "She's terrified."

"I merely ask for the truth. If she refuses that simple request—"

"Because *I* gave it to her," said Serilda.

"You?" asked the Erlking.

"I spin gold, don't I? I'm blessed by Hulda. Leyna was trying to protect me."

"Why would that require protection?"

Anger pulsed through her. "Because it was *your* gold. I stole one of the bobbins on the third night that I was brought to spin for you. I did not think you would notice, and later, you told me that it was the poltergeist who had stolen it. You strung him up in punishment." She swallowed, not having to fake her fear. The story was a mix of lies and truth. She had stolen a bobbin of thread, and Gild had been punished for it—among other things. But that bobbin had been given to Pusch-Grohla and the moss maidens, not Leyna.

Though she would eat her own tongue before she told that to the king. As far as she could tell, Pusch-Grohla was one of his most hated adversaries. A woman as ancient as the forest itself, who had made it her duty to hide and protect the creatures of the Aschen Wood that would otherwise be the king's to hunt.

The king narrowed his eyes at Serilda, as if trying to ascertain if she was telling the truth.

Serilda lifted her chin, daring him to contradict her. He had no proof otherwise.

As if this occurred to the king at the same moment, his lips pinched sourly. "That was quite a gift, to be bestowed on one so young and"—his glare slid to Leyna—"careless."

"Careless?" cried Serilda. "She was attacked! By one of *your* monsters."

The king shrugged, as if this argument meant nothing.

"Regardless," Serilda went on, "as I am now the queen, I suppose it is within my right to bestow gifts as I see fit."

The Erlking lifted an eyebrow at her—a warning to remember her place.

Serilda crossed her arms defiantly over her chest. "You aren't going to punish me for the theft. Not now that you've made such convincing marital vows. Are you, *my love*?"

The king's gaze darkened.

But before he could respond, Leyna dared to wriggle out of Serilda's hold. She took a step toward the Erlking and lifted a trembling palm up to him. "Please, my lord. Might I have it back?"

The king stilled, studying that uplifted hand. Though he appeared as calm as a frozen lake, Serilda could see something churning in his eyes.

"No," he finally said, the word as final as a gravestone. Leyna drew back, startled. "This gold is rightfully mine. And you, child, are a fool for coming here. A fool for thinking that you might ask something of *me*, the Alder King, when the only gift your presence has earned tonight is a swift and efficient death."

It happened so fast that Serilda did not have time to think. The way the king slung the crossbow off his back with the grace of one who had done so a thousand times. So close to Leyna, he did not even have to aim. A blink and an arrow was nocked. A gasp and the trigger was pulled.

She heard the hollow thump even as she started to scream. As her hands reached to shove Leyna out of the way.

But her hands passed right through the girl.

Just as the arrow had.

Serilda's scream died on her tongue.

She was too late, but so was the king.

Or perhaps he had timed it that way on purpose. He seemed unperturbed and unsurprised as he tossed the bow again over his shoulder. Then he sauntered right through Leyna's hazy figure to collect the bolt that had struck the grass.

Heart in her throat, Serilda fell to her knees and reached again for Leyna, but she could not touch her. Though the sun had not yet climbed over the castle walls, the highest tower windows were sparkling gold in the morning light. Beyond the castle, the sun had risen. The solstice was over. The veil had fallen, and Leyna, still alive and mortal, was on the other side.

Leyna stood petrified, her eyes wide but no longer seeing Serilda or the Erlking or the caged beasts. Serilda knew from her own experiences of being inside the castle when the veil fell that Leyna was now seeing the castle as it was in the mortal world. Crumbling, decaying, overgrown and wild and abandoned.

And haunted.

Soon Leyna would see the ghosts. Not as they were here—mild-mannered, gracious, tragic figures. But as they had been the night the dark ones stormed into the castle and massacred them all. There would be screams and blood and sobs and shadowy figures falling to blades wielded by invisible enemies.

There would be monsters, too. Creatures like the nachtkrapp and the drudes that were not trapped on this side of the veil as the dark ones were. They seemed to become extra restless when an intruder was inside these walls.

"Run," said Serilda, wishing she could grab Leyna and shake her. "Run. Get out."

"She cannot hear you," said the Erlking, examining the tip of his reclaimed bolt before sliding it back into the quiver.

"I know she can't hear me," Serilda retorted, her fury at his last stunt writhing inside her. Was it a stunt? Had he meant to kill her? She hated that she couldn't tell.

Leyna's breaths were coming in quick, uneven gasps as she put a hand over her heart, where the king's arrow should have struck her.

A caw echoed over the gardens. Serilda and Leyna both glanced up to see the eyeless raven perched on the wrought-iron gate.

It was enough to shake Leyna from her stupor. "S-Serilda?" she said, glancing around. "Are you still there?"

"Just go," said Serilda. "What are you waiting for?"

Another cry from the bird. This time it flapped its wings, showing off its tattered feathers.

Leyna took a couple of steps away from it, wrapping her arms around her body. Though the day would turn sunny and warm, the morning carried a sharp chill. Dew clung to the grasses. Mist would soon be rising over the gardens as the sun's rays swept across the grounds.

Leyna squeezed her eyes tight. "Serilda, if you're there . . . if you can hear me . . . I want you to know that I miss you. And I'll never forget you. And . . ."

The nachtkrapp squawked again. Leyna jumped, her eyes snapping open again, and her last words came out in a rush. "And I hope you'll enjoy the cakes!"

Then she turned on her heels and ran as fast as she could through the gardens.

Serilda clasped her hands together, watching until Leyna's small form disappeared behind the foliage. "Please let her be all right."

The king snorted. "I find your affection for these human parasites to be most disconcerting."

She glared at him, but her pulse skipped when she saw that he wasn't looking at her. He was inspecting the small golden figurine, turning it over in his hand. With a flourish, he tucked it into a pocket on his leather jerkin and smiled at her.

"What an odd little treasure you are, my queen," he said, holding a hand out to her. "Come. Let us bid the court good night and retire to our bridal suite."

She snarled. "I would rather retire to a pit of worms."

He laughed, frustratingly jovial. "Do not tempt me, love."

In a sweeping gesture, he gathered her into his arms and carried her toward the castle keep. Serilda began to struggle, but then she remembered that Leyna was not the soul she needed to worry about. With a growl, she crossed her arms over her chest and allowed the king to show her off as he strolled through the revelry, many dark ones still dancing and enjoying the feast, many ghosts tirelessly refilling goblets of wine.

The wedding guests cheered and hurrahed as their king and queen passed, but the raucous cries were quick to die down as they slipped into the echoing corridors of the castle.

As soon as they were out of danger of being seen, Serilda punched the Erlking in the nose.

He recoiled, though probably more from surprise than pain. Still, he made no effort to stop her as she swiveled out of his hold and landed in an awkward heap on the carpet. She skittered back to her feet, ridiculously pleased as the king pressed a finger to his nose. He was not bleeding, but then, they didn't bleed, did they? Only . . . smoldered a bit.

"I can find my own way from here, thank you," she said, adjusting her leather tunic.

"I had no intention of carrying you all the way. You needn't have struck me."

"Believe it or not, it was the highlight of my evening."

"Oh, I do believe it," he said, his eyes flashing. But—not with fury. If anything, he seemed amused.

Which made her anger only burn hotter. Serilda drew herself up until she was nearly nose to nose with him.

Well—nose to chest, as the case might be.

"You have made me your queen," she said, enunciating each word. "I hope you weren't wanting one of those meek, pathetic mortals you so despise, because a queen I intend to be."

The Erlking held her gaze, frustratingly unreadable as his grin softened.

"No," he finally said, with a hint of a purr. "A meek and pathetic mortal is not the queen I want. Rather unexpectedly, it would seem I have chosen well." He tilted closer, his long hair sliding from his shoulder and brushing against her arm. "You must be a gift of fortune."

Serilda stilled at the reference to Wyrdith, her patron god. She held his gaze, trying to not be afraid, even while her thoughts tumbled. The king had always believed that she was blessed by Hulda. So, what was he saying? What did he know? Or did his words mean anything at all?

The king's grin brightened again, flashing sharp teeth. He pressed a single rose-petal kiss to her cheek, and every vein in Serilda's body froze solid.

She yanked herself away from him. "I would ask that you reserve such affection for the court."

"As it pleases you . . . Your Majesty."

With a furious shake of her head, Serilda stormed off down the hall, toward her own chambers. The Erlking's haughty laughter followed her the entire way.

THE
THUNDER
MOON

THE
THUNDER
MOON

Chapter Eleven

ore than a month had passed since Serilda had been crowned the Alder Queen. In that time, the Erlking had taken to parading her about like a prized pig at the harvest festival—as pleased to show her off now as he would be when it came time to slaughter her. The feasts continued, many lasting until the sun rose over the castle walls. Wine and ale flowed like rivers, music filled the castle halls, and the servants ran about tending to their masters as well as they could, but Serilda could tell they were all exhausted and annoyed with the ongoing revelries.

She was exhausted, too. Tired of smiling. Tired of the king's ice-cold fingers trailing along her throat or her scarred wrist whenever they had an audience. Tired of lying, lying, always lying.

The one night that should have been a respite—the Golden Moon that had risen not long after the solstice—offered little reprieve. The hunters had wasted most of the night on an impromptu archery contest that had delayed them nearly until sunrise. By the time they'd finally left, Serilda and Gild had had a mere few hours to search for their bodies until the wild hunt returned. Their search had turned up nothing more than a handful of enormous spiders that had probably been haunting this castle for as long as Gild had.

But then, the very day after the Golden Moon, Serilda had the most brilliant idea. She and Gild had already been to a room where she knew the Erlking was hiding something. That eerie place not far from the hall with the stained-glass gods, where drudes had attacked her both times she'd gotten too close.

There was an enchanted tapestry in that room, along with a cage hidden beneath a curtain of gossamer fabric. At least, when she'd first seen it, she'd believed it was a cage, but lately she had convinced herself that it might be something else entirely.

Like a coffin. Perhaps for keeping the body of a cursed prince?

There was only one way to find out, and now she was tapping her fingers impatiently against the brocade gown that weighed about as much as the king's warhorse. This time, as the Thunder Moon approached, Serilda had tried to take matters into her own hands. She had spent the past couple of days ensuring that the hunters would have everything they needed as soon as the veil fell. She had worked with the blacksmith, the stable boy, and the head cook, confirming that blades were sharpened and horses were groomed and evening bread was served long before nightfall—but not so early that she risked the hunters taking in too much drink and becoming lazy and useless as the moon rose.

She had worked so hard to make sure that the wild hunt would depart the moment the veil fell, and her efforts had even earned her the approval of her lord husband, who had twice complimented her emerging interest in the hunt.

But alas. Her efforts had backfired.

While the dark ones had polished off the last of their evening bread, hours before, the Erlking had stood and raised his glass and made a declaration. As his wife was so keen on learning about the ways of the hunt, she ought to be treated to a spectacular demonstration of the hunters' prowess and skill. Serilda didn't know what that meant, but it had sent everyone, hunters and servants alike, into a flurry of activity.

The demonstration was to take place the following morning in the menagerie. That was all anyone would tell her, and she'd been forbidden from observing the work herself. The king did not want his surprise ruined.

And now, once again, she was waiting and waiting for the hunt to finish their preparations and *leave*. Serilda did not care one whit about surprises or the hunt's prowess. Sunrise was not that far away, and at this rate, she and Gild wouldn't have any chance to search for their bodies at all, and they would have to wait four more weeks.

Four long, agonizing weeks.

Serilda couldn't help feeling that the Erlking knew she wanted him gone and was only doing this to provoke her. The wild hunt had been riding out beneath every full moon for centuries. Surely they could be more efficient than *this*.

"Why do you appear so anxious, my dear?" muttered the Erlking, casting a sideways look at her as he pulled on his black leather gloves.

"Just wondering how much longer I have to wait out here. It's been a long night."

"Are you so eager to be rid of me?"

"Yes," she said, without hesitation. "Always."

He peered at her like he wasn't sure if he should punish her for this statement or laugh.

Finally—*finally*—the king ordered the drawbridge to be lowered, revealing the mortal world across the lake. The city of Adalheid was dark, the residents sequestered in their homes, hiding from the wild hunt they knew would come roaring through.

"Perhaps you should stay back this night, Your Grim," said one of the dark ones. Serilda glanced up to see a man with bronze-colored skin smirking at her. "Your bride appears positively morose to see you leave."

Serilda was tempted to start throwing rocks at the nosy demon, but she fluttered her lashes instead, like the simpleminded, coquettish mortal girl they believed her to be, and said sweetly, "I would never wish to keep my husband from his true love—the hunt. Though I shall eagerly anticipate his return."

The Erlking gave her a subtle nod, eyes alight with approval.

"Have a lovely time," she called. "Try not to kidnap anyone. Children especially. Except for the *really* naughty ones—like the ones that wipe their earwax on their little sister's favorite dress. Those ones are fine to take. Oh, and the ones who—"

"Serilda," hissed Nickel, giving her a forceful shake of his head.

"Right," she said, smiling up at the hunters. "Best not to take any children. Or any mothers, for that matter. It's terribly traumatic for a child." This was said with more than a little resentment. Serilda's mother had been taken by the hunt when Serilda was barely old enough to toddle about. For months, Serilda had wondered—even hoped—that her mother's spirit might have been brought back to this castle. But after weeks of inspecting the face of every female ghost she passed, searching for dark hair and a chipped front tooth, she became convinced that her mother wasn't here among the castle specters. Serilda had lost hope that she would ever know what had become of her, because even if her mother was alive, Serilda was trapped here and would never see the outside world again. That, too, was the Erlking's fault.

Hans cleared his throat. "How about they just don't kidnap anybody?"

"Ah. Yes. Hans makes a fine point. It is a terrible habit."

The Erlking, who had been ignoring her as he strapped a series of hunting knives to his belt, met her gaze.

"I will not make a promise I cannot keep," he replied, looping an arm around her waist and tugging her against him. It took all Serilda's strength not to grimace as his cold lips found the corner of her mouth.

He released her quickly. In another moment, the hunters mounted their steeds. She caught one of them watching her, and fear spiked through her that they might have noticed her revulsion.

But it was not a dark one, but rather a castle ghost—one of the few who joined the dark ones on their hunts—the headless woman, whose spirit Serilda had once seen sobbing with guilt on the other side of the veil. She held Serilda's gaze now with an understanding nod, before giving a flick of her reins.

The king lifted the hunting horn to his lips. Its haunting cry echoed off the castle walls. The hounds were released, the embers beneath their fur burning like bonfires.

Then they were gone, tearing across the cobbled bridge, disappearing in the silver-dappled streets beyond.

Serilda made a face and wriggled her arms, trying to rid herself of the cloying feel of his touch. "Great gods, I thought they'd never leave."

She spun back toward the keep, only to find her path blocked by five small ghosts watching her with curious eyes.

"What are you so impatient about tonight?" asked Fricz, arms crossed over his chest. "Got big plans?"

"That don't include us?" added Anna, sounding hurt.

Serilda sighed. "Don't be silly. I just really like it when they leave. Don't you?"

The children couldn't argue, but she could see that she hadn't convinced them.

"Nothing to worry about," she added, squeezing their shoulders as she slid past them. "There's just been something I've wanted to look into is all. I'll be back in our chambers in plenty of time to get ready for this . . . *demonstration* they're putting on. Do you know what it is?"

"Not really," said Hans, "but the dark ones seem all eager about it, which makes me very suspicious."

"We'll know soon enough," said Serilda, glancing up at the sky. "Come, it's late. Well . . . early, I suppose. Why don't you get some rest until morning?"

Without waiting for their response, she hastened off into the keep.

A ghost was knocking cobwebs from the chandeliers in the entry, keeping her from slipping up the staircase that led to the second story. Instead, Serilda strode into the great hall and busied herself inspecting the tapestries until the servant had moved on. Once she was sure she would not be seen, Serilda darted into the stairwell that led up to the hall of gods, as she had taken to calling it. This corridor was the home of seven stained-glass windows, each depicting one of the old gods. A faint glow from the Thunder Moon shone through the panes.

Serilda paused at the landing. The hall was empty.

Pressing her hands down the folds of her gown, she made her way along the corridor, eyeing the glass portraits. The last window depicted Wyrdith, god of stories and fortune. The god who had granted her father's wish and cursed her with the wheel of fortune on her eyes.

She paused to study the figure, dressed in a yellow cloak trimmed in crimson and orange. A cascade of hair spilled nearly to their ankles—black in this light, but during the day, the glass had a deep amethyst tint. The god held a golden feather quill in one hand, a long scroll in the other. But rather than looking down at their work, the god was peering toward the sky with a somber, contemplative expression.

As if deciding someone's fate.

Everyone's fate.

It was odd to see this figure—this god—captured in a window that had been crafted hundreds of years ago, and imagine that they had such influence over Serilda's life. Her penchant for storytelling, which had once brought her so much joy. Her habit of lying, which had landed her here in the Erlking's castle. The neighbors' superstitious whispers that followed her through childhood. So many misfortunes that may or may not have been her fault.

Yet here was Wyrdith, wearing old-fashioned robes and holding a quill so ridiculously long it could only have come from some mythic creature. Serilda did not think even the Erlking had a bird hung up on his walls that could have produced a feather like that.

It was a bit pretentious, actually.

"Why did you do it?" she murmured to the portrait. The god did not respond, but kept staring off into the distance, oblivious to the plight of their mortal godchild. "Why not just grant the wish, give my father a child? Why curse me at all? Why fill my mind with these stories?" She thought of the tale she had told of the prince who had killed Perchta. A true story. Gild's story. "Why are some of the stories coming true?"

"Communing with the gods now, are we?"

Serilda turned around to see Gild holding two slender golden swords. "So far, the conversation has been rather one-sided."

Gild's gaze drifted toward Hulda, who was pictured with a giant spinning wheel, strands of golden thread wrapped around the spindle. "Meddlesome beings, aren't they? Throw about their curses and gifts and then . . . never heard from again."

"Wyrdith could have loaned me that quill, at least." Serilda gestured to the enormous feather. "Imagine the stories I could write if I had a feather twice as long as my arm."

"Are you saying that a golden longsword isn't your truest wish?" He lifted one of the swords. "Guess I'll be keeping this, then."

"One of those is for me?"

"I thought I'd feel more comfortable with this gods-awful idea if you at least had a weapon this time."

He handed her one of the swords, and she was surprised at the giddiness that sparked inside her when she wrapped her hands around the engraved handle. It depicted a gilt tatzelwurm—the symbol of the royal family of Adalheid. Gild's ancestors.

"Where did you get this?"

"The armory," he said. "Where the good stuff is kept. But bear in mind that, while drudes are averse to gold, it's still an ornamental sword. The blade isn't very sharp, so keep that in mind if we run into trouble."

"I suppose I'll have to bludgeon the little beasts to death." She tested a few different grips on the sword's hilt until she found one that felt somewhat natural. Though it was not a large sword, it was heavier than she'd expected.

That was when she noticed the wooden kitchen ladle hanging from Gild's belt. "What are you doing with that?"

He looked down and held the bowl of the spoon up toward the candlelight. "What do you mean? I could bludgeon something with this as well as a sword."

"Sure. You could also serve up a hearty bowl of stew."

His cheeks dimpled. "I like a multipurpose weapon."

"I'm serious. Why are you carrying that thing around?"

"It's the only thing I've ever gotten from the Erlking, and I won it from him in a fair bargain." He shrugged. "I'm never letting this go."

"A fair bargain? You traded me!"

"Yeah, but . . . look at the quality of this spoon! It could be hung up on the wall, a piece of fine art."

She rolled her eyes. Then, realizing that they were both stalling, she heaved a sigh. "Are you ready?"

"Not at all." Gild scanned the corridor that branched off this main hall. A corridor that was cast in shadows, murky and impenetrable. The castle was always creepy at night, no matter how many torches and candelabras were lit. But this hall was perhaps the most frightening of all. Here lived real monsters. Monsters that had twice attacked Serilda when she'd come to explore this dark corridor that she felt inexplicably drawn to.

This was the part of the castle that the drudes had laid claim to. Horrid beasts, with bloated, purple-gray skin, spiraling horns, and serpents' tongues. But the worst thing was the damage they could wreak with their piercing, deafening shrieks.

They were living nightmares. They could make a person see their greatest fears, as if they were real and inescapable. Serilda still shuddered to remember the visions the drudes had shown her. Everyone she loved—Gild, her father, the children, Leyna and Lorraine—being tortured. Murdered. Disembodied heads hung up to decorate the Erlking's walls . . .

It didn't help that even Gild seemed afraid of them, despite having once fought off two drudes with the same golden sword he carried now. Gild never seemed scared of anything, not even the Erlking himself, but his dislike of the drudes clung to him as thick as the shadows that clung to the castle's corners.

"This is the perfect hiding spot," she said, "precisely because no one wants to come here, not even you. And we know *something* is in that room. Something those monsters are protecting. Something the king doesn't want anyone to find. We have to check."

"Sure, if you want to be a midnight snack for a drude," said Gild, tapping the flat edge of his sword against his shoulder. "This is a big castle. I'm sure there are lots of places we haven't searched yet."

Except he didn't sound sure. He had been here for centuries. He'd had lots of time to accidentally stumble onto his not-quite-dead corpse.

She paused at the corner, eyeing the hall. In the dimness, she could barely make out the line of heavy wooden doors, shut tight, and tall candelabras that had not been lit, so that the end of the hall disappeared into darkness. Their destination was down there. The room that had called to her since the first night she'd stepped into this castle. The room with the tapestry that she'd never gotten a good look at, the one that seemed to glow with magic.

"I'm only saying," Gild continued, "that the Erlking wouldn't have given my body some fancy, ceremonial resting place. Throwing it into the depths of the dungeons is more his style. He might have tossed it into a pit or bricked it up behind a wall. For all we know, he could have thrown my body into the lake ages ago. I've probably been devoured by wild carp."

Serilda shook her head. Even though the Erlking would have gotten vast amounts of pleasure from watching Gild's body being picked apart by fish, she had the distinct impression that their bodies needed to be kept intact, or the curse would have been incomplete. The arrows were important, she was convinced. When he cursed her, the Erlking had stabbed a gold-tipped arrow through her wrist. Once they found their bodies, she suspected they would only have to remove the arrows that tethered their spirits to this castle in order to break the curse.

Simple.

Utterly simple.

Or so she kept telling herself, when she had to tell herself something to maintain hope. She knew they couldn't kill the Erlking—immortal and invincible as he was. She knew he would never let her go willingly, not so long as she bore the child he meant to give to Perchta. And he would certainly never free Gild, who he loathed beyond reason.

This was the only way. Find their bodies, break the curse. True, they might fail, and even if they *did* succeed, it was likely the Erlking would hunt them down and drag them right back. But Serilda couldn't sit around pretending to be the queen of the dark ones and bemoaning her fate. She had to try something, and this was all she could think to do.

Except she'd had so little time to search. Serilda was often at the mercy of the Erlking, being paraded before the court and forced to go along with their mimicry of courtship and betrothal, while Gild was free to travel anywhere in the castle he wished to go.

And he'd gone almost everywhere. Sneaking into every room, from private chambers to wine cellars, larders and armories, chapels and dungeons and tombs. Serilda was worried they might be running out of places to search, but then she thought of how vast the castle was. How labyrinthine. There must still be plenty of secrets for it to give up.

"You haven't been devoured by fish," she said, tightening her hold on the sword and grabbing a lit torch from a bracket on the wall. "I believe our bodies are here, and I don't wish to waste the next three centuries searching for them, when they might be right down that corridor. Come on, Gild. We have to do this, before the hunt returns."

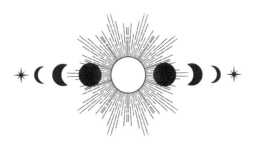

Chapter Twelve

Gripping the golden sword, Serilda stepped into the shadows. But she'd barely entered the corridor when Gild maneuvered his body in front of her.

"Hey," she whispered. "I'm capable of defending myself."

He shot her an irritated look. "I've been trained in sword fighting. Have you?"

"Trained? You don't remember anything from your previous life. How do you know?"

"All princes are trained in combat," he said with a cocky grin. "And what sort of prince would I be if I—"

He was cut off by a scream and the beat of wings.

Serilda stumbled backward. Before she could even think to raise the sword—ornamental or not—Gild lunged against the attacker. In the flickering torchlight, Serilda saw a flash of gold and the glint of talons. She heard the frantic beating of leathery wings. A drude.

Gild swung the sword, knocking the beast against the wall. It wailed and tumbled to the floor.

A second screech split the air.

Serilda spun around, but she could not pinpoint where the sound had come from.

Then the beast was upon her, diving down from the rafters, its sharp-toothed mouth gaping open. Serilda screamed, but it swung past her and landed on Gild's arm, its talons digging through his sleeve. Gild let out a roar. His sword clattered to the ground.

The first drude spread its wings. Hissing, it leaped upward and landed on Gild's other shoulder. Talons pierced cloth and skin. Its jaw unhinged. It released a horrific scream into Gild's face.

Gild lurched backward, crashing against the wall. Unarmed, he struggled in vain to knock the drudes free. Sweat beaded on his brow. His expression twisted as the nightmares claimed his mind.

Serilda heard the shriek of a third. She scanned the hall, but the beast was invisible in the darkness.

Stuffing the torch into an empty sconce, she raised her sword. Acting on brutal instinct, she wrapped her forearm around the neck of the drude that clutched Gild's arm and swiped the blade across its throat.

The monster's head snapped back, all the way back, so that its slitted eyes were staring straight at her, its face upside down, its pointed tongue flicking at the air as a thick gurgle filled its throat.

Its grip on Gild's arm loosened. With a grunt, Serilda tore it away and threw its body to the floor.

Gild was no longer fighting. His cheeks were stained with tears, his arms hanging limp at his sides. The first drude was still attached to his shoulder, infiltrating Gild's mind with its nightmares as blood leaked from his wounds.

With a guttural cry, Serilda threw herself at them and drove the sword through the creature's back, directly between its veiny wings. She cut upward, the blade barely missing Gild's shoulder as it impaled the creature.

The drude yowled and thrashed.

Serilda yanked out the blade. Blood, viscous and smelling of rot, splattered across her arms as the beast fell to the floor.

The monster turned and scrabbled for her, claws reaching. Tongue whipping against the air. Wetness slicking the corners of its mouth.

Serilda stepped back as the creature's strength drained away. It slumped forward, convulsing.

"Gild," she breathed, stepping over the drude and reaching for his arm. His linen shirt was covered in blood. His pupils dilated to near black, his gaze unfocused and darting around the hall. His whole body was shaking so hard that he nearly ripped himself out of Serilda's grasp. "Gild, it's me!"

A hiss cut her short.

The third drude, bigger than the others, stood at the opening to the corridor, wings outstretched.

With a shuddering breath, Serilda curled her fingers around the sword's hilt.

The drude launched itself into the air, wings beating. It landed briefly on one of the chandeliers, then jumped to the wall, talons digging into the stonework. Shards of rock clattered and rained onto the carpet as it skittered forward. Up the wall, across the ceiling, like an enormous spider.

She tried to mimic the stance she'd seen Gild take, as the gems from the hilt dug into her palms.

The drude dropped toward her.

She swung. The blade missed, but forced the drude back. It struck a door and clung to it, needle-claws embedded in the wood.

Serilda backed away, her whole body shaking. Daring to remove one hand from the sword's hilt, she fumbled against the wall. Searching—

The drude screamed and leaped again.

Not at her—at Gild, still in a daze. Lost in whatever nightmare was clouding his thoughts.

Serilda's hand found cool metal. She pressed on the latch and shoved open the door.

Then she hefted the sword as hard as she could over her shoulder and threw it spearlike at the monster. The point pierced one of the drude's wings, dragging it down to the floor. The creature howled.

Serilda wrapped her arms around Gild and hauled him through the doorway, slamming the door shut behind them with her foot. Releasing him, hands trembling, she fumbled to latch the door. The lock fell in place with a loud *thunk*. She let out a shaky cry of relief.

"Ha!" she yelled—half victory, half bewilderment. "Who's trained in sword fighting now?"

She spun around, an astonished smile on her face.

It quickly fell.

Gild had dropped into a crouch. His palms were pressed into his eyes.

As Serilda watched, he let out a groan—almost a wail. A sound that was broken and frightened and hollow.

The nightmares hadn't released him yet.

Exhaling sharply, she went to him and knelt down. "Gild," she whispered, her tone the same that she had started using with the children on nights when they awoke with visions of nachtkrapp and hellhounds haunting their dreams. "I'm here, Gild. It's only a nightmare. You can wake up now."

He groaned again, but a moment later, his gaze started to clear. His eyes focused on her, wide and uncertain and glistening. He swallowed hard.

"Gild. It's me. You're all right."

Reddish-gold lashes fluttered a few times, as if blinking could physically clear the visions from his mind.

Then his arms were around her, crushing Serilda to his chest. She gasped in surprise, but also from the sheer force of his embrace. He held her so tight she could feel every one of his sputtering breaths against her neck.

"Serilda," he said, his voice choked. "You were . . . you had a sword. And you could have killed the Erlking. He was *right there.* But instead, you turned, and you stabbed *me.* And the look on your face . . . like you hated me. Like you'd always hated me." He shuddered. "It was awful."

"It wasn't real. It was the drudes," she said, the words lost in the hair that tangled around his ears.

He pulled away from her. Enough that he could grip the sides of her face in his palms. Enough that he could see her. Whole. Fine. Inspecting the golden wheels in her eyes. The planes of her cheeks. Her mouth—

"Serilda—"

His lips crushed against hers. Intense and wanting and needing. Fingers in her hair. Gild, engulfing her. All her senses, sparking and frantic.

Just as quickly, it was over. Gild broke away, muttering apologies before he'd managed to take a full breath. "I'm sorry. I wasn't thinking. I shouldn't have—I didn't mean to—"

Serilda grabbed his arm. To silence him. To steady herself. "Don't," she said, breathless. "Please. Don't."

They were both shaking. His fingers buried in the brocade of her skirt. Serilda gripping his bloodied shirt, only becoming aware of it when she realized that her hands were sticky.

They stared at each other, breathless. Scared. Serilda found the courage to sink into him, pressing her cheek to his, and Gild, after a long hesitation, allowed his arms to come around her again. Gentler now.

She wasn't sure who needed the comfort more.

"I can't tell you how many times I've wanted to kiss you," she said. "Or wanted you to kiss me. Every day. Every time I see you. And I know . . . I understand why there's this distance between us. I know what it would mean, if . . . if he ever found out . . . but it doesn't keep me from wanting."

Gild didn't respond at first. He held her, but didn't move for a long time.

Until, all at once, she felt his taut muscles start to relax with a quiet sigh. "It's nice to know I'm not the only one."

She sniffed. She hadn't realized she'd started to cry. The tension of the battle, short but vicious as it had been, finally catching up with her.

Gild pressed a kiss to her temple. "I've spent a lot of time thinking how hard this is for me. To see you . . . going to him. To think of you . . ." He swallowed hard. "But I haven't spent enough time thinking of how hard it is for you. Serilda . . ." He pulled away, studying her. "I hate that he's trapped you here. I hate everything about this. But you have to know that I would do anything for you. I—" He stopped himself, and Serilda felt a yawning in her chest where her heart should have been. Something like hope, at what she thought he wanted to say.

Instead, he heaved a tired groan and slid his palms down her arms until he was holding her hands. Then he raised her hand to his face, pressing the backs of her fingers to his cheek, his eyes closed.

He had done this once before, on the first night they'd met. It was a small thing. A gentle caress. A piece of stolen affection, for the boy who had been given so little.

It made Serilda want to start crying again.

And kiss him again.

And tell him the truth. About her and the Erlking. About her unborn child.

But that was too dangerous a path. She didn't know for sure how Gild would react. If he would be happy or afraid or a mix of too many emotions to count. But she did know that if Gild was aware of the child, and that he was the father, he would never go along with this ruse. He would never pretend that the child belonged to the Erlking. And if the Erlking found out that Serilda had told Gild the truth . . . she could only imagine what he might do to the children that she was desperate to protect.

So she dragged in a sharp breath and looked toward the locked door, saying nothing.

Silence from the corridor outside, which made her wonder if perhaps she had managed to kill the final drude after all.

Returning her attention to Gild, she took in the blood streaked across his shirt. "You're hurt," she said, reaching toward the wounds. She paused, her fingers hovering above them. "Maybe I can find something to use as bandages or—"

"I'll be fine," he said, a weary smile replacing the heartbreak on his face. "I heal fast. And look, Serilda. We did it. We're in." With a groan, he climbed to his feet, bracing himself against a wall. "Since we did risk our lives to get in here, maybe we should have a look around."

Chapter Thirteen

Serilda approached the tapestry first, the one hung just inside the door's alcove. It was destroyed, cut through by blades or talons, and hung in tatters. Despite its ruinous state, Serilda had always been curious about the tapestry, which had glowed on the mortal side of the veil, as if sustained by some unknown attachment. In a castle that was little more than crumbling ruins, it had remained vivid and whole, untouched by time.

But thanks to the drudes, she'd never had a chance to fully regard the haunting image. Holding her breath, she took hold of two of the largest scraps. She lifted them up, piecing together the destroyed image. Gild joined her and, without asking questions, held up the remaining loose shreds to fill in the gaps.

Together, they took in the scene. It was almost charming. A royal family standing in a garden. Lanterns hung from tree boughs all around them. A king, a queen, a prince, and a princess.

A lovely family portrait.

Except that the king and queen, bedecked in royal finery and bejeweled crowns—were dead. Skeletons, with dark hollow eyes in their skulls and white teeth locked in eternal grins. The queen's bony fingers were wrapped around her daughter's hand, holding fast.

The prince and princess, on the other hand, seemed very much alive.

With her golden curls, the girl was the mirror image of the child painted inside of Gild's locket.

"My sister," Gild breathed, taking the locket from beneath his shirt collar and opening it to compare the two likenesses. Serilda thought she was a little younger in the locket's painting, but it was the same girl, clear as dumpling broth. The same golden ringlets tumbling around her face. The same impish smile. Serilda wondered how she hadn't noticed the similarities between her and Gild the first time she'd met him. It wasn't on a surface level—the girl's hair was blond and neatly styled, while his was cinnamon red and always a mess. Her eyes were vibrant blue; his brown and flecked with gold. They were both pale-skinned, but the princess did not have a fraction of the amount of freckles that Gild did.

But there was something more intrinsic that tied them together. Humor and jubilance and a spark of up-to-no-good.

Her attention returned to the prince. The one in the tapestry.

Gild.

"Are you sure that's me?" said Gild, sounding disappointed.

"Positive."

He grunted. "I look like a pompous asshat."

She laughed. "Why? Because you're properly dressed for once? Or because you actually combed your hair?"

He shot her an irritated look. "I'm wearing a ruff collar. Do you know how itchy those are?" He scratched his neck, as if it were strangling him even now.

"You were probably forced to pose for a portrait for *hours*, so the weaver had your likeness to work from," she said. "You must have been miserable."

He smiled wryly. "I imagine so."

"On the mortal side of the veil," said Serilda, "the tapestry isn't destroyed like this. Almost like it's been preserved by magic." She traced her fingers along one of the rough edges. "Why do you think it's ruined here?"

"Probably destroyed by those rotten drudes." Gild glanced back toward the door. They were both tense, waiting for another attack. But there was only silence. "Or, I don't know. Maybe the Erlking destroyed it. Didn't want me seeing any portraits of my family."

"That would make sense," Serilda mused.

Gild turned away. "Or maybe it's just this creepy castle being creepy, as it likes to do. Come on. Our bodies could still be around here somewhere."

As one, they faced the other great mystery of this tucked-away room.

A sheer curtain hung from the rafters and chandeliers, draped across the large cage that had long ago caught Serilda's eye, disguising whatever was inside.

She slid past Gild, rubbing her hands down the sides of her gown. The curtain pooled at her feet, undisturbed for ages, gathering clumps of dust in its folds. As she came nearer, the shape of the cage inside became more evident, and hope gathered in the pit of her stomach. It stood hip-high and was long enough to be a coffin. Large enough to hold what they were searching for.

This could be it. Their bodies, waiting to have their spirits returned. Their curses broken.

Inhaling, she searched the folds of the curtain for an opening. It took a moment, as plumes of dust were shaken into the air around them, but finally she found it.

She pulled the curtain aside.

Her eyes fell on a cage and she froze. Her lips parted in a startled gasp.

"What in Wyrdith's name is that?"

Gild's hand found her elbow. They both stared, speechless, into the cage. For it was indeed a cage—not a coffin, not a jeweled box meant to keep the mortal body of a cursed prince.

Just a cage, with bars crafted of shining gold and a floor that might have been a solid sheet of alabaster, though it was difficult to tell, given the thick ooze that had pooled in the bottom of the cage and dripped slowly over the sides, hardening over time like globs of candle wax.

And inside, nestled among that sludge, was a . . . chicken?

Serilda dared to take a step closer. It looked like a chicken, its fat body perched in one corner of the cage, wings folded back. Its feathers were a mix of fiery orange and periwinkle blue, with a pure white comb atop its head, and for a chicken, it was rather lovely. But beneath the plump body there were no tail feathers, but rather the back end of a red-and-blue snake winding around the edges of the cage, longer than Serilda was tall.

More striking even than the serpentine tail was that the creature had no eyes. For a moment, Serilda thought it might have hollow sockets like the nachtkrapp, but as she stared, she realized that it *should* have eyes, but someone, or something, had carved them out. The wounds had healed into uneven scars in its flesh.

"Another taxidermy?" Gild whispered.

Serilda considered. "Then why keep it in a cage?" She was whispering, too.

After another long moment, in which they both slowly relaxed from their surprise, Serilda began to feel silly. "Why are we whispering?"

"Not sure," Gild whispered back. "I can't tell if it's dead or asleep. But look. What is that?" He pointed to the creature's side, where something was sticking out from beneath its iridescent wing.

Serilda leaned closer. "An arrow?"

The sight reminded her of the rubinrot wyvern hung in the great hall, still struck through with the arrow that had supposedly killed it. A hint of pity tugged at Serilda's gut. Biting her lower lip, she carefully reached between the bars of the cage. She could barely wriggle her hand through the gap.

"Do you think that's a good idea?" said Gild.

Serilda wasn't sure at all. But the creature didn't move—didn't so much as flinch—when she grabbed hold of the arrow and tugged.

It was stuck.

She cringed.

"Maybe I should just leave it," she said. And then she did the exact opposite. She pulled harder.

This time, the arrow tore out of the creature's flesh.

She and Gild both gasped.

"I'm sorry," she breathed, as a rivulet of blood started to drip from the wound. "I'm so sorry!"

But the ... *thing* ... did not stir.

Slowly, Serilda relaxed. She held the arrow up to the light, seeing it tipped in shiny black. With a shrug, she tossed it to the floor.

"Why do you think it's being kept in here?" asked Gild, "and not out with the menagerie?"

"I have no idea. I can't even tell what it is."

After a long silence, Gild responded, "The legendary chicken-snake."

A snicker escaped from Serilda before she could stop it. She glanced at Gild over her shoulder. He returned a teasing smile. "As good a guess as any."

Shaking her head, she turned back to the cage.

And screamed.

Gild yelped and pulled her tight against him. They both backed a few steps away.

For in that breadth of a moment when they'd been distracted, the creature had moved. Without a sound—no squawk, no rustle of feathers, no soggy plodding through whatever that mess was on the bottom of the cage—it had deserted its corner and come to stand right in front of them. If it had not been blinded, Serilda would have thought it was peering at them through the bars. Instead, after a second, it tilted its head to one side, as if listening.

"Do chickens have ears?" Gild whispered.

"Hush," she replied.

And thus began a very awkward, very tedious staring contest.

The creature did not move.

She and Gild did not move.

She could not fully understand the fear that curdled in her stomach, the instinct she felt to hold perfectly still, lest it could find her. It was trapped in a cage. It didn't have eyes. It was a *chicken*. Mostly.

And yet, she felt an overwhelming terror as she took in its pointed yellow beak, long scaly toes, and the vibrant tail whipping back and forth against the golden bars. Though she could not explain it, this bizarre little monster conjured as much fear inside her as had the drudes, the nachtkrapp, even the enormous bärgeist. And if the way Gild's fingers were digging into her sides was any indication, Gild felt it, too.

Finally, gathering up every ounce of courage, Serilda cleared her throat and murmured an uncertain hello.

The bird . . . *thing* . . . bobbed its head, every bit like the chickens she'd often seen pecking around farms, searching for worms.

It opened its beak. But it did not cluck.

Instead, it hissed.

And sent a glob of goop, as thick and disgusting as the substance beneath it, straight at them. Serilda and Gild jumped away. The substance landed on the hem of Serilda's gown.

The fabric began to hiss as the slimy liquid burned a hole into the brocade. It sizzled and smoked, releasing a putrid odor into the room.

Serilda's eyes widened.

Within seconds, the hole in the material began to spread, scorching through the first layer of thick, luxurious fabric, eating away at the intricate design of golden lily flowers. Spreading along Serilda's calf, up past her knees, revealing the petticoat beneath. She cried out and backed farther away from the cage, but she could hardly escape her own gown.

"Gild!" she cried, as a drop of the venom touched the petticoat, and that, too, began to disintegrate into ashes. "Get it off! I have to get it off!"

Before she'd even finished talking, he was yanking at the laces on the back of the dress.

"Cut them!" she screeched, watching the fabric burn away. Ashes up to her thigh. Soon it would be at her hips, her waist, and then there would be no keeping it off her skin. "Gild!"

"I don't have anything to cut with!" he hollered, hands scrabbling, yanking at the ties. "Almost. Almost."

One last yank. The dress's bodice loosened. Serilda pulled her arms from the sleeves as Gild shoved the dress past her hips. She fell onto her backside in an effort to scramble out of the material as fast as she could. As soon as the heavy brocade gown was off, she took hold of the petticoat's muslin and ripped, tearing off the skirt, including the panels being ravaged by venom. She kicked the tarnished material away. The gown landed on top of the pool of gossamer curtains, and together, Gild and Serilda watched as the dress dissolved. Then the muslin skirt. Then, even the curtains that had kept the creature's cage hidden.

Within minutes it was all destroyed.

Every last thread.

Serilda and Gild pushed themselves back against the door and stood, panting. An acrid stench hung in the air, stinging the back of Serilda's throat.

Only once its destruction had run its course did the little beast lie down again, tuck its head into its puff of chest feathers, and give a few satisfied flicks of its long tail.

"Well," said Gild, his voice haggard, "I guess that explains why it isn't out in the menagerie."

Serilda let out a high-pitched squeak of a laugh.

She and Gild glanced at each other.

Then, having forgotten about the drudes—or perhaps mutually, silently agreeing that they'd rather take their chances with the nightmares—they unlocked the door and fled.

They had just started down the hall of gods when Serilda screeched to a halt.

"Gild, wait!" she cried, grabbing his arm. "I can't go down there. Look at me."

Gild's gaze swept up and down her twice before understanding brightened his eyes. "The hunt isn't here."

She heaved a sigh. "I know, but there are plenty of dark ones who would love to tell him that I was spotted running through the hall wearing nothing but my bloomers!"

An amused grin broke over Gild's face. "You could be starting a new trend."

"Be serious." She whapped him on the shoulder.

"This wouldn't be a problem if you'd been practicing your—" He snapped his fingers and disappeared.

Serilda rolled her eyes and turned around, fully expecting him to have reappeared right behind her.

But he hadn't.

She frowned and spun in a full circle, searching.

Gild did not come back.

She let out a disgruntled noise. "Gild!"

No response.

Flailing her arms, she huffed and glowered at the nearest god, for no particular reason other than she had no one else to blame for her current predicament. The window depicted Solvilde, god of sky and sea, blowing wind into the sails of a large ship. As with the others, the artist had chosen to depict the god regally—in flowing robes that changed from crimson red to a pale blue, like a sunrise, and a crown of pearls shimmering brightly against their dark skin. But Serilda imagined Solvilde would dress in something practical—airy shirts and comfortable breeches, leather harnesses for carrying their important gadgets. Compasses and telescopes and the like. She'd always pictured the god to dress something like a pirate.

"Ask and ye shall receive."

She whipped around. Gild stood in the hall, a swath of burgundy velvet in his arms.

Serilda could have melted with relief. "Thank you."

"Nothing to it. Was hoping I'd get a chance to pick through your undergarments, too, but the twins were there, watching me like little owls. Children are terrifying." He faked a shudder.

She rolled her eyes. Gild pretended to be frightened of children, but he was the first to wrestle with her five when they were bored, the first to spot Anna when she practiced her handstands, the first to hold Gerdrut's hand when she got scared. She wondered if he was always so good with little ones. She thought it might be due to something buried deep inside him—forgotten experiences of caring for his little sister.

"You wouldn't dare pick through my undergarments," she said, snatching away the dress.

He made a noncommittal shrug. "Thought you might want a new one of . . . those things." He made an awkward gesture toward her legs.

"A chemise?" She sighed. "I'll have to go without. Turn around."

Gild lifted his eyebrows at her. A touch of pink was making the freckles on his face more pronounced, but there was something daring in the look. Something roguish. And in that moment, Serilda felt a thousand unspoken words sparking in the air.

They had never talked about what had happened between them, the third night she'd been asked to spin straw into gold. The night his kisses had burned trails down her throat. The night she'd had absolutely no qualms about letting him see her without her chemise, her bloomers . . . without anything.

But Gild didn't press the point.

With a smirk clinging to the corners of his mouth, he swung himself around to face the wall. "Let me know if you need assistance," he said in a singsong voice.

"I'll be fine," she muttered. Her fingers twitched with memories and urges that had never fully gone away.

"If you insist," he said. "I just know how queens get used to having others dress them, pamper them . . ." He raised his arms in an exaggerated stretch. "Just want you to know that my services are available."

"Stop talking, Gild," she said, her whole body flushed now.

He answered with a laugh.

Even as she tore off what was left of her chemise and shimmied into the gown he'd brought, her skin, bare against the dress's fabric, tingled with memories of where his fingers had once traveled. The backs of her knees. The sensitive skin along her rib cage.

She gave a ferocious shake to her head as she straightened the gown's fabric. "All right, you can turn around. Will you do the laces?"

"Ah, so you do need my help?"

She cast her eyes to the ceiling. "You're insufferable."

"You seem to like me anyway."

She paused, half turned around, and faced him again, catching the hand that had been reaching for the laces. She held his gaze and he froze, the teasing glint fading in his eyes.

"I do, Gild," she said earnestly. "I do, so very much."

His mouth opened, but she didn't give him a chance to respond before she leaned forward and pressed her lips against his, trying to fill the kiss with all the words she wasn't allowed to say. She might be married to the Erlking, but she wanted *him.* Only him.

Her eyes were watering when she pulled away. Gild watched her, his expression both hopeful and . . . heartbroken.

Without a word, Serilda turned her back to him.

She was both relieved and disappointed when Gild cinched up the laces with as much integrity as a gentleman could. He did not let his fingertips trace the triangles of bare skin, or linger at the nape of her neck. He did not lean closer, letting his breath dance against the back of her ear. He did not embrace her from behind and start to undo his hard work.

And everything he didn't do left Serilda boiling over with a yearning she'd spent the past months shoving deep, deep down into herself.

"There you are," he said, quietly stepping back.

Serilda faced him again. "Thank you."

He must have seen it in her eyes. He must have known. She couldn't have hidden her desire from him if she'd tried.

His eyes darkened, but for once, he had no cocky remark.

Serilda swallowed.

They were alone.

No one would know if she stole one more kiss. One more embrace.

No one had to know.

She took a step forward. "Gild, I—"

"They're waiting for you," he stammered, as his hands came up to her arms. Not to pull her closer, but to hold her back.

She froze. "What?"

"The children. Everyone. They're waiting for you." Gild gave a fleeting smile. "We wouldn't want anyone to worry."

Chapter Fourteen

R eady the hounds," ordered the Erlking from atop his raven-black steed. "Hunters at the ready." He shifted the horse and glanced up, his gaze meeting Serilda's. But the look was brief. In the next moment, the hounds began to howl, and the Erlking's attention shifted back to the hunt's spectacle.

Serilda was so bored, and it was a constant struggle to remind herself to act regal. Don't yawn. Don't squirm. Don't give any indication that she would rather be anywhere than here.

Especially when she was as much a spectacle as the hunters themselves.

In honor of Her Majesty's first appearance watching the hunters' demonstration, the Erlking had ordered a lofted set of stands built in the corner of the hunting arena, complete with a large shade canopy and plush benches. The carpenters had worked on it all night long. And here Serilda had sat for the better part of the afternoon, with her five attendants beside her and a host of phantoms doting on her with cups of fruit-filled water and trays of buttery pastries. Which would have been rather nice, she supposed, if she hadn't felt like a peacock on display. Because it wasn't just her and the kindly ghosts. It never was. She was also surrounded on all sides by the king's court. Those beautiful, vicious creatures, with their eyes that followed her every move and their quiet, mocking laughter.

Serilda didn't care so much what they thought of her. But she hated always feeling like she was sitting in a pit of hellhounds, waiting for them to tire of toying with her and finally devour her whole.

Below, the hunters had situated their horses into formation around the arena, which was really just a large forested portion of the gardens that had been walled off.

"Let us provide an entrancing show," said the Erlking. "I would not want you to embarrass yourselves before your queen."

Though he sounded serious enough, Serilda could hear some of the hunters' scoffs even from her high perch. A couple of the dark ones in the stands cast her wry looks.

"I'm bored," groaned Anna, cupping her chin in her hands. "How long do we have to sit here?"

"Not much longer," Serilda lied.

"You said that an hour ago." Anna started to kick at the rail in front of them. "When they were finishing the archery competition."

"And the hour before that," piped up Fricz, "when they were parading the dogs around like prized ponies."

"And the hour before that—" started Hans, but Serilda raised a hand to stop him.

"I know," she said. "I think this is their final demonstration. Besides, it looks like it might start raining soon." Though the morning had been filled with sunshine, dark clouds had begun to gather on the horizon. She had never been so eager for a storm.

She was as antsy as the children, made worse by a sleepless night, a heavy gown, sweat dripping down her back, and the fact that she couldn't mindlessly kick the rail no matter how much she wanted to because, again, she was the queen.

She didn't care how impressive the hunters were or their smoldering hellhounds. She just wanted to retreat to her chambers and take a long nap.

Anna's kicks became more vehement, and Serilda reached over and placed a hand on the girl's knee to still it. In response, Anna crossed her arms over her chest and sank into a sulk.

Down below, the king nodded at Giselle, who stood before the cage of the bärgeist—the great ghost bear. A hulking figure, ten feet tall, covered in oily black fur, with eyes that flamed like coals. Though an imposing figure, it was not as beautiful as some of the other creatures in the menagerie. The bärgeist appeared ancient, with great chunks of its black fur falling off in places to reveal gray, withered skin beneath. A couple of missing teeth did not make its enormous maw any less terrifying. It had one missing ear and jagged scars crisscrossing that side of its neck all the way down to its front paw. It looked like it had lived for a thousand years—and each century had been more cruel than the last.

"Release the bärgeist!" shouted the king.

Giselle, with the help of three servants, lifted the iron bar from the door of the cage. As the latches groaned and the bear paced back and forth on legs as wide as tree stumps, the hounds began to snarl and pull at their chains.

Serilda swallowed hard, hoping that their hastily constructed platform wouldn't come toppling over should the bärgeist decide to ram into them.

"What if they can't capture it again?" whispered Gerdrut.

"Then we'll have a ferocious half-dead bear wandering around the gardens," said Fricz.

"Maybe it will eat the Erlking," said Nickel, "and solve at least one of our problems."

Anna twisted her lips to consider this, but ultimately shook her head. "Not much of a solution if it just makes a bigger problem to deal with."

"I'll take my chances with the bear," muttered Nickel.

Down below, the bear was crawling on all fours out of the cage. The hunters gave it a wide berth, those on foot hiding in the trees and brush, while those on horseback lingered closer to the edges of the arena. The bear walked with slow, stocky movements, sniffing the air, its patchy fur bristled with distrust.

Until, without warning, the bear stood on its back legs and roared. Its yellowed fangs flashed in the sunlight. When it landed back on its forepaws, the ground trembled, the vibrations even felt through the floorboards of the stands.

Then the bear was charging through the false forest, searching for an escape.

"Hold!" shouted the Erlking.

No one tried to stop the bear as it sped around trees and trampled vegetation, knocking over saplings and crushing ferns and ignoring the brambles and twigs that caught in its fur.

It reached an outer wall.

The bear came to an abrupt stop, staring at the impenetrable stone before it. Then it roared again—the sound shaking Serilda's bones.

The bear spent a moment sniffing around the wall, even attempting to climb it.

With a frustrated snort, the bear charged back into the forest. This time, heading toward the castle.

Still, the hunters did not move. How far would they let it go?

She wondered if there was any chance the bear might actually escape. If it found the southern gate, the bear might be able to climb over it. Could it get to the courtyard and across the drawbridge into Adalheid? Or could it leap into the lake and swim for a distant shore? What if the bear made it out into the mortal realm?

She felt bad for the bear—but not so bad that she wanted it loosed upon the people she cared for.

"Why aren't they doing anything?" asked Anna, who had stood now and was leaning both hands against the rail to see better.

"They are biding their time, waiting for the creature to exhaust itself. It will be easier to capture once it has relinquished hope."

Serilda and the children turned toward the raspy voice. A woman was sitting in the next row of benches. Alone.

Serilda recognized her immediately. The headless woman, as she had always thought of her. Not a dark one, but a ghost—one of the few who often joined the wild hunt, who had been down in the arena practicing swordsmanship and archery earlier that afternoon. She wore a scarf around her throat, perpetually drenched in blood, as was the front of her tunic. In the mortal realm, when Serilda had once been fleeing from the castle, she had seen this woman's ghost. Had heard her crying, saying it was all her fault. Serilda had watched as the woman's head was cut off by some invisible blade. Even now, Serilda shivered when she thought of it. The decapitated head, eyes staring, mouth open, whispering—*Help us.*

The memory accosted her every time she spotted this woman, though she didn't think the ghosts knew what their haunting selves did on the other side of the veil.

"They're playing with it," said Hans, disgusted. "Making it think it has a chance."

"Precisely," said the woman. "It is one of the king's favorite games."

Serilda shivered, thinking how the wild hunt had once allowed her to believe she might escape, too. She and her father had fled to a nearby town, hoping they could hide until the full moon was over. She had thought they stood a chance—just like the bärgeist below.

"How long will it take the bear to . . . give up?" she asked.

The woman met her gaze. "Impossible to say. This is the first time the bear has been outside its cage in hundreds of years. How it reacts is anyone's guess."

"Why aren't you down there?" asked Nickel. "You're a hunter, too, aren't you?"

The woman smiled at him, her expression soft. "I am a hunter," she said. "But I am not one of *them*, nor will I ever be." The contempt in her tone was obvious.

"You don't like the wild hunt?" said Fricz, twisting so far around in his seat that he was nearly sitting backward.

"Oh, I enjoy the taste of freedom it offers, but not as much as I despise the sensation of being trapped yet again when we return." The woman paused before adding, "We ghosts are given few choices. I suspect you know that yourself, young squire."

Fricz's curious expression dimmed.

"His Darkness takes me with him because I have skills he values on the hunt," she went on. "If given a choice, I would not keep such company, even if it meant abstaining from the one thing I've ever been good at."

Serilda considered this, wondering if she could ever abstain from telling stories—the one thing she had ever been good at. Probably it would benefit her greatly if she did, but she had promised herself in the past that she was done with her tales and her lies and yet, somehow, her mischievous tongue always betrayed her, and usually got her into deeper and deeper trouble.

"M'lady, I might not perch quite so precariously if I were you," said the woman.

Serilda turned to see Anna sitting on top of the rail, her back toward the arena. Serilda gasped and reached forward, grabbing Anna's arm and pulling her back. "You could fall!"

Anna huffed. "At least it would be something to do!" she said, facing the spectacle and leaning her elbows on the rail, refusing to sit back down on the bench.

Serilda shook her head and wished doubly hard for this day to be over. She was glad to see that the storm clouds had gotten nearer. Any minute now they would roll in front of the sun. A shadowy mist in the distance suggested a heavy rain was coming, too.

"Forgive my forwardness, Your Majesty," said the woman. She had stood and come around the bench and now gestured at the spot Anna had deserted. "I wonder if I might join your company?"

Serilda blinked, studying the woman more closely than she had before. She was fair-skinned, with keen blue eyes and yellow hair braided into a neat crown atop her head. Her posture was stiff and regal, her build athletic and strong.

Now that she thought of it, this woman had always seemed different from the other ghosts of the castle. She was a hunter, but not fully welcomed by the dark ones. She was a ghost, but not a servant. She had earned respect for her skills, and yet—just like Serilda—her skills had also earned her the position of an outcast.

"Of course," said Serilda, scooting closer toward Gerdrut to make room. "We would be honored by your company."

The woman smiled, almost shyly, as she sat. "I am Lady Agathe, huntress and weapons master."

"Weapons master?" said Serilda, her eyebrows lifting.

Agathe nodded. "I have few memories of my mortal life, but I was once tasked with training the castle guards, among other responsibilities."

Serilda thought again of the shadowy figure weeping in the castle entrance. *I taught him as well as I could, but he wasn't ready. I failed him. I failed them all.*

It was as though a piece of the castle's tragic past fell into place. No wonder Agathe blamed herself, at least in part, for failing at her duties. She had trained the castle guards. She must have been a great warrior herself. And yet, against the dark ones, Adalheid had fallen. The very people she had meant to protect had been slaughtered, including herself, and the royal family. Surely Agathe would have known the king and queen, even Gild. Perhaps she had been the one to teach him sword fighting and archery.

"It must have been a great honor for one of your talents," Serilda ventured, "to be given a place among the wild hunt."

Agathe grinned sourly. "They should be honored to have *me.*" Then she cut a look toward Serilda, her eyes twinkling. "Rather like they should be honored to have such a queen on the alder throne."

Serilda felt her cheeks warming. She was a miller's daughter. She still did not see herself as much of a queen, and she wasn't sure she ever would. "I doubt many see it that way."

"They are fools."

A roar from the arena drew their attention back to the bärgeist. The bear had reached the western wall and was eyeing some of the taller trees, likely contemplating whether they would hold its weight if it tried to climb them.

The hunters, too, were on the move. Creeping through the foliage. Surrounding the bear like a trap, their moves as silent as moonlight.

"I don't understand why you aren't down there," said Serilda. "Surely your skills would be valuable in practice as much as in reality."

"I am useful on the hunts," said Agathe, "but this is for sport. A way to build skills and to practice with the golden chains. It is also entertainment for the dark ones. To show the court what their hunters can do." She glared at a group of dark ones who had gathered close to the rails. "It would not be appreciated for a human ghost to upstage their beloved hunters before such an audience. Before the queen herself." She chuckled under her breath. "The king would not risk that."

Serilda could not help grinning at her. Agathe's words were arrogant, but her tone held a quiet confidence. Could this woman, once a mortal, truly be a better hunter than the demons? It was difficult to imagine, but Serilda had seen firsthand how the Erlking gave Agathe more respect than he afforded most of the ghosts in this castle, or even some of the dark ones.

"Watch now," said Agathe.

Down below, the king—barely visible in a patch of fig trees—gave a signal with his arm.

The hounds raced forward. Yelping. Howling. A blur of black fur in the trees.

The bear growled, putting its back to the wall. It sniffed the air, red eyes flashing.

Serilda leaned forward, hoping the bear would fight back. That it would destroy some of those awful hounds.

But the hounds did not attack. Instead, they stopped just beyond reach of the bear's massive claws, ducking and dodging as it swiped at them. It took Serilda a moment to realize that the hounds were herding the bear. Forcing it away from the wall and back into the tree line.

The bear continued to snarl and swat, even as it lost ground. The hounds were too quick, too well-trained. Serilda wondered if they were intentionally trying to confuse the bear, the way they darted in and around it, growling and nipping at its fur, coming at it from every direction. Then a hound leaped onto the bear's back and buried its fangs into the bear's flesh. The bärgeist roared and flung the hound off—

And the arrows began to fly.

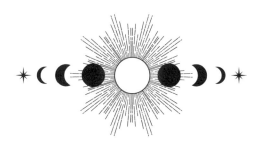

Chapter Fifteen

Serilda had been so focused on the hellhounds she hadn't noticed the hunters.

Three arrows struck the bärgeist in quick succession. Two in its shoulder, one in its side. The bear roared again, the embers in its eyes kindling with rage.

But it didn't charge at the hunters.

Instead, it turned and ran, fleeing for its life.

It had not gone far before a net woven from golden chains snapped taut in its path. The bear crashed into it, its limbs quickly entangled.

Agathe rose to her feet, and Serilda was quick to join her. She and the children gathered close to the rail, watching in horrified awe as the bärgeist struggled to claw its way free. The hunters strained to pull the chains taut, securing the net around its massive body.

"It isn't enough," murmured Agathe.

Serilda didn't respond. She was trying to see what Agathe saw. Trying to discern what was happening in that mass of black fur and howling dogs and glittering chains.

It surely seemed like enough to her.

Around them, the stands erupted in applause. Serilda did not cheer, nor did the children. Nor did any of the servants, who had stopped distributing food and drink to watch the hunt.

Nor, she noticed, did Agathe.

It had not really been a fair battle. The bear hadn't stood a chance. It had been a beast in a maze, with no hope for freedom.

What was the purpose? To taunt this poor creature, who had already spent an eternity in confinement? The violence was grotesque, and Serilda couldn't fathom why anyone would wish to see it. There wasn't any glory here.

A small hand slipped into hers. She looked down to see Gerdrut watching the hunt with tears on her face. "Are they going to kill it?"

Serilda frowned. "I don't know."

"No, child," said Agathe. "They intend to put it back in the cage. So that, once it is healed, they may hunt it again and again."

Gerdrut shivered.

A sudden shadow eclipsed the sunlight. The clouds were gathering over the castle.

Serilda searched out the Erlking. He was still astride his horse, but his expression was not celebratory. He was watching the sky, as if the storm were a personal slight.

Then his attention dropped back down to the bärgeist and his scowl deepened.

"I don't understand," said Serilda. "Why is His Grim not pleased?"

"Those chains were enough to capture the tatzelwurm," said Agathe. "But they cannot hold the bärgeist. Which means they will not hold a gryphon."

"A gryphon?"

Agathe nodded. "It is the next creature that His Grim has set his sights on capturing."

Serilda tried to picture such a regal beast in the flesh—eagle wings and lion claws—the vision straight from one of the books she had borrowed from the schoolhouse in Märchenfeld.

Below, the bärgeist had stopped struggling against the bindings.

"It looks like they are holding to me," murmured Serilda.

"Wait," said Agathe.

But though the crowd held their breath, and the hunters held the chains and dug their heels into the soft dirt, the bärgeist did not move. Too afraid, or too discouraged, to fight back.

"But how did they capture it before?" asked Serilda. "The king hunted the bärgeist without golden chains. And so many others. The rubinrot wyvern, the . . ." She stopped herself before she could mention the creature she and Gild had seen, not sure if that was meant to be a secret. "So many others."

"My understanding," Agathe said slowly, "is that the bärgeist was captured by Perchta, the great huntress."

Serilda's head whipped around. "What?"

A shadow fell over Agathe's face. "I mentioned how I have few memories of my mortal life, but there is one clearer than the others. The night the dark ones came. They stormed the castle with weapons, yes, but also came with their beasts. The nachtkrapp. The drudes. Alps and goblins and the rest." Her voice grew quieter. "And the bärgeist. They unleashed it in the great hall and watched as it tore through our ranks like a sickle through wheat. I remember being in the throne room, and I wanted to chase after it, to try to stop the monster, but I . . . I didn't. I couldn't." Her brow furrowed. "I think, perhaps, I was defending something in that room. Or someone. But I don't remember . . ."

"The king and queen," said Serilda, laying a hand on the woman's arm and biting back the grimace at the sickly sensation. Agathe stiffened, looking down at the touch, briefly astonished. "I believe the king and queen died in the throne room during the massacre. You were probably trying to protect them."

Agathe shook her head. "I don't remember a king and queen—"

"Nobody does. It is a part of the curse on this castle, that the royal family be forgotten. There were a prince and princess, too."

"A prince and princess?" Agathe fidgeted with the bloodied scarf at her neck. Then she inhaled sharply, a deep frown scrawling across her features. "So I failed them, too."

Serilda's insides tightened. "That isn't what I—"

"It doesn't matter anymore," interrupted Agathe. "You asked about the wyvern. It was captured later. Perhaps . . . a hundred years ago? It is difficult to track the passing of time, but I was on that hunt. The king had an arrow he had been saving for that particular beast. I believe it was one of Perchta's, perhaps the very last of her arrows. The huntress had a special poison that she dipped her arrows into on important hunts. It could subdue her prey. Rendered beasts immobile. That is how we captured the wyvern, even without the golden chains. I do not believe the king has any more of those arrows." She cocked her head, peering at Serilda. "The wild hunt is most formidable. But even today, the hunters talk of Perchta as if she were still their leader. Not even the Alder King can replace her in their minds."

"She sounds terrifying," said Serilda.

Agathe laughed. "Yes. I agree." Suddenly, her body went rigid and she pressed forward against the rail again. "Look."

Serilda and the children leaned in as shadows stretched across the arena. The bärgeist was still hunched over protectively, its back like a mountain with jagged, bristled fur, the golden net looped around its front legs and up around its right shoulder. Three arrows jutting from its flesh.

Serilda did not know what Agathe had seen. It still seemed to her that the hunt had won. The bear was captured.

The hounds fell back and the hunters crept forward, weapons drawn.

A gust of wind whistled across the gardens, shaking the branches in the orchard. With it, the first sprinkles of rain.

"They *are* going to kill it!" said Gerdrut.

"No," said Agathe. "They will try to get it to move. They are not strong enough to haul it back to the cage, so they will use pain to encourage it to walk. If that fails, they might have to hook the chains to the horses, but even that—"

One of the hunters leaped forward, preparing to jab a spear into the bear's hindquarters.

But just before they did, the bear reared up on its back legs. The hunters holding the chains slipped through the dirt, dragged forward by the beast's incredible strength. Some dropped the chains. The hunter with the spear leaped backward as the bärgeist turned on him and lunged, cutting through the hunter's abdomen with one swipe of its claws. Smoke seeped out of the wound, spilling like dark fog around the hunter's ankles. The man cried out in pain and collapsed. The bear launched its massive form over him and bolted back into the dense forest. With the golden net still on its shoulders, it managed to drag a couple of determined hunters along with it, until they were forced to relinquish the chains and let it go.

"Yes!" cheered Gerdrut.

And then—a scream.

It happened so fast, Serilda barely saw Anna's figure leaning too far out one moment—then toppling over the rail in the next.

She cried out and peered over the edge. Anna lay sprawled on the ground, and for one heart-wrenching moment, Serilda remembered it all over again. Finding her body on the side of the road, just outside the Aschen Wood. Still in her nightgown, mud streaked across her face, a gaping hole in her chest where the nachtkrapp had eaten out her heart.

Horror and despair crashed over her, and Serilda wanted to scream and rail and lash out at anyone who dared cross her path—

But then, a groan.

Anna's eyes flickered open. "Still . . . alive," she said, with a half smile.

Serilda wilted. It wasn't true, but it was enough to assuage the horrible pain of losing her all over again.

Until Gerdrut shrieked, "Anna! The bärgeist!"

Serilda's eyes widened. The beast was stampeding through the forest, heading straight for Anna, who looked as though she could barely move.

"It can't kill her," Serilda whispered beneath her breath. "It can't kill her, not again."

But it could hurt her.

Movement flashed in Serilda's vision. Agathe planted one hand on the rail and threw herself from the platform. She landed on her feet and sprang forward, grabbing a fallen branch from the ground. She positioned herself between Anna and the bärgeist seconds before the hulking black form crashed into her with a ferocious growl. Limbs and fur and claws and snarling and blood and then—

"Kill it! Now!"

Arrows, from every direction. The bärgeist roaring. Fighting. Clawing.

Finally—the bear released Agathe and faced the hunters. Agathe collapsed beside Anna, covered in blood, gripping the stick. Her other arm appeared mangled and twisted.

The bärgeist gave one last swipe at a hound that dared get too close, but missed. It swayed on its hind legs a moment, then collapsed to its side, heaving with every breath. Blood ran thick from too many wounds to count, dripping slow like molasses, matting its black fur. Its great body shuddered one last time, before falling still.

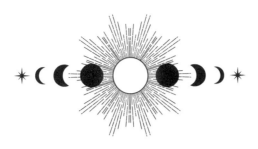

Chapter Sixteen

Serilda elbowed her way through the dark ones who stood watching. She flew down the rickety steps, her feet hardly touching the boards, and shoved open the protective gate.

"Anna!" she cried. "Lady Agathe!" She fell to her knees between them, not sure who she was more worried for. Anna had not made any attempt to sit up, and Agathe . . . if Agathe were alive, well . . . she would be dead already.

"I'm all right," said Anna, though Serilda could tell she was hurt. "Just . . . maybe . . . a broken bone. Or . . . sixteen. But I'm all right."

"I shall be as well." Agathe did a better job of hiding her pain as she held her destroyed limb against her stomach. "It is not the worst wound I've experienced."

Sadly, Serilda knew this to be true.

"What is the matter with you?" yelled the Erlking.

Serilda balked. Her emotions were strung so tightly, she was in no mood to be yelled at. But as she glowered up at her husband, who had appeared like a specter on his black horse, she saw that he was not looking at her, but Agathe.

"She is only a ghost!" he went on, gesturing at Anna. "She cannot be killed! And now, because of your foolishness, we have lost the bärgeist!"

With great pains, Agathe forced herself to her feet. "Forgive me, my lord. But it was not I who gave the order for the bärgeist to be killed." She met his gaze without flinching. "After all, I am also *only* a ghost."

The Erlking snarled. "Any other ghost, I would gladly have let it maul to pieces." His nostrils flared and it seemed to pain him to add, "But you are worth more to the hunt. At least . . . you *were*." He scowled at her arm with disgust.

"I am honored that you think so," said Agathe, not sounding honored at all. She bowed her head. "The arm will heal in time, but I would not see the child harmed any more than she has already been. Our queen seems so attached to her attendants. I did not wish to see Her Majesty disappointed."

The king snarled at Serilda. Then, as if remembering their ruse, he appeared to physically swallow his anger. After a long, steady exhale, he dismounted from his horse. "Of course," he said bitterly. "We would not wish to disappoint Her Majesty. Though the bärgeist is a great loss for us."

"Fret not, my lord," said Serilda, kneeling beside Anna and helping the girl sit up. "I have no doubt you will find another. What is one mythical beast to the wild hunt?"

She smiled, and the king returned a glare. Serilda understood his irritation more now that she knew it had been Perchta, not the Erlking, who had captured the bärgeist in the first place. And now, the Erlking had no more of Perchta's poisoned arrows, nor enough golden chains to capture anything larger or more ferocious than the tatzelwurm, and one of his most skilled hunters was sorely wounded. Despite her concern for Anna and Agathe, Serilda was pleased at the king's growing frustration.

"Agathe," he said, "see that your wounds are tended to. I would have you in good spirits by the Straw Moon."

Serilda heard a snicker. She glanced over her shoulder to see that the rest of the children had joined them in the arena.

"Good spirits," said Fricz, elbowing his twin. "I think that was a joke."

The Erlking took in the hunters and servants and the rest of the court.

Then he cast his gaze skyward. The raindrops were fat but scattered, a mild annoyance. But the clouds were so dark it might have been dusk.

"Before we end the day's pageantry," said the king, fixing his calculating attention on Serilda, "my queen and I have a most fortuitous announcement. As we are all gathered, I see no reason to withhold our happy news."

Serilda froze. "Happy news?"

The Erlking held a hand toward her.

Serilda hesitated, but seeing that she had no real choice, she deserted Anna and went to him, taking his hand as dread hardened in her gut. "My lord, everyone wants out of the rain—"

"They can wait," said the Erlking. "They will all want to share in our joy."

She swallowed, knowing with utter certainty what *happy news* he planned to share.

She wasn't ready. She'd thought she would have more time to prepare herself. She'd thought, somehow, she might even be able to prepare *Gild*. But all she'd done was avoid the inevitable and hope that maybe it would never come to pass.

And now here she was, hand in hand with the Erlking, facing the entirety of their court.

Not ready, not ready, I'm not ready . . .

Silence had fallen over the arena but for the gloomy droplets smacking the ground, the plants, the canopy over the stands. The hunters were restless, still weary from the fight with the bärgeist. The children watched with curious, expectant faces.

"It is with greatest delight," started the Erlking, lifting Serilda's hand and pressing a kiss to her knuckle, "that I share with you the most glorious news." His eyes glittered as he watched Serilda squirm. "My queen, gem of my heart, has informed me that we are with child."

Even expecting them, the words struck Serilda like a bolt to the chest.

We are with child.

She wanted to pull away from him. To tell them it wasn't true. The child wasn't his. The child would never be his.

But she kept her expression placid.

God of lies, help me see this through, she thought. And then, to even her surprise, a tiny smile dared to creep across the corners of her lips.

She could do this. She had to do this.

"By the grace of Eostrig," said the Erlking, with a clever twist to his mouth making it clear that he meant this as a taunt, "we shall have a new prince or princess to celebrate by the new year." He lifted their entwined hands into the air. "Raise a cheer for our Alder Queen!"

A cry went up among the gardens, though it was unclear how many of the dark ones were truly rejoicing at the news. After ages without a royal heir, they must think that such an addition was frivolous. They were immortal. They needed no progeny to pass on their legacies.

As the cheers died down, the king dismissed their audience. While hunters began gathering their weapons and chains and the servants started tearing down the stands, Serilda tried to extricate her hand from his grip, but the Erlking held fast.

"Was there more?" she said, not hiding her irritation.

"You are not pleased? But you so enjoy being the center of attention."

"Whatever gave you that impression?"

He considered her. "One does not barge into a haunted castle and demand a bargain with the Alder King unless they have some appreciation for the dramatic."

Serilda glared at him. "It might have been nice to have some warning." She again tried to pull away. He again refused to loosen his grip. "I wish to retire," she said through her teeth. Then she leaned closer to him, lowering her voice to a growl. "You would not keep your pregnant wife from her rest, would you?"

"Of course not. I just think there is something you are forgetting."

"And what is that?"

He lifted an eyebrow. "How much we adore each other."

With his free hand, he cupped Serilda's ear and neck, tipped her back, and claimed her mouth with his.

Serilda went rigid.

The moment he attempted to deepen the kiss, she bit him.

The Erlking pulled back with a hiss, though he managed to hide it from anyone who might be watching.

Then, as if brought on by the Erlking's anger, a bolt of lightning shot from the sky, striking the keep with a boom of thunder so loud it rumbled the castle grounds. Serilda jumped from the king's arms and clapped her hands to her ears.

The rain became a torrent. Thick, heavy drops that struck like pebbles. It had been too warm lately for Serilda to require her dutiful wool cloak—the one Gild had once mended for her after a horrific drude attack—but as the storm began in earnest, she wished she had it with her.

"The children and I will retire now," said Serilda, yelling to be heard over the storm.

But the Erlking was not paying any attention to her. His focus was on the sky, drawn with suspicion as the rain soaked his clothes. "It can't be . . . ," he murmured.

More lightning streaked from the clouds, making the hairs on Serilda's arm lift from her chilled skin. One bolt hit the Erlking's statue in the gardens, sending it toppling to the ground.

"Hunters!" bellowed the Erlking, reaching for his crossbow. "Gather the chains and follow me! Quickly!"

Serilda did not know what he thought they were going to be hunting in this storm, and with the veil down no less, but she was more concerned with herself and the children and poor Anna. She found them huddled in what shelter they could find beneath a plum tree. Anna had managed to get to her feet, and had her arms slung around Hans's and Nickel's shoulders.

"Anna, can you walk?"

"Y-yes," she said. "I think so."

"Good. Let's get inside for some warm cider."

There was no point trying to maintain her regal dignity with her gown already drenched, so they hurried as fast as they could into the keep, dodging the hunters, who were running about as if they were preparing for a war, not trying to get out of the rain.

As soon as they had ducked into the shelter of the keep, Fricz shook his head like a puppy, sending raindrops scattering across the carpets. "Have you ever seen a storm like this before? One that came on so quick like that?"

"Not in memory, no," said Serilda. "But we are in the season of the Thunder Moon."

Outside, another boom of thunder made the torches on the walls flicker.

"It's all right," said Serilda, picking up Gerdrut, who was terrified of lightning storms. "We'll feel better when we're dry and warm. Nothing to be frightened of."

"Is it true?" asked Hans, who seemed less bothered by the storm than the others. "Are you really going to have a baby?"

Gerdrut pulled her face out of the crook of Serilda's shoulder. "With *him*?"

Serilda sighed heavily. "It's true enough. But I don't wish to speak any more about it."

"But, Serilda—" started Hans.

"Not a word," she said. "This is the way things have to be, and that's all there is to it."

A silence fell over them, likely due more to her abruptness than anything else. She hardly ever snapped at them.

Until, just as they had passed back into the castle corridors, Gerdrut cleared her throat. "I can rub your feet, if it helps? Mama's feet were always hurting her."

At this gentle suggestion, a sudden, unspeakable sadness welled up inside Serilda. Gerdrut's mother was even now pregnant with her second child— Gerdrut's first sibling. That child would be born soon, and Gerdrut would never meet them. Would never get to be the big sister she had so longed to be.

"When Mama was carrying Alvie," said Anna, referring to her two-year-old brother, "her back hurt her a lot. She was always asking me to plump up her pillows and make up some chamomile tea. I can bring you some, once we get to your room."

"And we'll make offerings to Eostrig," said Hans. "Praying for an easy childbirth. The Erlking probably won't like us getting the old gods involved, but that's all the more reason to do it, if you ask me."

"And you know, I'm supposed to be your messenger," said Fricz, "but you never use me to run messages. You'll have to start, though. Can't have you overexerting yourself, walking about the castle just to tell the cooks that you'd like squab for supper or what have you."

"Squab?" said Nickel. "When has our Serilda ever requested *squab*?"

Fricz shrugged. "You know how ladies get when they're with child. Always wanting things they never wanted before. Ma said all she wanted when she was pregnant with us was rye flour. Not bread, not pastries—just the flour, straight from the mill."

"Well, that explains some things," muttered Hans.

"Is there a midwife here at the castle?" asked Nickel. "We can't let you give birth without one."

"I'll ask around to the maidservants," said Anna. "I'm sure someone must have experience birthing babies."

"I don't know," said Fricz. "Don't think there's been much birthing of anything around here for a long time."

They carried on, but Serilda was hardly listening. She placed her hand on her stomach, wishing she could sense the baby inside of her. But her stomach remained stubbornly flat. She had been so focused on breaking the curse and avoiding her lord husband as much as possible that she had given little thought to the passing of time, but surely she should be feeling different by now. Shouldn't she? A swell, a bump, some sign of the life inside her?

But she felt nothing.

Her feet were not swollen. Her back did not ache. She'd never once craved squab or rye flour or anything other than copious amounts of sweets, but there was nothing unusual about that.

"Serilda?" asked Gerdrut. "Are you feeling all right?"

The worry was so evident in her voice that Serilda stopped walking and stared at them. The children stared back, eyes full of concern.

"What's the matter?" said Hans. "Are you in pain? Should I fetch someone, or—"

"No, *I'll* fetch someone!" barked Fricz. "I'm the messenger!"

"That isn't it," said Serilda, trying to cover her anxiety for her baby with a laugh, which turned into a sniffle as tears pricked at her eyes. "It's only . . . I love you all so very much." Dropping to her knees, she pulled them toward her, careful to be gentle with Anna and her wounds. She ignored how her skin crawled at their touch and pressed her cheek against Gerdrut's hair. "Never in the world has a queen been so fortunate in her attendants."

A quiet descended on them, as Gerdrut snuggled her face into Serilda's neck.

Until Fricz groaned loudly and complained, "I think the baby is making her emotional."

Serilda grinned and pulled away, ruffling his hair.

"What baby?"

Her laugh hiccupped.

"Gild!" cried Gerdrut, throwing herself into his arms. Of all the children, she had become especially fond of the poltergeist. "You missed so much excitement!"

"Yes," said Gild, returning the embrace but not the smile. "I overheard some of the cooks talking about the bärgeist and the storm. And one of the queen's attendants fell into the arena?"

"That was me," said Anna, leaning on Nickel for support. "I'm all right. Not dead. Well . . . not dead*er*."

Gild flashed a distracted smile at her. "It must have been terrifying."

"Not so bad," said Anna. "Agathe was there. She protected me from the bärgeist."

"She's the weapons master," added Fricz. "We'd never met her before, but she sat with us in the stands, and when Anna fell, she jumped down and fought back the bear. It was fantastic!"

"Do you know her?" asked Serilda.

"A little, but not well," said Gild. "She's always been quiet, solitary. Wicked fast with a sword, though. I've seen her in practice, and training with the dark ones. Wouldn't want to cross her, I know that much. I'm glad she was there, Anna."

Serilda wanted to tell him that Agathe might have been the person who had trained *him* in weaponry, so long ago, but the look he was giving her made the words die out on her tongue.

Gild continued, "After the storm started I saw a bunch of hunters running toward"—his voice turned extra meaningful—"the, uh, the hall we were in? This morning?"

Her eyes widened. Was it possible that this vicious storm had something to do with the weird chicken-snake creature she and Gild had awoken? Was that what had made the Erlking so anxious?

"Also," Gild added, denial etched onto his face, "I heard something about the queen's announcement?"

He was waiting. Horrified, but also hopeful that he might be wrong. That perhaps he had misunderstood. She could see it written plainly on his face.

But in the end, she didn't have to tell him. Gerdrut did it for her.

"We're going to have a baby!" she cried, bouncing on her toes. "At least, Serilda is. But I'm going to help take care of it!"

"Ah," said Gild, nodding stiffly. "I see. Congratulations."

Serilda watched him carefully, wishing he would hold her gaze for longer than half a second. Then maybe he would see the truth that she could not speak aloud.

The child was *his*.

But he avoided her eye.

How many times had she opened her mouth to tell him the truth, before he could hear the lie and be devastated by it? It might not have surprised him. He believed she'd been intimate with the king for weeks now. He believed that was the king's entire aim in marrying her—to father a child with his mortal bride.

After today there would be no denying it. No pretending that she had not been in the Erlking's bed.

But it wasn't true, she wanted to scream. The Erlking didn't even *have* a bed!

"You . . . uh . . . probably should rest, then," Gild said.

"No, I'm not tired at all," said Serilda, which was true. Though she'd been exhausted during the hunt's demonstrations, she now suddenly felt wide-awake. A new idea struck her as she thought of what Agathe had told her. "We should continue our search, while the hunters are preoccupied with the . . . storm." She affixed Gild with an intent look.

"All right," he said uncertainly. "If you're sure."

"Just let me tuck in these little troublemakers. It's been a long night and an even longer day. Do you think you could find something for Anna's wounds? She thought she might have some broken bones."

"I'll check with the apothecary for something to help with the pain," said Gild. "You'll find that ghosts heal much quicker now than when they were alive."

"I can go," piped up Fricz. "Why does no one take my job seriously?"

"No, please," said Gild, backing away. "You all take care of Anna, and . . . and Serilda. I'll be back soon."

With a wan smile, he vanished. Serilda knew he wasn't only going to get help for Anna. He needed a moment to himself, to come to terms with her news.

It tore at her insides, the truth screaming inside her skull.

She shut her eyes and forced that truth down, down, down.

"Come along," she said. "We'll get comfortable, and then I will tell you a story."

It has oft been said that a god captured beneath an Endless Moon will be forced to grant a single wish, but in the beforetimes it would have been ludicrous to imagine one of the old gods ever being trapped by tricks or wiles. Just as humans are made of skin and bone, the gods are made of magic and starlight. They have the power to change their forms at will, with no earthly limitations on their figures. With nothing more than a thought and a wink, a god might become the smallest of insects or the greatest of sea serpents. For thousands of years, the seven gods inhabited the lands, the seas, the skies—sometimes as humans, sometimes as beasts. They interfered little in the affairs of mortals, preferring to keep to themselves, and to enjoy the freedom and pleasures their magic afforded them.

But that began to change, many years ago.

For you see, the dark ones had escaped from Verloren.

Velos had done all they could to stop them. The god of death had tried to keep the demons trapped in the land of the lost. But the demons managed to flee across the great bridge and through the gates into the mortal realm, and now they were free to wander the earth.

Unlike the gods, the dark ones did not keep to themselves. Nor did they wish to settle quietly among the human villages and live simple, tedious lives. They would not tend crops or spin wool or learn a trade. They saw themselves as superior to humans. They were stronger and faster and more beautiful, and above all else, they were immortal.

And the dark ones wished to rule.

Soon, the dark ones began to terrorize the poor, frightened humans. They took what they wanted without consequence. Their lives became endless sport, made possible by the servitude of the mortals who could not fight against them.

At first, the gods did not intervene, preferring to let matters settle themselves. But as the dark ones grew in strength and cruelty, the gods determined that something must be done.

They met at the peak of Mount Grämen on a cold winter's night, when a solstice moon hung full and heavy in the sky. There, they talked and argued and discussed a solution.

Tyrr wished to slaughter the dark ones and wash their hands of the whole matter, but Eostrig insisted that to do so would only send their spirits back into the ground, where all that maleficence would sprout up as something even more terrible and poisonous.

Freydon wished to send them back to Verloren, from whence they had come, but Velos knew that the demons would never go willingly, and to try and entrap them could lead to a war unlike anything the world had ever seen.

Hulda wished to imprison them in golden chains and drop them to the bottom of the sea, but Solvilde would not hear of the waters being so tainted.

And on and on and on they went, with no suggestions posed that would satisfy them all.

Until, finally, Wyrdith stood. The god of stories and fortune had thus far been silent, but now they took out the wheel of fortune from their heavy robes.

The other gods fell silent as Wyrdith lifted a hand and gave the wheel one power- ful spin.

They watched and waited to see where fate would land.

When the wheel finally stopped, the gods peered at the god of stories, waiting to hear what solution they had to offer.

"Fortune smiles on us," said Wyrdith, "for I have seen what we must do."

But even in speaking this, there was a sadness in Wyrdith's eyes, for they alone knew what must be sacrificed.

Wyrdith explained, and the gods, seeing that it was the only way, each willingly gave up a single thread of their own hallowed magic.

Wyrdith gave up their golden quill. Velos gave a tooth. Eostrig a horn and Hulda a serpent's scale. Tyrr gave a gem, Solvilde an egg, and Freydon a claw.

Hulda took the seven gifts and used them to spin an unbreakable yarn. They spun for hours, and when the yarn was finished, Hulda took it and began to weave. Again, hours passed. It was nearing sunrise when finally the work was complete.

Using the magic of the gods, Hulda had woven a cloak that would cover the world. A veil that was unbreakable and impenetrable, one that would forever trap the dark ones and keep them separate from the mortal realm.

As Hulda worked, the other gods grabbed hold of the edges of the veil and pulled it protectively around the whole earth.

But as the moon was descending toward the horizon, Perchta, the great huntress, saw what the gods intended to do. With moments to spare, she took her bow and an arrow from her quiver and aimed toward the sky.

She fired.

Though the veil was nearly complete, the arrow shot straight through the only remaining gap in the magical shroud and struck the full moon beyond. The moon began to bleed from its wound, and one single drop of moonlight fell onto the veil. Where it struck, Hulda found they could not complete that final stitch, forever leaving an opening in this otherwise perfect tapestry. An opening that would be visible only beneath a full moon and on nights when the sun and moon fight for dominance in the sky.

Determining that they had done all they could, and the veil, though imperfect, would nevertheless be enough to keep the dark ones from continuing their rampage through the mortal realm, the gods returned to their separate lands. Tyrr to the volcanoes of Lysreich. Solvilde to the coast of the Molnig Sea. Hulda to the foothills of the Rückgrat Mountains. Eostrig deep into the heart of the Aschen Wood. Freydon to the lush grasslands of Dostlen. Velos, to the shadowed caverns of Verloren. Wyrdith to the basalt cliffs at the northernmost edges of Tulvask.

There the gods lived in peace for some time, pleased when the veil held, for the dark ones could enact only so much harm on but one night of each moon cycle, and they felt they had succeeded in tempering this great threat.

Only Wyrdith understood the full extent of what they had each given up that night. It would be many years before the other gods understood that by giving of themselves to create the veil, their magic had been irreparably changed. In creating a prison for the dark ones, they were also entrapping themselves. Having given up a thread of magic, the gods found their abilities to change their physical forms now had a single limitation.

Forever after, on the nights of an Endless Moon, like the one beneath which *the veil had been created, the gods would no longer have dominion over themselves. Rather, they would be forced to take the forms of seven terrible beasts.*

After that, it became possible to catch a god on that long, dark night. Possible to hunt them, to capture them . . . and to claim that elusive wish.

Ever since, whenever the full moon rises on the longest night of the year, the hell-hounds can be heard sniffing and searching for their prey.

Seven gods made into seven extraordinary beasts.

It took four tales before the children fell asleep, so excited were they from the day's events. Anna fell asleep last, after struggling to find a comfortable position to lie in, and grimacing every time one of the other children shifted beside her. Gild had eventually returned with an elixir from the castle apothecary, and Serilda doubted Anna would have gotten any sleep at all was it not for the herbs easing her pain.

"Your stories," Gild whispered from the other side of the room, "are *not* for children."

Serilda blinked at him. She hardly remembered the tales she told, when the entire time she'd been half-focused on Gild and his reactions and wondering if he was thinking about her child and believing it was the Erlking's and what would she do if he asked her about it and how would she possibly maintain this lie until the Endless Moon?

So his statement caught her off guard.

"What do you mean?"

"Demons enslaving humans? Gods turning into beasts? And that one about the child being tricked into eating her grandmother's teeth? What is *that*?"

Serilda rubbed her palms into her eyes. "I hardly know what I was saying."

"Has it ever occurred to you that you could just, you know . . . read them a story? I was flipping through this book earlier. There are some pretty good ones in here." He picked up the book of fairy tales that Leyna had stolen from Frieda's library. She'd been so distracted these past weeks with thoughts of her baby and her curse and the five children and doing her best to play the part of the Alder Queen, she hadn't been much in the mood for fairy stories that ended in *happily ever after*. The farthest she'd gotten in the book was the opening page, a note to the reader about how the stories were collected by a contemporary scholar who had spent years traveling around Tulvask gathering and transcribing household tales that she believed to coincide with true historical events. Normally, it was the sort of thing that would have intrigued Serilda, but now she could only think about what a luxury it was for this scholar to travel about the country, listening to stories and writing them down and never fearing that one of those story's villains might kidnap her and curse her and keep her trapped in a haunted castle.

"I really liked this one," said Gild, flipping to a page with a woodblock print of a prince and a farm boy, their hands cupped together, holding a tree sapling between them. The title was written in flourishing calligraphy: "Hardworking Stiltskin and the Northern Prince."

"It's got a good moral," Gild added. "For people who like that sort of thing."

"Maybe *you* can read it to the children, then."

"Maybe I will." He shut the book and peered at her. "You look tired, Serilda. Maybe we should just—"

"No, I want to search for our bodies. I want to help you. Are the hunters still preoccupied?"

Gild scratched behind his ear. "Last I checked, yes. But, Serilda . . . I've probably gone over every inch of this castle a dozen times, at least, every inch that I know of. There's a surprising number of storage rooms in the basement, and I've checked them all. Plus the chapels, the towers, the dungeons, every garderobe, which was *not* enjoyable. The studies, the tower attics . . . I even went to the bottom of the water well." He shrugged. "Nothing. He wouldn't have left our bodies somewhere anyone could just stumble onto them, least of all me. Wherever he's hiding them, I don't think it will be a place that I can easily pop in and out of, not if I don't even know it exists. I'm not discounting the possibility of secret passageways or rooms, but if that's the case . . . short of tearing up the foundations . . . I don't know where else to look."

"Actually, I had a thought earlier. Though it will probably amount to nothing."

"More likely it will amount to something creepy and awful," said Gild. "That seems to be where your thoughts typically go."

She rolled her eyes. "What about the throne room?"

"What about it?"

"When I was speaking with Agathe today, she mentioned how she recalls being in the throne room during the massacre, and how she couldn't leave, I think because she was protecting your mother and father."

Gild fidgeted, as he always did when she brought up the family he couldn't remember.

"And I realized how so much that happened that night revolved around this one part of the castle. Your paren—er, the king and queen were murdered there. The princess was . . ." She trailed off, remembering the awful vision of the child hanging from the rafters. She shook her head. "It's where the Erlking lured you when you returned, and where he cursed you . . . and where he cursed me, for that matter. When you or I go beyond the walls of the castle, the curse brings us back to the throne room, every time. Now, this might be nothing, but . . . in the mortal realm, there's something different about the throne room. Everything else in the whole castle is decrepit and marred by age, but the dais and the thrones . . . it's like they're trapped in time. Unchanged in hundreds of years, while everything crumbles around them. There's some sort of magic there. What if . . ." She shrugged. "What if it has something to do with the curse?"

"Except . . . our bodies aren't in the throne room," said Gild. "We would have seen them. It isn't like there are a lot of hiding places."

"Aren't there?"

He opened his mouth, but hesitated. He leaned back on his heels, considering. "The walls," he murmured. "Or . . . possibly the floor?"

"Specifically," said Serilda, "I think they could be under the thrones. I wonder if maybe the magic needed to sustain our bodies is . . . somehow leaching up from the floor. And that's what's preserving them? I could be wrong. I have no idea how any of this works, I just—"

"No, no, it makes sense." Gild smiled. "We should explore it, on the Straw Moon."

She shook her head. "I'd like to go now. While the Erlking is busy dealing with the . . . that thing. That we woke up."

"The legendary chicken-snake," Gild said, without humor.

"I know it's risky, but . . ." She trailed off. She wanted to say that they were running out of time. Months were going by too fast, and soon her child would be born and the Erlking would capture a god and wish for Perchta's return. But she didn't know how to bring up her pregnancy to Gild. She didn't know what to say to him. So instead, she finished lamely, "It isn't like anyone really goes in the throne room. I've never seen the Erlking there, aside from when he cursed me."

Gild inhaled slowly. "It shouldn't take long to check."

She smiled at him gratefully, but it quickly fizzled. Serilda stood, wringing her hands. "Gild . . . about the announcement . . ."

"You don't have to."

She hesitated. "I don't have to what?"

"Whatever it is you're about to do. Explain or apologize or . . . just . . . talk about it, even. I mean . . . That didn't come out right. If you want to talk about it, of course, we can. I want you to feel like you can talk to me. But only if you need to. You don't owe me anything, I guess, is what I mean. I just . . ." He dragged a hand through his hair. "I just want to be here for you, Serilda. However you need me to be."

She wished these words made her feel better, but they didn't. If anything, his attempts to support her and care for her through all of this only made her feel worse.

"Thank you," she breathed.

His brow drew together. "There is the, um, the matter of the . . ."

He didn't finish, and Serilda didn't know what he was talking about.

The matter of Serilda being in love with him? The matter of her husband being a murderous bastard? The matter of—

"The bargain," said Gild. "The . . . deal that we made."

Ah. That matter.

"I haven't told him," said Serilda.

"I figured as much."

"I never thought . . . when we struck that deal . . ."

"Neither did I."

Serilda pressed her lips together.

Gild wiped his palms nervously down his tunic.

"Nothing we can do about it tonight," she said.

"Agreed," said Gild. "We should focus on the important things. Not that this child . . . *your* child . . . isn't important."

"To the throne room, then?"

He nodded vigorously. "I'll meet you there."

He blinked out of sight, and Serilda was grateful to have a moment to catch her breath and recover from that painfully awkward exchange. Could she really survive until the winter solstice without telling him?

She shut her eyes. "Wyrdith help me."

Chapter Seventeen

The throne room was ornate, with two rows of massive stone pillars on either side, each one carved with the body of a tatzelwurm slithering down from the ceiling. Gilt moldings and tapestries hung on the walls, and a row of windows facing the lake, with the mountains in the distance, let in a wash of sunlight during the day. At night, chandeliers with hundreds of candles cast a golden glow across the walls.

The space was grand, no doubt, but Gild had been right. There were no obvious places to hide a body. No cabinets, no wardrobes, no stone tombs conveniently left lying around.

"It's so different on the other side of the veil," said Serilda. "Imagine cobwebs and rats' nests and the furniture toppled and broken—what remains of it, at least. Thorn bushes cover a lot of the ground. Windows are broken. But the thrones are unchanged . . . as if something is protecting them." She approached the dais, where the two chairs stood, upholstered in cobalt blue, with tall backs and lion claw feet. "They still look exactly like this. Not even a speck of dust on them."

Gild walked around the dais, studying the thrones from every angle. He stomped one foot against the stone floor. "I'm fairly certain the floor here is solid stone. But . . . underneath the dais? Who knows."

They both moved to one side of the dais—a platform raised up on three steps and covered in a rug woven into a pattern of intricate gold knots.

Together, they crouched beside the platform and pressed their hands against the edge.

"On three," said Gild. "One. Two. Three!"

They pushed.

And groaned.

And strained.

Serilda was moments from giving up when, finally, the platform shifted. Her foot slipped and Serilda smacked her knee on the stone floor, but there was no denying that the dais had moved a few inches.

Just enough to reveal what appeared to be the edge of a hole beneath.

She sucked in a breath.

Their eyes met, charged with renewed energy. They tried again. The dais moved easier this time, allowing them to push it back one inch after another.

They stopped when their feet reached the edge of the hole. From what they could see, it was nearly a perfect rectangle, the same size as the dais that had kept it hidden. The stones from the floor had been removed, and the bedrock dug out from below, leaving rough walls and a pit that was nearly four feet deep.

Serilda's breath left her. She grasped Gild's arm, both of them kneeling at the ledge.

Serilda had never seen so many bones. The pit was full of them. Femurs and hip bones and collections of tiny finger bones amid the bleached-white skulls. In contrast, the two bodies, which looked as though they were merely sleeping, stood out like crimson roses against a bank of snow.

They were perfectly preserved, and yet they had not been treated with any sort of care, these two bodies.

She recognized the prince, even though he had been tossed facedown into the pit. He wore a vibrant green cloak with gold embroidery, fine leather boots, and a tailored doublet. The cloak he wore was wound in and around some of the bones, and Serilda could picture the skin and flesh and clothes of those beneath him slowly rotting away, while he was kept in this magic spell, untouched by time.

Cursed.

She could not quite think of the body lying there as *Gild*. The way he was dressed so regally, yet so old-fashioned. A prince from three hundred years ago. And the way he was almost dead, when Gild had always struck her as so very alive.

Then there was the second body. A girl.

It should have been Serilda's body, but it wasn't.

Serilda felt strangely hollow as she stared at the child. Perhaps a bit taller than Gerdrut, with similar golden curls. They might have been sisters, except that this child was a princess. Gild's sister, also carelessly tossed into the pit. She lay on her side, one leg awkwardly crooked behind her, a tumbled curl concealing half her face. But her cheeks were rosy, flushed. It was as though at any moment, she and her brother could awaken and look around and be terrified to find themselves thrown haphazardly into this mass grave.

Serilda shuddered. Once she was able to stop gawking at the bodies of the prince and the princess and face the horror of the rest of the grave, she noticed a dagger with a jeweled hilt. A gem-covered broach. Near a skull in the corner—a crown.

The dark ones had not bothered to search these bodies and take their valuables. They'd only wanted to be rid of them.

She blinked back a rush of tears. These were not just any remains, with their gaping eye sockets and grinning rows of teeth and scattered bones buried amid luxurious fabrics. This was Gild's family. His mother and father, the king and queen who had once ruled this castle. And the others—servants, courtiers, guards? How many of the bodies left here to rot had once belonged to the ghosts that still prowled these halls?

She knew it couldn't be everyone who was murdered that night. She doubted more than a couple dozen people could have fit into this hastily constructed pit back when they were more flesh than bones. Perhaps these had died here in the throne room. The dark ones had not cared about preserving any sense of dignity, any rites of burial. They had only cared to be rid of the bodies as efficiently as possible. It was likely the people in this pit were here because the Erlking needed a place to keep the bodies of the prince and the princess, and it was easier to drag the rest of these corpses into this hole than to carry them to the drawbridge.

She wondered if Agathe was among them.

She wondered what the dark ones had done with everyone else. Thrown their bodies into the lake? Or were there other graves like this one, scattered and unmarked across the castle grounds?

"These were my people," Gild whispered beside her. His expression was hollowed out, a cross between disbelief and horror. "The . . . *prince's* people. Our court, our servants. He killed them and then just . . . just discarded them. As if their lives had no meaning."

Serilda slipped her hand into his, but his fingers stayed limp in her grasp, as if he couldn't feel her or refused to be comforted.

His head lowered, and when he spotted Serilda's fingers entwined with his, he gave a small jolt of surprise. He met her gaze, and she had not seen him so devastated since . . .

Well. Since the Erlking had declared that she would be his bride.

"He tossed them aside like rubbish," he muttered. "He didn't want the castle for its wealth . . . He didn't want anything but revenge. He killed all these people just to hurt me. He killed my parents"—his voice hitched, but he plowed forward, his sorrow morphing into anger—"just to hurt me. And now I can't even remember them. I can't even properly mourn them."

"You're mourning them now," she whispered.

He gave a furious shake to his head. "I failed them. Every one of these—"

"No, Gild. There was nothing you could have done. You weren't even here when it happened, and even if you had been, the dark ones took everyone by surprise. They're immortal. They're expert hunters. They have magic, and . . . it wasn't a fair fight." She leaned against him, tucking her head against his shoulder, though he only tensed. "None of this is your fault. All you did was try to save your sister."

As soon as she said the words, she wished she could take them back.

He had tried to save her, but he had failed.

But he couldn't have stopped the massacre. Serilda knew it weighed on him, that he wasn't even there when it happened. The Erlking had done it all as an act of vengeance because Gild had slain Perchta and sent her spirit back to Verloren.

He paid for it dearly. Was still paying for it. Would always be paying for it, if they didn't find a way to put an end to their curse.

"Why is she even here?" he said, his voice rising. "You told me she was dead."

Serilda pulled away. But despite the anger in his tone, she knew he wasn't mad at her. He was glaring into the pit, at the bodies—those forgotten, those cursed—his breaths coming in struggled gasps. "She's not dead. Serilda. She's not dead."

Serilda regarded the princess again. She couldn't make sense of it. She had seen the princess's body strung up, not far from this very pit.

Her eyes widened.

Her body.

She had seen the princess's body, *this* body, hanging there.

"He'd already cursed her," she whispered. "Her spirit had already been separated from her body. But then . . ."

"Where is she?" Gild finished for her.

"I don't know."

Serilda wished she could do something, anything, to help ease his pain. She watched him take the locket from beneath his collar and squeeze it in his fist, eyes locked on his sister's corpse. His sister who was not dead.

"Don't."

Serilda stiffened. "Don't what?"

He sniffed, though no tears had fallen. "Don't give me that pitying look. I'm not sad. I don't even remember her. And we don't have time to be sad, anyhow."

She lifted an eyebrow. "More than three hundred years and you're suddenly in a hurry?"

"I don't care about me, and I don't care about her! I don't know her. I care about you. About getting you and . . . and your child away from the Erlking as quickly as possible."

Her heart softened. Of course it was her that he was worried about.

"It is all right to care about her, too, you know," said Serilda. "To miss her, even."

"I don't *remember* her," Gild repeated, his voice uncharacteristically sharp. "You can't miss someone you don't remember."

"That isn't true. I miss my mother every day, and I have no memories of her either."

Gild's eyes flashed at her, full of regret. "I'm sorry. I didn't think—"

"It's all right, Gild."

He dropped the locket and dragged both hands down his face. "I forget, sometimes, that he took your mother, too. That's all he does. Take and murder and destroy. He needs to be stopped. I want to stop him, to figure out how to . . . to kill him. Or send him back to Verloren. I don't know. I don't know what I can do, but . . . I hate him. I despise him."

Serilda wanted to ease his pain, but she didn't know what to say. It wasn't just Gild's family. It wasn't just hers. It wasn't just the children or this castle full of ghosts. How many lives had been stolen too soon? How many families ripped apart by the wild hunt? How many forest folk slaughtered? How many magical creatures hunted and killed?

And it would go on forever.

What if there was no stopping him?

Pulling away, Gild lowered himself down into the pit. He was cautious and slow, trying his best not to disturb the remains of those buried there, but it was impossible to avoid the bones. Serilda cringed at each crunch and clatter as he made his way to the bodies.

He stopped beside the prince and rolled the body onto its side. It was surreal to see Gild's identical double splayed out amid the bones. The same wavy copper hair, the same constellation of freckles, the same cheekbones and shoulders and elegant fingers. Only his clothes distinguished the two, along with the fact that this version of Gild had not caused any trouble in three hundred years.

An arrow with a gold arrowhead and silky black fletching pierced the wrist in the exact spot where Gild had a scar.

Gild stared into the prince's face for a long moment, and Serilda could not begin to guess what he was thinking.

With a pained sigh, Gild took the golden ring from his finger, the one Serilda had once traded to him in exchange for spinning straw into gold. Neither of them realized it at the time, but the ring had been rightfully his. It bore the royal seal of his family—a tatzelwurm coiled around the letter R—and Serilda suspected he might have once given it to Shrub Grandmother and the moss maidens in payment for their healing magic. Before the curse. Before his memories had been erased.

Now Gild took that precious ring and pressed it onto the prince's finger. Then he lifted the chain from around his neck and slipped it over the prince's head, tucking the locket inside the fine leather jerkin. "I think these things belong to you," he said. "The true prince of Adalheid."

Serilda bit her lip. She wanted to ask if he was *sure* he wanted to give those precious items up—the only things he had that connected him to his former life. But her throat felt swollen shut and she was afraid to speak, as if she were intruding on a sacred moment that didn't really belong to her.

Gild turned and faced the girl. His sister.

Unlike the prince, who seemed uninjured but for the arrow, the princess bore purple bruises around her throat. Serilda's chest tightened at the sight.

Taking one of the girl's small hands, he lifted it toward the light, revealing a gold-tipped arrow through her slender arm.

"She should be here," said Serilda. "Tethered to the castle. So, where is she?"

Gild had no answers. All they knew was that if the girl was somewhere in this castle, haunting it like Gild himself was, surely he would have known.

Serilda did not know how to feel about this new information, and she could tell that Gild was struggling with it, too. In many ways, death could be a mercy. But the Erlking had not killed the princess. He had separated her body from her soul, but where was she tethered to? Could he have left her in Gravenstone, his castle deep in the Aschen Wood? Had this child been left alone, abandoned, for centuries?

"She looks exactly like her portrait," Gild said. "Maybe a bit older is all." With painstaking tenderness, he began to rearrange the princess's body. He rolled her onto her back and straightened the wrinkles from her faded nightgown. He folded her hands atop her stomach and brushed the curls off her brow.

When he was finished, she really did appear to be sleeping.

Finally, he looked up at Serilda. "Where is *your* body?"

"I don't know," she whispered. "He must be keeping it somewhere else."

Gild sighed, frustrated. "We need to put the platform back. If the Erlking knew what we'd seen, he would move the bodies somewhere else."

Serilda frowned. "Gild . . . you can take the arrow out. Untether yourself. Break the curse. You can do it now."

He held her gaze, confused. "And what about you?"

She shook her head. "You can't be worried about me. This is your chance to get away, to be free of this place—"

He scoffed. "And leave you here by yourself? Not a chance. As soon as I break my curse, I'll be trapped on the other side of the veil, without you."

Serilda wanted to argue, but his tone was decided, and she could tell he would not be persuaded. A part of her was relieved.

But his words also brought a sting of guilt. She didn't want to be the reason he was trapped here. And even if they did find her body . . . would she leave with him? Could she ever abandon the children like that?

"Gild," she started, attempting to sound reassuring and logical, "we don't know if we'll ever—"

"We will," he said, making his way back to the edge of the pit. "We'll find your body, too, Serilda. When we leave, we'll be leaving together."

Rarely did she see him so stoic. So determined.

Slowly, she nodded. "All right."

Gild climbed out of the pit and began to walk around to the other side of the dais to push it back into place.

"Wait," said Serilda. "You should take this." Reaching down, she picked up the crown that lay near the corner of the pit. Delicately crafted of gold filigree, inlaid with emeralds and pearls. "You would have been king."

He laughed, though it lacked his usual humor. "I don't want that. I haven't done anything to earn it."

Then a change came over him. A shadow. A tension. It showed in the set of his shoulders and the tilt of his chin.

"But I want to earn it." An unfamiliar glint entered his eye as he scanned the pit again. His parents, his court. So many who still wandered its halls, locked into servitude of the Erlking.

"Let's break these curses, Serilda. And let's find a way to make him regret ever having come to this castle."

A throat cleared, startling them both.

Gild vanished.

Serilda spun around.

Agathe stood in the doorway, covered in new bandages, her arm in a sling. Smiling crookedly. "I might be able to help with that."

Gild poked his head out from behind a column. He looked from the weapons master to Serilda. "Help with . . . putting the thrones back where they go? Or help with breaking the curse?"

Agathe's grin widened. "Both."

Chapter Eighteen

Agathe knew where Serilda's body was being kept.

Serilda couldn't believe it. *Didn't* believe it.

As she and Gild hastened after the weapons master, she felt hope warring with disbelief.

They had found Gild's body, and now they were on the verge of finding hers as well. After months of searching, it seemed almost too easy. Could it be a trick?

They stepped out of the keep, across the courtyard, and to the bailey, the grounds splattered with mud and puddles from the recent downpour, though the rain had long ceased. Agathe did not lead them to some crypt or dungeon or tower or mysterious wing of the castle blockaded by an iron door and a series of intricate locks.

She led them to the carriage house.

Which is when Serilda began to suspect that, yes, the ghost was toying with them.

Agathe lifted the bar across one of the huge carriage house doors and gestured for Serilda and Gild to enter.

Serilda tensed again, filled with the overwhelming sense that she was being lured into a trap.

Agathe smiled at her, as if amused. "Afraid of carriages, my lady?"

"My body is in here?" said Serilda, disbelieving. She glanced at Gild. "We never thought to check the carriage house?"

He shook his head, equally baffled. "Never."

Serilda squared her shoulders. Lifting the hem of her gown, she swept inside. Before her stood a row of carriages in a long, dusty room, the air stifling and damp from the summer storm. She recognized the small carriage that had first come to Märchenfeld and summoned her to the Erlking's castle, back on the Hunger Moon. Its body was made from the rib bones of an enormous beast, the interior hung with heavy black drapes, giving it the appearance of a lustrous cage.

Then there was a carriage with walls of stretched leather and silver night-raven statues perched at each rooftop corner.

And one with wooden walls carved so ornately into pillars and tall cloaked figures it looked like a mausoleum on wheels.

The largest carriage stood at the end of the row, and it was this one that Agathe led her toward. It was more a wagon, really, with a large storage compartment built out of alder wood. It reminded Serilda of a luxurious version of the wagons that had come through Märchenfeld to round up dead bodies when a plague had spread through the village years ago. She'd been only four or five at the time, and what she remembered most were the distrustful glares cast her way and the superstitious rumors that followed after her in the village square. For surely, what could have brought such misfortune upon their town, but the unholy, god-touched girl?

It was not until years later that Serilda learned the plague had also swept through much of Tulvask and parts of Ottelien, and therefore could not possibly have been her doing.

To this day, burial mounds from the plague victims could still be seen dotting some of the fields outside of town, now overgrown with grasses and wildflowers.

It was this she thought of—those forgotten graves, those wagons laden with decaying bodies—as the weapons master undid the latch on the back of the carriage and pulled open its double doors.

Inside was a box—not unlike a coffin, but with no lid. And inside, nestled atop a bed of crimson cloth, lay Serilda's body.

She had been preparing for this for months, yet it was impossible not to feel that first jolt of wonder. Even though she had witnessed her body detaching from her spirit and crumple to the throne-room floor when the king first cursed her, it was so easy for her to forget that she no longer inhabited a physical form. After all, she still felt. She could still distinguish between hot and cold, soft and firm. Tears still pricked her eyes when she was sad. Heat still crept up her neck when she was embarrassed.

But now, looking into the face before her—her *own* face—the reality of it was jarring.

More jarring still was that the body before her was undeniably with child.

Her hands had been positioned so they rested just above her swelling stomach, rounded and pronounced in her reclined position. The same mud-spattered dress Serilda had worn the night she'd come rushing into the castle and become the king's prisoner was still draped softly over her figure, pronouncing every curve.

Serilda placed a hand to her own stomach, but there was no child there. Her baby's spirit was not inside her. It was growing here. In this body, in this carriage house. She would never be physically connected to this child. Not so long as she was cursed.

She was startled at the wave of despair that crashed upon her at the thought.

Her gaze drifted to the arrow struck through her wrist.

She took in an unsteady breath. "How can the child survive like this? How can it be growing when I am not . . . I am not able to care for it?"

"Our bodies are being sustained by magic," said Gild. "It must be protecting the child as well."

"But it's *growing*," she said. "It isn't just . . . existing, like you and me. What will happen when it's time to give birth?"

Gild didn't answer her question.

Instead, he settled a hand on her back. "Serilda. I think we're running out of time."

Her breath quickened.

They knew where both of their bodies were. They could break the curses, both of them.

They could be gone *tonight.* It didn't matter how the king intended for her to bring this child into the world. By sunrise, she could be back in her body again, and she would have her child, and Gild, too. She would have Gild and she could tell him everything.

They could be free.

She shut her eyes, and allowed herself to have this one moment, in which there was hope. In which this awful mess she'd made for herself was resolved.

When she opened her eyes again, her vision was blurred with tears.

She turned to Gild.

He gazed back at her, unsurprised. "We're not going to break the curses tonight, are we?"

She swallowed. "I can't leave."

"The children."

She wiped a tear from her cheek. "I can't abandon them. It's my fault they're here in the first place." She glanced at Agathe, who was watching Serilda with heartfelt sympathy. "The Erlking promised me he would release their souls to Verloren if I . . . if I do what he wants me to do."

"You mean, bear a child for him," said Gild with a snarl.

"I wondered if you were not as enchanted with the marriage as he would have us believe," said Agathe. "You seemed too sensible to be in love with that monster."

"No," said Serilda with a wry laugh. "I'm definitely not in love." As soon as she said it, she caught Gild's eye, and heat flushed through her cheeks. She looked away. "But I am trapped. I am so grateful you've brought me here, but . . . I can't break my curse. Not until I know the children will be all right."

"I understand," said Gild. "Just as I can't break my curse until I know *you'll* be all right."

He squeezed her hand, their expressions pained as they realized how much they had hung all their hopes on this moment. Finding their bodies. Snapping the arrows, untethering their souls, setting themselves free.

But it had only been a distraction.

It was never going to be that easy.

"In that case," said Agathe, "the solution is quite simple, isn't it?"

They both frowned at her. "What do you mean?" asked Serilda.

Agathe adjusted her bloodied scarf. "You must free the children. You are a gold-spinner, are you not?"

Serilda's eyes widened in shock, before she realized that Agathe was asking *her*, not Gild. "Y-yes. But what does that have to do with anything?"

"Well," Agathe started, "ghosts are magical creatures, just like the beasts we hunt. They are affected by god-spun gold. It is said that if you tie a strand of god-spun gold around a ghost beneath a full moon and call upon Velos . . . well. It will . . . you know." She waved her good hand through the air.

Serilda, mouth agape, glanced at Gild. He looked equally perplexed.

"It will . . . what?" said Serilda.

Agathe sighed. "Free their souls. Allow them to pass on to Verloren."

"*What?*" shouted Gild, startling them all. He clamped a hand over his mouth, but quickly dropped it to his side again and stepped closer to Agathe. "Are you telling me that all these ghosts . . . This whole time I could have . . . They could have been freed? All this time?"

"Well," started Agathe, "you need god-spun gold for it to work." She looked past him to Serilda, then she stilled. "Oh. I'm sorry. I forgot. You can't spin anymore, can you? His Grim has been so upset that we don't have more chains . . ."

"Uh . . . no," said Serilda. "I can't. It's complicated."

"I'm sorry," said Agathe. "I thought I was being helpful."

"You have been," said Gild, dragging his hands through his hair. He started to pace, frenetic energy pulsing through him at this new information. This incredible, unexpected gift the weapons master had given them. "You've been very helpful."

"But *you* had access to the golden chains," said Serilda. "Couldn't you have freed yourself during the hunt?"

Agathe laughed. "The king is very protective of those chains, so I'm not sure I could have managed to sneak even a single strand without his notice. But"—her expression grew serious—"I don't think I would have, even if I'd had the chance. You mentioned before it's your fault those children are here. Well. It's *my* fault the rest of us are here. I am to blame for the massacre that happened within these walls. I failed in my duty to protect the people of this castle. I let the dark ones through. I let them kill us all."

Serilda shook her head. "No, Agathe. They are immortal. They have magic. It is not your fault—"

"Thank you, my queen, but I am not asking for comfort or absolution. I have lived with my failings for long enough. My point, I suppose, is that—while I may not remember the dynasty I once served—I do remember an unbreakable loyalty. A pride in serving one family, one kingdom. The Erlking took that away from me, and has kept me and so many others prisoner all these years." Despite her dark words, a small smile touched her lips. "You, poltergeist . . . and now, *you*, my queen, seem to be the only ones who are able to . . . How do I say it? Fight against him. It gives me hope to think that someday, perhaps, I will be able to fight back, too. Then I will finally be able to atone for my failures."

Serilda felt emboldened by her words. She was tempted to tell Agathe the truth about Gild, the so-called poltergeist. What would Agathe think if she knew that this mischievous boy was none other than the prince she had once been so loyal to?

But Serilda knew she couldn't say anything. It could too easily make its way back to the king, and then he would know that Serilda had figured out the prince's identity. They were already risking so much letting her help them. Serilda didn't know what the Erlking would do if he knew she'd been working with the poltergeist to find their bodies.

But maybe it wouldn't matter. Agathe had given them an incredible gift, a way to free the children, to free *all* the ghosts . . . and ultimately, to free themselves.

Not knowing what else to say in response to the woman's story, Serilda managed, "Thank you, Lady Agathe. You don't know how much you've helped us tonight. Between protecting Anna from the bärgeist, and now this . . . you are a true gift. I promise, this will not be forgotten."

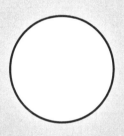

THE
STRAW
MOON

Chapter Nineteen

One more meal with the Erlking.

That was it.

That was all.

She had only to survive one more evening bread with that insufferable, arrogant, wicked man. And when the meal was over, the wild hunt would depart beneath the Straw Moon, and she and Gild would be able to set free not only her five beloved attendants, but every single ghost in this castle.

Though Serilda knew better than to praise the day before the evening, she couldn't help but feel they were *so close*.

Gild had been sequestered in his tower for weeks, ever since Agathe had told them how to overcome the Erlking's hold on these spirits, spinning strands of gold from the fur of the dahut kept in the menagerie, and the hair of the goats kept for milk and cheese, and green summer grass from the castle lawns, and any other fibers they could get ahold of. Serilda didn't know if the spirits, once released, would take the gold ropes with them into Verloren, so they didn't want to rely on having to reuse the same ropes over and over again. They needed enough for everyone. And they needed to be most secretive about it all. Even the children couldn't know what they were doing, for fear their false allegiance to the Erlking would force them to confess the plan.

No—they would wait until the hunt was gone, and then they would move forward. The Straw Moon was rising and they were ready.

She had only to get through one more meal. Now that the pregnancy had been announced, there was no longer any purpose in feigning intimacy behind closed doors, and so the Erlking had frequently requested her presence in the dining hall instead. Usually it was just the two of them and a handful of servants, but when they were seated at opposite ends of a massive table, Serilda could pretend she was alone.

Except, when she swept into the dining hall that night, she knew immediately that things were different. And in this castle, Serilda had come to associate anything different with a quietly brewing threat. Her husband was a man of habit. When things changed, it usually meant he was plotting something. And when he was plotting something, it was usually against *her*.

She took in the dining hall, already on edge. The great table had been pushed to one side, and the Erlking's high-backed mahogany chair was instead placed at a small round table set for two. Silver dishes and cutlery with pearl handles stood out against a dark velvet tablecloth puddled on the stone floor. A tall candle in a silver candlestick sat in the table's center, surrounded by a wreath of lavender and lobelia. An assortment of platters overflowed with late-summer delicacies. Blackberries and tangy cheese drizzled with honey and pistachios. Roasted quail served with sweetened mustard. Tarts filled with apples and walnuts. Pears soaked in mead.

"My wife," said the Erlking, setting down a goblet of crimson wine and standing to greet her.

Serilda's eyebrows shot upward. This, too, was new. The Erlking never stood for anyone, least of all her.

"What is this?" she asked as he pulled out a chair for her.

"I've been distracted of late," he said, "and have not been giving you enough attention. It would not do to neglect my duties to you and bring into question my great affection, given our very young romance. And, of course, your special condition."

Serilda's frown deepened. "What is this really?"

He laughed. "Were you always this suspicious?"

"Indeed not. But being cursed and locked up in a haunted castle has a way of changing one's perspectives on the world."

His fingers drummed against the back of the chair. "Take a seat, love. I mean only to enjoy a fine meal with the mother of my child."

The words made her shudder, but Serilda forced herself to cross the dining hall and accept the proffered seat. The Erlking filled a goblet of water from a crystal carafe and added a few juniper berries with a flourish. Serilda watched them sink to the bottom of the glass with mounting trepidation. Then the king prepared her plate, scooping berries and pears alongside slices of quail breast.

To her annoyance, her stomach growled. Which was a strange sensation, as she was convinced that, without her physical body, she actually had no use for food. But she craved it all the same.

"These are some of my favorite foods," she said in surprise.

"Yes. I requested them from the cooks."

She shot him a simpering smile. "Tell me. What delicacies would you prefer? Puddings crafted from the blood of your victims? Cakes sprinkled with the milk teeth and finger bones of lost children?"

His eyes glinted. "Don't be grotesque, my sweet. I only eat the teeth of the elderly, once they've gone a little rotten. They're softer, not so difficult to chew." He pinched his fingers together in imitation of chewing, and Serilda gaped. That was a joke. Right?

While he prepared their plates, Serilda let her gaze drift around the room, where it landed on the massive taxidermy bird on the wall above a long buffet. It was the hercinia, a magic creature with wings like a fiery sunset, that even in death continued to glow faintly in the dim room. The first time she had been brought to this castle, the Erlking made a point of showing her this prize that the hunt had captured in the Aschen Wood. He had also made a point of telling her how both her head and her father's would soon decorate the wall to either side of the fabulous creature if she failed in her task of spinning straw into gold.

Remembering it, Serilda started to laugh.

The Erlking paused from placing a strip of veal on her plate. "What has amused you?"

"You," she said, "and how you once threatened to cut off my head, standing in this very room. And now you are cutting my meat for me. If one cannot find amusement in that, then they are hopeless."

The Erlking peered at the hercinia. "It was really the moss maidens' heads that I wanted then."

Serilda grimaced. "I remember."

He placed the plate in front of Serilda and took his seat. "Perhaps I shall have them still."

She didn't respond. She suspected he said it mostly to make her uncomfortable.

"Shouldn't you be preparing for tonight's hunt?" she asked, breaking apart a dark-crusted roll, releasing a burst of sweet-smelling steam.

"The hunt can wait. I am enjoying the company of my beloved." He grinned, and in that look she searched for his usual smirk, his taunting laughter.

She looked for it, but it wasn't there, only a memory of it where it ought to be.

"Charming," she mused. "I had not known you for a romantic."

"No? Then I have not been treating you as I ought to." Setting down the knife, he peered at Serilda a long moment, then reached across the table and, with the affection of a man enchanted, tucked a lock of hair behind her ear.

The shiver that overtook Serilda's body swept all the way to her feet.

As he pulled back, she felt herself frozen to the chair.

What was happening?

"All right," she said, her voice hardening to ice. "Out with it. What is this truly about?"

He chuckled again. "Ever quick to question my motives."

"Can you blame me?"

"Not at all. In fact, there is a small mystery I hoped you might help me solve." He reached into a pocket and pulled out a black-tipped arrow.

Serilda stilled, recognizing the weapon she had pulled out of the venomous chickenlike creature. The one that had then nearly killed her and Gild, even from inside its cage.

The king set the arrow between them on the table. "This was found in a room on the second floor, amid a great deal of destruction. Curtains, furniture . . . everything but a particularly resistant golden cage was completely annihilated. Even some of the inner walls suffered damage. I've had carpenters working all month to try to reinforce them." He cocked his head to one side. "You wouldn't happen to know what caused that destruction, would you?"

Serilda hummed to herself, as if considering the question. "Well," she said slowly, reaching forward and picking up the arrow as if to inspect it, "I have heard of these before. If it is what I think." She held the arrow toward the candlelight. "Ah yes. What you have here is the mythical black arrow once carried by Solvilde, god of sky and sea. When its powers are called upon, the very air around it will spark with the energy of a thousand bolts of lightning, unleashing fire and chaos upon whatever it touches." She clicked her tongue and set the arrow down again. "You dark ones really should be more careful with your treasures."

A slow smile curled over the king's mouth. "Actually," he said lowly, "it was not lightning that caused the destruction, but rather the venom of a basilisk."

The word made Serilda sit straighter.

A basilisk.

Of course. How had she not realized it before?

In modern fairy tales, the beast was often likened to an enormous serpent, but in older folklore it was depicted as much less frightening—though no less deadly. Part snake, part chicken. A look from it could turn anyone to stone, which explained why its eyes had been cut out. And its venom was strong enough to . . .

Well.

To burn through castle walls, evidently.

"Oh," she said. "So . . . this *isn't* the mythical black arrow of Solvilde?"

"No, though I suppose it could be called the mythical black arrow of Perchta. After she was taken from me, I have used what weapons of hers that were left behind in our hunts, when necessary. I doubt I could have captured the basilisk without it. What is strange, though, is that the basilisk was kept tranquilized for many decades. I cannot imagine who would ever dare to remove the arrow and risk the beast's temper."

"No," said Serilda, shaking her head. "Who would be so careless?"

The Erlking held her gaze. She did not flinch as he took the arrow and slipped it back into his pocket. "No matter. The threat has been dealt with, and this arrow may yet come in handy again for a future hunt."

Serilda swallowed. "The basilisk—did you have to kill it?"

"Would it bother you if we had?"

She hesitated, unsure how she felt. The creature was a menace, but it was also glorious. Odd though it was, its feathers were the prettiest she'd ever seen, and for such a small creature to be so feared was admirable, even aspirational.

"I don't like unnecessary killing," she finally said.

"No?" The Erlking grunted in surprise. "It is one of my favorite pastimes." He raised his goblet to his mouth and took a sip. When he lowered the glass again, his expression was more scrutinizing. "Have I been unkind to you, miller's daughter?"

She stilled. It took a long moment for her to believe he meant the question in truth. "You murdered five children from my village. Your ravens ate out their hearts. All because I wouldn't give you what you wanted."

His brows creased in confusion. "I murdered *them*. Not you."

"You cursed me!" she yelled, holding up her wrist to show the scar. "You plunged an arrow through my arm and trapped me here for all time."

"Which is an improvement, is it not?"

She guffawed. "An improvement over what?"

"Your *life*. Here you are a queen. You live in a castle. With servants and attendants and . . . feasts." He gestured to the food before them. "You cannot tell me you dined like this in Märchenfeld."

He said the name of her village as though it were overrun with rats and refuse. When in reality, despite some superstitions and mistrust from the townsfolk, Serilda always felt it to be quite a nice little village.

Which was entirely beside the point. Was he really so dense as to think any part of this life was preferable to the one he had stolen from her?

She leaned across the table. "My servants are tortured souls who would sooner follow Velos's lantern than bring me a pair of slippers. My attendants are the very children you killed and continue to use as a threat against me. And no, I never did dine like this in Märchenfeld, because I was enjoying hearty turnip stew by a cozy fire beside my father, who you *also killed.*"

He studied her a long moment, before leaning across the table and placing his cool palm over her hand. Serilda tensed. She had not realized during this tirade that she'd been gripping her dinner knife like a weapon.

"And yet," said the king softly, "have *you* been treated poorly?"

Serilda did not know what to say. He seemed genuine, and she had the strange sensation that he was trying to please her. With this meal, the candlelight, this conversation. But to what ends? He never gave anything without wanting more in return. It felt like a trap, but one she could not see clearly, and therefore did not know how to avoid.

"Not at all," she finally said, allowing her mood to brighten as she pulled her hand away. "I have been treated with utmost kindness and respect. Every day in these walls has been abundant with delights previously unknown to this simple mortal."

It was a credit to her godparent that the Erlking nodded, as if pleased to hear this. She barely kept from rolling her eyes when he turned his attention to a strip of wild boar on his plate.

"I have sometimes wondered," he said, dipping the meat into a dish of gravy, "if you have had cause to miss your paramour."

Serilda stared at the dripping meat on the end of his knife. "Paramour?"

Sliding the meat off between his teeth, he gestured with the knife point down the front of her dress.

It took her another moment to understand.

Ah—the father of her child. The one that, as far as the Erlking knew, was nothing more than a farm boy she'd had a tumble with. Nothing meaningful. Nothing of importance.

"No," she said, scooping some buttered peas onto the edge of her own knife. "Why would I?"

He made a noncommittal noise in his throat. "Ladies can be sentimental."

She shot him an irritated glare. "We are not the only ones."

"What was he like?"

She shrugged. "What do you wish to know?"

"Was he charming?"

She pictured Gild—she couldn't help it. But then she tried to swipe the image away, worried that even to think of him would give away the truth she wished to keep hidden.

Instead, she thought of Thomas Lindbeck, Hans's older brother. She had once thought herself in love with him; it felt like a lifetime ago. She wondered distantly whether he married the girl he'd been sweet on. If he was running the mill in her and her father's extended absence. Had life gone on in Märchenfeld, or would the scars of losing five innocent children to the wild hunt haunt them for as long as it would haunt her?

"He was . . . charming enough."

"Handsome?"

She wished—oh, how she wished—she could feign neutrality, as the question itself was asked as if it meant nothing. But again, she found herself thinking of Gild, and she could not keep the heat from climbing up her neck and spilling across her cheeks.

"He does not compare to you, my lord, if that is what you're asking."

His eyes sparked. "And did you love him?"

Love.

The word came like an arrow, straight through her chest, wholly unexpected. How could she answer such a thing? Already she could feel the hollow place inside her expanding, searching for a flutter of a heart, and she could almost, almost feel it.

Did she love him?

Did she love Gild?

If she were being honest with herself, she did not think she had been quite in love with him that night they had lain together. She had wanted him. Yearned for him. Yearned to experience something with him that was entirely new to her, to both of them. She had not regretted their intimacy then, and despite all that had happened since, she could not regret it now.

But had she loved him?

Not exactly. Love grew out of shared memories, shared stories, shared laughter. Love was a result of knowing the many things a person did that annoyed you to the ends of the earth, and yet, somehow, still wanting to hold them at the end of every day and be held by them at sunrise every morning. Love was the comfort of knowing someone would stand by you, accept you, despite all your eccentricities, all your faults. Maybe loving you, in part, because of them.

She hadn't had that comfort with Gild, despite what they'd shared, despite how just thinking about him made her tingle with anticipation, eager to be near him again.

It might not have been love then. But a seed had been planted, and in the months since, it had continued to grow. It grew with every passing day. Blossoming into something unexpected and frightening and true. Her yearning had morphed into tenderness. A desire, so powerful, to see him free, to see him happy—regardless of whether or not he could be free and happy with *her*.

Was that love?

She didn't know. But she did know that she had no other words that came close to describing what she felt for Gild.

"You had me convinced that you felt hardly anything for him," said the Erlking, pulling a dark purple grape off its stem with his sharp teeth. "Now I see. I wonder what else you might have lied—"

"You *don't* see," she said, surprised at the flare of anger inside her. "You couldn't possibly."

"I might surprise you," he said, a teasing new tilt to his mouth.

"Why are we even discussing this? What does any of it matter?"

"Call it curiosity about the child as much as the father. I like to know what to expect."

Serilda swallowed hard. She'd tried not to think too much about what traits her baby might have. Gild's copper hair? His freckles? His incorrigible smile? Or would the child take after her—with cursed eyes, a penchant for lying, and a stubborn spirit that so often got her into trouble?

"You are wrong, you know." The melancholy in the king's voice startled her more than his words.

"About what?" she snapped, unwilling to release her anger so quickly.

The king chuckled. "Believe what you will. But I do know what it is to love, and what it feels like once that love is lost."

Chapter Twenty

The king's statement hung in the air between them. It was the most vulnerable he'd ever been in Serilda's presence, and to her annoyance, it drove all her fury out of her in one crystallizing breath.

His eyes slid toward hers, peering through lush black lashes. "But I am only a demon. That is what you call us in your tales, is it not?"

She shuddered, not daring to admit it, though he did not seem particularly hurt.

"Perhaps you do not believe that love between demons can be real."

Her lips parted, but no words came out. She didn't know what to believe. Everything she'd seen of the Alder King and his court had been cruelty and selfishness, nothing ever like love, as far as she could tell.

But she remembered the story of the Erlking and the huntress. Somehow she knew, if ever given the chance, he would realign the stars themselves to be reunited with her.

"You're going to try to bring Perchta back," she whispered.

The Erlking did not smile. Or frown. Or move. He stared at her, watching for *something*, though Serilda didn't know what it was. Only when she shivered again did he blink and draw back. Neither realized that he'd begun to lean toward her, his elegant fingers on the tablecloth mere inches from Serilda's.

Serilda shook her head, feeling like she'd been caught in a daze.

"You believe," said the Erlking, "I have the power to bring a spirit back from the clutches of Verloren?"

"I believe you will try."

He didn't deny it.

"I believe," she went on, watching him carefully, though his expression gave nothing away, "you mean to capture one of the old gods during the Endless Moon. And when you have them, you will wish for the return of Perchta, and you will give my child to her."

She held his gaze, waiting for the acknowledgment that she was right. She was rewarded by a sharpening of his eyes.

"You are clever," he mused.

"Only observant," she said. "Perchta was taken three hundred years ago. Have you been attempting to capture a god all this time?"

He shrugged. "Hasn't everyone?"

"I don't think so, no."

He smirked. "They would, if they had the means."

"The gold."

"The gold," he agreed.

"But you don't think you have enough."

His jaw twitched. "I can be resourceful."

Serilda was surprised he did not try to deny his plans—but again, what would be the point? What could she do about it?

"If you should succeed, won't she be jealous once she learns that you have taken a mortal wife?"

His brow pinched and Serilda realized he didn't understand what she meant. Then his expression cleared and his face lit up in the candlelight.

"My Perchta," he drawled. "Jealous. Of *you*?"

Serilda had never been more offended by so few words. She straightened her spine. "I am your wife, am I not?"

He barked a laugh. "You mortals care so much for your arbitrary titles. I find it rather quaint."

This time, Serilda did not hide the roll of her eyes. "Yes, yes. We silly mortals. How adorable we must be when viewed from a place of such superiority."

"I find you rather refreshing."

"So glad I could please you, my lord."

The Erlking stopped smiling only long enough to take a sip of wine. "Now it is *you* who cannot possibly understand," he said, idly swirling the goblet. "Everything I am belongs to the huntress. It has always been that way, and it will never change. I could never give of myself to another, for there is nothing to be given. So, no, Perchta will not be jealous. Rather, she will delight in the child I can give her, the only gift I couldn't give to her before."

"But you have given her children before, and she tired of them all. And what then? Are you going to murder my child, or abandon them in the woods?"

"You know the stories well."

"Everyone knows those stories. Living so close to the Aschen Wood, they are some of the first stories we tell our children. A warning to stay away from you."

The king shrugged. "I brought her children, but never a newborn. Perhaps her maternal affection needed to develop from infancy."

Serilda clenched her knife tighter. "Nonsense. All children deserve to be loved. All children deserve a mother or a father who will care for them and protect them, unconditionally. Not someone to dote on them for a time, only to lose interest when parenthood no longer suits them. Those are not the actions of someone who wishes to be a mother. That is the opposite of a mother. That is someone who cares only for themselves."

The Erlking's gaze darkened with a warning, and though she had *much* more to say on the topic, Serilda forced her lips tight.

"I suppose we shall see," he said quietly. "If all goes well."

If all goes well.

If he did capture a god and wish for the return of Perchta. If he did give Serilda's child to that monster.

"What is the point of any of this?" she said. "You have what you want, so why bother with candles and flowers and"—she swung her knife over the table spread—"*romance*?"

"Is that what's bothering you?"

She snorted. "I cannot begin to account for the many things that are bothering me."

"Ah yes. Because you are a prisoner, cursed, trapped in a haunted castle, those beloved rodents you call children are dead, and so on and so forth. Forgive me for having forgotten your many complaints." He sighed, sounding bored. "I merely thought it might be nice to enjoy a peaceful evening together. Husband and wife."

"Jailer and captive."

"Do not be defensive. It makes you sound human."

"I am human. And my child will be, too, if you hadn't realized that yet. They will have human emotions and needs. You want to know what to expect? Well, there it is. All the messy, illogical, ridiculous things that humans experience every day of our lives. Because we have hearts and souls—something you cannot fathom, no matter how much you think you know what love is."

The king listened to her tirade, his haughty expression back, icy and hardened once again.

"Is that all?" he finally said.

She exhaled sharply through her nostrils. "No. That is *not* all," she snapped. But she quickly came back to herself, remembering the importance of this night. All that she and Gild had been working for. "But it grows late, my lord. You must get ready for the hunt. To catch yourself a new bärgeist or a . . . gryphon, or what have you."

"Ah, so you've heard about our gryphon?"

"I've heard you don't have enough gold for that either," she shot back, wishing he would stop dragging out this conversation. Wishing he would just leave.

"Perhaps not," said the king, evidently unbothered. "We could always just kill it. Mount its head . . . right there, perhaps." He pointed to the stone mantel behind Serilda, but she did not turn to look. "But that would be a shame. There are beasts meant to be hung on walls, and there are beasts meant to be admired in full flesh and blood. I would not wish to kill the gryphon, and you're right, I do not believe we have enough chains to subdue it." He cocked his head to the side. "Perhaps I shall bring back a gift for you, my darling."

"I pray you will not."

"Come now. There must be some magical beast that would entice you. What mortal child hasn't dreamed of riding a white unicorn through the southern meadows?"

"A unicorn! That sounds a rather tame goal compared with gryphons and bärgeists and tatzelwurms."

He grinned. "So says one who has never tried to capture one. They are trickier beasts than you would expect."

"Of course they are." Serilda leaned forward conspiratorially. "They are drawn to innocent maidens and children, my lord, whereas you are constantly surrounded by murderous demons. Perhaps you keep the wrong company."

"I shall take it under advisement. Though I wouldn't want to make it too easy. There is no satisfaction in that." He traced a fingernail along the edge of his goblet. "Innocent maidens and children, you say. What a novel idea."

"You aren't really going to hunt for a unicorn, are you?"

"Why not? It is a worthy prize." His lips curled. "Those two attendants of yours. The little one and the"—he waved his hand languidly through the air—"the one that never holds still. You aren't needing them tonight, are you?"

Serilda stilled. She wanted to believe he was teasing her, but she could never be sure.

"I didn't mean it," she said. "No one actually believes that unicorns are drawn to children. It's a silly myth is all."

"There is truth to be found in silly myths."

"Not this one. Unicorns are too clever for that. You'd be better off searching in the darkest parts of the forest, where the sun never falls. Unicorns do not like to compete with sunlight. They make their homes in glens with lots of . . ." She surveyed the offerings on the table. "Blackberry bushes. And stinging nettles. And an oak tree. They always have to be near an oak tree, because it is the only wood that can withstand them sharpening their horn. Everything else will wither and die, straight down to the roots." She shrugged at him. "At least, that's what I've been told. See? No children necessary."

The Erlking stared at her a long moment, inscrutable.

Then he stood and—most disconcertingly—dropped to a knee beside Serilda and took her hand into his. "You are a prize," he whispered, pressing his lips to her fingers.

Serilda pulled away, horrified.

All at once, her story of the tatzelwurm came back to her. It had been nothing but a ridiculous lie, and yet, that very night, the hunt found the beast precisely where she'd said it would be. Had she done it again?

"My lord—"

"Come," he said, rising to his feet and downing the rest of his wine in a single gulp. "We mustn't tarry. The moonlit hour has gold in the mouth."

Serilda frowned. "You mean *morning* hour. The saying goes . . . oh, never mind."

He dragged her out of the keep and into the courtyard, which was bustling with activity, as it always was on the night of the hunt. But Serilda could tell as soon as she stepped outside that something was different.

It was not only hunters and hounds and horses being prepared. There were also dozens of carriages and wagons hitched to bahkauv, odd bull-like creatures. She saw the stable boy and nearly all the castle's servants hurrying about, checking carriage wheels and greasing axles, others loading crates and cargo into the wagons.

"What's going on?" said Serilda.

"I have made new accommodations for us," said the Erlking. His grin turned slippery as he took Serilda's hand, tucked it into the crook of his elbow, and led her away from the keep. "No need to look so fretful."

"I'm not fretful," she said with a growl. "I just find it unspeakably annoying how everything you say comes with more layers than an onion."

"Forgive me. I hate to ruin a surprise. In short, my love, we are leaving."

"Leaving?" She gawked at the hunters checking their weapons, and also a number of dark ones who did not usually attend the hunt stepping into enclosed carriages. "Leaving Adalheid?"

"I sent word to your little attendants earlier this evening," he said. "I suspect they'll be arriving with your things . . . Ah yes. Here they come now."

Serilda spotted Hans and Fricz carrying a trunk between them. Anna and Gerdrut followed after, their arms full of cases and woven bags. Though it had only been four weeks since Anna had fallen into the arena, her wounds had healed quickly, as promised, and she seemed to have no trouble carrying the heavy luggage.

The children stopped at a carriage, the one that had reminded Serilda of a mausoleum, where Nickel was helping to hitch up a horse.

"I don't understand. Where are you taking them?"

"Taking *them*? Don't be ridiculous. What need have I of such parasites? If you hadn't noticed, they make abhorrent servants. I've seen the way that small one styles your hair, and if I am being frank"—he fixed her with a meaningful look—"it is difficult for me to tolerate."

Serilda scowled. "I do my own hair."

He blinked. "In that case, I wish you wouldn't. As to your question, they are here to accompany you. They are your attendants, are they not?"

"But . . ." She shook her head, squeezing her eyes shut in exasperation. "I cannot leave. I'm trapped here."

"Is that what has you so upset?" He stroked a fingertip along the inside crook of her elbow. "Do you not think I have prepared everything?" He lifted his voice. "Manfred! See to it that wagon there is given our two most dependable beasts and a contingent of guards. It carries my most precious cargo. I would hate for something to happen to it."

Manfred, who had been checking something off on a small scroll, gave a firm nod. "Of course, Your Grim. I will see to it."

Serilda peered past him, to see the carriage the Erlking was referring to.

A heaviness settled over her. It was the large, luxurious wagon that Agathe had shown her in the carriage house. The one that held her body inside.

Leaving.

Somehow, it was possible for her to leave Adalheid. And it was happening. It was happening now, tonight.

"No," she said, squinting up at the castle windows, searching for a sign of Gild. "Not tonight. Your Grim, be sensible." She clutched the Erlking's arm. "If you wish to travel, should we not go under the protection of the veil? Why leave tonight, when the Straw Moon is high? You should go hunting, and I will . . . I will be better prepared to leave tomorrow. If you'd given me any warning I could have been ready, but I . . . I simply can't leave tonight."

He smirked. "Did you have very important plans for the evening, my dove?"

She swallowed. "N-no. I only—"

"Giselle!" he barked, startling Serilda into silence.

The master of the hounds appeared, looking more sullen than usual.

"You are in charge of this castle in my absence," he said. "I expect my court to answer to you as they would to me."

"An honor, Your Grim."

"Take special care of the menagerie," the Erlking added. "I hope to have new acquisitions for it upon our return."

Giselle bowed. "And you are sure your hunters can manage the hounds? They have a specific feeding schedule and require regular exercise outside of the hunts and—"

"Calm yourself, Giselle. You are fretting as much as the mortal."

Serilda and Giselle both made disgusted faces at each other.

"The hounds will be well taken care of, I assure you. And for your willingness to stay behind, I promise you will be rewarded."

Giselle pressed her lips into a thin line. "Whatever my king requires of me." She bowed again before turning away, heading off to check on the waiting hounds.

"Now then," said the Erlking, taking Serilda's hand into his and tracing his frigid thumbs over the scar on her wrist. A lance of ice shot up her arm, into the cavity of her chest. "Are you ready?"

"For what?" she breathed, her insides suddenly coated in winter frost.

The Erlking stepped closer, so she had to crane her neck to hold his gaze. Before she knew what was happening, she felt the unexpected yet familiar tug of magic. A crackling deep in her belly. A sparking in the air. The fine hairs lifting on the back of her neck.

"*I dissolve the binds tethering you to this castle,*" he said, his words echoing inside her skull. "*Though your spirit remains outside the confines of your mortal body, you are no longer trapped. As the keeper of your soul, I gift to you freedom from these walls.*"

As the last of his words flickered on the air between them, Serilda felt the same searing pain as when he had first placed the curse upon her, shooting up from the scar where the arrow had pierced her flesh. She cried out in surprise, crumpling forward, and might have collapsed had the Erlking not caught her.

The pain did not last.

Her next breath, though shaky, allowed her to stand again. "Why would you do this?" she said, bewildered. "I don't understand."

"You will," he said blithely, stroking her hand between his, the picture of a doting husband. "There is nothing more for you to do but to make yourself comfortable. Your carriage awaits." He started walking her toward the carriage where the five children were waiting for her. Hans stood holding Serilda's favorite, travel-worn cloak. There was uncertainty on their faces. She could tell they were as baffled by this unexpected outing as she was.

"Here you are," said the Erlking, taking the cloak from Hans and draping it over Serilda's shoulders as she tried to disguise her growing sense of dread. He tenderly checked the clasp, before helping Serilda up onto the driver's bench. "You should have a fine view from here."

"Your Grim." Agathe appeared, her expression inscrutable as she looked up at Serilda, then turned her attention back to the Erlking. She held up a golden chain, looped a dozen times around her fist, and a long sword in a scabbard. "The weapons you asked for."

The king took the chain and the sword and secured them to his belt.

"The hunters are ready," added Agathe.

"Good. Let us depart."

"Wait!" cried Serilda.

The Erlking lifted an eyebrow at her.

"Please," she pleaded. "Tell me what is going on."

"Isn't it obvious?" he said. "We are going hunting."

With that, he sauntered away. He was quickly surrounded by his fellow hunters. The stable boy brought him the black war steed.

Hans climbed up onto the driver's bench beside Serilda. Tonight he would be her coachman. Nickel helped Gerdrut inside the carriage, before he and Anna and Fricz climbed in as well.

"What is happening?" she whispered. "Where are we going? How is it that I . . ." The words left her.

Hans took ahold of her hand, the touch comforting, even as it made gooseflesh rise along her arm. He didn't reply, his lips pinched tight, and Serilda wondered if there was something they knew, but the Erlking had forbidden them from telling her.

As the carriage began to rumble over the cobblestones, joining the line of horses and wagons being pulled toward the drawbridge, Serilda craned her neck to search the castle keep again. The windows glowed with firelight, but there was no sign of Gild.

The carriage passed into the shadow of the gatehouse. The sound of the horses' and bahkauv's hooves changed to melodic clomping as they stepped onto the wooden bridge.

She held her breath.

The carriage wheels rattled and creaked and thundered onto the bridge.

She emerged from the shadows of the gatehouse, and she did not vanish.

Her spirit was not dragged back to the throne room in the heart of the keep.

She had left Adalheid Castle, and somewhere in this dark parade, her body had left it, too.

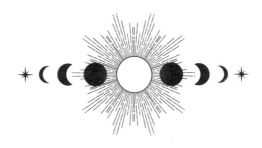

Chapter Twenty-One

Serilda continued to stare at the castle until the carriage hit the road into Adalheid. Her attention swiveled toward the path that ran along the lake. In the distance, barely visible in the light of the Straw Moon, she could just make out the pretty blue front of the Wild Swan Inn. She gripped the edge of the driver's bench, itching to dart from the carriage. She was free. *Free.* And her friends were so close. Leyna. Lorraine. No doubt they were tucked into their beds already, their doors and windows latched on a night when the wild hunt should have been storming past, not this hastily assembled parade.

How far could she get before the dark ones caught her and dragged her back?

Probably not far, she reasoned. Their traveling party was enormous, and Serilda wondered if every single ghostly servant was among them, for when she looked back, it seemed that their wisping forms trailed along the road as far as she could see. She knew some of the dark ones had stayed behind at the castle, but all the hunters seemed to be here, hemming her in on all sides. She was outnumbered and surrounded, like always.

The Wild Swan passed from view and the carriage continued on, past darkened buildings, pens with goats and chickens shut up for the night, flourishing summer gardens.

Serilda faced forward. She didn't want to see the bakery, the cobbler, Frieda's library . . . She yearned for this town with every passing moment, but forced herself to stay still until the caravan had passed beneath the shadow of the city gates.

"Serilda," said Hans, releasing one of the reins to settle a hand on her wrist. "Are you all right?"

"I'm not sure," she answered. "Do you know what this is about?"

He shook his head. "We were told to pack your belongings and expect to be gone for a month or more."

"A month! But where . . . ?"

Hans shrugged. "He doesn't confide in *us*."

"No, nor to me." Serilda's thoughts spun wildly as she tried to make sense of it. One minute she'd been worried that she may have unwittingly given the Erlking some clue as to where to find a unicorn, and the next she and the children were being carried off through Adalheid to gods knew where.

Soon the tree line of the Aschen Wood rose up to greet them. Even in the heat of summer a mist was shrouding the base of the forest, as if there was never a time in which this magical place was not just a little bit dreary.

The sounds of the wagons became stifled as they made their way into the woods. Their progress slowed as the shadows engulfed them, the path lit by lanterns hung from each carriage, though their light barely cut through the encroaching darkness.

With a shiver, Hans knocked his palm twice on the carriage wall. "All right in there? Gerdy?"

It took a moment, but Gerdrut's voice squeaked back, "I'll be glad when we're through."

"Me too," said Hans. "Stay brave."

Sorrow overtook Serilda as she realized that the last time—the *only* time—Gerdrut and the others had been through these woods, it was when they'd just been taken by the wild hunt. The night they were murdered.

Even Hans seemed shaken by the memory, reminding Serilda that, despite all his efforts to be the steady, pragmatic eldest of their group, he was still a child himself.

"It will be all right," said Serilda.

Hans looked at her. He held her gaze a long moment, his dark eyes glinting with torchlight.

"Will it?" he asked.

"I'll make sure of it."

She could tell that Hans wanted to believe her, but he didn't. Not really.

They slipped into a long silence, listening to the sounds of the wheels and gazing out into the woods, though all she could see was a black void beyond the torches. It would have been better to wait until morning, she thought. Even the Straw Moon barely touched this part of the forest, where the tree canopy grew dense overhead.

Suddenly, the caravan came to a stop.

"The queen!" someone shouted from up ahead. "Bring forward the queen!"

Hans put an arm in front of Serilda, as if to protect her. An impulse she appreciated, even if they both knew it was useless.

A second later, the king came galloping from the front of the caravan, pulling a second horse beside him. He drew up short and dismounted in front of the carriage. "Your services are required."

She traded looks with Hans. "Should I bring one of my attendants?"

"That won't be necessary." The Erlking held a hand to her.

Clearing her throat, she stood and accepted his assistance onto the second horse.

"What's happening?" said Anna, a whimper in her tone. She and Fricz were poking their heads out through the carriage's window.

"Nothing to worry about," Serilda said. "I'll be back soon."

Her horse required no command from her as she and the king trotted toward the front of their parade, where the hunters waited.

"The darkest part of the forest," said the Erlking, gesturing toward the shadows. "No sunlight falls here. No moonlight touches this hallowed ground." He paused, cutting a sharp look toward Serilda. "But we have given our hounds the scent of blackberries and nettles, and they detect none here."

Serilda stared at him, incredulous. "Are you serious? Did we really come here looking for a unicorn?" She let out a wry laugh. "I was making it up, my lord. I do that sometimes."

"I've noticed." He brought his horse closer so that his knee brushed hers. "Humor me."

"What do you want me to say?" She gestured flippantly toward the woods. "Continue east for fifty paces until you come to the babbling brook where rest the bones of a squirrel—the sad remains of a wolf's dinner. Then follow the path of late-season foxglove until you come to a ring of toadstools where once a forest pixie sat embroidering constellations on an oak leaf that always points like a compass toward the unicorn's meadow?"

The Erlking stared at her, expressionless. "That will do. Hunters, continue on. Fifty paces east."

Serilda threw her hands into the air. "Nonsense. With sauce!" she bellowed. "It's nothing but gibberish! There is no unicorn! No toadstools, none of it! I'm lying! And they aren't even very good lies!"

"We shall see."

And so they did. Fifty paces east where, to Serilda's amazement, they came to a small bridge over a babbling brook. One of the hunters held a torch toward the water, and were those bones in the stream or merely small white stones?

"There," said another, gesturing to a path that cut off from the main road, so narrow that Serilda wondered whether the carriages could pass.

Evidently so. They plowed forward, and soon saw tall spikes of foxglove flowers littering both sides of the path.

Serilda pressed a hand to her temple, overcome with an odd dizziness. How was this possible?

Not long after that, before they could seek out toadstools and embroidered oak leaves, the hounds caught a scent and dashed off. The Erlking spurred his horse forward, and Serilda's mount hastened to follow. The shadows of the forest blurred past. Every now and then the trees and ferns were illuminated by a shard of moonlight cutting through the dense foliage.

Nothing was familiar. Everything was strange and impossible and topsy-turvy.

This wasn't right. She was suddenly overcome with the sense that she should not be here.

But she could not escape. Not only because the Erlking would never allow it, but also because she would be immediately lost in these scraggly woods, filled with monsters and magic.

"Blackberries!" someone cried. "There are blackberries up here! And an oak tree."

The Erlking grinned smugly. "Nonsense with sauce," he muttered.

When they caught up to the hounds, they had indeed reached an oak tree. It was the biggest oak tree Serilda had ever seen, its trunk wider than the carriages that trundled in the distance, trying to catch up.

Serilda gaped, knowing that she shouldn't be surprised at this point that her ridiculous lies were coming true, but . . . really? This particular bunch of lies had been exceptionally ridiculous, even for her.

"I found this," said one of the hunters, holding up what appeared to be an oak leaf, embroidered. The hunter tossed it into the air and it fluttered down, down to the forest floor, landing with its tip pointing toward the tree.

The oak tree—the more Serilda thought of it—seemed awfully familiar.

But that was impossible. The only time she'd trekked through this forest was when the schellenrock and the moss maidens brought her to see Pusch-Grohla, the Shrub Grandmother. She remembered that day so clearly. Everything they had discussed. The thinly veiled threats against her life if she ever dared to betray them to the Erlking.

But now that she thought of it, why couldn't she remember how she'd gotten there? Where was *there*?

A babbling brook. A salige that tried to attack her. The hollow clatter of the schellenrock's coat. A village among the trees. Pusch-Grohla seated upon a tree stump.

Her words came back to Serilda.

Should you ever try to find this place again, or lead anyone to us, your words will turn to gibberish and you will become as lost as a cricket in a snowstorm.

Serilda didn't remember this oak tree, but suddenly, she knew where she was.

She knew where she had just brought the wild hunt.

Not to the lair of a unicorn, but to something far worse.

Her eyes widened with horror.

"Your Grim," she said, reaching for the Erlking's arm. "I've just remembered—a story I heard when I was a little girl. About a unicorn that liked to sleep among a cluster of birch trees off the banks of the Sieglin Riv—"

"That's enough," said the Erlking. "I appreciate your enthusiasm, but that will do for now."

He leaped from his horse, landing soundlessly amid the brush.

"Wait!" said Serilda, sliding off her horse with much less grace.

The Erlking did not wait. He approached the oak tree and peeled back a layer of vines and moss that clung to the wide trunk, revealing a narrow hole in the tree's roots, tall enough for Serilda to walk through, though the Erlking had to duck. She noticed that he took care not to touch the tree's bark, and she thought of an old superstition—that oak could keep evil creatures at bay.

"Light," he called, and a hunter appeared with a torch. The Erlking took it and held it high, revealing the hollow insides of the trunk, like a small cavern.

Hung on the other side was a tapestry. Serilda's breath caught as the Erlking held the light to reveal the image woven with fine threads. A white unicorn standing proud in a vibrant glen, surrounded by every creature of the forest, from the simplest squirrel to the most alluring water nix. The image was breathtaking, a vibrant work of impeccable art.

"Lovely," said the Erlking.

Then he brought the torch flame to the fabric.

"No!" Serilda cried out. "Please!"

The tapestry caught fire like dry leaves. The flames spread. Black smoke quickly filled the cavern within the oak tree, and the Erlking pushed Serilda out of the tree as the fire began to consume it from the inside. Smoke rose, blocking what little moonlight tried to find them through the tangled branches overhead. Twigs crackled and splintered and fell. Heat pressed against Serilda's face, driving her back toward the line of hunters.

It did not take long for the entire tree to become engulfed, and for the fire to spread, jumping across the branches into nearby trees.

"Gods alive," she breathed. "You will destroy the whole forest."

Beside her, the Erlking grunted. "It would be worth it."

She looked at him, aghast.

"Oh, calm yourself. The forest will live. You see, the fire is already containing itself. It will only destroy what this tree was meant to hide."

She didn't understand. The flames were spreading, and quickly. Ash was falling down like snow across the forest floor—

Ash.

Blanketing the world before her.

Revealing—not a dense forest—but a village. A village built of tree houses and vine bridges and homes nestled among the roots.

The fire was not burning down all of the Aschen Wood.

It was burning down Asyltal.

As the great oak tree collapsed into itself, releasing a flurry of blinding sparks, Serilda saw the figure standing amid the flames and destruction.

Grandmother to the moss maidens. Protector of the forest. Pusch-Grohla.

She was glaring, not at the Erlking, but at Serilda.

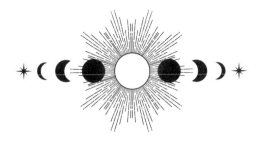

Chapter Twenty-Two

I should have known better than to let live a human once you had seen our home," said Pusch-Grohla. Her long white hair hung in tangles and knots, run through with sticks and bits of moss and even a clump of hardened mud. Completely out of place was the elegant pearl diadem that rested on her wrinkled brow.

"I'm sorry," Serilda gasped. "It was an accident—"

"Yet bring them here you did. Which should not have been possible. I made sure that you would not be able to find us again."

"I didn't mean to! He was asking about a . . . a unicorn. I just made up a story, I swear. I never would have betrayed you!"

"The unicorn *was* a nice touch," drawled the Erlking, striding into the clearing. "All this time, hidden behind one of Hulda's tapestries. Clever gods." He glanced around. "Have your children scampered off in fright? I had expected more from the so-called forest folk. I thought you were raising them to be warriors of a sort. Or—let me guess." He tilted his head back, peering around at the towering trees. "They're tucked away, hiding in the branches, waiting for just the right moment to heroically throw themselves into battle." He lifted an eyebrow. "I *do* hope that moment comes before it all burns to the ground."

"With or without our home," said Pusch-Grohla, "we will fight you and your selfish path of destruction."

He chuckled. "Not if you're dead."

In one motion, he unsheathed the longsword and swung it at Pusch-Grohla. She blocked it with her staff and where metal struck wood a swarm of white-winged moths fluttered into existence. They flurried at the Erlking and in that moment's distraction, a war cry sounded out.

Hundreds of moss maidens appeared from the surrounding woods, horns and antlers flashing gold in the light from the consuming fire. They wielded bows and daggers and spears as they charged at the hunters, who rushed forward to meet them with their own eager weapons.

Serilda screamed and crouched down, trying to protect herself with raised arms, but no one paid her any attention as the world was thrown into chaos. The ground rumbled and she fell to one knee, thinking it was hunters' horses rushing into the fray. But then she noticed enormous tree roots breaking through the forest floor and lashing at the hunters like snakes. Soon, the roots were joined by vines whipping down from the burning branches. Brambles winding around hunters' legs. Birds appeared from the trees to hurtle toward the invaders with sharp beaks and sharper talons. Spores from enormous fungi mixed with the fire's smoke, choking and blinding anyone who came in contact with them.

But though the forest magic was strong, the hunters were brutal and well-trained and immortal. In the frenzy of battle, they focused their attention on the moss maidens, meting out blow for blow.

Screams everywhere. Of pain. Of rage.

Then—*Serilda!*—little voices calling her.

She blinked to clear the dust from her eyes.

The five children were hiding between the wheels of a carriage. Though she was afraid to move, Serilda forced herself to skitter forward. Dodging a hunter's knife and a moss maiden's hatchet, she threw herself beneath the carriage, panting. "Is anyone hurt?"

"We're all right," Hans answered for them, though Gerdrut was crying as both twins tried to shelter her with their arms.

From this vantage, Serilda had a better view of the turmoil. The fire continued to spread, forming a barrier around the glen that had been the village of Asyltal. Every now and then a branch would splinter above and fall, crashing down with a surge of sparks.

The ghosts were mostly seeking shelter themselves, hiding inside or underneath the carriages, their cursed tie to the Erlking keeping them from fleeing into the woods.

All except Agathe. Like the hunters, she was in battle mode. A broadsword in her hands, she moved like a dancer through the fight, cutting through moss maidens with dazzling speed and grace. Oh, how Serilda wished the skills of the weapons master could have been used against the dark ones, and not the forest folk.

Serilda couldn't watch.

Turning away, she spotted the large wagon, not far off, sheltering a handful of cooks and scullery maids. She recognized that wagon. *Her* wagon. The one harboring her body.

Could she get to it? Break the curse? Reunite her spirit with her body and free herself for real? No one was watching her.

But . . . no.

The children were still trapped, enslaved to the Erlking. She could not abandon them. She had to . . .

She gasped and swiveled her attention to the Erlking. He was advancing on Shrub Grandmother, who was fighting back with an onslaught of forest magic. Roots winding up his legs. Tree saplings grasping at his arms. Wildflowers sprouting from the king's own scabbards and pockets when he reached for his weapons. No matter how quick or ruthless the Erlking was, Pusch-Grohla always had a trick to throw him off or slow him down. Where any warrior might have been frustrated, the Erlking was grinning, his blue eyes bright and zealous.

He still hadn't used the long golden chain tied in a loop at his belt, as if he was saving it for a special occasion. She knew the hunters had more, somewhere, from when they had captured the tatzelwurm and fought the bärgeist, but she had no idea where they might be keeping them. But the Erlking's chain was *right there*, glinting in the firelight.

If Serilda could somehow get that chain, she could use it to free the children.

"Stay here," she said, crawling out from beneath the carriage.

The children's dismayed cries followed her, but Serilda ignored them. She thought only of the Erlking and that chain and how she had to get closer to him without being stabbed by an errant dagger or impaled by a wayward spear.

At least the hunters and the moss maidens were so focused on killing one another they paid no heed to the girl ducking and crawling and sprinting through their midst.

She threw herself behind a stone to catch her breath. She was close now. The Erlking and Shrub Grandmother fought not a dozen paces from her.

He was intent, so focused on his quarry.

But Serilda could sense the battle was nearing its end—and the dark ones were winning. Bodies of fallen moss maidens littered the ground, along with all manner of forest beasts. Bats and badgers, foxes and owls. Lifeless eyes peering up into the night. Bodies punctured with bolts and arrows or cut through by swords. The moss on the forest floor was soaked through with blood, and everywhere fallen tree branches and burning embers mixed with carnage.

Even Pusch-Grohla was losing ground, having been continuously beaten back by the Erlking's advances until her back hit the trunk of a towering pine tree. Its upper limbs were burning. Ash swirled around them.

The Erlking grinned and lifted his sword, the point hovering at her throat. "Have your tricks finally run out, you old hag?"

To Serilda's surprise, she spied a glistening tear in the corner of Pusch-Grohla's eye as she took in just how much devastation the fire had caused.

"Please . . . Solvilde," Shrub Grandmother whispered, her throat scratchy from the smoke, "if you ever cared for anything beyond yourself, help us."

The Erlking laughed, a cruel, cold sound. "The great Pusch-Grohla, begging for what? A rain cloud? A thunderstorm?" He clicked his tongue. "Unfortunately, Solvilde has not been in a position to answer hopeless prayers for a very long time."

Holding her breath, Serilda left the relative safety of the stone and crept closer, her eye on the looped chain.

Shrub Grandmother's face contorted. "What have you done with them?"

"The same thing I'm about to do to you." He lowered the sword. His other hand reached for his belt.

He unhooked the chain at the same moment Serilda caught hold of the loop.

The Erlking started and turned toward Serilda, sword raised. But he froze when he saw her, both hands gripping the chain.

"I won't let you hurt her!" she yelled. "She only wants to protect the forest. *You* are the villain here! You can't do this!"

One corner of the king's mouth lifted with amusement. "Never has a mortal surprised me as you can."

With a single tug on the chain, he pulled Serilda toward him and wrapped an arm around her waist. Serilda cried out, refusing to let go even as her hands and the chain were trapped between their bodies. The Erlking craned his head, his breath dancing across her cheek.

"Don't forget your place."

With a snarl, he shoved Serilda away, yanking the golden chains from her grip. They tore across her palm, leaving wicked gashes in her skin. Serilda fell to the ground. "No!"

The Erlking swung his sword—not at Pusch-Grohla, but at a series of enormous thorns that had shot up from the ground right where he and Serilda had been standing. She was certain that one would have impaled her had the Erlking held her even a second longer.

"Enough!" the Erlking roared. With a flick of his wrist, he unwound the golden chains and sent them flying at Shrub Grandmother. They whipped around her and the burning tree, trapping her against the trunk.

She released a guttural, inhuman sound, more howl than scream. She thrashed against the bindings, but with her struggles, the chains only wound tighter.

"Go on," said the Erlking. "Keep fighting. I'm rather enjoying this."

Shrub Grandmother snarled and spat a glob of mucus at him. It landed on his leather jerkin, where it hissed like some sort of burning venom.

The Erlking groaned. "Disgusting creature."

Pusch-Grohla's nostrils flared and she lifted her chin in defiance.

Then, to Serilda's surprise, she whistled a fluttery, melodic tune, like an enchanted birdsong, that echoed long and loud across the glen.

Hope lifted inside Serilda. Was she calling for reinforcements? Some unexpected ally from the forest who would rush in and destroy the hunters where they stood?

No.

Her hope quickly fizzled as she saw the remaining moss maidens, battle weary but still alive, turn and flee into the forest, obedient to their grandmother's order.

"They are retreating," one of the dark ones yelled. "Your Grim!"

"Do not pursue," rumbled the Erlking's voice as the moss maidens disappeared like fireflies at dawn. "We have what we came for."

He regarded Pusch-Grohla, who had stopped writhing against her bonds. Her expression remained obstinate. As the Erlking approached her, she bared her teeth at him, and Serilda remembered how odd her mouth had looked to her the first time she'd met Shrub Grandmother. As if the few teeth she had left had been taken from a horse and crammed behind the chapped lips of a crone.

"What an easy victory," said the Erlking. "I had hoped to slaughter many more of your daughters before you called them off. Where will they go, I wonder, now that Asyltal burns to the ground." He made a point of surveying the flaming trees. The air was so thick with smoke it stung Serilda's eyes, but the dark ones seemed unbothered by it.

"You do know that all of this could have been avoided," the Erlking went on. "We could have been . . . well, not friends. But cordial acquaintances. All those years ago. If only you had lent your aid when I first came to you. If only you'd placed a child into Perchta's womb. Do not tell me your magic could not accomplish it. By denying us, by denying *her*, you brought this plight on your forest and your own children."

Shrub Grandmother snarled. "Perchta is a soulless heathen. Any child placed in her womb would have withered from the poison in her blood. If by some miracle she carried a babe to term, then it would have been born a monster and grown into a beast the likes of which I cannot begin to imagine. I would never give my blessing to such an ill-suited mother. I do not regret my choice, and I never shall."

The Erlking held her gaze a long, quiet moment. "Then I suppose we are at an impasse. Pity." He reached up and tapped a finger against the pearl diadem on Pusch-Grohla's brow. "I will be requiring that horn."

"And I will be requiring a strong mug of winter-berry cider," Pusch-Grohla shot back, "but it is the dead of summer and we don't always get what we want."

"I usually get what I want just fine."

The Erlking reached into his quiver and pulled out—not a gold arrow, but one tipped in black. Identical to the one Serilda had pulled from the basilisk.

Pusch-Grohla had only enough time to gasp when she saw it, before the Erlking plunged the tip into the flesh where her throat met her shoulder.

Serilda screamed.

Pusch-Grohla threw her head back, teeth bared in agony.

With a flick of his hand, the Erlking undid the golden chains that bound her and stepped back. Pusch-Grohla collapsed to her knees amid the ash-covered tree roots.

She began to change.

Serilda's eyes widened as the old woman's body morphed, her withered hands turning into glossy black hooves, her long hair becoming a milk-white mane.

She had barely blinked, and then there was a unicorn before her, majestic and proud, lying on folded legs. From the pearl in the center of Pusch-Grohla's diadem emerged a spiraling horn, longer than Serilda's arm and glistening like fire-filled opals.

As a woman, Pusch-Grohla had been one of the ugliest creatures Serilda had ever encountered. But as a unicorn, she was magnificent. So much that tears pricked at Serilda's eyes to see her there with the arrow buried in her pearlescent coat.

No sooner had she transformed than the Erlking once again threw the chain around her, capturing her neck in a golden loop. She shook her head in a half-hearted effort to dislodge it, but it was no use. She was beaten.

"I do like you better when you cannot speak," said the Erlking. Glancing over his shoulder, he snapped his fingers. "Child, come here."

A moment later, Gerdrut stepped forward, her round face streaked with tears and ash.

"Please," whimpered Serilda. "Leave her be. She's been through enough."

"I am not going to hurt her, dear wife," he said, beckoning Gerdrut closer. She did as she was told, though her whole body was trembling. "But this part requires an innocent. As I said, most myths do have some truth in them."

Gerdrut gave a violent shake of her head. "Please. I don't want to." Her voice broke.

"But you will anyway." He flicked his fingers and Gerdrut approached the unicorn, her sobs becoming louder as she grasped the unicorn's horn in both of her tiny hands.

"Wait," said Serilda. "No. Don't make her do this. Don't. *Please.*"

The Erlking ignored her. He nodded at Gerdrut.

The child squeezed her eyes shut and pulled as hard as she could, snapping off the horn at its base. The unicorn reared back, but held by the golden chain it had nowhere to go.

"I'm sorry," said Gerdrut through staggered cries. "I'm so sorry!"

"Well done," said the Erlking, holding out a hand. "Finally you've made yourself useful."

Gerdrut gave him the horn, then fled into Serilda's arms.

The Erlking held the horn up to the firelight with a triumphant grin, while embers and debris drifted around him. "You see, if I had tried that, it would have turned to dust in my grasp. That would have been a shame, wouldn't it?" He gestured toward the waiting hunters. "Load the unicorn onto one of the carts, and be quick about it. I wish to be home by sunrise."

Chapter Twenty-Three

Serilda felt numb as the caravan left the smoldering remains of Asyltal and countless bodies of fallen moss maidens behind. Smoke clung to their party. Fine flakes of ash had settled into gray-black snowdrifts on the tops of carriages and wagons.

The hunters had suffered many wounds, from missing limbs to deep gouges that revealed decaying flesh beneath their shimmering skin. Serilda saw them pulling arrows from their sides and tying strips of cloth around cuts that sizzled and smoked almost as much as the forest floor.

Despite this, their attitudes struck her as ebullient. She had never seen them grinning so widely with their crimson lips and sharp cheekbones. She had never seen their eyes glowing so bright.

They moved through the forest as victors.

Their attitude was in sharp contrast to that of her and the children and the other servants in attendance. They might have been marching to their own funerals.

Serilda was so lost in painful memories—replaying the awful snap of the unicorn's horn over and over again—that it took a long time for her to notice the brightening sky, occasionally glimpsed through the trees, and to realize they were not heading in the direction they had come.

Still astride her horse at the front of the parade, she frowned at the Erl-king. "You said we were going home."

His eyebrows raised. "And we are."

"This is not the way to Adalheid."

"What indication have I ever given that Adalheid was my home?" After a hesitation, he added, "Or *yours*, for that matter. She who adores her superstitious little village."

"Gravenstone," she said, ignoring the slight. "We're going to Gravenstone."

"As I said." His teeth flashed. "Home."

"But why now? As I understand, you abandoned Gravenstone three hundred years ago."

"I abandoned nothing. My castle was taken from me, and now I finally have the means to reclaim it."

Serilda's hands tightened in her horse's mane.

For a while, they carried on in silence, made more pronounced by the steady clomps of their horses and pack animals, the creaking wheels of wagons and carriages behind them, the sounds of a forest beginning to wake up as night bled into morning.

"We tried to return to Gravenstone," said the Erlking, surprising her after such a long silence. "It was never my intention to stay in Adalheid. I wanted nothing more than to leave the ghosts and that . . . *prince* to his eternity. After the veil fell, we made our way back to Gravenstone, and we found it . . . changed." He seemed almost melancholy as he spoke. "In our absence, Pusch-Grohla had placed a spell over the castle grounds, forming an impassable barrier. Her only motive was to keep us out. To never allow us to return to the castle that was rightfully ours. To never again allow access to Gravenstone or—" He cut off so abruptly a chill swept along Serilda's spine.

The Erlking did not know she was aware of part of this history. As he spoke, she thought of the prince's tale—Gild's tale. After he shot an arrow into Perchta's heart, the sun rose while she lay wounded on the bridge to Gravenstone. On the mortal side of the veil, there was no longer a castle for her to flee to. Instead, there was a gate. The gates to Verloren.

As the prince watched, Velos emerged and reclaimed Perchta, stealing her away to the land of the lost. After that, Pusch-Grohla had arrived and sealed off the gates. Evidently, in doing so, she had sealed off the entrance to Gravenstone as well.

"That's why you went after Pusch-Grohla," murmured Serilda. "You need her to break the spell on the castle."

"I need the *horn* to break the spell," he clarified. "I have another use for Pusch-Grohla." His expression eased. "Though I won't say it isn't gratifying to have the old hag in chains."

Serilda looked away, her guilt returning in force. She was still trying to piece out the idea that Pusch-Grohla was actually a unicorn and the Erl-king had known about it, but that seemed an unimportant mystery, given all that had happened.

The road narrowed, branches scraping at the sides of the carriages. It felt as though the forest was fighting them. Fallen logs across the path. Thick roots that made the horses stumble. Thorns lashing out at the intruders. The tree trunks grew closer together, as if they were an army of soldiers closing their ranks. Serilda felt a prickle of unease as the Aschen Wood grew increasingly dense, blocking out any hint of the sky, the mountains, the world beyond.

With a crook of the king's fingers, the ghost servants scurried forward to clear the way, beating back the forest with shovels and scythes.

They broke through the tree line, all at once, revealing an amethyst sky overhead and a sight that stole away Serilda's breath.

Before them stood two trees—an ash and an alder—their trunks spiraled around each other as if trapped in an eternal embrace. They were too enormous to be real, so tall their tops vanished into the clouds. A canopy of branches spread like an enormous umbrella in every direction, disappearing into the misty forest. At their base, a labyrinth of gnarled roots so vast it might have covered the entire city of Adalheid.

The ash tree was flourishing, its delicate, tear-shaped leaves a vivid summer green.

The alder, on the other hand, appeared to be dying. Most of the leaves had fallen from its withered, gray-tinged branches, filling the spaces between the massive roots with a brittle carpet of brown and ochre. It was if the ash were slowly draining the alder of life.

The alder tree, Serilda realized. The tree that had sprouted up from the depths of Verloren and burst into the mortal realm, forever creating a chasm through which the dark ones had escaped, forever earning their leader the title of the Alder King.

But—there was no castle.

Her jaw fell with the realization. Those massive, tangled roots . . . they had grown over the castle, hiding it from view and keeping out anyone who would wish to enter.

That was the spell that Shrub Grandmother had put on this place. Her own life-giving ash tree fighting for dominance with that of the Alder King, preventing the dark ones from returning.

The Erlking urged his horse to a canter, while the caravan spilled out into the clearing. The world here was eerily silent compared with the bird-song and whistling breezes of the forest.

Serilda glanced back, searching the crowd, until she caught sight of the children. She tried to flash them an encouraging smile, but they were too busy gaping up at the trees to notice.

The Erlking dismounted and approached a gigantic root that wound along the ground like a mythical serpent, its girth almost as tall as the king himself. He pulled the unicorn's horn from the scabbard at his belt. It shimmered in the dim morning light.

She bit her lip. The horse whinnied and she placed a hand on its neck, then felt silly for trying to tame a horse who was probably more magic than actual beast. Still, at her touch, the steed did seem to calm.

The king lifted the gleaming horn overhead, and did she imagine how the ash tree shuddered and trembled, as if frantic?

Then the Erlking drove the horn into the root.

Somewhere in the caravan, the unicorn let out a horrendous bellow, as the branches of the ash tree shrieked.

There was no other word for it. Serilda clapped her hands over her ears. All around the clearing, the roots of the ash tree began to blacken and shrivel. They died quickly, those nearest the Aschen Wood crumbling into the earth. The decay spread inward. The roots turning to dust.

As they fell back, they revealed the castle long hidden beneath.

Gravenstone.

Chapter Twenty-Four

As the ash tree disintegrated, a cloak of gray dust clung to the castle walls and spread across the field and into the forest. The tree's delicate branches gave way last, crumbling to the earth—fading away into sand and chalk and nothingness before they hit the ground. Only the leaves lingered behind, tossed like an emerald blizzard in every direction. Already a slight wind was kicking the dust and the leaves into eddies, casting them out into the woods. Serilda suspected that one good rain would wash it all away, and no one would ever know that this castle had been hidden for so long.

Left behind was the alder tree. Still vast in size, but still sickly and weak.

The castle was equally forlorn. Serilda had always imagined it to look something like Adalheid, with its tall towers and striking spires silhouetted against the sky. But where Adalheid was tall and elegant, Gravenstone was more of a sprawling fortress. Rather than an imposing wall, its outer structure was an open colonnade supported by two rows of thick black columns that stretched out as far as she could see. A dreary fog was spilling out of the colonnade, disguising whatever lay beyond.

The castle would have been further protected by a swamp moat that had been a part of as many stories as the castle itself, with its legion of bog monsters and poisoned waters. But now that deep ditch lay dry and empty, filled only with dead alder leaves and rot.

Still gripping the unicorn's horn, the Erlking spent a long moment staring at his castle. Glancing around, Serilda took in the expressions worn by the dark ones. She had never seen anything that would mimic *joy* on their faces, but this might have been the closest yet. Pride, perhaps.

Finally, the king strode forward. His boots struck the onyx-black bridge over the empty moat, where carvings of scaled dragons curled along each edge.

A moment later, he passed between two of the enormous columns of the colonnade and was swallowed up by the mist.

Serilda hesitated. Should she follow? Was it dangerous? No one else was moving.

"I am the queen," she whispered, and drove her heels into the horse's side. It leaped forward, nervous in a way that made her even *more* nervous. After all these horses had seen and been through, she expected them to be unshakable. What was waiting in that castle that could unnerve these beasts, who had long hunted beside hellhounds and demons?

The horse cantered at its own hesitant pace. As its hooves clomped across the bridge, Serilda's eye was drawn to a spot where the ancient stone seemed darker, as if stained.

She shuddered, wondering if that was where Perchta had fallen.

Thinking it brought a shot of pain to her own chest.

How she wished Gild were here.

Gripping the horse's reins until her fingers ached, she passed through the colonnade and found herself facing a palace made of stone and wood. Stone and *roots*. It was as if the castle and the alder tree were one. Inseparable. Forged together when the alder tree first rose from the depths of Verloren, and now its roots ran like veins through marble. The structure was vast, sprawling in both directions, each of its two stories lined with narrow arched windows, inlaid with obsidian and quartz. A series of wide steps led to the main entryway, ornamented with towering sculptures of horrifying monsters, all wings and fangs and stone.

And there was the alder tree, rising into the sky from the very center of the palace.

The Erlking was nowhere to be seen, but the towering entry door, carved of glossy black stone, stood wide-open. Shadows spilled forth, almost tangible in their thickness.

Footsteps startled her. Serilda glanced back to see some of the ghosts making their way across the bridge—some on mules and bahkauv, others on foot.

"Sh-shall I take your steed, Your Luminance?" asked the stable boy, his gaze darting in every direction. "Suppose there's got to be a stable around here . . . somewhere."

"Thank you," said Serilda, accepting his hand as she slid off the horse. "Did we bring food and supplies for the animals?"

"Yes, my lady. In one of those wagons." His expression was bereft as he continued to take in the lichen-covered outer walls. "Quite a lot, actually. Suppose he means for us to stay here some time." He swallowed, clearly not happy about it.

Serilda couldn't blame him. In one night, the Erlking had uprooted them, taking his contingent of servants away from the only home they had ever known and depositing them in this strange and sorrowful place.

"It's all right," said Serilda, laying a hand on the boy's shoulder, refusing to shudder when her palm threatened to slip right through him. "We'll make the best of it that we can."

The stable boy met her gaze. He straightened, and Serilda realized he was nearly as tall as she was. He often looked so frightened and unsure, it was easy to forget that he could not have been much younger than she was when he'd died.

"Course it will be all right," he said, a touch of color blooming on his cheeks. "We'll make it so. For you, Your Luminance."

A startled laugh escaped her, until she realized that he was speaking in earnest, then she suddenly wanted to weep. "I am not sure I've done anything to earn such loyalty, but I shall certainly try to."

Bolstered by the boy's words, Serilda climbed the steps to the yawning black door. Her gaze drifted up to the gargoyles perched on the upper ledges—alps and drudes and all manner of nightmares staring down at her, their eyes made from shining black stones.

She stepped into the darkness. Silence greeted her. Not just any silence, but the silence of a tomb that had spent centuries hidden from the outside world. The air smelled of loamy earth and unfurling ferns, as if the castle itself were rooted in the ground. She even detected a hint of wood smoke, though perhaps that was the smoke from Asyltal still clinging to her cloak.

Serilda waited for her eyes to adjust. Slowly, the dim light filtering through opaque windows showed her an entry hall. The walls were dark stone. Alder roots made up the beams and rafters. There were no furnishings here, as if the castle itself did not want its visitors to get too comfortable too soon.

Her attention fell to the floor, and where she expected to find the Erlking's footsteps set into three centuries' worth of dust, she instead found wood floors that gleamed as if freshly polished. In fact, though an ominous silence hung over the castle, it did not feel neglected. She spied no cobwebs hanging from the wall sconces, no bird nests in the rafters, no drips of water running down the walls. She even spied a floral arrangement inside an alcove—a large clay vase bursting with vivid azure cornflowers and vibrant red poppies.

They were not dead. They might have been picked that morning.

Serilda thought of the thrones in Adalheid, preserved by some spell, trapped forever in a moment of time while the rest of the world crumbled around them. She suspected some similar magic had held this castle, too, preserved and unchanged.

Waiting for the return of its master.

Her footsteps echoed hollowly as she made her way down the cavernous passage, where three tall doorways with pointed arches yawned open into what she thought might be the great hall. Scattered pieces of furniture were arranged over fur carpets. She could picture lords and ladies whiling away their evenings playing cards and bone dice by the fire. At least, she could picture the royal family of Tulvask playing card games and dice. The dark ones probably spent their time here tossing the bones of small birds and predicting their own miserable fortunes based on which way they fell.

The fireplace stood empty, but she imagined she could still feel a hint of warmth from its ashes, as if it had only recently been extinguished.

Here, too, she found the Erlking.

He stood in the center of the room staring at a tapestry that took up an entire wall.

"Here you are," said Serilda. "The stable boy was wondering where he should secure the animals. And I think all the ghosts are feeling at a loss as to what to do with themselves. A bit of direction from their king might not be amiss."

He did not answer. Did not blink. His face was serene, but his focus intent.

Serilda scowled and paced over the lush carpets to his side. She squinted at the tapestry that so mesmerized him. She expected that his tastes in decor would mimic those in Adalheid, where there was no shortage of paintings and tapestries depicting a wildly idealized interpretation of the wild hunt brutally slaughtering some mythical beast or another.

But this tapestry did not show the wild hunt.

It took Serilda a moment to realize that she was staring at an image depicting the caves of Verloren. Stalactites dripped from molten rock. In the background, hints of a green-gray waterfall filled a steaming basin.

In the center of an underground chamber, wrapped in a passionate embrace, stood the Erlking himself—and Perchta, her skin blue-silver, as though she had the moonlight inside her. Her hair was as white as his was black, falling in lustrous waves to her hips. Dressed like a hunter, a warrior, she looked strong and invincible, every bit the match for the terrifying Alder King.

It might have been romantic if not for the drudes that surrounded the couple, the exact image of those nightmare creatures that had attacked Serilda and Gild in Adalheid, with their bulging stomachs and curved talons and leathery wings. In the tapestry, they were torturing the two dark ones. Even while the Erlking and Perchta lost themselves in a kiss, the monsters were gnawing on the flesh of their legs and shoulders. One drude had ripped open a hole in Perchta's back and was dismantling her spine, vertebrae by vertebrae, while another had reached a clawed hand into the Erlking's stomach and was pulling out his intestines in one long blackened rope. Another was about to jab a talon into Perchta's ear. Another held a burning candle beneath the Erlking's elbow. All the drudes were leering, their enormous eyes full of a sickening delight.

Serilda's insides churned. Why, she wondered, would anyone wish to keep something so grotesque in such a prominent place?

She turned to the Erlking, prepared to ask exactly this—but his expression gave her pause.

It was not an expression she had ever seen on him before, and it took her a moment to place it.

Confusion.

Serilda looked from him, to the tapestry, and back again, one truth becoming clear.

He had never seen this tapestry before.

She cleared her throat. "My lord? Shall I . . . ask the servants to have it removed?"

His gaze cleared. It took a moment for the sheen of ice to fall over his eyes. "I think not. The likeness *is* remarkable." A muscle in his jaw twitched, and he offered Serilda his elbow. "Come, my queen. Let us find proper accommodations for you and your retinue. We shall be here at least until the Mourning Moon."

"The Mourning Moon?" said Serilda, allowing herself to be led back toward the entry hall, where she could hear their entourage carrying in supplies from the wagons. "But that's two months away."

"Your Grim?" said Manfred, appearing in the doorway.

The Erlking sighed. "The stables are by the west wall."

"No, my lord, we did find the stables. But we were wondering what you would like to be done with the unicorn."

The Erlking's eyes brightened. "Ah yes. It is fine in the cart for now, but make room for it in the stables. Have the carpenters and blacksmith construct a cage to hold it."

"Yes, my lord. And the poltergeist?"

Serilda's breath caught. Her body stiffened.

The Erlking shot her a sly look. "I had almost forgotten," he said, though his tone suggested he had not forgotten anything. "Bring him here. He and I need to have a discussion." His lips curled upward. "After that, he can stay in the dungeons."

Chapter Twenty-Five

A servant came to light the fire in the massive hearth, but it did little to fight off the chill that had seeped into Serilda's bones. She sat perched on the edge of a sofa, feeling the steady passing of time with every stilted breath. The Erlking was ignoring her. Since Manfred had left, there had been a stream of servants and dark ones coming in and out of the great hall, and the king barked orders at them as if he'd been rehearsing for this moment for the last three hundred years. Linens were to be washed and hung to dry, and all the beds made up by nightfall. They needed to take stock of the wine and ale and any supplies left behind in the pantry. The animals required tending, and the wagons and carriages had to be checked for loose wheels and broken axles before being put away. A full sweep of the castle was already underway, conducted by the hunters, to ensure no forest critters had taken sanctuary in the castle during their absence, and evidently there was a lot of debris in something called the lunar rotunda that the Erlking insisted they start clearing immediately.

Where the castle had felt ominously still when they'd first entered, now the halls bustled with activity.

Serilda waited. For the children. For Gild. Watching as the Erlking paced back and forth in front of the horrendous tapestry. Every time someone entered the room, she tensed, expecting it to be him. The prince. The poltergeist. Her Gild, who should not have been able to leave Adalheid any more than she could.

But, as if the Erlking was determined to make her suffer, it was never him.

"Nothing so far, Your Darkness," said a hunter, tapping a curved blade mindlessly against his shoulder. "Though it will take a few days to thoroughly search the castle."

"Yes, fine," said the Erlking with a wave of his fingers. "Alert me as soon as you find them. *Any* of them."

"Who are you looking for?" asked Serilda once the hunter had been dismissed. "I thought this castle was abandoned."

The king sighed, as if her presence suddenly exhausted him. "There were servants left behind. Not ghosts, but monsters. They should be here."

"It was three hundred years ago. Do monsters not die?"

"Some live far longer than that. Others breed, like any beast. This castle should not be empty."

She shrugged. "Maybe they escaped."

He snorted, as if such a suggestion were ludicrous, and merely repeated, "It should not be empty."

"Well," said Serilda, "it is not as though we are lacking for help."

A grunt sounded from the hall, and at once, every nerve in Serilda's body started humming. *Gild.*

She forced herself to remain tranquil as he was dragged through one of the arched doorways, even though it caused her physical pain to resist the urge to lurch from her chair and race toward him. He had gold chains around his neck and wrists and binding his ankles, but she could not tell at first whether he was hurt.

He wasn't alone. Agathe held the chain of golden threads that connected to his wrists like a leash. Behind them, the five children crept in, hugging close to one another. Their eyes brightened when they spied Serilda and she waved them over. They instantly surged forward and crowded at her sides along the sofa.

Gild's eyes, too, met hers, but he quickly shifted them away. He lifted his chin, doing his best to ignore the height difference as he glowered at the towering Erlking.

Gild's practiced smile emerged. That taunting glint in his eye. "I was just thinking I could use a vacation. Would have preferred a cottage by the sea, rather than some abandoned ruins in the middle of nowhere, but still nice to have a change of scenery. Did you do the decorating yourself?" His gaze fell on the tapestry. "You and I have very different tastes."

"Well?" said the Erlking, ignoring Gild and focusing instead on Agathe.

"We found this in the tower after we captured him," said the weapons master, avoiding Serilda's eye as she opened a large satchel. "Along with a spinning wheel."

The Erlking took the satchel and from it pulled out a handful of wound golden threads.

Serilda's insides squeezed.

The gold. All the golden threads that Gild had spun this past month, in preparation for freeing the ghosts from the castle and sending them to Verloren.

She gawked at Agathe, but Agathe remained focused on the Erlking, expressionless.

Had the weapons master been forced to betray them?

She was still a ghost. Still under the Erlking's command.

How foolish had they been to believe their plan would not get back to him.

"But this is impossible," drawled the Erlking, inspecting the threads. "My wife can no longer spin gold, so how has new gold been spun?" He cut a haughty look toward Serilda, which was when the first hard stone settled in her gut. This wasn't a surprise to him.

How long had he known?

"Perhaps," he went on, "these were spun by the elusive *Vergoldetgeist.*" He sauntered around Gild, twisting the golden threads so they shimmered in the light. "That is what the human child called you, is it not? The Gilded Ghost. When I heard the name, I was certain I had heard it before." He tapped the threads against his lips, as if deep in thought. "A long, long time ago. Rumors of a ghost that dropped little trinkets into the lake and left them there for the people of Adalheid to collect. Sounds like nonsense, does it not? A silly myth, nothing of importance. But when that child visited us on our wedding night carrying god-blessed gold, a gift from Vergoldetgeist, I began to wonder. For these rumors would have begun long before my fair wife graced us with her talents. I did not want to believe I had been misled by my beloved, yet there it was. Luckily"—he grinned—"it was an easy suspicion to confirm."

He crooked a finger, and at first, Serilda thought he was summoning her. But then Hans stood and approached the Erlking, his movements stilted.

Serilda tightened her grip on Anna's and Gerdrut's hands, all of them watching as the Erlking took one of the loops of golden thread and wrapped it twice around Hans's body, crossing it at his heart.

"Velos, master of death," said the Erlking, his voice becoming lofted and bold, "I hereby free this soul. Come and claim it!"

Serilda gasped. What was he playing at? Would he really free Hans so easily?

The echo of the Erlking's words faded away. They waited.

Nothing happened.

The Erlking chuckled. "What foolishness." He clicked his tongue as he unwound the golden threads and tucked them back into the satchel. "Did you really think they could be freed so easily?" He focused on Serilda now, his gaze darkening. "Humans are such hopeful little simpletons. One suggestion was all that was needed to persuade you to spin a bit more gold. Or should I say"—he reached for Gild and gripped his chin fiercely with his fingertips—"it was all the persuasion Vergoldetgeist needed." He shoved Gild's face away and rounded on Serilda. "Poor miller's daughter. It was never you, but the poltergeist. Hulda-blessed, all this time."

He nodded at Hans, who returned to his seat on the sofa with a distant, hazy expression.

Serilda looked at Agathe, who was staring blankly at the fire. "You lied to me," she murmured. "You told me the gold would free their souls. Was it just a cruel trick?"

Agathe shut her eyes briefly, but when she opened them again, that sad, listless expression was gone, replaced with cool ferocity. "It was never about you or the poltergeist," she said. "His Grim offered me something I had to accept."

Serilda's eyes widened. She didn't want to believe it, and yet . . . "You did this by choice?"

"I couldn't risk you knowing I had asked her to plant this idea into your minds," said the Erlking. "I needed her to act . . . naturally."

Serilda shook her head. "But you showed me where my body was being kept. You helped me. You—"

"I had to earn your trust," Agathe said softly.

Serilda stared at her in dismay. "What could he have possibly offered you, that you would betray us like this?"

"Atonement," said Agathe, as if it were the simplest answer in the world. "We both blame ourselves for things that have happened to people we sought to protect, so I think you will understand better than most." She looked meaningfully at the five children gathered to either side of Serilda. "I would do anything to make reparations to the people of Adalheid. I failed them all, but I will not fail them again." She adjusted the bloodied scarf at her throat. "His Grim has promised that if I help with this matter, he will free all their spirits to Verloren on the Mourning Moon."

"He's lying!" Serilda shouted, launching to her feet. "You know he's lying!"

"Do not be so quick to cast accusations, my queen," scolded the Erlking. "After all, how many lies have *you* told?"

She snarled at him, the comment piercing the empty cavern of her chest, but she quickly turned her attention back to the weapons master. "You don't understand what you've done. It isn't just me you've betrayed, or these children." She gestured at Gild. "*This* is your prince. The prince of Adalheid that you once swore to protect. You failed his family and you failed him, and now you've failed him again."

Agathe's eyes narrowed. Her gaze slid toward Gild, taking in his oversize linen shirt, his messy hair, perhaps trying to picture him as anything other than a meddlesome ghost.

Serilda could admit it—*prince* had once seemed far-fetched for Gild, until she'd gotten to know him.

"I wondered whether you knew," mused the Erlking. "How long have you known he was more than just a gold-spinner?"

Serilda bit the inside of her cheek. Should she lie? But what did it matter now? The Erlking knew all their secrets, everything she had worked so hard to keep from him.

No.

No, that wasn't true.

He still did not know that Gild was the father of her child. He still did not know about the magical bargain in which she'd promised him her firstborn.

"Not until the day I came to rescue the children," she admitted.

"Ah yes. That day didn't work out as you'd planned either, did it?" The Erlking laughed, as if he were recalling a pleasant memory. He went on, enjoying his captive audience as he started to pace. "I should have realized the truth of his abilities long ago. I knew that one of the royal children of Adalheid was Hulda-blessed, but I'd believed it to be the young princess. It is, in fact, why I had sought her out as a gift for my Perchta." He shook his head and cut a look toward Gild. "Astounding that you could keep it a secret for so long. And yet, all it took was one pathetic mortal girl for you to become careless with such a gift."

Gild had been silent for this exchange, his eyes glued to the carpet and a muscle twitching in his jaw. Serilda understood that to say anything would be to say too much. But she hated seeing him like this—trapped in golden chains—both of them realizing that the Erlking had been toying with them for weeks and they'd had no idea.

"And you," said the king, turning his cruel smile back on Serilda. He stepped closer, studying her. She waited, determined to be brave—for the children, if nothing else. "God-blessed, but not by Hulda," he murmured quietly. "My bride, the storyteller. Always so quick with a lie on her tongue. You do not even know of the gift you possess, do you, my dear? Fortune and fate . . ." He said these last words with a lilt in his tone, as if singing a long-forgotten song. "Your eyes are not a spinning wheel, are they?"

"No," she breathed. "They are not."

"The wheel of fortune . . ." The Erlking cupped her face in his frosty hands. "Well? Are you feeling fortunate, godchild of Wyrdith?" He lowered his voice as he leaned his forehead against hers. "Because I am feeling *very* fortunate. Here, I thought I would be forced to wait until your child was full-grown before I had another gold-spinner. I was prepared to be patient. To wait for one more Endless Moon . . . But now, you have given me another gold-spinner at my disposal, you wonderful mortal, you." Tilting her head down, he pressed a kiss to her forehead.

Serilda shuddered and pulled away. "I have given you nothing," she spat. "And you are a bigger fool than I if you think he will ever spin gold for you! Gild is not one of your ghosts, to be manipulated and controlled. You cannot force him to do this."

"I can be very persuasive."

"No," said Gild, the word thick with hatred. "I can spin gold for my own gain when I wish to, but when someone else demands it, the magic won't work. Not without a price." Even bound in chains, he managed to stand tall, facing the Erlking not as a poltergeist, but as a royal prince. "And there is no bargain that would compel me to help *you*."

The Erlking beamed. "On the contrary. I suspect it will be quite easy to reach an agreement. Perhaps I could pay you with kitchen utensils? You were so very fond of the soup ladle."

Gild's jaw twitched. "Tempting offer, but I think I'll pass."

"And I think you'll reconsider," said the Erlking. He slid his fingers down Serilda's arm and took her hand into his, threading their fingers together. She shuddered. "Not so long ago," the Erlking went on, "I believed these hands to be touched by Hulda. Such a precious gift. But now I know . . . you don't really need them, do you?"

Without warning, he grabbed Serilda's thumb and yanked backward, snapping the bone.

Pain rushed through her. Sparks and stars flooded her vision and she started to crumple forward, but the Erlking embraced her, holding her aloft. Distantly, she heard the children crying. Gild roared, calling her name.

"There, there," murmured the Erlking into her ear. "You will heal quickly, just like these sweet spirits. And for every day that goes by in which our god-blessed prince refuses to spin more gold, I shall break another finger, and another." He shrugged. "For your sake, I hope he is not so stubborn that we will have to consider other bones as well."

He released her. Serilda stumbled, trying her best to bite back her anguish, even as the children gathered around her.

"Do we have a deal, poltergeist?"

Chapter Twenty-Six

Serilda did heal quickly, somewhat to her chagrin. Within a few days, her bone had righted itself, just as Anna's bones had after her fall into the arena. But Serilda could not be grateful. She had not seen Gild since that awful day in Gravenstone's great hall, but she had to assume, so long as the Erlking wasn't having her tortured, that Gild was behaving as the Erlking wanted. Which meant that somewhere in the dungeons beneath this spooky castle, he was spinning gold for the hunt.

All so the Erlking could capture a god and wish for the return of Perchta.

It made her sick to think about, so Serilda tried to push it from her mind. There were plenty other things to think about, anyway, as she attempted to settle into their strange new home.

She had been given a set of rooms in the northwest corner of the castle, right across the hall from the Erlking's chambers. They were lavish, with burgundy drapes hung on a four-poster bed and a hearth that was so big Gerdrut could have lain down inside of it—which she did after Fricz dared it of her.

Fortunately, the Erlking gave her and the children a surprising amount of freedom. While he had falsely doted on Serilda in Adalheid, he seemed to have forgotten her entirely in Gravenstone, keeping up pretenses to their romance only by sharing their evening bread together. Even then, he hardly spoke to her.

A welcome change.

He and the hunters were usually preoccupied now, either muttering to themselves in dimly lit parlors or studying enormous maps spread out in the dining hall. Discussing upcoming hunts, approaching full moons. She heard much talk of tree roots and brambles, rockslides and castle walls having caved in. She heard that the blacksmith had been ordered to make pickaxes and shovels and sickles that would cut through the thickest of brush. She saw servants pushing carts overflowing with broken stones and bundles of dead branches. She gathered that they were trying to repair some part of the castle sublevels that had caved in and been overtaken by the forest, but why the dark ones cared about having a few more cellars and storerooms when the castle was enormous as it was, she couldn't fathom.

Eager to distract the children, Serilda used their unexpected boon of freedom by creating a game in which they explored a new corner of the castle every day, and whoever discovered the strangest or most interesting thing that day would be dubbed the game's winner.

Anna claimed victory first. They had found the kennels where the hellhounds were kept and, with nothing else to do, decided to stay for the afternoon feeding. It was a grotesque display of raw meat and slobber and a dozen unnatural beasts snarling at one another to prove dominance, which was exactly the sort of thing that Anna, Fricz, and Hans found enthralling, and Serilda, Nickel, and Gerdrut managed to tolerate.

And it was Anna who first observed that the hounds were acting different. That they seemed . . . *anxious*.

The hunters had to actually coax some of them out of their kennels to claim their meat, and throughout the feeding, a few of the hounds appeared continuously agitated. They'd abandon a slab of meat to peer around with wide, burning eyes, or even duck back into their kennels.

"What's wrong with them?" Anna whispered.

"Maybe they're scared of the ghosts," said Hans.

Serilda frowned at him. "What?"

"This place is haunted," he said, perfectly matter-of-fact. "Can't you tell?"

She stared at him a long moment, expecting him to realize why this was such an ironic statement. When he didn't, she sighed. "Hans . . . *you* are a ghost. You're all ghosts."

He rolled his eyes. "I don't mean ghosts like us. Whatever was left behind at this castle . . . I think it's angry." He blinked at Serilda. "You can't feel it?"

Which is when she realized that the five children *could* feel it . . . whatever *it* was.

She swallowed. "Well, let's just hope it's angry at the dark ones, and not us."

The next day, Fricz claimed the most interesting discovery.

He had spent the morning helping the stable boy reorganize some of the outbuildings, where he found the wagon that had transported Serilda's body from Adalheid to Gravenstone. With no more reason to keep it a secret, Serilda had told them that first night about Agathe's betrayal, and when Fricz saw the wagon, he'd hoped that maybe he'd found her body, too.

But it was empty.

He brought Serilda and the others to see it, to be sure it was, indeed, the same wagon, now with no sign of the open coffin.

"Where do you think he's moved it . . . her . . . *you* to?" asked Anna.

"Who knows?" said Serilda, trying not to feel defeated. "Maybe we'll stumble across it, if we keep exploring."

They knew it was unlikely. Gravenstone had even more nooks and passageways than Adalheid.

"It doesn't really matter," she said with a sigh. Then, hearing how crushed she sounded, she plastered on a smile. "I could never leave you, anyway."

The children stared at her, frustrated and dismayed.

"What is it?" she asked.

"Serilda," said Nickel, in the same tone he might use to explain to

Gerdrut why it actually *is* necessary to wear gloves during a blizzard, "if you ever find your body again, you've *got* to break your curse."

She glanced around at their resolute faces. "But I couldn't."

"You *have* to," Nickel insisted.

Hans jumped in. "As long as you're here, the Erlking has something to hold over Gild. He'll keep spinning straw."

"And then the Erlking will win," said Gerdrut, earnest and wide-eyed.

Serilda's breath caught. She looked at each of them, horrified at the thought of leaving them behind. "But how could I ever leave you? It's my fault you're here. If I abandon you—"

"No, it isn't your fault," said Hans. "The wild hunt took us."

"Because of me!"

"Because they're monsters," said Hans. "Because they've been kidnapping people for hundreds . . . maybe thousands of years. Are you going to blame yourself for all those deaths, too?"

Serilda sighed. "You don't understand."

"No, *you* don't understand." Hans's voice grew louder. "We love you, Serilda. We don't want you to be trapped here, and we hate seeing you as his . . . his *wife*." He grimaced. "If you ever have a chance to leave here, you have to take it, with or without us. If not just for yourself, then"—he gestured at her stomach—"for the baby."

Serilda swallowed.

They all understood now that her unborn child was growing inside her physical body, but that Serilda's belly would not swell until she was mortal again. She wanted to argue with them, to insist that she couldn't possibly abandon—

Gerdrut launched herself at Serilda. She buried her face into Serilda's stomach and wrapped her arms around her and said in her muffled voice, "*Please*, Serilda. It would be better for us if you were free. If we didn't have to worry about you all the time."

Her mouth ran dry as she squeezed Gerdrut against her. Never had it occurred to Serilda that they might worry for her as much as she worried for them.

Finally, she dragged in a long breath.

"All right," she whispered. "If I find my body, I will try to break the curse and get away."

Serilda didn't have much hope of ever seeing her physical form again. Not until it was time to give birth, she supposed, and by then it would be too late for her to break the curse, save her child, and disappear. Gravenstone was a labyrinth, full of dark halls and winding stairwells. Wherever her body had been hidden now, she was sure it was somewhere secure and protected. Somewhere she was not meant to go.

(

On the third day, the children were summoned to help with washing and hanging all of the castle's drapes and table linens, leaving Serilda to explore the castle on her own.

The Erlking had mentioned a library over their evening bread. He said it was filled with ancient tomes collected long ago, and it was this that Serilda sought to find. Her lord husband had given vague directions—the south wing, past the lunar rotunda, turn before you reach the solarium—but Serilda was hopelessly lost. She had found neither rotunda nor solarium, just a never-ending chain of parlors, sitting rooms, and galleries filled with more disembodied heads than a chicken farm.

Serilda was making suspicious eyes at an astoundingly impressive stag with great silver antlers when she heard a distant giggling.

She spun around, straining to listen.

The sound came again.

"Gerdrut?" she called, stepping into a dim study. She saw no one, only paintings of gloomy, stormy oceans on the walls. "Anna? Is that you?"

Another giggle, farther away.

Serilda hesitated. It *did* sound like a child, but was it one of *her* children?

She passed through to the far side of the room and entered a long corridor. To the left, a rumor of sunlight filtered into the hall. She squinted into the unexpected brightness and drifted toward it, stepping out into an enormous circular room with a domed ceiling.

Her breath snagged. The walls were painted deep sapphire blue and scattered with constellations of shimmering stars. Though the ceiling was mostly glass, the panels between the panes had been illustrated with the moon phases, along with the annual moons around the edges, from the Snow Moon at the start of the year to the final Dark Moon at its end. What, this year, would be called the Endless Moon, as the Dark Moon crossed with the winter solstice.

Serilda stared, amazed. This must be the lunar rotunda the Erlking had mentioned.

It wasn't just the moon phases, but an entire calendar depicted on these walls. As she craned her neck to peer up at the glass ceiling, she wondered how the moon passing overhead would fall across these shimmering walls. How the stars would swim in and out of view as the nights passed by.

But while the rotunda ceiling was glorious, the room itself was in disarray, the floor littered with detritus and signs of labor. Hand-drawn carts half-filled with rock and debris. Chisels and axes scattered about the tiles.

And once again, she heard a strange noise. Not giggling.

More like . . . whispering.

A distant sound.

Like a group of children hidden behind a curtain and unable to keep quiet.

Serilda swiveled around.

The door was set back into a shadowed alcove, easy to miss. Not a door at all, she saw, moving closer, but the opening of a cave. Blackness spilled forth from that hole. The walls around it were rough-hewn rock and dirt and thick, tangled roots.

Something was moving. Writhing, crawling along the walls.

Snakes?

Breaths coming in quick gasps, Serilda approached the cave on hesitant feet.

No, not snakes. It was brambles. A mess of thorn-covered vines slithering across the broken tiles on the rotunda floor. Masses of them had been hacked away, leaving broken thorns and splintered edges behind.

But they still appeared to be alive. Reaching for her. Writhing in the light, as if seeking the sun's warmth.

Serilda . . .

She froze. That was not a child's voice.

That voice belonged to an adult. A man. Someone familiar—

Her pulse drummed in her ears.

She had heard wrong. Her mind was playing tricks on her, cruelly taunting her.

It came again. Her name.

Serilda . . . ?

Louder now. More uncertain. More . . . hopeful.

"Papa?" she breathed, the word tenuous and fearful. She was sure the whisper was coming from this opening. She was sure it was her father calling to her.

But it was impossible.

He was dead.

She had seen him, turned into a nachzehrer, a flesh-eating monster. She had seen Madam Sauer drive the shovel through his neck.

He could not be here, in this awful castle in the middle of the Aschen Wood.

He could not be there, just beyond that yawning blackness.

Seril . . . da . . .

With a strangled sob, Serilda leaped forward and grabbed one of the vines, meaning to yank it away from the opening, to clear a path through the cave's mouth.

Pain lanced through her palm. She hissed and pulled back. A thorn had dug into the flesh below her thumb. The wound was slight, but burning, as she pressed it to her mouth to stop the bleeding.

Her gaze lifted. She stilled.

The brambles had begun to grow together, clustering in vicious knots over the cave's mouth, forming a thick barrier.

She drew back, shaking.

"Get away from there!"

She spun around, startled to see a hunter marching toward her, pick-axe in his gloved hand. She cried out and scrambled away. Away from the hunter, away from the thorns.

"Foolish human," he muttered. "Did you let it touch you? That will cost us hours of work." He snarled at her. "Get out of here, before you ruin anything else!"

Serilda opened her mouth, wanting to tell him what she'd heard, wanting to ask where this cave led to, what was down there?

But the dark one had already turned away from her, inspecting the vines that had knotted back together as he shook his head in irritation.

She knew she would not get any answers from him.

Besides, the whispers had gone quiet now. She had probably imagined it all.

Without waiting to be yelled at again, she ran from the room. Only once she'd caught her breath did she consider whether or not to tell the children about the discovery. She didn't want to scare them—they were already frightened enough—but she also knew that cave with its slithering vines would have no competition for the most interesting discovery of the day.

Chapter Twenty-Seven

The children had taken to sleeping in Serilda's rooms with her, as they had in Adalheid. She didn't mind. She wanted to be alone at night about as much as they did, and was glad for the company. If she ever lost out on a bit of sleep because she was squashed in the middle of five small, cold, slippery bodies, she never complained.

What did upset her, though, were the children's nightmares, which had become nightly occurrences since their arrival in Gravenstone. Before, they had all slept like groundhogs. But now it was almost nightly that one of them awoke in tears.

A thrashing body was the first thing that pulled Serilda from her slumber. In her half-dreaming state, she squinted into the shadows of the room, trying to remember which of the children had fallen asleep at the foot of the bed, where the troubled groans were coming from.

Rubbing hazy sleep from her eyes, Serilda sat up, trying not to disturb the others.

"Gerdrut?" she asked, reaching for her shoulder. "Gerdy, wake up. You're having another nightmare."

But her hand did not find Gerdrut's satin nightgown.

Instead, she felt something . . . leathery. A thin membrane and brittle bones.

She gasped and yanked her hand back. A hiss sounded in her ears.

She half crawled, half fell over Anna to get out of the bed so she could light the candle on her nightstand. As soon as she did, her gaze fell on the shadowy shape.

A creature with enormous yellow eyes and bat-like wings. Its talons digging into Gerdrut's shoulders as its tongue snaked toward her face.

Serilda screamed.

Instinct took over as she lunged for the drude, swinging the candle at it. But the wick flickered and went out, plunging them back into darkness.

Serilda screamed again, and her scream was met with the children's, scrambling terrified from their sleep. She struggled to relight the candle, while desperately trying to think what she might use as a weapon when there was little more than hairpins and a washbasin in this room. The water pitcher. It would have to do.

But by the time the candle sprang back to life, the drude was gone, and five children were flailing madly about the room, hiding behind the mattress and tugging on bedcovers, trying to protect themselves, though no one had any idea what was happening.

Her door was cracked open.

Serilda flew toward it, just as the Erlking yanked open his door on the other side of the hall.

Ignoring him, she peered down the hallway, one way, then the other.

The drude was perched behind one of the unlit chandeliers.

"There!" Serilda cried, pointing.

The drude hissed and leaped, spreading its wings. It landed on the wall and skittered across the stone, claws scrabbling for purchase, trying to make it to the far window.

No sooner had it found the window's ledge than a dagger struck, pinning one of its wings to the wooden ledge.

Serilda pressed her hands to her chest, surprised yet again when she felt no heart racing beneath them. She looked at the Erlking, whose hand was still outstretched. His eyes were narrowed, his face calculating.

"Th-thank you," she stammered. "It attacked Gerdrut."

The Erlking brushed past her. He was wearing flaxen trousers and, disconcertingly, no shirt, and his silver-pale skin glowed in the dim candle-light as he approached the struggling beast and pulled out his knife.

The drude collapsed to the floor, but immediately popped up onto its hind legs and bared its teeth.

Unperturbed, the Erlking wrapped his fist around the wounded wing and squeezed.

Serilda heard the crack of bones and flinched.

As the monster shrieked, the Erlking lifted it to eye level and studied it for a long, awful moment.

"We have been looking for you," he said. "Why have you been hiding from my hunters?"

In response, the drude hissed again, its forked tongue darting at the Erlking's face.

Serilda could not tell whether the Erlking expected an answer, but he seemed neither surprised nor disappointed as he used the point of the dagger to unfold the uninjured wing, inspecting the creature from every angle.

"I want to know what has happened since we left," he said. "Where are the rest of my monsters?"

The creature's eyes brightened until they were almost golden orange. Its talons clicked.

"Go ahead," said the Erlking. "I do not fear your nightmares. Show me."

Serilda's lips parted. The Erlking *wanted* the drude to enter his mind, to give him—not a nightmare—but the truth of whatever had come to pass here since the dark ones had been gone.

But the drude did not.

Instead, the small beast took its talons and drove them into its own chest.

The Erlking's eyes widened and he dropped the drude to the floor. He stepped away, and together he and Serilda watched as the life bled out from the beast in rivulets of dark, viscous blood.

"Well," said the Erlking, with a sharp edge to his tone, "I suppose it had nothing to say."

Serilda let out a shaky breath. "I . . . I need to check on Gerdrut."

Without waiting for his response, she darted back to the bedroom.

The children were gathered on the bed, holding one another. Protecting one another.

"Gerdy," said Serilda, sitting beside Gerdrut and taking her hand. "Are you all right?"

Gerdrut gave her a weak smile. "I'm all right."

"Good. It's over now. The drude is dead. It won't hurt you again. And I swear . . . it was a nightmare. Only a nightmare."

A haunted look crept over the child's expression. She glanced at Hans, who gave her an encouraging nod.

"She was telling us about the dream," Nickel explained. "Go on, Gerdy. Tell Serilda."

Serilda braced herself. She had been the victim of a drude's attack before. She had seen things in those visions that still sometimes woke her, shivering, in the middle of the night. She had heard tales of the drudes causing so much terror that a person had literally died of fright.

She hated to think what that beast had done to this poor, sweet child . . .

"Go on," said Serilda. "I'm listening, if you want to tell me about it."

Gerdrut sniffled. She'd been crying, and Serilda's heart would have broken, if she'd had one.

"I saw m-my grandmother," said Gerdrut.

Gerdrut's grandmother had passed on to Verloren just over a year before. She had always been a kindly lady, the sort that had extra sweets for the children on holidays, and who was one of the few that had never turned a suspicious glare on Serilda.

"She was helping me make dolls out of leftover muslin scraps," Gerdrut went on. "I was cutting out the pieces and she was adding buttons and flowers. And then . . ."

Serilda bit her lower lip, waiting for the moment when the dream turned to nightmare.

"She hugged me," said Gerdrut, falling forward with a sob. "And told me how much she loved me and couldn't wait to be with me again. She said she was waiting for me, and that someday we'd be together again. And I . . . I miss her so much, Serilda."

As the other children swooped forward to embrace Gerdrut, Serilda leaned back, confused.

"That . . . doesn't sound like a nightmare."

Gerdrut shook her head, still crying. "It was . . . such a lovely dream!" she said between her sobs.

Serilda opened her mouth, but closed it again. She looked from Gerdrut to the other children, then finally to the closed door.

It didn't make any sense.

"All right," she finally said, taking in a deep breath. "All right, my loves, we should try to get some more sleep, if we can." She stood and did her best to straighten out the covers and get them all to lie back down. "Snuggle in now, and I will tell you a story."

"Will it be a happy story this time?" asked Anna.

Serilda laughed, before she realized that Anna meant the question in seriousness.

"Well," she said hesitantly, "I suppose I can try."

The veil had been created. Without full access to the mortal realm, the dark ones could no longer torment the humans, and a sense of balance was restored. The gods returned to their solitary lives.

But Wyrdith was unsatisfied.

Stories are only half told until they've found a listener, and though Wyrdith had long preferred the brutal beauty of the ocean as it crashed into the northern basalt cliffs, they found themselves growing more and more unhappy. And so, the god of stories decided to venture out among the mortals.

Wyrdith took to traveling throughout the human world.

They would take the shape of a common sparrow and perch on a windowsill, so they might listen to the tales a mother told to her children.

They would don the guise of an old man and hunker into the corner of a public house to listen to the local fishermen tell their tall tales of whales and merfolk.

There was a time when Wyrdith even disguised themselves as a traveling minstrel, performing for peasants and royalty alike. In between their own performances, they took note of the stories told in every village they passed through.

The more they heard, the more enamored the god became with humans, who could find as much pleasure in a quiet bedtime tale as they could in an epic adventure. Their stories were full of joy and struggles, victories and defeats, but always there was an undercurrent of hope that filled a place inside of Wyrdith that they had not known was empty.

One could say the god began to fall in love with those mortals.

A year came to pass in which Wyrdith gathered with the villagers of a small town on the autumnal equinox to enjoy Freydon's Harvest. But that year, there was more worry than joy, for the harvest had been so poor that the villagers feared they would not have enough food to last them through the winter.

Rather than cast blame on Freydon, god of the harvest, the villagers accused Wyrdith. They were sure the trickster god had spun their wheel and this year, the wheel had dealt them a great misfortune.

Wyrdith was baffled, for they knew the wheel was not to blame.

Unable to understand why Freydon would abandon their responsibility to ensure a bountiful harvest, and angry that blame had been put at their own feet, Wyrdith took the form of a great bird and flew off to find the god of the harvest.

Freydon was enjoying a simple life on the eastern plains of Dostlen, where they tended a tidy garden and spent afternoons fishing at the delta of the Eptanie River. They were most surprised to see their old friend, the god of stories, and gladly invited Wyrdith to sit with them in the shade of an ancient fig tree to enjoy a game of dice and a cup of pear cider.

But Wyrdith was too angry to be appeased.

"This year's harvest was abysmal," said Wyrdith, "and the people are suffering! Why have you not made the grain plentiful and the orchards abundant? Why have you forsaken the good villagers who rely on you?"

Freydon was most taken aback by Wyrdith's ire. They set down their mug and leaned forward with an almost pitying expression. "My dear friend, I have not interfered in the affairs of mortals for many centuries."

Wyrdith did not understand. "But only last year, the autumn harvest was most bountiful!"

"Yes, as it has been for more than a decade, I am told. But that is because the rain fell and the sun shone and the farmers properly tilled their land and sowed their seeds."

Wyrdith's eyes widened. "I see," they said. "So I should speak with Hulda, who must have made the farmers lazy this year. And I should speak to Eostrig, who must not have blessed the new-planted seeds. And I should speak with Solvilde, who betrayed us all with a summer of drought."

At this, Freydon gave a boisterous laugh. "No, no, you do not understand. The others have sequestered themselves in their own sanctuaries, as I have, preferring to avoid the cycle of blame and blessings foisted upon us for so long. The seeds and the rain—they have their own will now. As for the farmers, if they gave in to laziness, they have only themselves to blame."

Seeing that Wyrdith was still confused, Freydon sighed. "Tyrr has not meddled in a human war for eons, yet wars go on just the same. There are conquerors and there are the conquered, as there ever were, but now it is the humans who strike their own path. Likewise, Velos may still guide souls on the bridge to Verloren, but they have not impressed their will on who should die and when they shall pass for ages. And yet, death comes for all mortals regardless." They shrugged. "We are the old gods, Wyrdith. The world has gone on without us. Mortals have gone on without us. They may invoke our names and leave their offerings and whisper their prayers, but it is up to them, ultimately, to devise their destiny."

Seeing that Wyrdith's expression had twisted into something hollow and sad, Freydon frowned. "Do not despair, my friend. There will be struggles. There will be tragedies. But humans can thrive better without our interference."

"That is not what troubles me," said Wyrdith.

"Then please unburden yourself to me."

"That I cannot do. For you see, it is suddenly clear to me why it is always my name that is cursed when misfortune comes to good people, through no fault of their own. I see now that I am the only one who truly loves these mortals. But to them, I shall always be the trickster god with the unfair wheel—and, I fear, for that, they shall never love me back."

Freydon placed a hand on Wyrdith's shoulder. "You are more than fortune and fate. You are the world's historian. You are the keeper of stories and legends long forgotten. If the mortals cannot love you for your wheel, they will love you for that." Freydon's eyes gleamed. "For there is not a soul alive—even among the gods—who does not enjoy a good story."

Wyrdith left Freydon feeling disconnected from both the world of the gods and the world of mortals, wondering if they did not belong to either. Yet, they could also see the wisdom in Freydon's words. Humans did love a good story, and if that was all Wyrdith could offer to them, then that is what they would give.

The god of stories returned to the world of mortals. They continued to live among them for many years.

Always listening to tales well told.

Always gathering the legends and lore of the greater world.

Always prepared to spin their own stories to any who would listen.

And sometimes—just sometimes—Wyrdith would look into the faces of their audience, cherubic children with rosy cheeks or old women with foggy eyes or young men weary from days in the fields, and the god would see love radiating back at them.

For a long time, that was enough.

THE
HARVEST
MOON

Chapter Twenty-Eight

Weeks after telling the tale of Wyrdith, Serilda still couldn't stop thinking about it. All her life she'd had a complicated relationship with the godparent she'd never met. The god who had cursed her before she had even been born.

Despite all the trouble stories had brought her, she loved telling them. She couldn't help it. The way star-crossed romances and unexpected villains wound themselves around her heart and made her feel like she was floating above the world as the story wrote itself. Made her feel like she was a part of something important, something eternal.

Never before had she wondered if the old god felt the same way. Did they also live for the rush of a perfectly executed resolution? Did they yearn for the reveal of a mystery, the unfolding of destiny, the troubled path of an impossible quest?

And did they ever wonder, like Serilda so often did, if their stories ultimately brought more harm than good? Stories might be an escape, but in the end, that's all they were. In the end, reality always crashed back in.

She couldn't help wondering where the god might be now. Had they eventually tired of mortals and gone the way of the other gods, taking on the life of a recluse? Or were they still wandering about the kingdoms, enthralling princes and peasants alike?

Serilda had never met a traveling bard, but her father told her that one had come to town when he was a young man and spent three straight nights spinning an epic tale about a hero knight who crossed land and sea, battling monsters and warlocks, in order to rescue a princess who had been turned into a constellation of stars. Papa said that story was all anyone would talk about for weeks after. When the bard traveled on, the children of the village had cried.

Could it have been Wyrdith?

For some reason, the thought sent a happy flush along Serilda's skin. After her birth, the people of Märchenfeld had grown wary of stories, out of fear of the cursed girl with the golden eyes. But she liked to think there had been a time when they, too, had gathered in the village square to hear a tale of enchantment.

It was just as Freydon had said. *There is not a soul alive who does not enjoy a good story.*

The days were long in Gravenstone, and at least these ongoing questions helped Serilda keep her mind from wandering to Gild, locked up somewhere, all alone, forced to spin day and night. Her insides had been tied in a constant knot as she dwelled on every horrible thing that might be happening to him. She imagined a flea- and rat-infested bed, and then wondered if he'd been allowed any sleep at all. She pictured his hands raw and bleeding from handling the straw. She could hear his sardonic voice, telling the Erl-king what he could do with his spun gold, and Gild's groans at the beating that would follow.

It was enough to make her sick with worry, especially when she was helpless to do anything for him. She yearned for a distraction.

The children had been kept busy at first, working beside the other ghosts to dust and shine and clear away the cobwebs. But once the work was done, they had to find new ways to entertain themselves in this dismal place. They invented board games and begged the castle's musicians to teach them songs on the zither and mandolin. They spent hours crafting paper lanterns that they planned to fill with candles and hang from the boughs of the alder tree on the Mourning Moon, a tradition they'd cherished in Märchenfeld.

Hans was also helping Gerdrut make her first poesiealbum, filling a book-let of loosely bound pages with paintings and dried flowers, snippets of poetry and happy memories. Nickel had taken to drawing, and Anna was back to her old self—immutable and energetic and bounding off the walls when the boredom got to be too much. Meanwhile, Fricz was determined to learn how to cheat at bone dice.

All in all, they made the best of it, though the air in the castle felt oppres-sive in a peculiar, intangible way. There were secrets hidden in these walls. Mysteries in the flickering candlelight. Adalheid might have been haunted, but it was Gravenstone that filled Serilda with a lingering dread whenever she made her way through the unfamiliar halls.

It could have been her imagination, but it seemed that even the dark ones were uneasy. They spoke of their things being moved or stolen when no one was around—and for once, no one could blame the poltergeist. The hell-hounds howled at all hours, as if trying to commune with monsters no one else could see. The stable boy said the horses, too, were jittery, always whin-nying and wild-eyed. And there were strange noises. Whispers and scratch-ing claws and hollow knocking that filled the corridors but had no obvious source.

Perhaps, after so long away, Gravenstone was no longer their home. Perhaps they'd grown too comfortable in Adalheid. Or perhaps it was the mysteries of the place that had them rattled. The angry presence that had all the ghosts looking over their shoulders. The phantom whispers. How the entire castle felt more like a mausoleum than a sanctuary. The Erl-king's court might have been used to living in a haunted castle, but there was something about Gravenstone that troubled them all, and it had gotten worse after the drude attacked Gerdrut.

Even though the drude had, in fact, *not* attacked her. In the days that fol-lowed, Gerdy's story did not change. It had not been a nightmare at all, but a dream. A happy dream that filled her with hope to think that someday *this*, their real-life nightmare, would end. Someday she would have peace and rest and be with her family again.

It made Serilda unspeakably sad to hear such poignant, bittersweet words spoken by a child so young.

But more than that, it made her confused.

Why in the name of the old gods would a drude sneak into their chambers to give a little girl a dream about her deceased grandmother?

She had not told the Erlking the truth of Gerdrut's vision. He was already in a sour mood. He, too, had been unusually tense since their arrival. His eyes shifted about the rooms, as if he expected the very shadows to attack. Or . . . speak. Or sing or dance or whatever it was that dark ones were afraid of shadows doing.

Serilda didn't mention her father's voice calling her from the opening in the lunar rotunda, either. She found her feet leading her in that direction more than once before she forced herself to turn away.

Her father was gone. He had been taken by the wild hunt, thrown from his horse, and left to die on the side of the road, because the Erlking had not valued his spirit enough to bring him back to the castle. Her father's corpse had become a nachzehrer—a rotting, mindless creature that had attacked Serilda, hungry for the flesh of his own kin. He might have killed her if Madam Sauer hadn't saved her. Afterward, they had thrown his body into the river. He was dead. He was never coming back.

Whoever, or whatever, had been calling her was not her father.

"Your Luminance?"

Serilda started from her reverie, staring out the parlor window at the Aschen Wood, to see Manfred at her side.

"The honor of your presence has been requested by His Grim."

She shivered at his words, exactly the same as the first time she'd seen him, when he'd come to the gristmill with a carriage made of rib bones and summoned her to Adalheid.

"What does he want? Evening bread isn't for hours."

"It has something to do with . . . the poltergeist," he said.

She stiffened. A hundred terrible possibilities crashed through her. She had not seen Gild since the morning after the Straw Moon when he had been taken away in golden chains to the dungeons. As the Erlking had not broken any more of her fingers, she could only assume Gild was obeying the king's orders and spinning straw into gold, likely night and day.

She had not dared ask about Gild, for fear the Erlking would come to know the full extent of her feelings for him, but also because she could not stand to know if he was being beaten or tortured. At least, in her denial, she could go on imagining him as he had been the first night she had met him in the Adalheid dungeons. Cheeky and unkempt and utterly exasperating.

But she was not a fool. Spinning was laborious work, even for a poltergeist, and she could imagine how he loathed every moment, knowing that the Erlking had won.

She followed Manfred out of the room. Though it was a different castle, she could not help reliving her long walk to the dungeons of Adalheid, when she had been certain the Erlking would murder her come morning.

Funny, she thought, how so many things had changed, and so many things had not changed at all.

As they descended into the castle sublevels, she found herself surrounded by knotted, ancient tree roots. The alder tree, forming the foundation on which Gravenstone had been built.

The cell itself was crafted of iron bars, though, for she supposed even magical tree roots would yield beneath a sword or claws or . . . persistent fingernails.

She braced herself for the first sight of Gild. She would not cry, she vowed. Not if his face was swollen and bruised, not if his bones were broken or his clothes stained with blood. She would be strong, for his sake.

Then Manfred opened the door, she spotted Gild, and all expectations crashed to the floor.

He was sitting on a pile of straw, arms defiantly crossed, a stubborn tilt to his chin.

No blood. No bruises. No broken bones.

His eyes landed on Serilda and he leaped to his feet. "You're here!" he cried, reaching her in three giant steps and swooping her into his arms. Serilda gasped, too stunned to return the crushing embrace.

"You're all right?" she asked. Tears stung her eyes at her eyes as he pulled away, holding her at arm's length. "I thought for sure you'd be . . ." She trailed off, not wanting to put her fears into words.

"Could say the same of you," he said, inspecting her from head to toe. He took her hands into his, studying every finger. "I didn't know what he was doing to you. I kept thinking—" His voice hitched and he swallowed hard. "I told him I refused to spin anymore until I could see with my own eyes that you were all right." His next words were barely a whisper. "He hasn't hurt you?"

Serilda shook her head. "No. Not since . . . that first day. And you?"

"I'm fine. Great, in fact. Been spinning day and night, and I feel like my fingers are going to fall off, but look at all my new spoons." He gestured to a pile of wooden spoons thrown haphazardly into a corner. "Who knew His Grump could be so generous?"

Serilda was so surprised to find herself laughing that she nearly started to weep. "It's a fine collection."

He shrugged, his expression darkening. "It satisfies the magic's need to be paid, but somehow, I don't think Hulda would be happy about it."

"I'm just glad you're all right. I've been so worried. Thank the gods."

"You can thank *me*," said a sharp voice.

Serilda spun around as the Erlking emerged from a shadowed alcove.

"I assure you, the gods have little to do with my mercy."

Gild gave Serilda's hand a quick squeeze before releasing her, but the Erlking still took note of the action. His expression was serene, though, as he flashed them an expectant smile.

"There you have it," he said. "You wanted proof that she is not being harmed, and I have delivered it. Now, then. You have work to do, as do I. Manfred, take her away."

"Wait!" Serilda cried, grasping for Gild's elbow.

The Erlking raised an irritated eyebrow at her.

"Five minutes," she said. "Please, can we have five minutes?"

He scoffed. "Why would I allow that? Manfred."

Manfred stepped forward, but Serilda pressed closer to Gild, who instinctively wrapped his arms around her.

"You will allow it, or I won't spin anymore," said Gild.

The Erlking laughed. "As you wish. Don't spin anymore. I'll enjoy breaking out my wife's teeth with an old chisel. I'm sure I saw one lying around here somewhere."

Pulling away from Gild, Serilda thundered closer to the king. "A word with you," she growled, before storming off down the corridor.

The Erlking sauntered after her. "I am not in the habit of bowing to the demands of mortals."

She spun back to face him. "Yet follow you did," she snapped.

His eyes flashed, but she ignored the warning in them and stepped closer, until she had to crane her neck to meet his eye. "Do you think I won't tell the whole court that you are not the father of this child?"

The warning morphed into a growing threat. "Careful, miller's daughter. You know the consequences of going back on our bargain."

"Yet I would do it, to spite you. What would the court think, when they realize the child you intend to raise as your heir is nothing but the child of a nobody farmer? Human down to their bones."

The king's eyes narrowed, calculating. "A nobody farmer?" he said coolly. "Here I had begun to wonder if that was only one more lie."

His gaze flicked meaningfully toward Gild's cell.

Serilda scoffed. "What an imagination you have." She planted her hands on her hips. "I am only asking for five minutes to speak with him. To see that he is being well taken care of. *Five minutes*." She tilted her head. "What are you afraid will happen?"

A muscle twitched in his jaw. He slowly inhaled through his nostrils.

Without answer, he spun away and gestured toward Manfred. "I am needed in the rotunda," he growled. "Give them five minutes, and not a second longer. And do *not* leave them alone."

With one last warning look at Serilda, he swept from the corridors.

Though he tried to appear indifferent, Serilda could tell by the widening of Manfred's good eye that he was impressed by her bargaining skills. And, likely, curious to know what, exactly, had been said.

But he didn't pry. Instead, a glint of defiance came into that eye. "I noticed a horrific number of cobwebs in the corridor that mustn't be tolerated. I don't suppose you would mind if I go take care of that?"

Her chest warmed. "Not at all."

"Good. I'll leave the door parted a bit, so as not to *leave you alone.*"

She couldn't be sure of it, but Serilda thought the squint of his eye was an attempt to wink, before he left the cell, leaving the door ajar barely the width of his thumb.

"Always did like him," said Gild.

Serilda turned back, overcome—with gratitude, with relief.

With desperation. The clock was already ticking.

She threw herself into Gild's arms.

"What did you say to His Glumness to make him leave?"

"Nothing of importance. Come, tell me everything."

"I have nothing to tell," said Gild. "How long have I been down here?"

"Four weeks. Tonight is the Harvest Moon."

Gild groaned. "And I thought time passed slowly in Adalheid."

Serilda looked at the pile of straw, to the spinning wheel in the cell's corner. "How much have you spun?"

"Enough to capture every animal in the Aschen Wood," he said, rolling a kink from his shoulders. "I didn't even know I could get blisters anymore." He lifted his hands to show her the sore spots on his palms and fingers. "And I've got a permanent ache in my leg from stepping on that damned treadle. I'll be happy to never spin again after this."

"Gild—you shouldn't be doing this. He plans to catch a god. He's going to bring back Perchta—"

"Do I have another choice?" He wrapped one of Serilda's braids around his fingers. "I can't let him hurt you. Just like you can't let him hurt those children."

She slumped, frustrated with how easily the Erlking had manipulated them.

"Besides, let him bring back his huntress. I killed her once, didn't I? I can do it again."

"Can you?"

He laughed and shrugged. "Probably not. I've no idea how I did it the first time. Something about an arrow? I *am* decent at archery."

"It's also possible Tyrr had something to do with that."

Tyrr, the god of archery and war, was often credited with a lucky shot.

Gild groaned. "You want to give the gods credit for everything. But I don't want to talk about Perchta or the Erlking or spinning gold. Serilda . . . we're in *Gravenstone*." He fixed her with a meaningful look. "Have you . . . I mean . . . have you seen her?"

Serilda stared at him. "Perchta?"

He made a face. "My *sister*."

Understanding bolted through her. Serilda had thought of the princess often in the first days since their arrival, but since then she'd been distracted by haunting whispers and drude attacks.

She shook her head. "She isn't here. The castle was abandoned."

Disappointment clouded his face. "He took her because of me. He had heard that one of the royal children was Hulda-blessed, and he'd assumed it was her."

"She might have been a gold-spinner, too," she said. "Maybe it runs in your blood."

His mouth lifted on one side, and she had to admit that the possibility wasn't much consolation.

"What do you think she was like?" Serilda asked.

Gild's expression softened, and she knew he had thought of this often since learning that the girl in the portrait was his sister. "Silly," he said. "I think she was very silly. I know the painter tried to make her seem all proper, but I don't think that's right. I can imagine her sitting for hours, being told to hold still, stop fidgeting. But that wasn't in her nature." He began to smile as he spoke, but all at once, the look darkened again. "But I'm just making that up. Who knows what she was like?"

His hand dropped to his side. Serilda took it into hers, lacing their fingers together. "She must still be out there, Gild. Somewhere. Don't lose hope."

His expression turned wry. "The truth is, when I looked at her portrait, it didn't feel like I was looking at my sister. It just felt like looking at a stranger." He sighed. "She isn't here, but *you* are." He tenderly cupped her neck, stroking his thumb along her jaw. "You're all that matters to me."

"Don't say that—"

"It's true. You want me to have hope? This is my hope. You and me, Serilda. Someday. Away from these haunted castles. In some village, dancing in the sunshine, telling stories in the public house. Maybe it's impossible, but . . . it might be all I have left."

A tear slipped from her lashes. "Gild, I—"

Manfred cleared his throat, and even rapped lightly at the door before pulling it open. "I'm sorry," he said, his voice gruffer than usual. "I gave you six minutes. I don't think it would be wise to give you more."

Serilda lowered her head. Sniffed. Slowly released him.

Gild let his hands fall to his sides.

They shared one lingering look, before she let herself be led away.

Chapter Twenty-Nine

There had been little talk of the hunt since coming to Gravenstone, and Serilda had begun to fear the hunters would not ride out on the Harvest Moon. But, when the sun set and the moonlight filtered through the alder tree's boughs, to Serilda's relief, the hunt seemed eager to depart. The hounds were all but salivating, pulling at their chains to be free. The horses, too, pranced excitedly as they were led to the colonnade that acted as a boundary between the castle and the forest beyond.

Serilda spotted Agathe among them. The weapons master had been avoiding Serilda since her betrayal, and this night was no different. Agathe kept her gaze focused on the gates, turned resolutely from Serilda.

The Erlking and his steed were the last to trot by. He paused and studied Serilda, standing just outside the castle's black-stone door, gripping Gerdrut's and Anna's hands.

"I will know if you attempt to visit the poltergeist again," he said.

Her eyebrows lifted. "And what will happen if I do?"

The Erlking's gaze slipped meaningfully to the hollow cavity in Gerdrut's chest, then slowly back up to Serilda. "Leave him be. His work is not finished."

Serilda tipped her chin toward the hunters. Every one of them now wore chains of gold looped on their belts and overflowing from the packs on their steeds. "Unless you're planning to set sail for the Molnig Sea and capture a kraken, I suspect you have enough chains for whatever beast you might encounter."

The Erlking smiled. "I have always wanted a kraken." He twisted around in his saddle. "It could live in the lake at Adalheid."

She huffed. "I hope it drowns you all."

His grin widened. "I will have to take my chances another night. We have a different prize in mind for this hunt."

Serilda could tell he wanted her to ask what it was, which was precisely why she didn't. Instead, she dipped into a half-hearted curtsy. "Then fair hunting and good riddance, my lord."

"How quickly the blush of early love has faded," he said. "Such a shame."

With that, he pulled the hunting horn from his belt and released its sorrowful croon. Seconds later, he and the hunt had gone.

Nickel looked up at Serilda. "I don't care what he plans to do to us. I would love to go visit the poltergeist."

Serilda released Gerdy's hand to ruffle Nickel's hair. "I would love to visit him, too. Unfortunately, I do care what His Grim would do to you, and I won't risk it." She tilted her head back to look at the umbrella of tree boughs glowing silver with moonlight. "It would be a shame to squander such a perfect night, though, with the hunt finally gone. What shall we do?"

"Oh—hide and seek!" suggested Fricz. "Think how many great hiding places there are here."

Hans frowned at the castle entry hall. "Too many, don't you think? We'd never find one another. Gerdy would be lost until Eostrig's Day."

"We could limit how far we can go," suggested Anna. "Maybe just play in the courtyard?"

The courtyard stood in the center of the sprawling castle grounds, just inside the first colonnade, easy to find because that's where the alder tree grew. From just about anywhere in the castle, one could turn their head upward or look out a window and see the great trunk reaching toward the sky. It was a handy landmark, Serilda discovered, as she navigated the expansive fortress.

A sprawl of massive roots lay like a nest of vipers at the alder's base, so that only a narrow pathway of broken stones wound along the outer wall. Up close, the tree's illness was even more apparent. Its bark was crumbling and dry. The lowest hanging branches drooped limply toward the ground, many blackened and barren of leaves. As with the meadow outside the castle walls, a layer of brittle leaves filled the courtyard beneath the alder tree.

There were a few structures scattered along the far end of the courtyard—storage sheds and stables, a large smithy, a water well, and the like.

"Well," started Hans, scratching the back of his neck, "there aren't too many hiding places, but I suppose we'll make do."

"I know!" shouted Gerdrut, bouncing on her toes. "Let's play Thirteen! We haven't played that in ages."

This suggestion was met with exuberant approval, and within seconds Serilda had been dubbed the seeker. She shut her eyes and counted down from thirteen, listening to the rapid stomp of footsteps as the children raced to secure hiding places.

"Three . . . two . . . one!"

Her eyes snapped open. Serilda looked around, straining to listen for telltale squirming and giggles. Gerdrut was almost always the first one to be found, as she simply hadn't learned to hold still long enough. Anna was usually not far behind.

But from her place by the stone door, Serilda saw no one.

Hitching up her skirt hem, she took three enormous steps forward into the courtyard—all the movement that was allowed her.

No sign of the children.

"All right, I'm going to count again," she called, shutting her eyes. This time, she started at twelve.

Immediately, the patter of feet could be heard as the children raced away from their hiding spots and came to tag Serilda while she counted. She felt the flutter of little hands smacking her, before they each darted away again to find new havens.

"One!"

She opened her eyes and searched around. No one.

"Hmm," she said loudly, her fingers tapping her lips. "Where might they be?"

This time, she used her three steps to move to the left. Still, no sign of the children.

"Ready to go again?" she said. The countdown became shorter now, with only eleven seconds for the children to scramble from their places, tag Serilda, and find a new place to hide.

This time, when she opened her eyes, she was sure she saw a flutter of movement among one of the tree roots, but even after taking her three steps, she could not see the children.

"You are too good at this!" she said with a laugh.

She counted again from ten.

And again from nine.

Each time, taking three large steps, making a slow, winding path around the sprawling tree roots. Each time, searching what nooks and crannies she could see. But the children continued to elude her.

She started again from eight.

Giggles and racing footsteps. The brush of fingertips before the footsteps hastily retreated.

"Two . . . one!"

Serilda opened her eyes.

Movement caught her attention. A flash of golden curls disappearing behind the water well.

"Ha!" she cried, pointing. "Pout, shout, and sauerkraut, I see Gerdrut and she is out!"

"No!" cried Gerdrut. "You always catch me first!"

Serilda spun around as Gerdrut emerged from behind an empty wagon cart.

"Wait," said Serilda, turning back to the water well. "You were . . . I saw you . . ." She frowned and started toward the well. Though she knew the figure she'd seen had been smaller, she still called out for the blond-headed twins.

"Did you see us?" said Nickel, as he and Fricz both popped up from two barrels that stood side by side.

"Nah, you didn't see us!" said Fricz. "You're cheating!"

Serilda ignored him. Her pace picked up to a jog. Her pulse thundered in her ears.

But when she rounded the well . . . there was nobody there.

She stumbled back a surprised step, staring at the leaf-littered ground.

"What is it?" asked Hans.

He, the twins, and Gerdrut were making their way to her. Anna, always stubborn, apparently refused to give up her hiding spot.

"I thought I saw someone," said Serilda. "A little girl . . ."

A shiver swept over her. Could it have been . . . ?

Perhaps she'd been imagining things. Perhaps it had been a trick of the moonlight.

"Perhaps it was the queen's ghost," said Gerdrut.

Everyone looked at her.

"Who?" said Serilda.

Gerdrut shrugged. "That's what I call her, anyway. Some of the maids and I were told to beat the dust from a bunch of tapestries last week, and there was this one I really liked. It showed a girl who I think was my age? But she was sitting on a throne, surrounded by nachtkrapp. Only, instead of attacking her, I think they might have been her pets." She tugged on one of her curls. "I guess it sounds scary, but it wasn't really. It kind of made me think that I'd like to have a pet of my own. Anyway, I figure she must have been queen here once."

Serilda shook her head. "Gravenstone has never had a queen. Only the Alder King . . . and well, Perchta. The huntress."

"Oh." Gerdrut stuck out her lower lip. "Then I don't know who she was."

Serilda looked again at the empty place behind the well, but it offered no answers.

"If anyone sees or hears anything more about little girls or ghosts that didn't come with us from Adalheid, will you tell me?"

The children promised they would, when Hans gave a curious tilt to his head, peering up at the alder tree. "Is it just me, or does the alder look different now than it did when we first got here?"

They followed his gaze, studying the enormous tree, lit by the moon and torchlight. Serilda could see what he meant. The bark had been ashy gray before, but now had patches of vibrant white, almost like a paper birch. And high above, far past the low-hanging boughs, Serilda spied the first buds of new leaves beginning to unfurl.

Then they heard Anna calling from the far side of the courtyard.

"Serilda! Everyone, come here!"

They traded quick looks, before racing off in search of her. Anna stood in the open doorway of one of the stables, her eyes wide, a stick in one hand.

"I may have done something I wasn't supposed to do," she said, stepping aside to let Serilda pass.

Nerves immediately bunching in the pit of her stomach, Serilda stepped into the darkened stable, where just enough moonlight filtered in that she could see the bars of a cage erected within a stall, and inside, the sleeping form of the white unicorn.

She froze.

Strangest of all was not the cage or the unicorn. It was the flowers. The dirt floor of the stable was covered in tiny grasslike leaves and patches of the prettiest, daintiest white blooms.

"Are those snowdrops?" whispered Nickel as the children gathered in around Serilda.

"It appears so," she said. She crouched to get a better look, careful not to trample any of the buds. Snowdrops were the first flowers to appear at the end of winter, their little drooping heads oftentimes pushing up through the last drifts of snow. They were a small, dainty flower, not ostentatious like the beloved rose or exotic orchids or unique edelweiss, but they had always been one of Serilda's favorites, as they were the first to herald the coming of sunshine and warmth. "There shouldn't be snowdrops for months still."

"It gets stranger," said Anna, her voice wavering. "They . . . weren't here. Before."

"What do you mean?" asked Serilda.

Anna swallowed and tucked her hands behind her back. "I came in here to hide, and then I saw the unicorn, and it just felt so *sad*. It still had the Erlking's arrow in its side, and . . . and I thought it must be in pain, so I . . ." She pulled one hand out and Serilda saw what she first thought was a stick before recognizing the Erlking's black-tipped arrow—the one he had plunged into Pusch-Grohla—forcing her transformation into the unicorn.

Serilda's eyes widened. "Give that to me before you hurt yourself!"

Irritation passed over Anna's face, but she handed the arrow over without argument.

Serilda spun back to face the cage, expecting the creature to have turned back into Shrub Grandmother—but no—the unicorn remained, still asleep, its legs tucked beneath its body and its head tipped down serenely toward the earth.

"It didn't wake up, like I thought it would," said Anna. "But instead, this happened." She gestured down to her feet.

Serilda shook her head. "What happened?"

"The flowers. They weren't here at first, but then they just started popping up everywhere."

"Uh, Serilda? Anna?" said Fricz, peering out the door. "Those aren't the only flowers."

They stepped back out into the courtyard, and Serilda clapped an astonished hand to her mouth. A path was stretching before them from the door of the stable to the base of the alder tree, blanketed with—not snowdrops—but deep amethyst crocuses.

Gerdrut squealed and darted off. "Tulips!" she cried, falling to her knees beside a patch of tulips painted in shades of orange and red. Not far beyond lay another patch of blooms in tones of pale pink.

Then Nickel pointed out a cluster of butter-yellow daffodils.

It began to feel like they were on a scavenger hunt, every step taking them farther away from the unicorn's prison, and every step revealing more blooms, as if they were sprouting fresh from the earth in response to their approaching steps. Finally, Serilda stood still, letting her gaze sweep around the courtyard, watching the first curl of bright green leaves poke their way from the soil at the base of the tree, or creep up between the jagged stones of the courtyard paths. They transformed in moments. From nothingness to tight little buds to flowers in full bloom, all in a matter of breaths. Their progression did not continue on through the drooping and fading and crumbling into death, though. The flowers stayed vibrant, filling the air with the perfume of springtide.

Beneath the Harvest Moon, the courtyard of Gravenstone transformed from a place of dreary decay to a lush meadow of wildflowers, the alder tree at its center practically shimmering with renewed magic.

"Can we pick some?" Gerdrut asked hopefully.

Serilda hesitated. She glanced back through the stable door, to where the unicorn lay in slumber. Would Pusch-Grohla be angry if they did?

Then she looked at the children, their faces bright with wonder.

She nodded as she tucked the Erlking's arrow into a pocket of her cloak. "Pick as many as you want. Fill our room with them. The servants' quarters, too—anywhere in the castle that could use some cheering up." She grinned. "A bounty like this is not to be wasted."

Chapter Thirty

All night long, Serilda and the children gathered bouquets of spring flowers beneath the autumn's Harvest Moon. They raided the kitchens for every bowl and goblet they could find, creating vivid arrangements that they placed in alcoves throughout the castle. Eventually even the ghost servants, caught up in the miracle of it all, abandoned their work to help.

As the hours passed, the courtyard grew increasingly lush, as if every flower they picked sprouted into three more, and soon the entryway and great hall and servants' quarters and their own chambers were flourishing with flower buds on every shelf and mantel and step, until the castle itself felt transformed. Like a magic spell, the flowers turned the gloomy halls and eerie rooms into spaces that were vibrant and fragrant and almost joyful.

By the time the sky began to glow with the coming sun, Serilda's back and legs ached in a way she couldn't recall them ever doing before her curse, Gerdrut had fallen asleep, nestled among a patch of forget-me-nots, and everyone was complaining of hunger.

A plan had just been made to retire to the kitchens for leftover stew and rosemary bread when the thunder of the hunting horn rolled over the castle walls.

Serilda sighed heavily. "All good things come to an end."

The hunt came storming through the colonnade, the king at their fore. Upon seeing the alder tree and the field of colorful spring flowers, surprise flashed across his face and he pulled his horse to an abrupt halt.

Serilda folded her hands demurely in front of her skirt and went to greet him, her slippers squishing against the bed of clover that had taken over the path. "Welcome back, my lord," she said, as the hunters gathered in bewilderment around the tree. "We have had quite an enchanting night."

A shadow fell across the Erlking's face. Without acknowledging Serilda, he leaped from his steed and charged toward the stable where the unicorn was caged.

Serilda ran to keep up with him. "I hope you won't mind that we had some of the servants place a few bouquets in your chambers. I wasn't sure what you might like, so we went with snowdrops and white irises, for a muted color palette. But there are lots of other choices, as you can see, so if you'd prefer—"

The door crashed open so loud, Serilda jumped.

The Erlking did not enter, but stood glowering at the unicorn.

It had not moved from its resting place on the floor of the cage, but its eyes were now open and staring balefully at the king.

He spun around, glowering at Serilda. "Where is my arrow?"

Serilda lifted her chin. "What arrow?"

"The one that had paralyzed the unicorn," he growled.

"Oh. That arrow. It was taken."

He drew closer, using his impressive height to intimidate her. But that tactic had stopped working a long time ago. "By whom?"

"The monsters."

Her voice did not falter. Her gaze was unwavering.

Suspicion pressed against his ire. "Explain."

"The children and I were playing not long after the hunt departed, when we heard a noise inside this stable. We came to check, just in time to see an alp pulling the arrow from the unicorn's side. It ran past us, and a second later, a nachtkrapp flew down from the alder tree's branches, grabbed the arrow, and took off, disappearing over the castle wall." She pointed to an arbitrary place, where her made-up night raven had gone. "The alp flew after it, but they seemed to be working together." She shrugged. "After that, the flowers began to grow."

His jaw worked. A muscle twitched at the corner of his eye.

Serilda did not fidget.

Then the Erlking looked past her shoulder. "*Where* is the arrow?"

She turned back and grimaced to see the five children standing there. She could see it in their faces—that moment of biting their tongues, trying so hard not be compelled by the Erlking's magic to give him what he asked for.

But little Gerdrut gave in first. "Anna took it out of the unicorn!"

"I didn't know what would happen. I just felt so bad for it!" added Anna.

"Then Anna gave it to Serilda," admitted Nickel, looking crestfallen.

"And Serilda put it in her pocket," said Fricz, looking angry.

The Erlking fixed his gaze on Hans, who only shrugged. "Your Grim."

With a glower, the Erlking held out his palm to Serilda.

She heaved a sigh, took the arrow from her pocket, and gave it to him. He dropped it into his quiver and turned away, gesturing toward one of the hunters. "Have the metalworkers construct a harness for the unicorn. Luckily, we now have enough gold that we can spare some."

"Must you?" asked Serilda. "The flowers aren't harming anything."

He snorted. "Flowers are only the beginning of that hag's bothersome magic."

Serilda was about to point out that this bothersome magic had revived the alder tree, when an earsplitting screech halted her tongue.

"What is that?"

The king's irritation quickly changed to a smug grin. "Our newest acquisition."

The rest of the hunters finally appeared as the whisper of sunshine touched the alder tree's boughs. The horses nickered and pawed at the ground, their eyes darting toward the beast in their midst, even as they attempted to shy away. The stable boy, for once, did not move forward to take the steeds from their riders, for he, along with all the rest of the court who had gathered to greet the hunters, stared with loose jaws at their prize.

"Is that," whispered Hans, "a *gryphon*?"

Serilda's mouth ran dry as she took it in. The beast was twice the size of the bärgeist, with sinuous muscles covered in golden fur, two immense paws on its hind legs, and daggerlike talons in the front. The regal head of a silver eagle stood taller than even the Erlking's steed, and Serilda could imagine that the wings, when spread, would cast a shadow like a storm cloud when it took flight.

But those wings were currently bound. The gryphon's body—powerful and magnificent—had been tied from beak to tail with layer upon layer of golden chains.

It was injured, too. Serilda could see a dozen arrows lodged in its back and wings, and a mottle of dried blood on its tawny fur. Even still, she knew that these alone would never have brought it down had the hunters not also managed to get the golden ropes around it. Despite its wounds and the smears of dirt caked across them—suggesting it had been dragged here over a vast distance—the gryphon continued to struggle. It frothed at the beak as it fought against its bindings, the chains cutting deeper into its flesh.

"Well?" said the Erlking. "What do you think?" The question was posed lightly, as if they had brought home a common stag. Pride illuminated his face. He swept an arm around Serilda's waist, drawing her closer, and she was so stunned by the sight of the gryphon she hardly noticed the way his touch left faint tinges of frost on her dirt-smeared gown. "Once again, I owe you my gratitude." Bowing his head, he placed his lips against her temple.

Serilda shuddered and jerked away. Her entire being roiled at his touch. At seeing this fantastic beast, broken and tormented. Another sickening prize for His Darkness to gloat over.

"What are you talking about?" she said. "I've never told a story about a gryphon."

"Are you so sure?" he said with a mild chuckle.

Serilda glared. Yes, she was sure.

But something about his tone gave her pause.

Never had she made up any lies or hints about a gryphon. *Never.*

"Your Grim," said a hunter, "it will take time to construct a cage that can hold it. What shall we do with the beast in the meantime?"

"Throw it in with the unicorn." His eyes twinkled, amusement in his tone. "They can help protect our castle from malevolent spirits."

"No!" cried Serilda. "The gryphon will eat it alive!"

At this, the Erlking broke into laughter, as did a number of dark ones.

Furious, Serilda swung an arm toward the beast, still screeching and pulling at its chains. "Look at it! Look at those claws! The unicorn won't survive a night with that thing!"

"Oh, how I would enjoy seeing them fight to the death," said the Erlking. "Though I am not sure I agree with your assessment as to whom would be the victor."

He started shouting orders to the hunters and servants. Soon, the great beast was being dragged through the lush flora covering the ground, its shrill screams making the hairs stand up on the back of Serilda's neck.

She glanced back at the unicorn. Its dark eyes met hers and flashed, and she wished she could guess at what it was thinking, and whether it was still Pusch-Grohla looking out through those dark eyes. Was this beast still intelligent, feisty, determined? Or was it just a magical horse with a broken horn?

Before she could feel certain one way or the other, the unicorn curved its head away from her, and she felt abysmally dismissed.

Chapter Thirty-One

Serilda picked at the knot of warm bread in front of her. It steamed when she pulled it apart, emitting the most heavenly aroma. But she had little appetite. She was beginning to feel like life with the dark ones was just one huge celebration after another . . . always in honor of another grotesque event.

It's the vernal equinox! Let us hunt the game and devour the banquet provided by this quaint lakeside village, while its residents cower in fear inside their homes!

A mortal bride has been cursed and coerced into marrying our Alder King—let us feast!

One of the most magnificent magical creatures of all time has been locked up for our viewing pleasure—huzzah!

The shadows deepened while Serilda picked at her food and listened to the melodies strummed on an old mandolin and a waldzither by a pair of ghosts who both had gaping wounds in their stomachs. Conversations mingled around her. The air in the castle remained stubbornly cool, despite the fires that had been blazing in multiple hearths for weeks. At least now the air carried a faint floral perfume down every corridor.

"You are not enjoying our hospitality?" murmured the Erlking, his breath gliding over her temple as he leaned close.

Serilda's jaw tightened. She looked down at her plate, where her fingers had pulled the roll into a pile of fluffy crumbs.

She flicked her fingers toward the pots of honeyed butter and platters of roasted goose. "I am accustomed to simpler fare."

The Erlking hummed thoughtfully. After a silence, he said, "The only food to be found in Verloren is that provided as offerings from the mortal realm. Prayers given at the altars to Velos or gifts sent with loved ones when they cross the bridge . . ." He chuckled, though his next words were tinged with resentment. "As you might expect, few offerings were ever left for us demons."

Serilda peered at him, realizing—in all her imaginings, in all her tales—she had given little thought to what captivity really must have been like for the dark ones, before they had escaped from Verloren.

"You believe we take it all for granted," he went on. "The feasts, the wine, the freedom of the hunt—to ride beneath each glorious moon." He shook his head. "But you are wrong. When you know what it is to have nothing, you can never take anything for granted. I assure you. Every morsel on our table. Every note plucked on a harp's string. Every star in the sky. To us, it is all precious." His smile turned curious. "It is not a terrible way to endure eternity. Would you agree?"

Hating to agree with anything he said, Serilda stuffed some bread into her mouth. After swallowing, she said, "I would like to see my body again. To check how my—our child is growing."

"You will, in time."

"When?"

He picked up a glass of deep purple wine and gave it a swirl. "When I believed you to be the gold-spinner, you convinced me that your child would inherit the same skill. Now I find myself wondering if he or she will be Wyrdith-blessed. As talented a storyteller as my wife."

She swallowed, hoping with every aching bone in her body, that she would live long enough to find that out as well. "I don't know."

The Erlking took a sip from his glass. "There was a time when the gods bestowed their gifts vigorously upon mortals, though it has become rare.

How did you receive your blessing? I doubt it had anything to do with your mother being a seamstress, as you told me before."

"I don't wish to talk about it," said Serilda. "Not Wyrdith nor my mother nor my father . . . It is none of your concern."

He tapped his fingernail against the table. "If you insist, my dove."

She scoffed.

"Shall I tell you of my parentage instead?"

Serilda went still. Slowly, she turned to him, brow furrowed. "You're mocking me. Dark ones don't have parents."

He shrugged. "Of a sort, we do. Born from the vices and regrets shed by mortals as they pass over the bridge to Verloren, letting their sins drain down into the poisoned river . . ." He said it like he was reciting poetry. "Depending on how naughty you humans have been, it can take hundreds of souls crossing the bridge and leaving their sins behind for a new dark one to emerge. But we all know where we came from. The sad and hurtful pieces that swirled in those dead waters, before they bound together to form . . . *us*."

He took his hunting knife off the table—no average cutlery for him—and twirled it in his fingers as he talked. "You know Giselle, the master of the hounds? One of her mortals liked to torture animals, especially stray dogs. He would blind them and force them to fight each other." He paused before adding, "Many of those in my court have scraps from the humans who came to bet on those fights."

Serilda dropped the last hunk of bread, disgust twisting inside her. "Great gods . . ."

He then pointed the knife down the line of hunters seated at one of the long tables, one by one: "A mortal who beat his wife, and one who beat his horse, a woman who beat her children. A military general who ordered an entire village burned to the ground, the people locked inside their homes. A woman who swindled a number of poor families out of their coin. A manor lord who refused to care for his serfs, leaving them to starve in the midst of a drought. And then there's the usual. Cheats and murderers and—"

"Enough," said Serilda. She swallowed the bile in her throat. "I've heard enough."

The Erlking, to her surprise, fell quiet.

They sat in a long silence while the feast continued around them. Serilda caught the eye of Agathe—sitting not with the hunters, but the ghosts. But the weapons master quickly looked away, her expression troubled.

When the Erlking spoke again, his voice was hushed. "The vices of only two mortals came together to make me what I am."

She swallowed. Dreading what he might say, but curious all the same.

"A king," he went on, "who ordered the mass killings of thousands of male children, for a fortune-teller had told him that a red-haired boy would one day be his undoing."

She sat straighter. It was impossible not to think of Gild, though this nameless king must have lived thousands of years before.

"Did he?" she asked. "I mean, did a red-haired boy—"

"No," said the Erlking, amused. "The king died of sweating sickness, at quite an old age. But it was too late by then. For the children."

She pressed a hand to her hollow chest. "And the other one?"

"A duchess," he said. "Quite talented at archery." He paused, a long, long moment. "In her older years, she developed a taste for using women, mostly poor, but whom she deemed prettier than herself . . . as target practice."

Serilda massaged her brow. "Why are you telling me this?"

"Because you, my fair queen, are not Wyrdith."

She frowned. "Of course I'm not Wyrdith."

His lips tilted to one side, but there was an unusual sadness as he peered back at her. "I want us to understand each other. I understand why you lied to me. Just as I understand you are more than your lies."

At these words, the strangest warmth flooded through Serilda, spreading out until it reached her fingers and toes.

You are more than your lies.

The Erlking tipped his chair toward hers. "In the same way that you are not your god-gift . . . In the same way that you are not your mother or your father . . . *We* are not the vices that created us."

She held his gaze a long time, debating whether or not to say the words that rose to the surface. In the end, she couldn't help it. "So," she said slowly, "you *haven't* stabbed your arrows into the flesh of helpless mortals? And . . . you *haven't* murdered children simply because they became inconvenient to you?" She shook her head. "Are you truly trying to convince me that you are not evil?"

She had not noticed that a wall between them had been opening up until it came crashing down once more. The Erlking slumped back in his chair and trailed his fingertip along the stem of his glass. "Forgive me for thinking you might understand."

A throat cleared, drawing their attention past the table. Agathe stood before them, her head bowed. "Forgive the interruption, Your Grim. I was hoping I might steal our queen away for a quick moment?"

"Whatever for?" asked the Erlking.

Agathe fixed him with an open stare. "I betrayed her trust. I feel I owe her an apology."

"Such a mortal sentiment. Fine." He waved his hand toward her, then glanced at Serilda. "If you are interested in hearing it, that is."

Serilda's hands clawed into fists beneath the table. She wasn't particularly interested, no. But then, it couldn't be any worse than *this* conversation.

She pushed back her chair and stood. She did not look at Agathe as she made her way out of the room, but she could hear the soft thuds of the woman's boots behind her.

Serilda stepped into a game parlor and crossed her arms over her chest.

"If he asks to know what we spoke of," said Agathe, "I will have no choice but to tell him."

"I know that," said Serilda. "But it seems you gave us up quite willingly before."

Agathe's expression was not haunted or guilty, as Serilda might have expected. Instead, she appeared resolute. "Is he really the prince?"

Serilda blinked. "What?"

"The poltergeist. Is he the prince of Adalheid?"

"Oh. Yes. He is."

Agathe paced to a window that looked out over the courtyard. "What else do you know about the royal family?"

"I thought we were here so you could apologize for what you did."

Agathe's nostrils flared. "I am not yet decided if I am sorry or not."

Serilda threw her arms into the air. "Right. Well. Thank you for rescuing me from a very awkward conversation with my lord husband, but if you'll excuse—"

"Please," Agathe said emphatically. "I remember *nothing*. Some of the servants, yes, but the king and queen? A prince? I cannot remember them at all. I would ask that you tell me who it was I failed when the dark ones came. I deserve to know."

"Why? You can't change what happened. You're only torturing yourself."

She shook her head. "How can one make amends if one does not know what wrongs were committed?"

Serilda groaned. "And this is all you care about? Not the fact that you tricked me? Or that Gild has now spun enough gold to capture every beast in the Aschen Wood? Or that you gave me hope—actual hope—that those sweet children might find peace?"

When Agathe spoke, her voice was faint. "I would see them given peace. *All* the spirits the hunt has collected. I wish peace for them all. That is why I betrayed you."

Serilda flopped onto a settee. "You cannot really believe that he will free them, simply because you asked him to?"

"I do not trust him, no. But . . . he has never offered this before. And if there is even the slightest chance he could have spoken truthfully, then I had to take it. I would take that chance again. You and the poltergeist, for all the ghosts of Adalheid." She swallowed, the movement making a droplet of blood seep out over the edge of her scarf. "I would do it again, my queen."

"Don't call me that."

"Then tell me about my true queen."

Serilda rubbed her temple, wondering if it was safe to tell anything to this woman who had betrayed her and Gild, knowing she might run straight to the Erlking. But then, the Erlking already knew the history of Adalheid, and he knew Serilda had figured out most of it. So what did it matter?

"I know very little about the royal family. All memories of them were erased from history. All their ancestors, lost. I only know that, during the time you lived in Adalheid, there were a king and a queen, a prince and a princess. And yes, Gild is the prince. The princess was taken by the wild hunt, and he rode after them and he shot Perchta and killed her, or . . . at least . . . gave Velos a chance to reclaim her for Verloren. The Erlking got angry and he attacked Adalheid in order to avenge Perchta's death. That's all I know."

Agathe turned her gaze back to the window.

"As for Gild," Serilda went on when the silence had become unbearable, "you might not think it to look at him, but he is skilled with a sword, even though he has no memory of learning how to fight. And he once shot an arrow into Perchta's heart, so he must have been a skilled archer as well." She hesitated, before concluding, "It's likely that *you* taught him."

Agathe lowered her head. "Yes," she said quietly. "I assume I would have."

Feeling the first twinge of sympathy, Serilda climbed back to her feet. "I know that Gild feels the same responsibility that you do. He believes that what happened in Adalheid is his fault. That he should have been there to protect everyone in the castle when the dark ones came. But it *isn't* his fault. And it isn't yours either."

Agathe laughed humorlessly. "And what of you? You blame yourself for the deaths of those five children, yet it was the Erlking who kidnapped them. His monsters that killed them."

"It was my lies that made them a target in the first place. Have *you* been cursed by the god of stories? Does every word out of *your* mouth somehow land everyone you love in danger?" Serilda pressed her hands into her sides, finding that she was suddenly shaking. "Unlike you and Gild, I *am* at fault for so much that's happened. And here I am. The Alder Queen." She shook her head. "Somehow as powerless to help anyone as I have ever been."

"Powerless?" said Agathe. "I have seen the way you talk to His Grim. You are stubborn and brave and—"

"And I'm going to get everyone killed," said Serilda. A second later, her shoulders slumped. "I already got them killed."

"Listen to me," said Agathe, pacing toward her. "Did you not once tell a story that tore a hole in the very fabric of the veil?"

Serilda frowned, thinking of the day she had gone to Adalheid, knowing that four of her beloved children were already dead, but still determined to rescue Gerdrut. "The hole was already in the veil. The story just . . . revealed it."

"To you? And you alone? That is power."

Serilda shook her head. "No, it's . . . it's another trick. Another trap. Another curse, if you ask me."

Even though, as she was saying it, she wasn't sure. Would she change anything about that day? Her determination to face the Erlking and demand the freedom of little Gerdrut? Even if, ultimately, she had failed . . . she did not know that she would act differently, even now.

Because there was still hope, she realized.

Pathetic, desperate hope. That somehow she could win freedom for the children. For Gild. For herself and her unborn babe.

Somehow.

She imagined she could hear the Erlking laughing at her. *Pathetic, foolish mortal.*

"Lady Serilda," said Agathe, "I do not wish to be your enemy. You and I, we are fighting for the same thing. The freedom of the innocent souls who are trapped in the court of the dark ones . . . in part, because of how *we* failed them."

Serilda swallowed. "He will not release them, Agathe. He will not do anything that does not suit him. You must know that."

"You are right. And yet, in my heart, I know that he spoke true. On the Mourning Moon, he will free their souls. All of them."

Serilda didn't know if she could trust Agathe, but if the weapons master was lying, she was as convincing as if she, too, had been blessed by Wyrdith. "And if he does?" Serilda asked, opening her palms wide. "What will be the cost of that? Because I assure you, any bargain that he is making . . . he intends to come out the victor."

Chapter Thirty-Two

Serilda typically preferred solitude on her birthday. The day was so close to the Mourning Moon—the anniversary of her mother's disappearance—that it brought a sorrow with it that Serilda embraced. No point in pretending she wasn't sad to have grown up without her mother, even all these years later.

But when she was young, her father tried hard to distract and entertain her on her birthday. He planned trips to the harvest festivals in Mondbrück and hours fishing by the riverside and afternoon picnics in the orchards, even though the mill was busier than ever and the weather was shiver-inducing.

Even though all Serilda wanted was to sit beneath her mother's hazelnut tree and feel a sort of self-indulgent pity for an hour or two.

Now she wanted nothing more than to go picnicking with her father one last time.

She had spent the night before lamenting that when the children had packed her things in Adalheid, no one had thought to bring the book of fairy tales Leyna had given her. She was desperate for a story to take her away from this place. So she decided to search for the library again, though it would mean braving the trek through the lunar rotunda.

This time, as she passed through, a few dozen ghosts and dark ones were hard at work—chopping at the persistent vines and clearing away buckets full of rubble from the cave. She could see lantern lights strung up beyond the entrance, and hear the sound of metal tools beating against the stone deep within the cavern. She was tempted to stop and ask what they were doing, but she didn't want to be a bother. And, if she was being honest with herself, she was afraid that she would hear that voice again. Her father, calling to her from deep within those fathomless shadows, when she knew it wasn't him. Couldn't be him.

She hurried past, speaking to no one and keeping as much distance between herself and the cave's opening as she could.

After that, she found the library without incident, and it was all she could have hoped for. Shelves upon shelves of leather-bound books, each one inked and colored painstakingly by hand, their spines stamped with gold, many so old their pages were brittle. There were scrolls, too, and loose sheaves of parchment and bundles of ancient maps drawn on stretched animal skins. Grimoires and bestiaries, books on alchemy and mathematics and astronomy.

After hours of climbing up and down the rickety ladders, Serilda had amassed a stack of intriguing titles—fairy tales and mythologies and a fascinating study on how artistic interpretations of the old gods had changed over the centuries. She claimed a tufted chaise beside the window, where outside she could see the alder tree, its leaves still a deep green, even while the forest beyond turned crimson and gold. The alder looked healthier every day, though the spring flowers had begun to shrivel and fade in its shadow.

Serilda had just finished reading a tale from far-off Isbren about a girl who fell in love with an ice bear when she heard footsteps in the hall. She shut the book as the Erlking's lithe figure appeared in the doorway.

"And here is my missing bride," he said. "Lost in a book. I should have guessed."

"Were you looking for me?" she asked, returning the book to the shelf she had found it.

"I have just been to see the poltergeist," he said, striding into the room and taking in the bookshelves as if they were long-forgotten friends. "I thought you might like to know that I finally have what I need."

Serilda shook her head. "You captured a gryphon. A unicorn. A tatzel-wurm. What else could you possibly want?"

The Erlking laughed. "The whole world, my love."

She fixed him with a glare. "No one should get to have *the whole world*. Not even you."

"Why limit your imagination?" he said, smirking.

Serilda hoped he would leave, now that he had delivered these annoying taunts, but instead he slipped into an armchair and threw his boots up onto the ottoman. Something about his mood made her tense. Since arriving in Gravenstone, the Erlking had often carried with him a melancholy air. Serilda did not know what to make of it. Was he reminiscing about Perchta, dreaming of the time when she would be with him again? Or was there simply something about this castle that weighed down a person's soul, dampening all sense of brightness, of joy?

But today, there was an unusual joviality to the king's movements, a flickering in his eye that made her uneasy.

"I was also speaking with your messenger this morning," he went on, "and he told me the most *interesting* news. It turns out that today is the birth date of our fair and beloved queen." He lifted an eyebrow at her. "How cruel of you not to give me warning. I was preparing a special gift to bestow on the Mourning Moon, but I think I shall give it to you early. I've sent word to have it brought to us."

"Should I be worried?" she muttered. "Historically, your gifts have not been well-received."

The Erlking laughed. "It is only a gift, from a king to his queen. Nothing more."

"There is nothing you can give me that I want."

"How ungrateful you mortals can be. Besides, you and I both know that isn't true."

She fixed an irate look on him. "You're right. Are you going to break my curse? Free the souls of my attendants? How about the rest of your court?

Or even the poltergeist? Would you do that if I asked? It *is* my birthday, after all."

Though Serilda was trying to needle him, the Erlking leaned back and rested his cheek against his knuckle, unperturbed. "If I were to make *all* your dreams come true, what would I have left to give you next year?"

"Next year? How optimistic of you."

"Don't discount my generosity so quickly, love." He crossed his legs. "I wonder. What *would* you sacrifice for your sweet little attendants to be granted freedom?"

She scowled. "That's the thing about gifts. One does not usually have to make *sacrifices* for them."

"That is not an answer."

She shook her head. "What do you want me to say? That I would give anything, my heart and my soul and all that I am, to see them go free?"

He shrugged. "Is that the truth?"

She scoffed. "You are despicable. To use them against me. They are *children*. They've done nothing to deserve being here."

"Yes, well . . . maybe someday you and I will come to an agreement."

A distant sound made gooseflesh rise on Serilda's arms. A long, crooning howl. She glanced toward the doorway. "Did you hear that?"

"Oh yes," said the Erlking, sounding bored. "The wolf has been going on like that all week. You haven't noticed?"

Serilda blinked at him. "The wolf?"

"Velos, guarding the gates to Verloren," he said, as if they were discussing the pastry shop on the town square. "This library is awfully close."

"Velos . . . guarding . . ." Serilda wanted to ask more, but words failed her.

The Erlking sighed. "As the Mourning Moon draws near, Velos becomes restless, now that the gates have been opened once more." He smiled wistfully. "I do hope the god will pay us a visit."

Serilda's words came out little more than a whisper. "Gravenstone grew

out of the gates to Verloren, and the alder tree that sprouted from its depths."
She turned in the direction of the lunar rotunda. The cave. The brambles.
The whispers.

Her father's voice . . .

"Come," said the Erlking, rising to his feet and extending a hand toward
her. "I can see you are intrigued. I will show you."

"Er—no. Thank you. I'm quite content here, with my poetry and fairy
tales."

He drew a step closer. "Are you reading fairy tales, miller's daughter?
Or are you living one?" He leaned closer, his voice dropping to a whisper,
mocking her words to him in the dungeon. "It is only the gates to the land
of the lost. What are you afraid will happen?"

She glared at him. Then, with a long inhale, she took his hand.

They did not have far to walk to the rotunda. The ghosts and dark ones
she'd seen before were gone now, and the room felt unnaturally quiet, as if
the walls were listening for the howls and whispers and voices that echoed
from below. The room was as magnificent as she remembered, with its towering walls and circular glass ceiling, the mural of stars and moons scattered
in every direction. But as Serilda's gaze fell on the cave opening, a cold wash
swept across her skin.

This time, the entrance stood unobstructed. There were still brambles
emerging from its depths, spreading along the walls like a kraken climbing
up from the depths of the sea, their thorns tearing into the stone and wood-
work. But all those that had been woven across the opening had been cut
back and removed. Now, one could walk right through that gaping hole.

She thought of all the ghosts that had been working earlier. The sounds
of chisels and picks echoing up from its depths. Were they clearing a path
to Verloren?

But . . . *why*?

Serilda dared approach only close enough to see a narrow stairway that
lay beyond the entrance, the jagged steps cut from stone and descending
steeply out of sight. A lantern hung just inside on the cave wall, but it was

unlit, and the light from the rotunda hardly penetrated the darkness beyond. She expected the air wafting up from the void to be dank and stale, to smell of decay. Instead it smelled like all the rest of the castle—fertile soil and wood smoke.

"I would have thought the gates to Verloren would be more grandiose, somehow," she murmured, feeling strangely disappointed.

"Oh, this is not the gate."

She turned to him. "But you said—"

"This staircase leads down to the gates. There is a chamber below. It was caved in when we arrived, I suspect due to Pusch-Grohla's magic. That chamber marks the end of my domain. It acts as a barrier between the upper world and Verloren. Beyond that . . . the gates. The bridge." He swept a languid hand toward the opening. "The land of the lost."

"You've been working to clear a path back down to that chamber, to the gates," said Serilda. "But why? Couldn't something . . . come out?"

"I suppose, if they were to make it past the bridge. But I daresay, Velos learned long ago to keep it better protected."

"Your Grim?" A ghost seamstress with a bloodied, bludgeoned skull stood in one of the rotunda's doorways, holding a large box. "As you requested."

"My gratitude." The Erlking swept forward and took the box from her. Relieved of her duty, she quickly spun on her heel and hurried away. The Erlking returned to Serilda, a giddiness in his eye. "Your gift."

Serilda peered down at the box. It was wrapped in gauzy fabric, a sprig of holly berries tied into a black bow.

"Poisonous berries," she said. "How . . . sweet."

The points of his teeth flashed. "Go on."

Serilda held her breath as she pulled out the holly with its sharp-pointed leaves and untied the bow. The ribbon slipped to the floor. She wrapped her hands around the box's lid and lifted.

Inside, she found a smooth field of bloodred velvet. She let her fingers dance across the surface, feeling the soft fabric. Gripping the folds, she pulled it from the box. A waterfall of crimson cascaded to the floor. Sleek black fur on the inside, red velvet on the outside, every hem embroidered with intricate designs of dainty lily of the valley flowers.

It was the most beautiful garment she'd ever seen. A winter cloak fit for royalty.

Setting aside the box, the Erlking reached for the clasp at Serilda's throat. As soon as it was undone, she gasped and stepped away, holding the velvet cloak over one arm while she grasped at the fabric of her old, beloved riding cloak with her other hand.

"You will not be needing that any longer," said the Erlking. "My queen need not wear something so tattered and worn."

She swallowed and looked down at the gray wool. Her father had bought it for her in Mondbrück years ago, and it had been a constant companion. Warm enough in the winter, while still comfortable for much of the fall and spring. Yes, it was tattered. Gild had even patched up a hole in the shoulder where a drude's talon had punctured it. And yes, it smelled a bit like Zelig, her old horse, who she hoped was now living a peaceful life on the pastures near Adalheid.

Yes, this cloak was fit for a peasant girl. A miller's daughter.

Not the Alder Queen.

But how the cavity of her chest yawned open when the Erlking took it from her. He tossed the gray wool alongside the empty box, then draped the new cloak around her with a flourish. The weight of it settled on her shoulders. There was a strange air of finality as he affixed the clasp at her throat.

"Much better," he whispered. "Do you like it?"

Serilda smoothed her hands along the velvet. Never in her life had she dreamed she would wear something so exquisite.

Never in her life had she felt so unworthy.

"I have seen lovelier," she said.

The Erlking grinned, because he knew what a liar she was. "I would have you wear it on the Mourning Moon."

She looked up, startled. "Will I be riding with the hunt?"

His hands landed on her upper arms, and the weight of them coupled with the fur made the cloak oddly stifling, even in this cold castle. "No, love. My hunters and I have something even more magnificent in mind."

Chapter Thirty-Three

Surprise!" shouted five chipper voices as soon as Serilda stepped into her chambers. The children gathered around a small writing desk, where sat a platter full of honey walnut cakes, Serilda's favorite dessert.

Immediately, the weight of the afternoon lifted. "What is this?"

"A birthday party!" shouted Fricz.

"*Your cloak!*" cried Gerdrut, rushing forward to feel the drapes of velvet.

Serilda was happy to undo the clasp and drape the fabric over Gerdrut instead, letting it smother her like a quilt. The girl squealed, hidden from view. "It's so soft!"

"It *is* magnificent," Serilda agreed. "A birthday gift from His Darkness. I'm not sure how to feel about it."

Gerdrut swam her way out of the fabric, but kept it wrapped around her body, the excess puddling on the floor. "I'll wear it if you don't want to."

Serilda laughed. "For now, consider it yours." She still held the bundle of gray wool. "Anna, would you please have my old cloak laundered and put away for me? The Erlking wanted to give it to the maids and have it cut up for rags, but I insisted it was too sentimental."

"Of course," said Anna, taking the cloak from her. "I'll do it tomorrow."

They sat down to enjoy the cakes, which they had requested from the kitchen staff weeks ago to ensure they didn't use up the supply of walnuts they'd brought with them from Adalheid before the queen's birthday.

"This is so thoughtful," said Serilda. "I wish I could give you something half as special."

"Really?" said Fricz. "They're just cakes. We didn't even bake them."

"Besides, you give us stories," Nickel said. "That's special enough."

Serilda's smile turned sad. She wished she could still think of her tales as the gift she once had, rather than the burden they had become.

"I have something for you, too," said Gerdrut, reaching into her pocket. "A fine gift for Her Luminance!" Her grin was sparkling as she held up her hand. In her fingers was clutched a small golden ring.

Serilda accepted it from her, and when she turned it toward the candle-light, the air caught in her lungs.

Pressed into the gold was a familiar design. A tatzelwurm wrapped around the letter *R*.

"Gild's ring," she breathed. "Were you with the poltergeist? Did he give this to you?"

"No," said Gerdrut, confused. "I found it. In that hall with all the tapes-tries. I was told to sweep the floors, and I found it stuck in a groove behind a table leg, covered in dust. Polished up nicely, I thought." Her smile became even prouder.

"Really?" said Serilda. "You found it here?" She tried to slip it on, but it got caught on her first knuckle.

"I know it's small," Gerdrut hastened to add, "but I thought maybe you could put it on a chain? Maybe . . . maybe Gild could make you one, or something."

Serilda pulled her close and gave her a tight squeeze. "I do love it. Thank you. Until I find a chain, will you keep it safe for me?" She took Gerdrut's hand and slipped the ring onto her finger. "A perfect fit."

The child flushed pink. "Are you sure?"

"I would entrust it to no one else."

Gerdrut clasped her hands against her chest. "I will protect it, I swear."

Serilda nodded. "I have one more request. Once we've finished this magnificent dessert . . . would you take me to see these tapestries?"

The lanterns and wall torches and candelabras were always burning bright in the castle, and the hall of tapestries was no different. Three grand chandeliers hung from the tall rafters in a line down the center of the impressive chamber, and a standing candelabra was positioned between each tapestry, illuminating each work of art in an amber glow.

And they were works of art.

Serilda had never before seen such skilled workmanship. The strands were so delicate, and each woven detail breathtakingly lifelike.

Most peculiar, though, was how many of the tapestries seemed to be taken from a story.

A story that Serilda had told. In some cases, a story she had *lived*.

A horde of dark ones, with the Erlking at their helm, charging over the bridge to Verloren while an enormous black wolf howled from the depths below.

Perchta dying in front of Gravenstone Castle, an arrow shot through her heart, while a princely Gild looked on.

Gild at his spinning wheel, surrounded by piles of straw while threads of glistening gold emerged onto the bobbin.

The Erlking preparing to stab a slender horn into a mass of tree roots, while a white unicorn watched with downcast eyes.

Then there were images that sent chills skittering down Serilda's spine. Stories she did not know.

There was the tapestry Gerdrut had told her about. The young princess— who was undoubtedly Gild's sister—sitting atop a throne crafted of thorns, with a crown of willow branches on her head. She was surrounded by monsters, but rather than attacking her, as the monsters in the Verloren tapestry had attacked the Erlking and Perchta, these creatures gathered around the child with respect and deference. As if they were guarding her.

The next tapestry was one of the largest in the hall. Serilda had to take many steps back so she could try to take in the image all at once.

To the left stood the Erlking beneath a glowing full moon. White snowdrifts lay at his feet, and in his hand was the end of a golden chain. That chain connected to a line of beasts that filled up the rest of the tapestry. Each one with a hanging head, their posture speaking of defeat while the Erlking lorded over them.

The basilisk.

The wyvern.

The tatzelwurm.

The unicorn.

The gryphon.

A black wolf.

And, lastly, a gold-feathered raptor, larger than any eagle or hawk Serilda had ever seen.

She stared at it a long time, her insides churning.

The Erlking had five of these beasts.

All but the wolf and the raptor.

What did it mean? Why was he collecting these seven magnificent creatures, when all he really needed the golden chains for was to capture one god on the night of the Endless . . .

Serilda's thoughts trailed off, replaced with distant humming that clouded her mind, replacing everything she had been so sure of. All this time. The Erlking wanted to catch one of the old gods. The Erlking wanted to make a wish. The Erlking wanted to bring Perchta back from Verloren.

But no.

She hadn't fully understood.

Seven gods.

Seven beasts.

She swallowed hard, inspecting the images until there could be no doubt that this was not an illustration of just any seven beasts. This was the very basilisk that she and Gild had fled from. The wyvern that hung in the great hall of Adalheid. The tatzelwurm that had tried to steal Leyna's golden figurine. The unicorn that had been the leader of the moss maidens for centuries. The gryphon who had, only weeks ago, been dragged through these castle gates.

Who were they? What were they? If the unicorn had been human—well, human-ish—could they all have been? Could they all be again, if they weren't trapped by poisoned arrows and golden chains?

Her gaze fell on the black wolf, and she remembered the story of the dark ones fleeing from Verloren, and the howls that could be heard echoing up from the gates in the lunar rotunda.

Velos. Velos became a wolf.

She scanned the others.

The unicorn. Pusch-Grohla. Protector of the forest, of maidens and mothers. With magic that brought trees back to life, that filled a courtyard with tulips and snowdrops. Could this be Eostrig, god of spring and fertility? Serilda had never heard any tales connecting Eostrig and Shrub Grandmother, and the wizened, scraggly old woman did not at all resemble the illustrations she had seen of the god, who was generally depicted as willowy thin, with strong hands and long bluish-purple hair. Eostrig was said to be both gentle and intimidating. Strong-willed, but kind.

Pusch-Grohla was intimidating and strong-willed, but gentle? Kind? Serilda made a face just thinking about it.

But then . . . she would not have marked her to become a unicorn, either, that most graceful of creatures. And Pusch-Grohla had known Serilda was pregnant, had mentioned her "condition," long before even Serilda herself knew.

She studied the tatzelwurm next, picturing the seal of Gild's family. *Maybe it runs in your blood.* The tatzelwurm had been drawn to the figurine crafted of god-blessed gold. Hulda. Hulda was Gild's patron deity. Hulda was . . . the tatzelwurm?

And what had the Erlking said to Pusch-Grohla? *Solvilde has not been in a position to answer hopeless prayers for a very long time.* The basilisk or the wyvern, who had been captured by the hunt years, perhaps even decades before. She pictured the seven stained-glass windows. Solvilde, dressed in vibrant orange and blue, the same colors as the basilisk's feathers. And Tyrr, with the ruby between their eyes, just like the wyvern.

And Freydon—

The gryphon. It must be.

She was sure that she had not told any stories of a gryphon. But she had told the tale of Wyrdith going to visit Freydon to demand answers about the terrible harvest. *On the eastern plains of Dostlen, where they tended a tidy garden and spent afternoons fishing at the delta of the Eptanie River.*

Another story. Another ridiculous tale. Another bounty of truths, betraying the location of a mythical creature to the wild hunt. A mythical creature who was actually . . . a god.

She would never tell another story again, she silently vowed. Not when everything, *everything* somehow turned into a boon for the Erlking.

Her legs were shaking as she walked closer to the tapestry, examining the final beast.

She thought back to the stained-glass windows at Adalheid, and how Wyrdith was so often depicted with a gold-plumed quill in hand. In beast form, Wyrdith was an enormous raptor with shining gold feathers. She could picture them as elegant as a falcon, as vicious as an eagle. But here, they were broken. Here, the Erlking had won.

"Why?" she whispered. "Why does he want all seven?"

"Serilda?"

She glanced over to see the children watching her with wide, fearful eyes. Had they realized the truth, too? Could they see what this meant?

No. Serilda wasn't even sure *she* fully understood what this meant. She wanted to believe this was her imagination running amok. Surely she was mistaken. This was just a tapestry, it didn't mean anything.

And yet, she knew she was right. She would have taken poison on it.

"We need to show you something," said Hans, one hand tense on Gerdrut's shoulder.

"It wasn't here before," Gerdrut said. "I swear. I didn't notice before . . . I would have told you if I had!"

It took Serilda a moment to shift away from the seven gods captured with golden chains and realize that whatever had upset the children, it was something entirely different from what had upset her.

"What is it?"

They guided her down to the end of the hall, where one final tapestry hung in the corner, barely touched by the candle's glow.

It took her a moment to realize she was looking at a portrait of herself. Dressed in black riding gear and her new crimson cloak, with her hair pinned back, she looked more like the Alder Queen than ever. But there was no mistaking the golden wheels in her eyes. It *was* her.

She was standing in the throne room of Adalheid, flanked by two columns, each wrapped by tatzelwurm carvings. In her arms was a swaddled baby.

Hope shimmered inside Serilda.

Brilliant, ecstatic hope.

It was her. Her and her child. She wasn't dead.

Her lips trembled and she had just dared to allow a hesitant smile to touch her lips when Hans put a hand on her arm.

"There's more," he said, and she remembered the children's stunned expressions. Not just stunned. *Horrified.*

Fricz picked up one of the standing candelabras. "We wanted to see it better," he explained. "And when you shine the light on it . . ."

He carried the candelabra so that it was directly in front of the tapestry, scattering the shadows against the wall.

Before her eyes, the tapestry changed.

It was no longer Serilda holding her child.

It was the huntress.

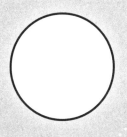

THE
MOURNING
MOON

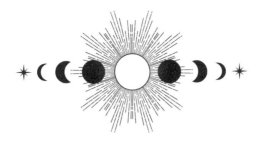

Chapter Thirty-Four

She would free the unicorn and the gryphon.

She vowed to do it as she lay awake on her birthday, thinking for once not of her disappeared mother, but something entirely different.

Serilda could do nothing for Solvilde or Tyrr or Hulda, not while she was in Gravenstone and they in Adalheid. But Eostrig, the unicorn, and Freydon, the gryphon. They were here, stabled in the courtyard. She did not know how she would open the cage or remove the golden harnesses that had been bound to their massive bodies. But she would find a way.

She could not let the Erlking have the gods. Not for one wish, and certainly not for seven.

They must be set free.

Tonight, she vowed. Beneath the Mourning Moon, after the hunt had ridden off.

How she wished she could free Gild, too. She missed him more with every passing day, a painful ache in her cavernous chest that never went away.

But she couldn't waste time trying to sneak into the dungeons. She couldn't reach Gild. Couldn't help him. She would have to do this on her own, and hope the gods had enough wisdom in their beastly forms that they would not try to devour her once she set them free.

There was one good thing that had come from her single-minded focus on freeing the two gods. In her scheming, she had forgotten to dread the onset of the Mourning Moon, when usually this entire moon cycle put her in a sour mood. She had come to expect the deep sensation of loss that always crept up on her during this saddest of days.

The Mourning Moon was meant to be a time of remembering ancestors who had gone on to Verloren. Paper lanterns were hung from trees and paraded through streets in honor of lost loved ones. Songs were sung and wine poured over graves. Families gathered together and told stories—not of loss, but of happy times when the people they missed had been with them. It was a somber celebration, but a celebration nonetheless.

For Serilda and her father, though, the Mourning Moon was not so much a time of remembering her mother, but a time of solidarity between the two of them. She and her father started off their moping as they broke their fast. They had practically made a game of it, to see who could wallow most despairingly, who could sigh the loudest, who could sulk with the most irrepressible glumness—to the point where they were both being so ridiculous, they had no choice but to laugh.

They even had a tradition, in which Serilda would borrow a book of poetry from Madam Sauer's schoolhouse, and she and her father would take turns reading the most tragic poems in the collection, full of words like *forlorn* and *wretched* and *nightingale*. Then they would dine on sweets from the local bakery for their evening bread. Anything with honey, anything with treacle, anything that would leave them both with upset stomachs, because that was better than upset hearts.

She was surprised to realize how much she cherished those memories. Days that should have been awful. That *were* awful. But that were strangely comforting, too.

Here in Gravenstone, there was little comfort, little joy, only her sadness creeping toward her on stealthy toes. A sadness that had begun to manifest in bitterness.

And impatience.

Why weren't they leaving?

She sat in the great hall, glowering at her husband. The dark ones were celebrating. Why? She didn't know. She didn't care. Historically, the Mourning Moon was one of their most prolific nights, with more innocent souls taken than on any other full moon of the year. But it was nearing nightfall, and the evening had turned into an unexpected revelry, with someone playing on a great pipe organ, and many of the hunters imbibing blackberry wine and partaking in table games that usually required some ghastly payment from the loser, such as cutting off the tip of their own ear.

Serilda had been sitting stick-backed on a settee for what felt like hours, her muscles growing stiff. She kept her eye on the children. They had hung their lanterns on the alder tree earlier that day, but would wait for nightfall to light them—the symbolism reminiscent of Velos's lantern, only it was said that their handiwork would bring the spirits of their loved ones back for one night, as opposed to Velos leading them away to the land of the lost.

But instead of lighting their lanterns and reminiscing about their loved ones, the children, like all the servants, were now bustling around with trays of food and carafes of amber liqueur.

She wished she could say her husband had been ignoring her—as he so often did during these soirées—but no. If anything, his attention had been relentlessly glued to her. Every time she glanced his way, he was watching, though she didn't know what he was watching for.

There it was again, that piercing gaze finding her in the crowd.

With a false smile, Serilda raised her glass of sage water in a mock toast. His teeth flashed in the candlelight, and to her regret, he abandoned the courtly woman he'd been speaking with and made his way toward her.

Serilda glanced around and made a hasty signal toward Hans, hoping she could catch him in conversation to avoid the attention of the king, but Hans was busy pouring ale into a hunter's goblet, and the next thing she knew, her husband was folding his long legs beneath the chaise and perching on the cushion beside her.

She couldn't keep a grumble from slipping out.

"Enjoying the celebration?"

"Who knew a castle full of demons could spend so much time drinking and eating and"—she gestured toward a table where a set of bone dice were clattering noisily across a game board—"playing games of chance."

"You mortals do not?"

She crinkled her nose. "It just seems an odd thing for you to celebrate. The Mourning Moon might have special meaning to us, given that *we* all have plenty of deceased loved ones to pay our respects to. How lucky for you that it is nothing more than a night of revelry."

"It was not always called the Mourning Moon, you know."

She frowned, hating—*hating*—that this comment sparked a bit of interest in her.

It sounded like the start of a story.

"Ah," said the Erlking, all too knowingly. "You didn't know."

"I have a feeling you're about to enlighten me."

He chuckled. Hesitated. But then—yes, continued. "Before the gates to Verloren were closed off, this was the night in which the souls of loved ones were allowed to return to the mortal realm. Beneath the glow of the full moon, they would cross the bridge. Humans would gather at their burial sites to give offerings and ask for blessings. Back then, it was called Velos's Moon." He said the name with obvious scorn. "Not that Velos had much to do with it."

"No? They weren't the one who allowed the souls to return?"

He lifted an eyebrow. "Was Velos not the one that took the souls in the first place?"

She frowned. "*Guiding* them toward a peaceful afterlife is not the same as *kidnapping* them."

He clicked his tongue. "You mortals love to cast us as villains, while Velos receives as much respect as any of those pompous deities. The god of death takes children still in the womb. They claim souls from plague, from childbirth, from starvation . . . How are they not a villain?"

"Perhaps it is because Velos treats us with respect. They do not cause the deaths, necessarily . . . They are only there to claim our souls and lead us to

Verloren once we leave the mortal realm. As we both know, souls left here are not happy. They don't belong here."

"You have too soft a heart, my queen."

"I wouldn't know. You took my heart so long ago, I've all but forgotten what it felt like."

He peered at her from the corner of his eye, his lips tilting roguishly. "I would like to show you the gates."

She stiffened. "To Verloren?"

"Yes. You were curious when we were in the rotunda before, I could tell. And on the Mourning Moon, they are a sight not to be missed."

Serilda started to laugh. The king almost sounded as if he wished to show her something romantic. A rose garden, a sunset. But no. The Alder King wished to show her the gates of death.

"I would rather not," she said. "I'm not dead *yet*."

He reached toward her, running a finger along the scar on her wrist. She jerked away. "So long as you retain the curse," he said, "you are immortal, too. You may never have cause to cross the bridge into Verloren."

She cast him a withering look. "And here I thought you intended to murder me as soon as I gave birth. Should I be rejoicing that you have changed your mind?" She leaned closer. "Could it be you are growing *fond* of me?"

He tilted his head and seemed to actually consider the question. Then he let out a long, pained sigh. "No. You're right. I will rid myself of you when you have served your usefulness."

Serilda sat back, appalled that he would speak so blatantly.

"Which is all the more reason," he went on, ignoring her reaction, "to enjoy our limited time together. It is the Mourning Moon. Perhaps you might see one of those loved ones you mentioned."

She held his gaze, trying to determine if this was yet another cruel joke. Was he offering to take her to the gates, to show her . . . her father?

Perhaps, even, her mother?

"No," she breathed. "I don't think I should."

"Does death frighten you?"

"Not as much as it used to." Then, a thought struck her, and she peered up at him again. "Does it frighten *you*?"

He sat back, just a bit, as if he worried the question itself could taint his answer. "For the last time, love. I cannot die."

She rolled her eyes. "You were trapped in Verloren for thousands of years. Aren't you afraid that Velos could capture you again, as they captured Perchta?"

His expression darkened until it all but smoldered. "Once I free Perchta, Velos will never claim us again." The words were tinged with his usual arrogance. That wicked twist to his mouth. Then, from nowhere—"I thought I told you to wear the cloak tonight."

She shrugged. "It gets too warm by the fire. Besides, you never cared how I dressed before, other than that ridiculous leather armor at the wedding. Why should you start now?"

Ignoring her, the Erlking waved at her nearest attendant—Fricz. "Bring the queen her cloak." He stood and took Serilda's hand, tugging her to her feet. "Where we are going, she might be cold."

Fricz ran off, leaving Serilda to frown at her husband. She thought of the howls she had heard, the whispers, the beckoning of her father's voice. "I don't *want* to see the gates."

"Liar," he said with a wink. "Just think what a great story it shall make."

Serilda's anger simmered. Largely because—*damn him*—he was right.

She squared her shoulders. "Fine. But if I see any opportunity to shove you into a pit you can't crawl out of, believe me, I will be taking it."

Chapter Thirty-Five

She expected a small contingency. Herself and the Erlking. Perhaps a few hunters, maybe even Manfred or Agathe.

She did not expect the entire bloody court to be joining them on this ill-advised excursion, but as they began making their way through the winding castle halls, it struck her that every single demon and ghost who had come with them from Adalheid was following along, filling the corridors in their wake. Manfred, yes, and also the stable boy, the cooks, the chamber maids, the gardeners, the carpenters. The children huddled close behind her, and she could tell from their confused expressions they had no idea what was happening.

Fricz was waiting for them in the lunar rotunda. The Erlking took the red cloak and draped it around Serilda as solemnly as one might bestow a crown.

"I'm having second thoughts," she said. "You go on ahead. The children and I will wait up here."

His only response was an aggravating smirk before he led her toward the cavernous opening, stepping over the dead vines that littered the tile as if they were nothing more than a child's playset left strewn about the floor. Without hesitation, he took a torch off the wall and disappeared into the shadows.

The moment he was out of view, Serilda gathered the children to her and started inching them back toward the corridor—but a sharp point jabbed into her side.

She froze.

A hunter leered at her. She gave her knife a twirl, then cocked her head toward the opening. "After you . . . Your *Luminance*."

"What's going on?" whispered Anna.

Serilda shook her head. "Nothing. His Grim is just . . . showing off again. You know how he does."

She approached the landing until she could see the flicker of the king's torch gleaming across a steep, narrow staircase. Brambles covered the walls and ceiling, but there was space to walk on the stone steps.

Pulling the cloak around her, she forced herself forward. She did not look back, but she could hear the children and the dark ones and the ghosts following behind her. Many brought torches of their own, and soon the stairwell was lit as well as any tunnel to the land of death could be.

Ahead of her, the staircase curved sharply and the Erlking disappeared from view. Serilda swallowed, tempted to reach for the wall to keep her balance on the uneven steps, but the threatening thorns kept her hands gripping the fur inside her cloak instead. The air grew cold, until she could see her own breath in front of her. There was dampness down here. Rivulets of water dripping down the walls, gathering on the branches, puddling on the steps.

And again—she heard the whispers. Voices rising up from the depths of the earth, blending into an indiscernible choir.

Until a new sound cut through them all. A howl.

Velos.

The god of death, who could transform into the great black wolf.

Serilda turned back so suddenly that Hans crashed into her. She barely caught his shoulders in time to steady him before he could grab one of the thorny branches.

The dark ones crowded into the staircase. Those nearest her glared and shouted for her to keep moving, but she ignored them.

She saw it now. The occasional glint of gold on their belts or hidden beneath their cloaks.

They were going hunting tonight, after all.

But if this was about trying to capture Velos, what did the Erlking want with her and the ghosts?

"Go on," said the hunter from before, flashing the hilt of her dagger. "Stop stalling."

Serilda peered down at the children, studying each of their beloved faces. "Whatever happens, you stay close to me."

She started her descent again. The stairs seemed never-ending and she could no longer see the glow of the Erlking's torch.

The whispers returned, growing louder, while her steps grew more hesitant, more hushed.

Beneath the knotted vines, the walls turned from stone to hard-packed dirt.

She was so cold. She could no longer feel her toes or fingertips and wished she did not have to feel grateful that the king had sent for the cloak.

Finally, she saw a glimmer ahead, illuminating the base of the steps.

She held her breath as she passed through an arch of brambles, thick as tree trunks, into a vast chamber. It was bigger even than the great hall above. Octagonal in shape, cavelike, with walls made of dirt and stone and clay and a ceiling that rose far overhead.

In the center of the room the Erlking stood near a flat stone altar, on top of which rested a wooden box.

A box she recognized.

As the dark ones poured in around her, sticking their torches into iron brackets on the walls, Serilda stared at the coffin where last she had seen her body. A wooden lid had been cut to fit the top, but she knew, she *knew*, her body was still inside.

So, this was where he had hidden it. In the very last place she would ever have dared to venture.

Serilda barely felt the slippery press of the children's hands grabbing her arms and hands. Trying to wet her parched lips, she tore her gaze from the coffin and looked past the altar. On the far side of the chamber, enormous glossy black monoliths had been toppled over into the dust, all pointing to where the roots from the alder tree climbed down the dirt walls, forming the foundations of the castle above.

Between two of the massive roots was an opening.

There, the roots were blackened and twisted with dead twigs and brambles like those climbing up the steps.

An abyss lay beyond that opening. Pitch-black nothingness at first, but the more Serilda stared, the more her eyes detected faint lights shimmering deep, deep in the darkness, pale blue and lavender fireflies shifting in and out of a thick fog. An entire ocean of shining black reflecting the constellations of a midnight sky.

Verloren.

Serilda felt a tension building up inside her. The sight beckoned her and repelled her at the same time.

She heard them again. Climbing up from those hallowed depths.

Whispers.

More distinct now.

Serilda . . .

Tears gathered in her eyes. She tried to nudge the children away. Back toward the stairs—

The Erlking noticed and cocked his head at her. "Don't be hasty, my queen. You've only just arrived."

"W-we shouldn't be here," said Serilda, not ashamed at the crack in her voice. "It's not . . . it isn't n-natural for the living to be so . . . so close to this place."

He barked a laugh and swept an arm around the room. "Who among us is living?"

Her gut tightened.

She was living, she wanted to say. She was not dead yet. Cursed—but not dead.

Before she could form a response, though, the voice called to her again.

Serilda . . . my sweet daughter . . .

Her lower lip trembled. She could not help taking half a step toward the gate before she felt Nickel's hand on her wrist, and the slickness of this cool, ghostly flesh made her wince. She shook him off before she realized she'd done it, and glanced back in time to see his hurt expression.

Regret coursed through her.

Get away . . . , urged the voice. *Run while you can . . .*

"Papa?" she squeaked, as the first tear slipped past her lashes.

"No," murmured Hans. "It isn't your father. It's . . . I hear my granddad."

Serilda stilled. "What?"

"He passed when I was eight," he said, so quietly. "But he's calling to me now." His eyes were on the gate, his expression part fear, but more longing.

"Telling you to run?" Serilda breathed.

Surprise shot through Hans's expression and he shook his head. "Telling me to come with him."

Serilda . . .

Serilda looked at the Erlking, who seemed to be watching her. Waiting for . . . something.

Swallowing, she walked past him, past the coffin, until she was close enough to see beyond the edges of the gates, into the mist that lay beyond.

In the distance, as if she were barely making out a moonlit reflection in a pool of ink, she could see a white bridge stretching out across—well, she wasn't sure. A ravine. A river. Golden candlelight illuminated the bridge's stark white stones. The mist gathered thick at its far end, obscuring what lay beyond.

Then—a single light. Moving closer. Swaying gently back and forth.

Hope leaped inside her, bright as a matchstick unexpectedly struck.

"Papa," she whispered, before she could stop herself. She took another step forward, but then a hand was on her elbow, holding her back. She shuddered and ripped her arm away from the Erlking's grip, her eyes locked on the swaying lantern, the figure emerging from the mist.

Crossing the bridge, step by unhurried step.

Tall. Slender. Wearing an emerald cloak trimmed in shaggy black fur.

Not her father.

And then she remembered what they were doing here.

"No!" she screamed, the sound ripping from her throat before she knew what she was thinking. "Run! Velos! He means to—"

Hands grabbed her, a palm pressing against her mouth, muffling her cries. She writhed, trying to pull away from the hand silencing her but, even more, from the smothering feeling of death and wrongness.

"I am sorry," whispered a broken voice.

Serilda stopped struggling. Tears were dripping down both cheeks now, her limbs tensed from revulsion.

She craned her neck to see Manfred peering down at her, his expression tormented.

With that look, Serilda felt the fight draining out of her. She couldn't fight Manfred. She didn't want to. He was not her enemy.

With a quiet sob, she turned her attention back to the gates.

Manfred hesitantly let his hand fall from her mouth, but he did not release her.

Velos had reached their side of the bridge. Serilda could not make out their face yet as they drifted up the steps. There was a subtle grace to their movements. A mesmerizing rhythm.

She had seen Velos once before, when she had drunk the death potion prepared by Madam Sauer. It had put her into a deathlike state during the night of the Awakening Moon. For a time, she had forgotten to take hold of the ash branch that would keep her spirit tethered to the earth until Madam Sauer could revive her. She had begun to drift away. She had seen Velos and their lamp, waiting for her. Beckoning to her. Prepared to walk with her soul into Verloren.

She had not been afraid then, and she wasn't afraid now. Not of this god.

She was afraid only of what the Erlking planned to do.

Velos stepped through the gate and peered serenely into the face of the Erlking.

With the lantern hanging from their elbow, the god reached up with their other hand and pulled back the hood of their cloak, letting it settle over their shoulders. Serilda stared, breathless, taking in the features that were somehow both youthful and ancient. The god had white skin that shimmered like pearls, a delicate nose and mouth, and short black hair that curled softly around their ears. Their expression held no cruelty, but neither did it hold much kindness.

Run, she pleaded silently, hoping the god might look at her and understand. But the god of death had eyes only for the Erlking. Not frightened. Not even wary. More . . . curious.

Slowly, the Erlking spread out his hands, revealing open palms. "The Mourning Moon greets you, Velos. I hoped we might conduct a peaceful discussion."

Velos tilted up their chin and Serilda noted the first touch of emotion on their sharp features. Not arrogance. Not amusement.

Resignation?

"I know what it is you have come to seek," said Velos, revealing sharp canine teeth. Their words were measured and thoughtful. "As you know, the price is too high, and you will not be willing to pay it."

"To the contrary," said the Erlking, whose own calm voice carried a roughened edge, "I am prepared to pay any price you ask."

Velos listed their head to one side. They did not smile. They did not laugh. They said, simply, as if it were obvious, "Then I would ask for *you*, in trade."

The arms around Serilda tensed. Her own gut spasmed.

The Erlking in trade for what? For—

No. Not what. For *whom*.

He was asking for the return of Perchta.

Chapter Thirty-Six

This wasn't supposed to happen now, tonight. Serilda had until the Endless Moon, which was still two months away. The Erlking could not demand a wish.

Though Serilda supposed he wasn't making a wish. He was making a request. Asking for a trade.

And what trade would the god of death accept?

Only the Alder King himself.

The Erlking smiled, just slightly. "I think not."

"Then there will be no bargain struck tonight." Velos bent their head, almost in deference or perhaps a mutual respect. Serilda knew that the dark ones held great animosity toward this god, who had once been their lord and master. But if Velos harbored any of that same hatred, she could not see it on their face. "I have much work to do beneath this moon," they went on. "You have my gratitude for reopening the gate, which makes my path into the mortal realm less treacherous. Please excuse me, for there are souls who wish to see their loved ones again." Their eyes slipped toward Serilda, locking onto hers for the first time.

She froze, feeling both lost and found inside that peaceful gaze. A gaze that held worlds and eternities.

"Including," Velos went on, "some who are here tonight."

The Erlking let out an annoyed huff. "I did not reopen the gate so my castle might serve as your toll road into the mortal realm. I am here to conduct business with you."

Ignoring the Erlking, Velos reached their hand toward the staircase and beckoned toward the shadows.

With a snarl turning up one lip, the Erlking stepped closer. "Do not think to bring those pathetic souls into my court. I have plenty of my own."

A figure shifted at the base of the steps, appearing on the near side of the bridge and drifting upward. Their body little more than a wisp of fog, but becoming corporeal as they moved closer to the gate.

Serilda's eyes narrowed. There was something familiar in the way the figure walked. Something in the way they carried their shoulders.

"Unless you want me to keep them all," the king growled, "I suggest you send them back."

The figure on the steps glanced up.

"Papa!" Serilda cried.

Manfred's arms tensed around her. Then, to her surprise, he let go. Serilda did not question if her freedom came from the ghost or the king. As soon as the arms fell away, she ran forward. Her father stepped through the gate. His soul solidified. He was whole. Not a nachzehrer. Not a corpse, his head cut off to stop his depraved hunger.

His eyes met hers.

A part of her worried she would rush right through him and find herself tumbling headfirst down the steps. But no—she reached for her father and threw her arms around him, and he was solid, he was real, he was—

Not alive. Of course not alive.

But not exactly a ghost either. He was more like her. A spirit. A soul, untethered by a mortal body.

He embraced her tight, squeezing her in arms made strong by years of working the heavy wheels at the mill.

"Papa," she said, sobbing into his shoulder. "I thought I'd never see you again." They were the only words she could get out before sobs took her over. She was crying too hard to hear his response, but he brushed her hair and held her close, and that was enough.

Then, all around her, a series of gasps and cries. Fear darted through Serilda and she released her father, spinning back toward the children.

But their cries had not been fear at all. Their eyes were shining with astonishment, with unparalleled joy. Little Gerdrut let out a squeal and lurched forward, passing Serilda in a delighted blur.

Serilda's father had not come alone. Gerdrut's grandmother was there, the same she had seen in her dream. And Hans's grandparents. And the twins' great-aunt and Anna's favorite cousin. And more, so many more. Spirits and souls gathered among the ghosts. The chamber became a cacophony of tears, laughter, disbelief. Everywhere Serilda looked she saw weeping and kissing and incredulous smiles.

Then, out from the gates, emerged two figures dressed in regal finery. A man and a woman, each with a slender crown atop their head. The man had a short beard and blond hair that fell to his shoulders. The woman—thick reddish waves and a spattering of freckles on her pale skin.

Serilda's breath left her. She knew those crowns. She recognized the man's doublet. She knew the woman's smile, warm and disarming and a tiny bit mischievous. It was Gild's smile.

The king of Adalheid swept straight up to Manfred, embracing him like an old friend. The queen made her way among the crowd, tears shimmering on her cheeks as she greeted the members of her court. She took every offered hand, kissed every cheek, opened her arms to every noble and servant as if they were equals. In death, perhaps they were.

The ghosts at first seemed baffled by the appearance of these two monarchs. They did not recognize the king and queen. They still did not remember them.

But their hesitation was short-lived, because the king and queen clearly knew *them*. Loved and respected them, even. It was not difficult to accept these grinning nobles as their true sovereigns, especially after centuries of serving the dark ones.

Pain spiked in Serilda's chest. Oh, how she wished Gild were here.

Meanwhile, the dark ones looked on, tapping their long fingers against their weapons and glowering impatiently.

Serilda scanned the thickening crowd of souls and realized that something strange was happening to those still crossing the bridge. Many of the spirits vanished the moment they passed through the arch of the gate, rather than entering the chamber beneath Gravenstone Castle. Were they being sent elsewhere, she wondered—to wherever their loved ones waited for them, weeping at graveyards or bent over candlelit offerings?

She turned back to Papa. "What about Mother? Is she with you?"

Her father's expression fell. "She is—" He hesitated, his voice catching. "I do not know. I have never seen her in Verloren. I do not believe she is . . . I don't think she's there."

Serilda blinked slowly.

Not in Verloren?

What did that mean? Was she still alive?

It was, somehow, both Serilda's greatest hope and deepest fear. That her mother was still out there somewhere. That she had not perished the night she'd been taken by the hunt. That Serilda might still have a chance of finding her.

And yet, that would mean the most hurtful truth of all. Her mother had left her and never come back. Not because she was forced to, but because she had wanted to.

Serilda shoved the feeling down deep inside. She made herself smile as she cupped her father's face. "It's all right. You're here. That's all that matters."

"For now," he said, embracing her again. "Even to have just one moment. To say goodbye. After all that happened . . ."

Serilda squeezed his shoulders, but even as she tried to make space in her heart for this unexpected gift—this precious moment with the man who had been everything to her for so long—her gaze snagged on Velos not far away. The god was turning back toward the gate, their cloak sweeping across the dusty floor.

"We are not finished!" said the Erlking, his voice sharp as a sword.

Velos paused, but appeared unbothered by the king's anger. "Are we not?"

The Erlking swept his arm around the chamber. "As you so value your beloved human souls, I shall give you the ghosts within this chamber."

Serilda stilled.

Every being in the room—dark ones and ghosts alike—went still.

Serilda extracted herself from her father's hold, unable to believe she'd heard correctly. The Erlking would give up his claim on all these souls? He would grant their freedom? An escape from the control of the dark ones?

On the Mourning Moon, just as he had promised Agathe.

"All," added the Erlking, his sharp gaze landing on Serilda, then dropping to the five children around her, all huddled together with their loved ones, "except for those five."

He might as well have driven a sword straight through her.

"No," said Serilda. "Please."

The king looked back to Velos.

Trembling, Serilda reached over and took hold of Gerdrut's hand, giving it a tight squeeze. The unfairness of it all was crushing. To know that he would trade every ghost he'd collected, every spirit imprisoned in Adalheid . . . all but the five she cared for most. All but the children. Only so he may still hold this power over *her*.

The god had not spoken, but Serilda could tell they were considering the offer. Surely, the god of death would see this as a great victory. To finally claim hundreds of souls who had been kept from their final rest.

But, in exchange, they would need to release Perchta.

The god's eyes sharpened. "I would have the children, too."

"No," said the Erlking. "I have other plans for them."

Velos shook their head. "Then I refuse your offer. It is not enough to release that plague back on the world."

The Erlking scowled. "Then name your price."

"I already have," said Velos. "There is nothing else you have to offer that I would trade for the huntress. Farewell, Erlkönig."

They began to turn away again, when the king's voice rang out, "I shall give you my court."

Sharp breaths echoed throughout the chamber.

The god hesitated. "Your court?"

The Erlking lifted his chin. "Every dark one that followed me down from Gravenstone."

Serilda sucked in a breath and glanced around. The dark ones were perpetually cast in a vague halo of arrogance and selfishness. But now they seemed uncertain, even rattled. Their eyes narrowed as their hands stealthily reached for blades and axes and bows.

Had the Erlking planned this all along? Had any of them suspected it? Would he really be so callous as to trade all of them for Perchta alone?

"The ghosts," said Velos, "and the dark ones?"

"That is my offer."

"Including your hunters."

"Yes."

The Erlking ignored those gathered at his side, so he could not have seen their hostile faces. Would they go peacefully if he ordered it? Or would they rebel against the king they had followed for centuries?

After an eternity of silence, Erlkönig asked, "Do we have a deal?"

Serilda's gut lurched. The whole court, gone. The hunters. The dark ones—who had haunted the roads, the villages, the Aschen Wood, for as long as fairy tales had been told. They would be gone. Forever.

Though she wanted to rage at the Erlking for holding back the children, she told herself that this was a victory. More than she ever could have thought possible coming into the Mourning Moon, when she had only flimsy hopes of freeing the gryphon and the unicorn.

So why did she feel more tense with every passing moment? Certain that the Alder King would never give this up so easily. Not for the huntress. Not without a fight.

Had she been wrong about the Erlking's plans to capture all seven gods? Or was this a trap?

"It is not so simple, Erlkönig," said Velos, sounding genuinely disappointed. "You must speak a true name to return a spirit from Verloren if you wish for them to be given permanence in the mortal realm."

"I am prepared to do so," said the Erlking. His voice became cutting. "Do we have a deal?"

Another hesitation.

"We do," said Velos with a solemn voice.

As soon as they agreed, furious cries echoed through the chamber. Serilda glanced around, awestruck, as the gold chains hanging from the hip of every hunter started to writhe and squirm. Like snakes, the bindings slithered around the dark ones, shackling their wrists, one by one. Tethering the demons to one another by a series of unbreakable chains.

The dark ones struggled against the bindings, but the Erlking ignored their outrage.

What could they do?

They were magical creatures.

This was god-spun gold.

How long had the Erlking been planning this? Had his talk of hunting beasts and needing more chains been to trick his own hunters? Is *this* what he had wanted the gold for—to ensure his own court could not run when he chose to hand them over to the god of death?

The betrayal seemed particularly ruthless, even for him.

The demons struggled. They wailed and screamed. They pulled on the chains. They did everything they could to escape this cruel fate.

But the Erlking had bargained them away, as if they had meant nothing to him. And when the chains snapped taut and forced them down the long set of stairs toward Verloren, the dark ones had no choice but to go.

Their horrendous shrieks echoed through the chamber long after they had disappeared on the other side of the gates.

Velos ignored their cries, nodding expressionlessly at the king. "Now the mortal spirits."

"First, you will summon Perchta."

Velos inclined their head. "Speak her true name and it shall be done."

The Erlking pulled himself to his full imposing height, his gray-blue eyes flashing.

His voice was quicksilver. He spoke so quietly that Serilda barely heard him. "I call to you, my Alder Queen. Harbinger of the Wild Hunt. Lady of the Final Feast. Mistress of the Embertide. Perchta Pergana Zamperi. Return to me, my love."

The lamp in Velos's grip flickered, then brightened to an unnatural bluish tinge. Then it extinguished entirely, plunging the tomb into darkness. Serilda gasped, clutching her father's arm on one side and Gerdrut's hand on the other, worried that either of them might disappear like morning mist.

The lamp flickered again, steadily returning to its warm glow, and with it the torches held by the ancient iron brackets along the walls.

The parade of souls had long vanished from the bridge below, traveling to wherever their loved ones awaited them. But now, a new figure emerged from the fog.

Serilda's lips parted. With an instinctual terror, but also wonder.

The woman from the tapestries. The woman from countless stories, countless nightmares.

Perchta, the great huntress, stepped through the gates.

Chapter Thirty-Seven

The huntress stood in their midst, a sickle of a smile on crimson lips. She wore bindings on her arms, shackles not unlike those that had appeared on the wrists of the gathered demons, though iron instead of gold.

"My star," she cooed to the Erlking. "Whatever took you so long?"

He did not return her smile, exactly, but there was something beginning to smolder in his usually frost-filled gaze. "It has been but three hundred years," he said calmly. "Barely a blink."

"I beg to differ," said Perchta. "But then, I was the one trapped, drowning in that vile river for all this time."

The Erlking's gaze shifted toward the god. "Release her bindings."

Velos inclined their head. "After you."

The king's jaw tensed. A moment passed, the air sparking with tension.

Finally, he cast a long, calculating look around the room, his gaze alighting on all the gathered ghosts, so many gripping the hands of loved ones and ancestors, newly returned for the Mourning Moon. Expressions full of a hope so intense it made Serilda ache.

A movement caught her eye and she glanced past the king, sure that in that moment she'd seen a shifting shadow, a shadowy figure moving along the walls. But now she saw only the gathered specters. The dim light playing tricks on her eyes.

With much theatricality, the king reached into his quiver and pulled out an arrow, tipped in gold. Exactly like those he had used to tether Serilda's and Gild's souls to the dark side of the veil. He held it out in the palm of his hand.

All around Serilda, a web of near-translucent threads appeared, silver black and strung in every direction. Each one reaching into the chest of every ghost gathered in the chamber. From Manfred to the stable boy, every scullery maid and gardener and seamstress. The blacksmith, the carpenters, the pages, the cooks.

And five strings connecting Serilda's own beloved attendants.

Hans, her serious and protective footman.

Nickel, her kind and attentive groom.

Fricz, her silly and stubborn messenger.

Anna, her bright and enthusiastic lady-in-waiting.

And Gerdrut, her earnest and imaginative chambermaid.

All connected with shimmering threads as delicate as spider webbing, each one attached to the king's arrow.

All but one, Serilda realized. Agathe, the weapons master, who had betrayed Serilda and Gild in trade for this very bargain.

She was nowhere to be seen.

"*I dissolve the binds that tether you…*" he said, his words echoing through the chamber. "*I release you from your servitude. I am no longer the keeper of your souls, but give you to Velos, god of death, so you might have eternal peace.*"

Those darkly glistening threads began to disintegrate. Starting at the shaft of the arrow and continuing outward along every strand, they crumbled away, fading into the air. Only the five strings reserved for the children remained, solid and tethered to the arrow's shaft.

Serilda followed one of the threads to Manfred and watched as the chisel that had been lodged in his eye socket for three hundred years evaporated into nothing. The gaping wound in his eye healed. The blood, the gore, gone—as if it had never happened.

And with that, the always-stoic Manfred began to cry.

He was not alone. All around, wounds were healing. Blood and bruises vanishing.

"My children," said Velos, with a new lightness in their tone. "You are free. Beneath the Mourning Moon, you may return to visit your families and descendants. As the sun rises, I shall guide you to Verloren, where you shall be granted peace."

With these words, the souls of the dead began to fade away. Not only the long-imprisoned court of Adalheid, but also those who had come to greet them. The grandparents, the cousins . . . the king and queen.

Serilda wanted to call out to them. Wanted to tell them about their son. She wanted to ask if *they* remembered him, when no one else did.

But she did not have time. As the final strands connecting each of them to the cursed arrow vanished, so too did the ghosts. One by one, each spirit fading away.

Mist on the fields, struck by sunlight.

"Serilda . . ."

Sniffing, she looked at her father, and his expression twisted her insides.

"No," she whispered. "Don't leave. Please . . ."

"I do not belong here," he murmured, glancing around at the underground chamber. "And neither do you." He cupped her face in his hands. "Be brave, my girl. I know you will be. You were always braver than I was."

"Papa . . ." She wrapped her arms around him, squeezing tight. "I'm sorry. I'm so sorry for everything. My stupid lies. Bringing the hunt to our door. What happened to you—"

"Hush. It's all right." He smoothed a hand along the back of her head. "You were always my greatest joy, you and that wild imagination of yours. So much like your mother." He sighed, and there was a deep sadness beneath it. "I would not change you for all the time in the world."

"I don't want to say goodbye. I don't want you to go."

He kissed her head. "It's not for forever. Be careful, my girl. Please. Be careful."

"I love you," she said, sobbing, pulling away to meet his eyes. "I love you."

He smiled and rubbed the tears from her cheeks.

And then he was gone.

Serilda sagged, wrapping her arms around herself like a shield. She felt carved out, as if a nachtkrapp had eaten her heart. She knew that seeing her father again was a gift, but it also opened up a wound that had barely begun to heal.

"Don't tell me *that* is the mortal girl you've dubbed the Alder Queen."

Her head snapped up. Through her blurry vision, she spied Perchta watching her with stony eyes. She had often felt that being caught in the gaze of the Erlking was a bit like being touched by an icy wind. But to be caught beneath Perchta's gaze was more like being plunged into an ice-covered lake.

"Such sentimentality is hardly befitting the queen of Gravenstone," came Perchta's biting voice.

Serilda stilled. She felt too numb to care for the insult, but not numb enough to ignore the threat in the huntress's vulture smile.

She shuddered. Suddenly the room felt too empty, too quiet. The hunters and dark ones, gone. The ghosts and visiting spirits, gone. Her father, gone. Leaving behind Serilda and the huntress, the Erlking and the god of death, and the ghosts of five children she still had not managed to save.

She did not want to cower before this demon huntress, but her sorrow had dimmed the embers she could usually feel glowing inside of her. She was not afraid of this woman. She was *terrified* of her. And she felt drained of courage, of stubbornness, of wit, of anything that might have allowed her to stand tall and face the huntress with dignity. She could only hold out her hands to the children, urging them to stay close to her, as if she could protect them now, when she never could before.

Perchta flashed her a knowing, cruel look that made the hair stand on the back of Serilda's neck. "Pathetic."

"It is done," said the Erlking. "Release the huntress."

Velos's expression darkened, but in the next moment, the shackles on

Perchta's wrists snapped open. They clanked to the floor and vanished in a curl of black smoke.

Perchta did not look down at her freed hands, but kept her stare fixed on Serilda, lips curving higher. Then, without glancing at her paramour, she reached her hand out and grabbed the front of the Erlking's tunic. She dug her sharp nails into the folds of the cloth and pulled him toward her. Her head turned in the last moment, capturing his mouth with hers.

Her eyes closed, her other hand burying itself into his long hair. The king wrapped an arm around her waist, deepening the kiss.

The kiss was passion and possession and even perhaps a tinge of revenge. Serilda did not know what to make of it, but she felt heat flooding her cheeks. She couldn't shake the feeling that part of the kiss was meant to be a warning, but for whom? Her? The Erlking? He had been so sure there could be no envy from Perchta, but she wondered whether he'd misjudged.

Perchta broke the kiss as quickly as she had started it. "Did you miss me?" she purred.

"As the moon longs for the sun," responded the Erlking.

"Vile," muttered Fricz.

The Erlking pulled away from Perchta, his gaze intensifying. "Welcome home."

"Yes," said Velos, an oddly victorious smile on their face. "Enjoy your hours in the mortal realm, Perchta Pergana Zamperi. For I shall be welcoming you back to join your brethren as dawn breaks upon the Mourning Moon."

The Erlking lifted an eyebrow, his knuckles tightening on Perchta's hip. "That was not our bargain. You have what I promised, and I shall keep what was promised me."

"I have freed the huntress, as requested." Velos lifted their swaying lantern. "But without a proper vessel, no spirit can be sustained within the mortal realm. She will be forced to return to Verloren at sunrise."

Serilda expected the king to snarl, to curse . . . but not to smirk.

And then, to laugh.

"Do you think me a fool? But of course I have a proper vessel."

He lifted his heel against the lid of the wooden coffin and shoved. It slid off and crashed onto its side, revealing Serilda's body within.

A shudder passed through Serilda at the sight. When she had seen her body before in the carriage house, it had been wearing the same drab, mud-speckled dress and boots that she had worn when she arrived at Adalheid Castle. But now her body wore a flaxen shirt—loose around her swelling stomach, the laces open at the throat. Riding breeches and black leather gloves, fine boots that rose over her calves, and a ruby-red cloak identical to the one Serilda wore spread around the body, more reminiscent of blood than velvet. Rather than her hair being kept in two disheveled braids, it was let loose to fall in waves around her shoulders. Her face had been washed of dirt, her lips and eyelids anointed with oil that made them glisten in the torchlight.

She almost didn't recognize herself. This was not some miller's daughter. This was a huntress, a warrior . . . a mother, round and glowing with the life inside her.

"I've gone through some bit of trouble to procure it," said the Erlking, "but I suspect it will do nicely."

Velos's expression twisted, but they said nothing as Perchta sauntered to the coffin and peered down at Serilda's figure. She trailed a finger up the body's shin and thigh, then slowly, slowly, over the protruding stomach. Though Serilda could feel nothing, she shivered, imagining the intimacy of the touch. Then Perchta's gaze shifted up to the Erlking.

"She is weak," she said, her voice biting.

Serilda let out an annoyed huff, which went ignored by everyone.

"In appearance, yes," responded the king. "But her strength of will has proven to be remarkably resilient." His lips turned upward with a hint of pride. "A trait I have no doubt will be passed on to our child."

Perchta swirled her finger in a full circle around the pregnant belly. "The baby *is* a thoughtful touch. A newborn . . . mine to keep."

"Carried by you," said the Erlking. "Birthed by you."

Serilda stood straighter. "No. That's *my* child!"

She took a step forward, but the moment Perchta met her gaze with such icy derision, Serilda felt her feet freeze to the stone floor. Her breath snagged.

"That's my body," she said, her voice trembling this time. "My child. Please. Don't do this."

With her gaze lingering on Serilda, Perchta stepped closer to the coffin and threaded her long fingernails into the body's hair. "I hardly would have recognized you." She let the hair slide from her grasp as she trailed her hand over the figure's shoulder and down her arm.

Serilda watched, gripped by an unspeakable fear, as Perchta's fingers danced down to the wrist where the gold-tipped arrow jutted up.

"Wh-what are you doing?" Serilda whispered.

The huntress smirked. "Accepting a most considerate gift."

"Stop," said Velos, a growl in their throat. "She is not willing. Therefore, the vessel is tainted. The spell will not work." They tightened their hand into a fist. "You have lost, Erlkönig. I am taking my prize with me, and I shall see the huntress at dawn."

"I do not recall you being so impatient, Velos," said the Erlking. "Are you so sure the spirit is unwilling?"

Velos held up the lantern, casting its light over Serilda. "You heard her as well as I. This human wants her body back, and her child. What reason would she have to agree to this?"

"What reason, indeed." The Erlking fixed Serilda with a knowing look. "I asked you once what you would sacrifice to see these children freed. It is time, miller's daughter, for you to make that choice."

Chapter Thirty-Eight

His words felt distant. Impossible. What he was asking of her . . . to *give* her body to Perchta, and with it, her unborn child? To allow the huntress's spirit to inhabit Serilda's physical form? For how long? *Forever?*

"Don't do it," Hans whispered beside her. "Serilda, you can't."

She shivered.

"What—" she started, then paused to wet her dry tongue. "What will happen to me?"

"Does it matter?" asked the Erlking. He swooped his long fingers toward the children. "They will be free, just as you wished. Velos can claim them right now. It is early enough on the Mourning Moon, they might even still have time to visit their families beyond the veil before they are called to Verloren. Is this not what you've wanted all along?"

It was what she'd sworn from the beginning. She would find a way to free these souls, no matter what.

But at this cost? Her own body, her own baby . . .

Could she live with this choice, knowing that she was responsible for allowing the huntress back into the mortal realm?

Her gaze dropped to the children, taking them in one by one.

Could she live with herself if she didn't do this?

Nickel gave a shake to his head. "Hans is right. You can't."

"I have to," she whispered, her lip quivering. She fell to her knees and held her arms to them. Her cheeks were wet, but she didn't know for how long she'd been crying.

"Serilda, no," said Anna, even as she fell into her embrace. They all did, excepting Hans, who stood a few steps off with a frown chiseled across his features.

"This is wrong," he said, emotion choking his words. "He's not supposed to win."

"He's not winning," said Serilda. "This is what I want. I couldn't protect you before. I have to do this now."

"Will we ever see you again?" murmured Gerdrut, pressed tight against Serilda's side.

"Yes," she said, not knowing if it was a lie. "Of course you will."

Perchta laughed, the sound like a wild creature. "We are standing at the gates to Verloren. I trust she will be following right behind you."

Serilda shuddered. Was that it, then? She would give her body to the huntress, and her spirit would just . . . fade away? Be guided off to Verloren, like her father and the ghosts?

She would never see her child, never look into their beautiful, precious face.

And Gild . . .

She would never see him again. Never tell him the truth. About their child. About her feelings for him.

Much as it would destroy her, there was no choice here, just as the Erlking had known there wouldn't be. The Erlking would never offer this again. She had to do it now.

"All right," she breathed.

"No," said Velos, the word barely a grunt. But they had struck their own bargains, and now it was time for Serilda to strike hers.

She met the Erlking's piercing gaze. "Free them, and I will do what you need me to do."

"Merely a word," said the Erlking, picking up the arrow with its five remaining threads. "Say that you give your body willingly as a vessel for Perchta's spirit, and our deal is made."

She took in the children. Cupped each face. Kissed every brow. She stood, and though Hans's jaw remained tight, he did not fight against her as she embraced him and pressed her cheek to the top of his head. "You won't be alone in Verloren," she whispered, "but I'll expect you to take care of them anyway."

He squeezed his eyes shut and sobbed. "We never blamed you," he said.

She swallowed around the lump in her throat. "I am so proud of you." She reached for the others. "So proud of each of you. I love you all very much. Be strong now."

She braced herself and stood tall again, even as her voice trembled. "I accept your offer. You may use my body as a vessel, in exchange for their freedom."

"Done," said the Erlking quickly, as if worried she would change her mind. Grinning, he spoke the undoing of the curse again.

I dissolve the binds that tether you . . .

As the threads began to dissolve, Serilda looked at the children. They stared back at her, uncertain. Afraid. Hopeful. As each fading strand reached the hollow places of their chests, they began to change. Like being washed clean, the blood disappeared from their tunics and dresses. Their ghastly wounds, healed.

"Serilda," said Nickel, "we'll miss you." He snuggled in close, and the others followed, burying their faces into her neck and settling their heads on her shoulders. Already, they felt solid again. Warm and soft and exactly like the children she had so adored.

"Don't forget us," whispered Gerdrut, pressing something small and cool into Serilda's palm.

"Of course not. Never." She sobbed and held them tight, pressing her lips into fluffy hair and ringlets and braids and—

Nothing.

Her arms closed on empty air. A void. A chill against her skin, where five of her greatest loves had been.

Serilda let out a cry, their sudden absence striking her like a dagger through her heart.

Not trusting the Erlking, she peered instead at Velos. "Are they . . . safe?"

Though the god wore a dismal expression, they nodded. "Erlkönig has released his claim. They are mine now."

She wilted at his words. In that sudden, unexpected loss, there was also a swell of unspeakable happiness.

She had done it.

They were free.

Even at this moment, their spirits might be back in Märchenfeld, seeing their families once more. Come dawn, they would pass through the gate into Verloren. It was precisely what Serilda had been wishing for, fighting for.

She swiped away her tears and opened her fist. Gerdrut had given her the small golden ring. The child's match to the same one Gild had, depicting his family's royal seal.

With a loud sniff, she pressed it onto her pinkie finger.

"And now," said Perchta, "I shall claim what is mine."

Serilda's head snapped up again. Everything was happening so quickly.

"Wait. My child. Please, let me say goodbye. Let me at least—at least feel . . ." She stumbled to her feet, hand outstretched, but she was too far from the coffin and the swollen belly that harbored her unborn child.

"I have waited long enough." Perchta leaned over Serilda's body, wrapped her fist around the arrow in the wrist, just beneath the fletching, and snapped the shaft in two, before yanking the arrow cleanly from her flesh.

Serilda felt a lurch in her chest, deep in the cavernous space where her heart should have been. Followed by a pain in her wrist—

The scar had opened up. Blood dripped down her hand. She clasped her palm over the wound. In the next moment, a swoon overtook her. A dizziness that made her stumble back, barely catching herself before she collapsed. The chamber tilted to one side.

Then, a release.

She was a snowflake caught in a flurry. Seeking somewhere to land. Somewhere to belong.

Her attention fell on Velos's lantern. An eternal flame, burning bright. It was a comfort. A promise. Warmth seeped into her, and all the world became that lantern light.

She took a step forward.

"Damn you, Erlkönig," growled Velos. The god was furious, but not at her.

She took another step, drawn forward, rather than repelled by that anger.

"It was not her time, and that child does not belong to you."

The Erlking responded, without remorse. "It was never Perchta's time. You should be pleased to receive such generous compensation. Our business is done. Take your new prisoners and go."

Velos shook their head. Though their expression was tormented, they nevertheless lifted the lantern toward Serilda. A gesture of welcome.

Serilda drifted closer. Ignoring the blood dripping from her wound, she held out her hand.

"Serilda—no!"

She hesitated. That voice. She knew it. She recognized the way the light inside her chest flickered at the sound.

A figure emerged from the shadows and threw themselves at the floor beside the coffin, snatching something off the ground. His hair copper in the dim light, his eyes wide and frantic when he looked up at her, gripping the broken end of the arrow that had once cursed her.

In his other hand, a golden sword.

"Gild?" she breathed, her hand dropping slightly.

Gild was here. How?

She shook her head, trying to clear it, but she felt so tired, so depleted.

"What is he doing here?" roared the Erlking. "Who let him free?"

Gild hurtled himself off the ground and rushed toward Serilda. He grabbed her hand, ignoring the sticky blood, and wrapped her fingers tight around the arrow's shaft. The black fletching brushed her palm.

Immediately, her dazed, untethered sensation lifted. She felt more solid, more complete. Not entirely intact, but not empty and searching either. Rooted once more to the earth.

"Ash wood," said Gild, as if that explained everything. "Don't let go."

Laughter rang out, echoing off the stone walls of the chamber. The sound a little feral, a little gleeful. But also a little like Serilda herself, when she was entirely too pleased by something unexpected.

Gild planted himself in front of her, sword at the ready, even though he was shaking. She looked past him to the source of the laughter and saw ... herself. Her body. Sitting up inside the coffin. Golden wheels gleaming in her open eyes. Long hair cascading across the ruby cloak, identical to the one on her own shoulders.

"Oh my," said Perchta, looking down at her new figure and resting her free hand on top of her stomach. "This is a novel sensation."

"It's only for a couple months," said the Erlking, kneeling at her side. "Then you will have a child, as you have always wished."

Perchta beamed at him, and Serilda felt like the ground was shifting beneath her feet. To see herself, her own eyes, gazing at the Erlking like that. Her own hands reaching, cupping the sides of his face. Her own mouth pressing hungrily against his.

A hand landed on her arm, startling her. "Come on," whispered Gild. "We have to get out of here."

He yanked Serilda toward the stairs. She stumbled after him, gripping the arrow shaft, still feeling like she could dissolve into nothing but dust at the first misstep. But the arrow was solid, and Gild's hand on her elbow was real, even if he, too, was nothing more than a spirit cursed and untethered.

Untethered.

No—Gild still had a body, somewhere, with an arrow through his wrist.

He still had the scar. He still had the curse that kept him in this world, half alive.

All she had was a broken arrow. Without that, her spirit would take the first opportunity to slink away to Verloren.

She opened her fist to see the splintered wood, the black fletching, but as soon as she did, dizziness enveloped her again. She stumbled, crashing into Gild. They were nearly to the stairs. He paused to check on her, when his attention caught on something else. His eyes widened.

"If it isn't the chivalrous prince charming."

Gripping the arrow shaft, Serilda spun around.

Perchta was on her feet now, striding purposefully through the chamber, straight toward them. Did Serilda imagine how the wheels in her eyes burned molten red?

"Three hundred years, trapped in that place. Because of *you.*"

Perchta lifted the other half of the broken arrow, holding it like a dagger in her fist. Even though Gild had a sword and Serilda knew her former body was not built for physical strength, she still felt a spike of fear.

Perchta bared her teeth and lunged.

Gild raised the sword.

A shadow jumped in between them, snarling. Serilda screamed and fell back, pressing against the wall. Gild was right beside her, his jaw hanging open, as they stared at the monster in their midst.

A black wolf, as big as the grinding wheel in her father's mill. The fur on its back bristled; its massive claws scraped against the stone floor.

The Erlking let out a triumphant shout, the sound as chilling to Serilda's ear as the low, earth-rumbling growl from the enormous beast. The god was protecting them, Serilda realized. Facing off against Perchta, the great huntress.

But if Perchta should be hurt . . . what would become of Serilda's child?

"It's Velos," murmured Gild, his tone full of awe. "The great wolf who guards the gates to Verloren—"

Serilda shook her head, tears misting her vision. "He can't hurt her," she said, clutching Gild's arm. "My baby . . ."

He blinked at her, momentarily confused. Then understanding struck him, followed fast by horror. He shifted the sword in his fist, looking back as Velos leaned down, jaws snapping.

"No!" Serilda screamed.

It didn't matter. Perchta was too quick, dodging out of the creature's reach and rushing forward to grab hold of its long, shaggy coat. Even with Serilda's unfamiliar body, even with a child growing inside her, Perchta was as quick as a fox, spry as a cat. She took the arrow shaft into her teeth and pulled herself onto the wolf's back, both fists clinging to its fur.

Velos howled, trying to shake her off, but Perchta cackled, her eyes lit with inhuman delight. "I have dreamed of this many times, you ancient mutt!"

A low, crooning noise reverberated off the stone walls—the king's hunting horn. The bellow was followed by a thunder of footsteps. At first Serilda thought they were coming from the castle upstairs, but then, a swarm of figures began to emerge on the steps leading to Verloren, flooding back in through the gates.

Not ghosts. Not lost spirits.

Dark ones.

The same who had been bound and reclaimed by the god of death. The golden chains shimmered on their wrists, but their looks of betrayal had transformed into looks of victory.

"Now, my love!" yelled the Erlking.

Perchta lifted her half of the arrow. The gold tip gleamed in the torchlight. Velos jerked upward, but when she would not be thrown, the wolf began to shift. For barely a moment, Serilda could see the beastly form beginning to grow smaller, the black fur lengthening, turning back into the god's dark cloak.

But then Perchta let out a war cry and drove the arrow down into the back of the wolf's neck.

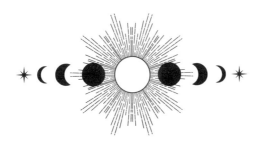

Chapter Thirty-Nine

An unworldly scream erupted from the beast's throat. A sound that shook Serilda to her core. A cry that made the earth itself tremble. The stone beneath them split—a single jagged cut snaking in from the gates of Verloren, like a bolt of lightning that shot straight across to the castle steps. Stone rattled and groaned as the earth split apart beneath them.

"Now!" yelled the Erlking. "Quickly!"

The dark ones surged forward, tearing the golden chains from their own limbs. They must have planned this. Practiced this. How they would fool the god into believing the chains had claimed them, when the Erlking never intended to uphold his side of the bargain at all.

With breathless precision, the hunters surrounded the great wolf and hefted the golden chains around its massive form. The creature bucked and struggled and snapped, but the dark ones were too numerous, and as soon as the chains were tight around its body, the fight drained away. Velos was left panting, the chains entrapping their body from throat to hind legs, rendering them helpless.

"Finally," said the Erlking, stepping forward to stare the great beast in the eye. "To conquer Eostrig was a joy, but to have the lord of death? I have waited long to have you at my feet. *Master.*" He snarled in disgust. "Did you really think I would give up my entire court? That I would sacrifice them to *you*?" He clicked his tongue. "You might be a god, but *I* am the Alder King. The dark ones are *mine*."

The Erlking lifted a hand to Perchta. She took it, as if she were a bride being helped from her wedding carriage. She slid from the wolf's back and into the Erlking's arms.

Around them, the walls groaned. The jagged crevice in the floor widened, yawning open. The gates shuddered. Motes of dust and pieces of rock fell from the trembling ceiling.

The edge of the destruction closest to the gates yawned open with a scream that burrowed into Serilda's head. She covered her ears. Even the dark ones cringed at the unholy noise, backing away as the ground tore itself apart.

The gates began to fall. Splintering wood and crumbling ash, collapsing down into the open earth. Beyond the gates, the stairway too trembled and began to fall. The bridge to Verloren—

"Come on!" Gild yelled, though Serilda could barely hear him above the chaos. He yanked her away from the destruction, through the archway. The walls shook as they ran upward. The stairs groaned, the cracks spread.

"What's happening?" Serilda cried.

"They captured Velos," Gild shouted back. "Maybe the gates were sustained by the god's magic?"

As they neared the top of the staircase, she noticed the walls were no longer trembling. The earth had stilled. But Serilda worried that it would follow them. That the gap beneath the castle would open so wide, it would swallow all of Gravenstone, taking them with it.

They had to get out.

Serilda was no longer tethered, no longer cursed. But could Gild leave? His body was in Adalheid, but with him imprisoned in the dungeons here, they had not been able to test what would happen if he stepped beyond these walls. Serilda had not dared to leave Gravenstone since their arrival, as she couldn't have taken the children with her. Besides, they were surrounded on every side by the Aschen Wood. Where would she have gone?

They reached the top of the steps and she spied the light of the Mourning Moon shining through the glass ceiling of the lunar rotunda, casting the walls in silver.

But no sooner had they run out into the rotunda than a swath of heavy cloth was thrown over them, cloaking them in darkness. Serilda screamed and shoved against the fabric, trying to find her way out of it, but it only tightened around her. "Gild!"

"Hold still!" he yelled. He drove the tip of his sword up through the fabric, then slashed downward, slicing a hole through it.

"Wait!" yelled a child's voice. "It isn't Erlkönig!"

Working his arm through the gap, Gild tore the fabric wide enough that he and Serilda could stumble free. The fabric—an enormous tapestry—pooled at their feet.

Surrounding them stood a horde of monsters. Nachtkrapp, drudes, hobgoblins. There were tiny sprites and shaggy waltschrats. Six-legged bukavac and long-nosed halgeists and an entire contingent of katzenveit, each wearing a tiny, bright-red cap. There were many monsters Serilda had no names for. Beasts with tusks and antlers, scales and wings, fur and enormous buggy eyes.

At their helm stood a human girl. A child with vivid blue eyes and curls of golden hair. Serilda would have recognized her anywhere, even though she looked so very different from the portrait inside the locket. This was no coddled princess. The girl before them was a warrior. Dressed in a mishmash of furs and scales herself, her curls pulled back and an expression of dark ferocity on her face, she reminded Serilda of the moss maidens. And like the forest folk, she, too, was heavily armed. Three blades at her hip, another on her thigh, a battle-ax clutched in her fist.

"You are not the dark ones," said the princess, with a disappointed sneer. "Where is Erlkö—" She broke off abruptly, her eyes widening. "You are the gold-spinner. And *you*." She jutted the ax blade toward Serilda. "His bride. What's happened to your hand?"

Serilda gawked at her. She'd forgotten about the wound, the blood dripping down her wrist. She was still clutching the broken arrow shaft so tightly, her fingers had gone numb.

Without waiting for Serilda's response, the girl gasped. "Give that to me!" she yelled, grabbing for Serilda's hand.

"No!" screamed Gild. "If she releases the arrow, she—" He cut off abruptly.

The princess had not taken away the arrow. Instead, she had deftly wrestled the small golden ring from Serilda's pinkie finger.

"This is mine!" she snapped, glaring at Serilda as if she were a common thief. "Where did you find it?"

"I . . . in the hall. With the tapestries. I didn't know—" Serilda's thoughts spun in every direction. "I-it's really you. Have you been here this whole time?"

A scream erupted from the staircase, followed by a distressed howl. *Velos.*

"What is *happening* down there?" said the princess. "We have been waiting to ambush the dark ones for hours! But it sounds like there's already a war, and we are missing it! Do you know how long we have been planning this? Come—everyone! Regroup!"

The monsters scrabbled for the tapestry, nearly knocking Serilda and Gild over in their rush to snatch it away. Shouts came from the stairs. Grunts and thundering footsteps.

"Resume your places!" barked the princess.

The monsters backed against the walls so they would not be visible as the dark ones emerged from below, leaving Gild and Serilda standing alone beneath the rotunda glass.

"Move!" said the princess. "They're coming! And for Hulda's sake, bandage that wound. You're bleeding all over the floor!"

Seeing that Gild was still dumbfounded and watching his sister—who, clearly, did not remember him—Serilda grabbed his elbow and dragged him against the wall, dismayed to see that she had, in fact, left a trail of blood behind her.

Mere seconds passed before the first dark ones emerged, racing to stay ahead of the collapsing chamber below.

"Now!" shouted the princess.

The monsters surged forward, as did their leader—ax swinging alongside talons and fangs.

The demons were caught unaware, and Serilda saw six of them fall within seconds, their wounds opening up to black clouds of putrid vapor. But these were immortal beings. These were hunters. And soon, they were fighting back, their numbers growing as more poured into the rotunda from the stairwell.

"They can't win," said Gild, his hands shaking as he affixed a torn strip from his shirt around Serilda's wrist, staunching the bleeding. "The dark ones will slaughter them."

Perhaps he was right, but it seemed the tenacious princess and her troop of monsters were well matched for the surprised dark ones, at least for now.

Then, in the midst of the fight, a group of dark ones emerged, pulling on golden chains. Their muscles were taut, their faces strained. The hunters gathered around to give them protection from the princess's monsters as they yanked the black wolf onto the landing.

"Great gods, what is that?" bellowed the princess. "And who . . . ?" She blinked. A dark one swung a sword at her, but the princess blocked it and cut through the dark one's arm, just above the elbow. The sword and limb fell to the ground. The dark one screamed and stumbled away, but the princess was ignoring him already, gaping at the red-cloaked woman who stood assessing the battle around her.

The princess cocked her head. She looked from Perchta to Serilda. Serilda to Perchta.

"Home, sweet home," Perchta mused. Then she reached up an arm and snatched a flying drude out of the air. In half a second she had snapped the creature's neck.

The princess screamed. "Günther!"

Her cry drew Perchta's attention. "Why, if it isn't the darling little Adalheid girl. Who would have thought you'd cause so much trouble?"

The princess backed away, bewildered.

Perchta picked up a mace that had fallen in the midst of the battle and joined the fight with revelry. She swung the weapon at anyone who came too close—taking down the flurry of monsters as fast as Serilda could take in every shaky new breath. It was a moment before Serilda realized the Erlking had emerged, too, and was standing over Velos's prone form, watching his love parry and strike, graceful as a dancer onstage.

"Hide," said Gild, pushing Serilda toward a corridor. "Get out of here!"

"What? What are you—?"

Gild ran into the fray with his sword aloft, cutting through the demons. At first, Serilda thought he was going after the huntress, and terror again seized her to think of her unborn child, so vulnerable inside the body of that vicious, bloodthirsty woman. But no, Gild was running for the princess, who had rejoined the fight. Gild drove his sword through the back of her nearest opponent and shoved the demon to the side, startling the princess, who had both her ax and a short sword raised to attack.

"You again!"

"Come with me! Quick!"

He grabbed her by the elbow and dragged her toward the alcove that Serilda had ducked into, and Serilda was certain that if the princess hadn't been so confused by everything that was happening, she would have taken off his arm as easily as she'd taken off that demon's.

"What are you doing?" asked the princess. "Hiding like cowards?"

"You cannot win this battle! They're immortal!" Gild gestured at a dark one who was even now getting back to his feet, despite the smoking hole in his chest. "And what do you think the Erlking will do when he captures you? Come on, we have to get out of here!"

He grabbed the princess by the arm and gestured for Serilda to start running. But even though he towered over the girl, as soon as he started to drag her away, she leaned back and kicked her heel right into his knee.

Gild cried out and collapsed.

"I will not leave my soldiers in the heat of battle!" she bellowed.

Gild gaped up at her, then gestured around. "Your *soldiers* are a bunch of monsters that are going to get themselves killed!"

The princess snarled. "We will drive out the intruders," she spat. "This is my castle! My plan!"

"And it's *their* lives!" he yelled back. "Look around. You've lost half of them already. How many dark ones have you killed?"

The princess drew herself up to full height with a stubborn clench to her jaw. But she did look around. The floor of the rotunda was littered with fallen beasts, big and small. And yes, there were wounded dark ones. Some with missing limbs, others hissing in pain and barely able to walk. But they would recover. They would go on fighting.

She swallowed hard, eyes suddenly shining—not with fury, but defeat. Her nostrils flared as she glowered at Perchta, who was whooping in an ecstatic frenzy as she cut down one monster after another.

"Who is that?" she breathed, glancing at Serilda. "*You* are the storyteller, the king's bride. So, who is that?"

Serilda swallowed. "Perchta, the huntress. The Erlking traded all the ghosts for her soul, and used . . . He is using my body as a vessel to hold her."

The princess paled. But her horror was short-lived. Squaring her shoulders, she lifted her ax toward the main corridor. "Retreat!" she shouted, stepping from the alcove. "My monsters—we must fall back! Flee this place! Escape while you can. That is an order from your queen!"

The monsters nearest her looked momentarily perplexed, but they did not disobey. Soon, the cries of battle were replaced with the chaos of retreat—dozens of monsters rushing for the halls, some crashing through windows and letting broken glass rain down through the castle as they fled toward the forest.

"Good. Come with us," said Gild.

But this time, the princess snatched her arm away from him before he could catch hold of her. Looking past him to Perchta, she snarled and lifted the ax.

"What are you doing?"

"I am defending my castle. I cannot leave it, and so I will keep fighting for as long as I am able." She cut a glare toward Gild as well. "They are not the only ones who are immortal."

Chapter Forty

The girl growled and prepared to charge at the huntress.

"We can break your curse!" Gild cried.

She stumbled and hesitated as, across the rotunda, Perchta spotted them in their alcove. With no more monsters to fight, the huntress started in their direction.

"What did you say?" asked the princess, not taking her eyes from the huntress.

"Your body is in Adalheid," said Gild. "If I can get to it, I can break your curse. Untether you from Gravenstone. But I need time. Please, don't challenge her. Not now. You have to hide!"

The princess slowly shook her head, still facing the huntress as she prowled ever closer.

"What do you care?" said the princess, knuckles tightening around the handle of her ax. "These demons . . . they come and they want to take *everything* from me. I will not allow it. Not again!" She raised her voice, speaking to Perchta and the Erlking, who stood by watching as if the battle were a great show performed for his amusement. "You might be the huntress, but your body looks very fragile, if you ask me."

Perchta grinned and smoothed one hand down the side of her belly. "It suits me more than I expected. Makes it all feel a bit more . . . *dangerous.*" She swiped a dagger from a fallen dark one and lifted it over her shoulder.

"I suppose you probably can't die, but there are other ways to punish such disrespect."

She cackled and flung the dagger. Gild launched himself at the princess. He knocked her to the ground, his body bracing for the impact of the knife.

In the same instant, a shape dropped from the sky with a shrieking caw. A nachtkrapp split the air between Gild and the huntress, catching the blade in its wing. It shrieked in pain and fell, skidding across the tile floor.

"Lovis!" cried the princess, struggling underneath Gild's weight. "No! Get off me!"

Perchta placed a hand to her cheek in mockery. "Oh, my darling beastie! How tragic!"

The princess roared, shoving at Gild. "I'm going to kill her! *I'll kill her!*"

"Oh, please do try," said Perchta.

Gild staggered to his feet and grabbed the princess, thrusting her behind him. He raised his sword.

Perchta snarled. "Even better. I have been waiting a long time to have my revenge against *you*, princeling."

"If you want him," called a new voice, "you will have to fight *me* first."

Agathe appeared with a short sword in each hand, cutting easily through any dark one who dared to enter her path, until she had placed herself as a shield in front of Gild and the princess.

Perchta lifted an unimpressed eyebrow. "And who are you?"

"A huntress and a warrior, like yourself. One who owes a great debt to the prince of Adalheid."

Perchta studied her. "You look like a sad little ghost to me. Why weren't you taken with the others?"

"I requested to stay. I had other business to attend to. Agathe's gaze darted toward the Erlking, who was leaning against the black wolf's shoulder as comfortably as one would lean against a wingback chair. "And yes, His Grim could force me to my knees. He could insist that I relinquish my weapons and put up no fight while you demons cut the head from my shoulders a second time. But I don't think he will." She fixed a wolfish smile on the huntress. "We wouldn't want to ruin the fun, would we?"

Agathe lunged.

Perchta cackled, weaving in and out of Agathe's attacks until she managed to grab a javelin off the ground. Weapon in hand, she met Agathe blow for blow, like two dancers in a choreographed match.

Agathe deflected the javelin's point, pushing back the huntress. "Your Highness, run! Get out of here, you fools!"

"Yes, run!" said Perchta. "But don't go far. I am not finished with you yet!"

Serilda tore her focus from the battle and saw that the princess was crouched over the nachtkrapp that had taken the dagger for her, tears streaming down her dust-covered cheeks. The night raven was an eyeless, soulless thing that had, somehow, come to love this girl. Or at least admire her enough to sacrifice itself to protect her. Serilda could hardly believe it was possible.

"Princess," said Serilda. "This might be our only chance. You've been hiding all this time. If you can just hide a little longer, we will go to Adalheid and break your curse."

"I am not a princess," she said, but much of the fire had gone from her voice. "I am the queen of Gravenstone. The only queen it has had for a very long time."

She took the blade from the bird's wing. It was still breathing, but barely. Its body twitched in pain.

"My dear Lovis, I am sorry," she whispered, before plunging the dagger into its heart.

Serilda flinched, though she knew this quick death was a mercy.

"Your sacrifice will not be forgotten," said the princess, her voice wavering. "Nor shall it go to waste." Inhaling deeply, she stood and looked around at so many fallen creatures. The floor was thick with blood, some red, but other splatters and pools made of sticky black or even shimmering gold. The monsters' blood. "None of these sacrifices shall go to waste." She faced Gild and Serilda with a fierce nod. "You're sure you can free me from these walls?"

"Sure, no," said Gild. "But I think I can."

"Then I would have you try. I know a back way out. Let's go." Without waiting for a response, the girl ran past them into the corridor.

Serilda glanced back at the battle one last time.

Perchta, wearing Serilda's skin as her own, moved with a grace and strength Serilda had never possessed. Though Agathe was a worthy opponent, Serilda knew she would not win this fight.

What would happen to her?

She had chosen to stay, to help them, when she could have gone on to Verloren with the other spirits. What would the Erlking do to her for this betrayal?

Then she saw the Erlking. Staring not at Perchta and Agathe—but at her. Intrigued. Curious.

He reached for the quiver on his back, pulling out an arrow tipped in black. Twice she had seen gods trapped by those black arrows—the basilisk and the unicorn. But she had seen the Erlking use a black-tipped arrow for something else, too. She had watched him kill a ghost. Free his spirit.

The Erlking loaded the arrow into his crossbow and leveled it at Serilda.

With a cry, she grabbed Gild and pulled him behind the corridor wall.

She heard the *thunk* of the crossbow firing, and ducked instinctively.

But he had not fired at her or Gild. Through the doorway they saw the arrow lodge itself into Agathe's side. She gasped in pain. The blood that leaked from the wound was not red like that coating her tunic, but oily and black.

Perchta, who had been prepared to thrust the javelin down through Agathe's calf, looked up with a snarl.

"Forgive the interference," came the Erlking's honeyed voice, "but I fear your prince is getting away."

"What are you two waiting for?" hissed the princess, reappearing down the corridor.

Beneath the lunar rotunda, Agathe's eyes met Gild's one last time. "Your Highness. Forgive me. I wanted to save the ghosts. I did not know . . . my loyalty to your family . . . my debt repaid . . ."

Gild shook his head, speechless.

"Go," breathed Agathe. "Run!" It was the last word she managed before her body convulsed and she went still. The black blood crawled along her body, devouring her whole.

Serilda grabbed Gild's arm and they ran.

Despite her short legs, the princess was quick on her feet, practically flying through the halls of the castle. Gild and Serilda panted after her, the red cloak billowing like a sail. Behind her, she could still hear Perchta laughing. Cruel and cold, in Serilda's own voice.

The princess led them into a series of narrow servants' passageways, down a flight of steps, past the kitchens, and finally outside.

They darted beneath the exterior colonnade and flattened themselves against a series of columns, listening for signs that they were being pursued. All Serilda could hear were the sounds of the surrounding forest. Wind knocking wooden branches and the thrum of insects and toads.

And a deeper sound. More distant, yet seeming to come from far beneath them. A groaning deep in the earth.

"Look!" cried Gild, pointing up.

The branches of the alder tree that formed a canopy over the whole castle were changing. The leaves were falling around them like a blizzard. It was autumn, made clear by the vibrant reds and oranges in the surrounding forest, but Serilda knew this was not the natural progression of an alder preparing itself for winter. She had seen it brought back to life by the unicorn, and now it was once again withering away into a hasty death.

"The alder tree grew from Verloren," said Serilda. "If Verloren is dying—"

The princess snapped around. "What do you mean, if Verloren is dying?"

Gild shook his head. "I don't think we have time to explain."

"Wait," said Serilda, watching as the alder's roots shriveled and blackened. "Eostrig and Freydon!"

"This isn't the time for prayers," muttered the princess.

Gild shrugged. "I might argue it's exactly the time for prayers."

"It's not that. They're . . ." Serilda glanced in the direction of the stables, but already, she could feel helplessness claiming her. The unicorn and the gryphon were too far away. Even if they could make it to the gods before Perchta and the dark ones caught them, she wasn't sure they could open their cages and set them free.

"Nothing. I'll explain later. Let's go."

"This is as far as I can take you," said the princess. "One step into the dried-up swamp and I will vanish, only to reappear at the drawbridge. Again and again. I cannot leave this castle."

"Not yet," said Gild. "Hide now, and I will free you. I swear it."

The princess lifted an eyebrow at him. "We shall see."

Pain lanced across Gild's face and Serilda could tell he wanted to reach out and embrace his sister, even if she was likely to slice him in half if he attempted it.

Then they heard Perchta's cackle from within the walls.

"We have to go," said Serilda. "You will hide?"

The princess snorted. "They will not find me."

Gild nodded, and together he and Serilda dashed through the colonnade, in and out of the dry moat, and sprinted into the Aschen Wood. Untethered to any castle, but still cursed. Still trapped on the dark side of the veil, unable to walk among mortals.

The shadows of the trees closed around them. A second later they heard whistling and footsteps crashing through the forest floor. Then Perchta's sing-song voice, "Run and hide, little princeling. This is my favorite part."

The hairs stood up on the back of Serilda's neck. They froze, trying to discern where she was as morning's faint light filtered through the autumn leaves.

A twig snapped.

They crouched into the brush. Serilda tightened her grip on the broken arrow shaft, while Gild kept his sword at the ready.

"This body might be slow and cumbersome, but I am still the great huntress," Perchta went on, a voice like a lullaby. "I will track you down and take pleasure as I flay the skin from your flesh. You cannot hide from me."

Serilda saw her then. Perchta slipping in between the trees like a phantom.

She swallowed, her body trembling.

She knew they couldn't run. They might be able to fight, but even Agathe had not been able to touch the huntress, and Serilda was afraid that hurting her might hurt the baby in her womb, too.

What could they do?

Escape was so close, and yet, as Perchta prowled nearby, she felt as trapped as ever.

She looked at Gild. He met her gaze, just as helpless, just as lost.

The leaves around Perchta's cloak whispered and crackled. Another step and she would see them—

Quick as a viper, Perchta reached through the shrubs and grabbed one of Serilda's braids. She cried out as the huntress dragged her to her feet.

From her cloak, the huntress produced a black-tipped arrow, perhaps the same arrow that had just seen shot into Agathe, reclaimed for a new purpose. An arrow that could kill ghosts. She pressed the point against Serilda's throat. "You," whispered Perchta, "were supposed to pass on to Verloren."

"Wait!" cried Gild, sword flashing.

Too slow.

Perchta drove the arrow through Serilda's throat.

Chapter Forty-One

Serilda cowered, her whole body seizing.

Gild screamed and swung his sword, slicing through Perchta's arm.

But Serilda felt nothing.

And the sword—it went through the huntress as if she were made of mist, leaving Serilda's mortal body intact.

Serilda's braid slipped out of Perchta's grasp and Serilda stumbled back, barely catching herself before falling to the forest floor.

The black-tipped arrow had passed right through her.

Stillness descended on them. Perchta, illuminated by the first filtered rays of morning light, stared in confusion into the place where Gild and Serilda stood.

"She can't see us," Gild whispered. "The veil . . . she's on the other side."

The huntress came to this realization at the same time. She examined the arrow in her grip, then scanned the warm flesh of her hands and arms.

"Is she . . . mortal now?" asked Serilda.

The huntress laughed again, sounding a bit more like Serilda now that her bloodlust had faded. "I suppose I shall have to wait a little longer to take my revenge. Until then, my prince."

Adjusting her cloak, she turned back toward Gravenstone.

Gild gawked at Serilda. "What happened in that cave? Are the dark ones *mortal* now?"

"N-no," said Serilda. "I don't think so. It must be because Perchta is in a mortal body. But the rest of them . . ." Her body sagged. "Velos knew."

"Did the Erlking know, too? Had he expected her to be on the other side of the veil from him?"

"I don't know." Serilda leaned against a tree trunk, still clutching the ash wood arrow in her fist. "I'm still trying to make sense of what happened."

"Me too." After a long silence, Gild whispered, "That girl is my *sister*."

Serilda took his hand and held it tight. "I'm sorry. She was there all along and I had no idea."

"Me either. She seemed . . . incredible."

"Ferocious, for sure."

"Yes, exactly!" He beamed, but it quickly faded. "I didn't get a chance to tell her who I am. Or even ask her name."

"You will. We will break her curse, Gild. You will see her again."

He swallowed and nodded, though she could see he was not comforted. "How is your wrist?"

Serilda checked the hasty wrappings, but could see only a tiny splotch of blood through the fabric. "I can hardly feel it."

Which was true, though she wasn't sure if that was a good thing or not.

"Surely the Erlking wouldn't bring Perchta back only to be separated from each other between each full moon." She looked at Gild, but he had no more answers than she did. With a sigh, she went on, "We should probably keep moving. Put as much distance between us and Gravenstone as we can."

Gild inhaled deeply. "And the sooner we get to Adalheid, the better."

She peered around at the forest, taking in the knotted branches overhead, the clusters of platter-size fungi sprouting from fallen logs, the corkscrew ferns and trailing lichen. It smelled of wild berries and loamy soil and rotting things and living things and growing things all around them.

"This way, I think," said Gild without much confidence, but Serilda had no better ideas than he did.

Picking their way through the brush was slow and treacherous. Serilda was grateful for the warmth of her cloak, though each time it snagged on brambles, it felt like there were claws reaching out to grab her.

After a while, Gild worked a piece of flaxen thread from the sleeve of his tunic and handed it to Serilda. "Use this to tie that arrow shaft around your neck. If you were to lose it . . ."

He trailed off.

He didn't have to finish. Serilda remembered the feeling of her soul being loosened from this realm. Of the yearning she'd felt to follow Velos's lantern.

"How did you get free?" she asked, taking the thread from Gild and looping it securely around the arrow, just below the fletching.

"The weapons master. Agathe. She said the Erlking told her he was planning to release the ghosts and let Velos have them on the Mourning Moon, but she asked to stay. She told him she preferred being a hunter, but really, she knew it would be her best chance to help me. I think she had an idea of what was about to happen. So she released me from the dungeons and gave me a sword and told me where the Erlking had taken you. She kept calling me *Highness*, and asking if I could forgive her. I didn't say anything. I thought it was another trap, that she was going to betray us again. But now . . ." He dragged a hand through his hair. "She really was trying to make up for what she did. I think she really would have stayed with the dark ones, too, as one of the hunters, much as she despised them. She was giving up her own chance to be free, just so she could help me." He sighed. "I hope she's at peace now."

Serilda swallowed hard as she knotted the string behind her neck and tucked the arrow beneath the collar of her dress. "Her spirit should be in Verloren, now. Free from the dark ones. And she succeeded—all the ghosts, the children, they're free, too." Her voice broke. Sudden sadness welled up inside her. She had not had any time to mourn her losses. To dwell on what had happened in that chamber. "Agathe was able to help you, the prince of Adalheid, and she did it all while being under the Erlking's control. It's remarkable, really. She chose to stand against him, when so few choices were given to her."

Meanwhile, what choices had Serilda made? She had given the Erlking precisely what he wanted. She had lost herself. Lost her baby. She could not help cursing the Mourning Moon for all it had taken from her.

"You know the worst of it?" Gild said glumly. "I ran out of that dungeon so fast, I completely forgot about my spoons." He sighed. "I worked really hard for those spoons."

Serilda laughed, but it was dull and fleeting. "All this time, I thought I knew what the Erlking was planning. What he intended to do. But I've been on the wooden track for months."

"Tell me what happened," Gild said, his tone gentle. "By the time I got down there, everything was chaos."

Serilda rubbed a palm into her eye. "It all happened so quickly. But I will try my best to recount it all."

So she began. From the Erlking leading them down into the depths beneath the castle to the arrival of Velos and the ghosts. She told Gild about seeing her father, and his parents, too, the king and queen. Gild shrugged at this, reminding Serilda that he still couldn't remember them, so it wouldn't have been much of a reunion even if he had been there. But she could tell that his cavalier response was a ruse. Memories or not, he would have loved to meet his parents, just as Serilda still yearned to meet her mother—the one spirit who had not come up from Verloren.

She told Gild about the negotiations and how the Erlking had offered to trade the ghosts *and* his dark ones in exchange for Perchta's spirit. How he had used Serilda's body as a vessel to hold her. But that his bargain had been false. He had never intended to sacrifice the dark ones, and as soon as Perchta was secured, the demons returned, trapping Velos in the form of the great wolf and securing the god with golden chains.

She left out only the part in which it was her own decision to trade the children for her body. What did it matter now? What was done was done.

Gild whistled softly. "Capturing a god. Sneaky bastard."

"It isn't just Velos," interrupted Serilda. "He's been trying to capture all of the gods. He has Eostrig and Freydon, and Hulda, and I'm pretty sure Solvilde and Tyrr, too, and now Velos. Which only leaves—"

"Hold on," said Gild, his face contorted. "I saw Velos turn into the wolf, but the others? How is that possible? It isn't even the Endless Moon."

"He's been hunting them for years. And lately . . . he's had help." She frowned. "Your gold."

She went on to explain what she had seen in the tapestry in the hall. The seven beasts . . . the seven gods. Gild was skeptical, and when she told him that she believed the basilisk to be Solvilde, god of the sky and sea, he couldn't help the amused glint that sparked in his eyes.

"Don't you dare laugh," said Serilda.

He laughed anyway. "You think the bizarre chicken-snake creature is a *god*?"

"It's a basilisk. And yes, I know it's . . . unusual looking. But it is one of the most feared beasts in all folklore. You saw for yourself how powerful its venom was."

"Yes, but still." Gild spread his hands wide. "It's part *chicken*."

"And Pusch-Grohla turned into a beautiful unicorn right before my eyes. And if Hulda is the tatzelwurm . . . well. It makes sense."

Gild snorted. "Does it, though? The tatzelwurm is part cat, part serpent, and you're telling me it's somehow responsible for me being able to spin straw into gold?"

"Yes," insisted Serilda. "The tatzelwurm is a revered beast. It is both elegant and fierce, and it is all *over* your castle. Statues in the gardens and climbing up pillars in the throne room, and of course, the tatzelwurm on your family seal. I think Hulda might have been your family's patron deity, which would explain your gift. So if Hulda transforms into a tatzelwurm . . . it makes sense."

"Sounds like the stuff of fairy tales."

She looked at him, aghast. "Don't you get it, Gild? This *is* the stuff of fairy tales. *You* are the stuff of fairy tales. Handsome princes who kill wicked huntresses and get themselves cursed inside haunted castles are the stuff of fairy tales."

He cocked his head, his eyes catching a bit of the light. "Handsome?"

She rolled her eyes. "Handsome *and* humble."

He winked and slipped his hand into hers to help her over a fallen log. "I'm not saying you're wrong. It's just . . . they're *gods*. They're magic and powerful and . . . and you're saying that he's caught four of them in almost as many months, when in all the centuries before, he only managed to catch two?"

"He did almost catch Wyrdith," she said. "On the last Endless Moon. The year my father found the god, wounded, and claimed the wish, asking for a child."

"All right, so the Erlking *almost* caught Wyrdith, but he didn't."

"No, but it shows he's been hunting them for a long time, and as you say, it isn't easy to catch a god. At first, he was using those black arrows. They have some sort of poison that can trap the gods. Force them into their beastly form and keep them . . . frozen, in a sense."

"Perchta's arrows," said Gild. "Probably what made her such a great huntress. But if he had those, why did he need the gold chains?"

"He didn't have enough. Two were being used to pacify Tyrr and Solvilde. I know he has at least one other. He used it to kill a ghost in front of me once. Let me think. The arrow we pulled out of the basilisk was probably the same one he used to trap the unicorn. And the one he used to kill that ghost could have been the same he used to kill Agathe."

"Which Perchta probably picked up and chased us with."

She nodded. "That's just three black arrows. Not enough to capture seven gods. He needed something else."

A shadow crossed over Gild's features. "And spun gold does the trick. He's been planning this from the beginning."

"Between your gold and my stories telling him exactly where to find them, we've made it easy for him."

He cursed beneath his breath. "I'd thought it was bad enough when he was hunting mythical beasts, but . . . the old gods? And I've been *helping* him."

"You've been protecting me," said Serilda, squeezing his hand.

"And great job I've been doing of that," he muttered, using the sword to beat back a thick patch of brambles.

Serilda sighed, but she knew there would be no persuading him not to feel guilty for his role in this. She felt responsible for it, too. If she hadn't lied about spinning gold in the first place . . .

"But *why*?" said Gild. "You only need one god to make a wish! Who would waste their time collecting all seven?"

"I don't understand either. I'd been certain that he wanted to wish for the return of Perchta, but he found another way to bring her back, which means that was never what he wanted the gods for. But now that he has her and his court and his castle . . ."

A beat of silence passed over them. Neither had any answers.

What else could the Erlking want?

"Do you think he'll come after us?" asked Gild. "Perchta might be on the other side of the veil, but it doesn't sound like the hunt is. And you know how he hates to lose."

"He would hate to lose *you*, perhaps," said Serilda. "But me . . . he got what he wanted from me. He has my body as a vessel for Perchta. He has my child . . ." Her voice wavered and she glanced at Gild, realizing that she could finally tell him the truth.

The unborn child held captive by those demons was *his* child, too. She no longer had to lie. The children were safe in Verloren. The Erlking had nothing more to hold over her.

But when she opened her mouth, the words caught in her throat. She hesitated.

"What?" said Gild, giving her a peculiar look. He stopped walking to face her. "You're going to start crying. Serilda." He cupped her shoulders in his hands. "I'm sorry. This has been all too much. But we'll figure this out. Together. All right?"

She smiled wanly. "Yes. Together."

Together.

Since the night she'd met him, there had always been something keeping them apart. The veil. The Erlking. A dungeon.

For all the horrid things that had happened, this, at least, was a blessing. They were together. They could figure this out.

She could tell him the truth about their child. She *would* tell him the truth.

But not yet. not when they were lost in an unforgiving forest that would just as soon kill them as shelter them.

"He won't have to hunt you down," she said slowly. "He'll know that you still want to break your curse, and for that, you need to go to Adalheid. He'll expect you to go back at some point. So it makes more sense for him to focus on hunting the gods."

"God," corrected Gild. "If you're right, then there's only one left."

A chill swept down Serilda's spine as she counted them in her head.

Tyrr—the wyvern.

Solvilde—the basilisk.

Hulda—the tatzelwurm.

Eostrig—the unicorn.

Freydon—the gryphon.

And Velos—the wolf.

The only god not yet captured was Wyrdith, the raptor. God of stories. God of lies. God of fortune and fate.

Serilda's own patron deity.

"We have to find them first," she murmured. "We may not know what he's planning, but we do know it will be awful."

"I don't disagree," said Gild, "but how do you intend to find a god?"

Serilda considered. How had the Erlking found most of the gods? Because she had told him precisely where to find them.

She thought back to the tale she had told of how the gods had created the veil, and where they had retired to once they were finished.

Wyrdith to the basalt cliffs at the northernmost edges of Tulvask.

"The cliffs," she said. "Wyrdith will be somewhere near the basalt cliffs to the north."

Gild's expression became troubled. "All right, the cliffs. We'll go north, then."

She met his gaze. Saw the torment behind his eyes.

"After we go to Adalheid," she said. "After we free your sister."

Gild opened his mouth, but hesitated. Then, a sorrowful smile flittered across his face. "Thank you."

"It isn't just about freeing her. Or you, for that matter. Wyrdith is only one god, but there are three others currently imprisoned in Adalheid. It certainly seems the Erlking will need all seven to do whatever it is he's planning. We need to try to free them. Hulda, Tyrr, and Solvilde."

"The chicken-snake," Gild said with a shudder. "Maybe we can let Erlkönig keep *one* god?"

Serilda rolled her eyes.

"And what if we succeed?" said Gild. "If we free these gods from right under the Erlking's nose? The hunt will find them again, won't they? I'm not usually the voice of reason, but they are immortal. The gods couldn't even keep them locked away. They had to make the veil to contain them, and even that lets them out once a month. It all just feels . . . so futile."

"Wait," said Serilda, standing straighter. She held up a finger, her eyes widening. "You're right!"

Gild scowled. "That we shouldn't even bother?"

"Not that. The gods couldn't contain the dark ones. They made the veil, but it has a weakness . . . the full moons. And what have the dark ones always wanted, more than anything?"

"To maim and torture innocent mortals until great epic poems are written about their wickedness and recited through the generations?"

"Well, yes," admitted Serilda. "But more than that, they want freedom. From Verloren. From the veil." She placed a hand to her throat, sure that she would feel a racing pulse there. But no . . . nothing fluttered beneath her skin. "The Erlking told me once that he wants the whole world. That's what he's gathering the gods for. He wants to destroy the veil, but he will need all of them to undo the magic."

"Gods alive," muttered Gild. "You could be right."

"With the veil destroyed, they would be masters over the mortal realm." Serilda tried to picture it. Their cruelty. How they would enslave the mortals, just as they had enslaved the ghosts. She had to stop them. Not just for herself. Not just for her unborn child. But for every innocent human who had no idea of the horrible fate that awaited them should the dark ones succeed. "Gild . . . we're the only ones who know about this. What if we're the only ones who can stop it?"

Gild laughed dryly. "I guess we'd better walk faster, then."

Chapter Forty-Two

They wandered for nearly a week. Traipsing through the forest, sleeping among tree roots, getting lost and turned around and finding their way before getting lost again. Being grateful that they didn't actually *need* food and water to survive, yet even more grateful when they managed to successfully forage for berries and ripe autumn fruits.

Creatures watched them from the shadows. Not just birds and foxes, but monsters, too. They sometimes heard the melodic clatter of a schellenrock's coat, the shrill cries of a distant bazaloshtsh. Twice Serilda spied the red cap of a wood spirit tucked among a cluster of mushrooms, and one evening they met a small, hairy waltschrat on the path that hissed and screeched and followed them for nearly an hour, throwing acorns and pebbles at their heels, scampering away only after Gild took out the golden sword and chased the creature off into the trees. The most frightening monster they stumbled across was a drekavac, which would have looked like a human baby if it weren't for the long brown fur and clawed hands. It snarled at Gild and Serilda from the boughs of a tree, and Serilda was sure it would attack them the moment their backs were turned, but after a long standoff, the creature scuttled off and disappeared.

Though the haunts of the forest lurked in every shadow, Serilda soon became desensitized to her fear. If anything, as the days wore on, she began to feel a kinship with the woods. She was nothing more than a spirit now, detached from her body and unable to cross to the mortal side of the veil. She was as much a monster as they were, she reasoned.

What did she have to be frightened of?

Finally, late one evening with a waning moon making its way overhead, they reached the edge of the Aschen Wood, emerging into a valley of fertile farmland.

They headed south, spending the night in a horse stable.

Late in the evening, two days later, they realized they should have headed north.

By the time they finally found their way back to Adalheid, they were tired and grumpy and sore, their mood in stark contrast to the city's festive atmosphere, which could be felt as soon as they stepped through the city gates.

Jaunty music came from the lake docks, mixed with laughter and cheers. The day was overcast, an autumn chill in the air, yet dozens of townsfolk were milling about. None of them could see Serilda and Gild passing by. Two spirits, trapped on the dark side of the veil. Serilda had been eager to return to Adalheid. To see Leyna and her mother, Lorraine. To see Frieda, the librarian, and all the people who had gathered around the fireplace at the Wild Swan and listened to Serilda spin her nightly stories.

She had not expected how lonely she would feel to be back among the townsfolk, but invisible to them. She could not touch them. Could not speak to them. Could not tell them that she was all right.

All right-ish.

They reached the docks. On the lake, the castle stood as imposing as ever beneath the autumn sun.

Gild slipped his hand into hers, a gesture that had warmed her many times these past days. "What are they celebrating?"

Serilda took in the jovial air of the crowd. It seemed the entire city was out on these streets, bundled in coats and hats to ward off the breeze that came in from the lake, but smiling as brightly as if it were a pristine summer's day. Tables were set up on the central square near the docks, displaying a grand banquet. Platters overflowed with cheeses and squash, cured meats and fish pies, roasted chestnuts and seeded pomegranates.

And flowers. There were flowers everywhere. Not only the usual pansies and herbs overflowing from window boxes, but also roses and chrysanthemums and frilly-edged kale leaves stuck into pots and buckets along the street, and more wired into a decorative arch that had been built on one of the piers.

"It looks like a wedding," she mused.

An exuberant trumpet melody blared from the musicians, bringing everyone to attention.

"Three cheers for the happy couple!" shouted the town's butcher, waving an arm toward the Wild Swan. "Madam Mayor and Madam Professor!"

The door of the inn opened and Lorraine and Frieda walked out. Frieda flushed pink, and Lorraine shook her head as if the pomp of it all were absurd, but both of them were beaming from ear to ear. Though their dresses were simple, Serilda suspected they were probably the finest they owned, and they each had a circlet of flowers over their hair.

They looked so lovely and so happy, their arms linked together.

Serilda clasped her hands together delightedly. "It *is* a wedding!"

Perhaps she should not have been so surprised. The first time she'd met Lorraine and Frieda, their feelings for each other had been obvious, though they'd both been far too shy to act on them. She wondered if it was Leyna, Lorraine's daughter, who had nudged them together.

As soon as she thought it, Leyna poked her head out the inn's door and cleared her throat meaningfully.

The butcher gave a boisterous laugh. "And Mistress Leyna, of course!"

Leyna pranced after her mother and the librarian, holding a posy of chrysanthemums. Lorraine reached back, took her daughter's hand, and together the three walked toward the arch of flowers while the townspeople gathered around them with enthusiastic cheers.

The wedding was both charming and raucous, a celebration for all. There were blushes and giggles and vows. An exchange of rings. Frieda even gave Leyna a golden bracelet as part of the ceremony, making a vow that she would never be a wicked stepmother like in the fairy tales. Leyna had looked near to bursting with glee when Frieda helped her with the clasp. Serilda and Gild stood apart from the crowd, watching it all.

When Frieda and Lorraine kissed, the cheers were so loud, Serilda thought her ears would ring the whole night through.

"A toast!" shouted Roland Haas, who had once given Serilda a ride in the back of his wagon, along with a whole lot of chickens. He raised a mug of ale and the crowd was quick to join him. "To the professor and the mayor, who are both so good and fair. Your joy all the world can see, and we hope you'll live in harmony. Should your love be ever doubted . . ." Roland hesitated, searching for a suitable rhyme. "Er—come talk to me and I shall *shout it*!" His quick-wittedness was met with *hurrah*s from the crowd and Roland gave a quick bow. "For though I be no poet, it is clear and we all know it. A love as grand as that before us should be sung far and wide by every chorus!"

His rhyming toast was met with raucous cheers and a number of drained cups.

The musicians started up again, blasting out a joyful ditty on block-flötes and reed pipes. Rose petals were tossed into the air. Dancing commenced as a group of fishermen performed an energetic jig right there on the cobblestones, followed by dozens of children linking arms and prancing in and around the onlookers. Soon, Lorraine and Frieda were ushered onto a bench, which was then hoisted up on the townsfolk's shoulders and paraded about while the crowd sang a traditional wedding ballad—the tempo too fast and everyone mostly off-key.

Serilda's cheeks hurt, but she could not stop smiling.

And yet—despite the joy that overflowed inside of her—she felt a deep sadness, too. Gild's hand was still in hers, and when she glanced up at him, his gaze was haunted.

He gave her hand a squeeze. "Wishing you could be a part of it?"

"Yes. You?"

"More than anything." He shrugged, feigning nonchalance. "I'm used to it, though. I've been wishing to be out here, on their side of the veil, for a very long time."

"Does it get easier?"

He frowned, considering. "I thought it had. But after I met you, it got a thousand times worse. I would have given anything to follow you out of the castle."

Serilda leaned her head against his shoulder. "We're together now."

"And now," he said, "I'd do anything to see you on the other side, with them."

She swallowed. If they succeeded in breaking Gild's and his sister's curses, then the two of them would be mortal again. Gild would be on the other side of the veil. Mortal again.

But Serilda would still be just a spirit, with no mortal body to keep her. She couldn't even rely on breaking her own curse anymore, not so long as Perchta inhabited her body.

"Gild," she said, turning her attention back to him, "after we free Hulda and Tyrr and Solvilde, I am still going to try to find Wyrdith."

His brow creased. "Why?"

"Because I have a wish to make."

Gild peered at her a long moment. "So, you're going to free three gods, and then run off and capture a fourth? Serilda, I don't think—"

"Not capture. This isn't about capturing anyone. Wyrdith cursed me before I was even born, and why? My father *helped* them." She leaned into Gild, tugging the cloak tight around her as a stark wind blew in from the lake. "Wyrdith owes me. And when I meet them, I'm going to make them grant my wish."

"Which is?"

"I want my body back," she said. "And my child."

My child. My child. My child.

The words rang in her head like the chime of a bell. Over and over and over.

"Gild, I need to tell you something," she blurted.

Gild tensed at her sudden intensity. "What's wrong?"

"Nothing. I mean, everything. Obviously. But it's not . . . I just need to tell you something. That maybe I should have told you a long time ago. I wanted to tell you. But I couldn't. I kept hoping you would guess, and then I wouldn't have to keep the secret anymore, but I don't know if you ever did. If you ever wondered . . ." She trailed off.

Gild was studying her, his brow furrowed.

She'd tried to tell him a thousand times since they'd fled from Gravenstone. She'd gone over the words in her mind, too many times to count. Practiced what she would say, tried to imagine his response. She'd opened her mouth and shut it, uncertain, again and again. The timing never felt right, stumbling through the woods, afraid that the wild hunt might find them at any moment.

Even now, she wasn't sure how to begin.

The music was suddenly too lively, too ebullient. Jarring to Serilda's ears.

"Not here," she said, pulling him away from the crowd and toward the marina, out onto the end of the one of the docks. The lake was empty of boats today, but the water was choppy from the wind. From here the music and laughter had to compete with the creaking of fishing boats, hulls thumping hollowly against the docks, waves lapping at their sides.

"Serilda?" said Gild, anxious at her long silence.

She took his hands into hers, even though her palms were beginning to sweat.

"What?" Gild pressed. "Just tell me, whatever it is."

She took in a long breath. "The child. My child. It's . . . they're . . . they're yours. Your child."

His frown deepened. "Because . . . of the deal we made? The gold, for your firstborn? Serilda, you can't think that I—"

"Because you're the father, Gild." She gulped, and said it again, quieter now. "You're the father."

He stared at her, his lashes fluttering. "What are you talking about? The Erlking—"

"Never touched me. Not like that. He—" She grimaced, wishing this conversation didn't have to be tainted with the Erlking and the awful arrangement they'd had. "He found out that I was with child, and at first he wanted to"—she shuddered—"*remove* it. But then I convinced him that the child might grow up to be a gold-spinner. After that he demanded I marry him and pretend the child was his, so when Perchta came back he could give the child to her, and no one would question that the child was his, was *theirs*. He said if I told anyone the truth, he would punish the children, and I couldn't . . . I couldn't let him hurt them anymore. I desperately wanted to tell you the truth, but I couldn't."

Gild pulled his hands away from her and pressed them back through his hair. "But there was only that one night. And . . . and I'm . . ." He gestured down to his body. His spirit body. "How . . . ?"

"I don't know. I don't understand it, either, but there's been no one else. The Erlking said that dark ones and mortals can have children. Maybe it works the same with spirits? I don't know. But I do know the child is yours. Well, ours."

He gaped at her a long moment. Then, without any warning, he collapsed down to the dock, sitting cross-legged with a deflated *whump.* "You could have told me to sit down first."

Grimacing, she knelt beside him and placed a hand on his back. "I'm sorry."

"Great gods, Serilda. A *baby.*" He massaged his temple. "I'm going to be a father."

To this, she dared not respond. She grimaced again, waiting.

"I mean, I would be lying if I hadn't thought . . . hadn't hoped . . . that maybe we would find a way to get your body back, and for you to have the child, and we'd be together and of course I would treat the child like my own . . . raise them like my own. If you wanted me to." Wonder crept into his voice. "But . . . they *are* my own. I'll be a father. I—"

He stopped abruptly. A second later, it came. The miserable groan as he pressed both hands to his face and cursed beneath his breath. "I would have been a father."

A silence fell over them, the lively music at odds with the thoughts plaguing them both.

Their child would never know them. Their child would have the Erlking and the huntress as father and mother.

Serilda struggled to imagine what that childhood would look like, but she knew it would not be filled with patience and compassion and love.

With a long exhale, Gild lowered his hands and met Serilda's gaze. "Even though I believed the child was his, there was a part of me that felt responsible for it. And not just because of our deal. But because they were *your* child . . . I already loved them. I wanted to be in their life. And now . . ."

Serilda sniffed. "What are we going to do?"

He stared at Serilda a long moment, contemplating. She saw the changes flashing through his eyes. Despair to hope to determination.

Without warning, he reached for Serilda and pulled her into his lap. She tumbled against him with a gasp and had barely caught her breath before he was kissing her. Arms cradling her, hands in her hair. Pouring a thousand promises into that touch.

He ended the kiss as quickly as he had started it. His cheeks were flushed beneath his freckles, his eyes flashing and resolute.

"We will find Wyrdith, and you will make your wish." He pressed his forehead to hers, stroking his thumbs across Serilda's cheeks. "Erlkönig has taken everything from us. I won't let him take this, too."

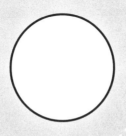

THE
HUNTER'S
MOON

Chapter Forty-Three

They had hoped to sneak into Adalheid Castle weeks ago, long before they had to fear the return of the Erlking and his hunters. But every time they tried, they found the drawbridge was up. The castle gates were shut tight. Unless they intended to scale the massive walls using grappling hooks—an idea which Gild was keen to try but Serilda doubted she had the strength for—they would have to wait.

So wait they did.

On the dark side of the veil—unknown to the people of Adalheid—they'd claimed an unoccupied room at the Wild Swan. The place had been busy with a constant stream of well-wishers coming to bestow gifts and unsolicited advice on the newly married couple.

Serilda, with Gild's help, found that despite being on the other side of the veil, there were small things she could do to influence the mortal realm. Just as Gild, the poltergeist, had slammed doors and knocked over candelabras, with effort she could rattle chandeliers and riffle curtains and even, if she really set her mind to it, slide a plate of fruit tarts across the table.

Using these skills, she tried her best to communicate with Leyna. To let the child know that she was here, beside her, with her.

But it was no use. Her efforts led to nothing more than the occasional confused frown and a suspicious glance around the room, then Leyna going on as if nothing peculiar had happened.

Which Serilda supposed might be normal for a girl who had grown up surrounded by tales of haunted castle and the wild hunt.

Then—finally, on the cold, drizzly morning of the Hunter's Moon—they looked across the lake and saw that the castle gates were open.

Serilda wilted with relief. She'd been sure, after waiting nearly a month, that the gates would not open until nightfall, and then probably only to welcome the return of the hunters.

"Perfect," she whispered. "The veil won't fall for hours still."

Gild had assured Serilda there were never any guards posted at the gatehouse or in the towers, as the dark ones, being the most terrifying creatures on this side of the veil, never had to worry about defending their castle against intruders. Still, they had both agreed that it would be wise to have a story to tell, in case they encountered any demons.

Serilda donned her red cloak and strapped the golden sword to her hip. Gild wrapped a scavenged rope around his wrists, handing the long end to her like a leash.

Together, they made their way over the bridge. Serilda kept her head high, her expression severe, almost eager to explain to any dark one who stopped them that she—their queen—had returned early from Gravenstone in order to return the poltergeist to his entrapment in Adalheid. His presence had been too bothersome, she would tell them, and the Erlking refused to tolerate his antics a moment longer.

If needed, she was prepared to deliver an entire list of the poltergeist's offenses, from tying together the laces of the Erlking's favorite boots to putting manure in the wine casks (two pranks Gild had gleefully insisted he'd really done), until whatever dark one got bored of listening and ushered them past.

And so Serilda could not help feeling disappointed when they made it all the way to the gatehouse and the only creatures to notice them were two nachtkrapp perched on the castle walls.

The courtyard, too, was empty. Serilda knew that all the ghosts had gone, and at least half of the dark ones. They'd expected the castle to be quieter and emptier than usual, with the hunt not yet returned, but the oppressive silence gave her chills.

Even when Gild loudly cleared his throat, no one appeared to question them.

"Gild," she whispered. "Can you . . . you know . . . *poof*?" She snapped her fingers.

His lips twitched. "Poof? Is that what you think I do?"

"You know what I mean."

He peered up at the keep, where the stained-glass windows of the seven gods looked dreary and miserable behind the curtain of rain.

A few seconds passed before he shook his head. "It isn't working. When Erlkönig revoked my curse and untethered me from this castle, it must have changed so I can't move around like I used to."

"No matter," she said, starting to untie his ropes. "I'll get Solvilde, you get Hulda, then we meet in the throne room to free your sister and release Tyrr."

As soon as the ropes fell away, Gild surprised her by pulling her to him and pressing a kiss to her mouth. She met the kiss in force, throwing her arms around his neck.

"Be careful," she whispered, breaking the kiss.

His expression softened. "*You* be careful. The legendary chicken-snake is not to be trifled with."

"Oh! I almost forgot." Serilda reached for the sword at her hip, but Gild placed his hand over hers.

"You take it."

"But—you're the one trained in combat."

"I think you can handle yourself just fine," he said, eyes glittering. "Besides, I'll feel better if I know you aren't unarmed." Gild tossed the ropes over one shoulder. "Meet you in the throne room?"

"As soon as possible. Don't do anything *too* foolish."

He winked at her. Then he was gone, darting around the side of the keep in the direction of the menagerie.

Serilda jogged up the stairs and into the castle keep. Now that the ghost servants were gone, she immediately noticed that cobwebs clung to the chandeliers and a layer of dust had gathered along the edges of the floor.

She turned toward the stairwell that led to the hall of gods, when she heard voices coming her way from the great hall. She slipped around a pillar, pressing herself to the wall as two women came into view.

"—have to peel our own potatoes for another month," grumbled one. "I'd rather pull out my own teeth with rusted pliers."

"What's one month, compared to eternity?" said her companion. "His Grim promised that by the Endless Moon, we will have more servants than ever before."

The woman scoffed. "We had plenty of servants. Ghosts. Mortals. What does it matter?"

"Well," said the second woman, "mortals don't bleed all over the carpets, do they?"

This brought a dark chuckle from the other's lips. "They do when I want them to."

Their laughter echoed off the walls as they wandered off toward the parlors.

Serilda was trembling with anger as she stepped out from behind the column. This proved it. The Erlking did mean to bring down the veil and enslave the mortals. The thought left a hollow pit in her stomach.

As soon as she could no longer hear the dark ones, she ran up the steps to the upper corridors. Sword in hand, she charged down the hall, prepared to knock aside any drude that dared attack her.

To her surprise—no attack came.

She reached the end of the hall without incident, her panting breath the only sound.

She planted one foot on the door and shoved it open. This part, she knew, was even more dangerous than facing off against a horde of drudes. She could not let the basilisk's venom touch her before she had a chance to free it from the cage and—

She froze, gaping into the room.

It was not the evidence of destruction that made her stop, though there were singe marks on the floor and one wall was still being propped up with wood scaffolding. The room was barren now, but for the tapestry of Gild and his family, which seemed to have escaped the venom's destruction unscathed.

No. What halted Serilda was the fact that the basilisk was gone, and in its place, wrapped in golden chains and laid atop the basilisk's cage, was a *person.*

Skin dark as polished basalt and feathery hair that shimmered in shades of turquoise, cobalt, and fiery orange. With a sharp nose and full lips, they cut a most striking figure, even asleep. Their appearance was enhanced by flamboyant clothes—boots that reached over their knees, a silky black shirt with wide sleeves beneath a long-tailed burgundy vest, and shining brass buttons everywhere a person might possibly think to add a button.

Serilda couldn't help noting, with a tinge of delight, that she'd been right. Solvilde really *did* dress like a pirate.

Lowering the sword, she stepped into the room.

She had not gone half a dozen steps when the god took in a long breath and gave an exaggerated yawn. Their eyes opened sleepily and they tilted their head to peer at Serilda with a tangerine-colored gaze. Though their eyes were intact, Serilda could see rough scar tissue all around the eye sockets, and she recalled how the basilisk had been blinded, supposedly so that its gaze couldn't turn anyone to stone.

"S-Solvilde?" she breathed.

The god of the sky and sea studied Serilda for a long moment, inspecting her from head to toe, giving particular interest to the sword. Then they slumped their head away. "Come and wake me again when a proper hero shows up."

Serilda frowned. "I'm here to free you."

"You are a wandering spirit."

Serilda looked down at her body, wondering how the god could tell.

"Maybe," she admitted, "but I'm also the one who pulled the arrow out of you before, so you wouldn't be trapped in your basilisk form anymore."

Solvilde made an unhappy sound in their throat. "Yes. Great victory, that was. I would clap for you if my hands weren't tied."

"Well, that's what I'm here to fix, isn't it?" She set the sword against a wall and moved closer to inspect the golden cords. "Maybe you shouldn't be so quick to judge."

"You haven't done anything yet but wave around a sword. Not even a real sword. That's clearly ornamental."

Serilda huffed. "You know, you were my favorite when I was a child. I'm regretting that now." She tugged on some of the chains, but they were locked down tight. If she could find where they were attached to the cage below . . .

"Let me guess," said Solvilde. "You liked to tell stories of sailors on the high seas, charming sirens, and battling sea monsters."

"Well, yes, actually. How did you know?"

Solvilde grunted. "Godchild of Wyrdith."

"Oh." Serilda lifted a hand to her cheek. Sometimes she forgot about her gold-wheeled eyes. "They were good stories, I'll have you know. Do you have any idea how these chains work? If I could just get them loose—"

"It's too late for that," said Solvilde. "You should probably run."

"Run? Why?"

A ring of steel echoed through the room. Serilda gasped and spun around, reaching for the sword just in time to block a tall candelabra that swung for her. Gold met iron and Serilda stumbled back. The dark one—a woman with amber-colored skin and enormous emerald eyes—advanced, swinging again with a throaty grunt. Serilda parried, but the force pushed her back again. Strike, block, swing, parry, every move pushing Serilda around Solvilde and the cage in the center of the room, until she had come full circle. She knew she was lucky that this demon was not one of the hunters, that not all dark ones were exceptional fighters.

But Serilda was no warrior either.

"Stand down!" Serilda said between panting breaths. "I am your queen!"

This brought a shrill laugh from the woman. "You were never our queen. You are a pathetic mortal." She pitched a glob of spit at Serilda's feet. "You think we couldn't tell His Grim was using you? He needed a mortal girl to carry a child. Once he's got that, he'll toss you out into the lake with the other rubbish."

Serilda scowled. "Well," she said, scrambling backward as the dark one lunged at her again, "he *does* need me to carry that child, and he will be very upset if any harm should come to me!"

"Unfortunately for you, a nachtkrapp arrived just after the Mourning Moon to tell us that Perchta, our true Alder Queen, has returned. So no, I really don't think His Grim will be upset at all to know I rid him of his pesky mortal wife."

Serilda cursed under her breath. She barely managed to block another thrust of the candelabra.

"Honestly, this could go on forever," bemoaned Solvilde. "Just fake a swing to the left and when she goes to block, trip her on the right, then run!"

Serilda gritted her teeth. "I'm not running. I came here to save you."

"And you tried your best, love. Much appreciated, truly. Don't be so hard on yourself."

Serilda's arms were shaking with the effort to hold back the dark one, to block another attack. When the dark one pulled back for another swing, she followed Solvilde's suggestions, swinging the sword to the left. The woman parried. Their weapons clanged, and Serilda swept her right foot around the woman's ankle. The demon cried out and fell backward, the candelabra flying from her hand and skittering across the floor.

"Nicely done!" said Solvilde, craning their head to see.

"I can't believe that worked!" panted Serilda.

"No time to celebrate. There will be more coming."

Serilda pivoted on her heels. "I'm so sorry to leave you like this!"

"Ah, thanks anyway for trying."

Serilda took their hand. "I will return for you if I can."

Solvilde smirked. "And they call me dramatic. Go! Go!"

With a regretful nod, Serilda retreated.

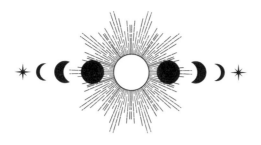

Chapter Forty-Four

She had to find Gild. He would know how to break the god's chains, or at least how to loosen them. Wouldn't he?

She raced down the steps to the entry hall, the dark one shrieking for her to stop. Serilda ran into the great hall and threw herself beneath a table, curling up as small as she could and trying to calm her ragged breaths.

She heard the dark one stop at the doorway, but the woman didn't linger. A second later, she charged off toward the throne room, screaming about there being an intruder in the castle.

Serilda shakily emerged from beneath the table. She would find Gild, help him free the tatzelwurm if he hadn't already, then they would make a plan for how to help Solvilde.

As she made her way through the castle, keeping to the shadows and servants' halls, she heard a distant commotion. Yelling and crashing and hasty footsteps.

She spun around a corner—and crashed into a figure running the opposite way.

She cried out, caught herself just before falling, and gawked at Gild's harried expression.

"Gild!"

He blinked wide-eyed at the sword that had nicked his sleeve in their collision. "They're coming!" he shouted, taking the sword from Serilda and grabbing her hand. He started back the way she'd come, dodging in and out of corridors as the footsteps behind them grew louder.

"Did you free Hulda?" she panted.

"No. They've got dark ones posted all around the menagerie like guards. One of them spotted me and gave chase, and they've got spun gold, Serilda! If they catch us—this way!"

His words were cut off by a scream. His hand was ripped from hers. The sword clattered to the floor.

Serilda spun around to see Giselle, the master of the hounds, wrapping a golden chain around Gild. His arms were pinned to his sides.

"Run!" he screamed, thrashing against his captor.

With a smirk, Giselle stepped closer, placing the heel of her boot on the sword's hilt. "If it isn't the poltergeist. How I have dreamed of this."

Down the corridor, more dark ones were coming, fast.

There was a moment of indecision. A terrible moment when everything went still and Serilda didn't know what to do. She couldn't leave Gild, but she also couldn't help him. She couldn't fight them all.

"*Run!*" Gild cried again.

She made a decision. Turning, she sprinted through the corridor, weaving in and out of parlors and studies.

The footsteps were distant by the time she reached the empty throne room. Serilda rushed toward the dais that held the two thrones and planted her feet against the polished stone floor. She braced both hands against the carpeted platform and shoved.

It slid forward with an earsplitting screech.

Every muscle strained. She shoved and shoved until she had moved the dais enough that she could get down into the pit full of bones and skulls. Crowns and jewels.

And two perfectly preserved bodies.

She tried not to think about the people who had been tossed here and left to rot away. Tried to ignore the way bones clicked against her ankles as she waded through them.

She reached the princess's body first. Serilda had barely caught her breath when she grasped the arrow lodged in the girl's wrist and broke it with a clean *snap*. The sound echoed through the throne room.

Then Serilda turned toward the prince. He still lay haphazardly across the bones in the pit, one arm flailed outward as if reaching for someone. His parents, maybe. Or his sister.

Serilda took hold of the arrow, tears blurring her vision, but she refused to doubt this choice. What it would mean. For him. For her. This hadn't been a part of the plan. They would break his sister's curse, which would return her to her mortal body, but they would wait to save Gild. Because as soon as she did this, he would be mortal again, and she would still be a spirit, her body given up to the huntress.

They would be separated, on all but those full-moon nights when the veil fell. Gild would be on the mortal side. Same as Perchta. Same as their child, once Perchta gave birth.

While Serilda was stuck here, and would be forever, if she never found a way to reclaim her body.

But there was no other way. She would not let him be trapped here, not again.

She took the arrow that had cursed Gild three hundred years ago and snapped it in two.

She stumbled back, two broken arrows in her hands, sweat dripping down the back of her neck.

She bit the inside of her cheek and hoped. Hoped that she was right. Hoped that this curse could be broken.

The princess's eyes opened first, at the same moment Gild dragged in a wheezing breath. He turned onto his side with a violent cough. The princess reached for her arm, to cover the bleeding wound, as she looked around, bewildered. She lurched upward, taking in the bones around her.

Catching his breath, Gild met his sister's gaze. They blinked at each other.

Then Gild scrambled to his feet. "No! *Serilda!* What did you do?"

She had freed him.

Shaking, Serilda stuffed the arrow fragments into a pocket inside her cloak. He couldn't see her. The Hunter's Moon had not yet risen. But it would, soon, and then the veil would fall.

"Where are we?" asked the princess. "What happened? Who is *this*?" She picked up a skull.

"Adalheid. Serilda broke our curse. I don't know. Come on." Gild started for the edge of the pit, having no idea that Serilda was mere inches from him.

"Adalheid!" cried the princess. "It worked? I'm out of Gravenstone?"

"Very clever, Your Luminance."

Serilda spun around to see Giselle waiting in a doorway, tossing a knife into the air and catching it in such a blatant display of arrogance that it made Serilda want to laugh.

Instead, she fought to mold her face into one of terror as she approached the side of the pit and climbed out on trembling limbs. Behind her, she could hear the princess's persistent questions and remarks, but she tried to ignore her and Gild. They couldn't see her. They couldn't see the dark ones. They couldn't help.

She was alone now.

"Please," she said, raising her hands in supplication, "don't hurt me."

"Why shouldn't I?" Catching the knife, Giselle pointed it toward Gild as he and the princess scrambled from the pit. "You just cost my king one of his most prized possessions."

"Yes, well"—Serilda flashed a smile—"it isn't the last thing I'll be costing him tonight."

Giselle frowned.

Serilda bolted toward the hall.

The knife flew past her, clattering against the wall. Serilda exhaled, glad that her guess had been correct. If Giselle were any good with a knife, she would have been a hunter, not left behind to care for the animals.

She passed the massive dining hall, a game room, then skidded through the doorway into the great hall. She rounded the massive fireplace. The rubinrot wyvern hung over the mantel, as hauntingly lifelike as it had always been, unmoved after all these years. Its slitted eyes seemed to follow her as she reached for the arrow embedded in its side.

Her fingers wrapped around the shaft, and with a determined bellow, she yanked it free. The arrow's black tip emerged, along with a chunk of flesh and shimmering scales. The force of it sent her flying backward and she landed on her rear end, panting as she gaped up at the massive beast.

Giselle chased after her, face contorted. "Why do you keep running, little mort—"

She cut off as the wyvern's head swiveled in her direction. Its slitted green eyes blinked. Once. Twice. A forked tongue darted out from between a horrible maw lined with rows of needlelike teeth.

With a low, vibrating growl, the wyvern yanked one wing and then the other away from the pins that had long held it in place on the castle wall. The beast shuddered with pain, but that didn't keep it from extending great clawed forelegs toward the floor. It prowled toward Giselle, who backed slowly away.

Serilda couldn't recall ever having seen a dark one afraid. *Truly* afraid.

Giselle raised a hand, as if she could reason with the creature. As if she could tame it with a few fatty slabs of meat. But she didn't even have *that* to ward off this massive beast.

Giselle pivoted on her heels. She started to run, just as the wyvern opened its jaws and spewed forth a rush of molten flames.

Serilda screamed and scurried backward as an almost unbearable heat surged through the room.

When the wyvern was finished, all that remained of Giselle was a black mark on the stone wall, and a tapestry smoldering away to ash.

Serilda's jaw dropped. She blinked once, twice, three times, before she managed to speak. "You killed her! You killed a demon! I didn't think they could . . . be . . ."

She trailed off as the wyvern swiveled to face her. It clomped closer on heavy, taloned limbs. Drops of oily blood splattered across the carpets from its open wound.

Serilda trembled as she lifted the black arrow, still tinged with the wyvern's blood. "T-Tyrr? My name is Serilda. I'm a godchild of Wyrdith. I'm not your enemy. I freed you."

Behind the wyvern, she caught sight of Gild and his sister creeping through the castle—though they were seeing a very different castle than she was. One that was long abandoned, left to decay under the burden of time.

She swallowed, wishing Gild could see her. Wishing he knew she was there.

But they were divided now, until the sun set. How much longer?

She met Tyrr's fearsome gaze again, and determined it was a good sign that the god hadn't yet burned her up like a roast pig.

The wyvern huffed, and a wave of heat scorched Serilda's skin. Its nostrils flared. Its eyes narrowed.

It took Serilda a moment to realize it was glaring, not at her, but at the arrow in her hand.

"Oh—this isn't mine!" she said. "I would never . . . um. Here." She broke the arrow over her knee, then tossed the pieces into the hearth. "Better?"

In the corridors, the thunder of footsteps rattled the walls. The clang of weapons.

"The dark ones are coming. Please—I need your help."

The beast prowled closer, so close she could see her own reflection in its faintly glowing eyes. And she could see it. A wisdom deep in those narrow pupils. An ancient magic, breathtakingly powerful.

Tyrr. God of archery. God of war.

"Please," she breathed, cowering. "Will you help me?"

The beast snarled, sending a breath of steaming air over her.

Then the wyvern bent its head low to the ground.

It took Serilda a long moment to realize it was encouraging her to climb onto its back.

"I . . . are you sure?" she said, scrambling to her feet.

The beast gave a shake of its head, but did not throw her off as she grabbed on to the row of scales on its back and hauled herself up between its wings.

Serilda had hardly grasped what was happening before the rubinrot wyvern was barreling toward the doors and launching itself out through the entry hall, stopping dozens of dark ones in their tracks.

Then the flames started, surging through the crowd. Serilda kept her head lowered against Tyrr's scales, afraid that the heat would blister her skin. But it did not last long. A second later, the wyvern was forging ahead, through the entry hall and onto the steps of the castle keep. The wyvern stretched its neck upward and roared at the gray twilit sky, trembling the stone walls all around them. Wings extended and, with two powerful thrusts, they were airborne.

Serilda bit her cheek against a scream and ducked her head along the muscled back, gripping the scales as tightly as she could. The clouds were dark gray, and though she could not see the sun, she knew sunset was near. As the wyvern swooped over the castle walls, she spotted two figures racing across the drawbridge.

Gild and his sister.

"There!" she said, pointing. "Can you land us in front of those buildings?"

At first, she didn't think the wyvern would listen to her. Then it banked hard to the side.

They dropped toward the ground. She felt the shimmer of the veil falling over the world just as they landed in front of Gild and his sister with a thump and a flap of enormous wings.

Gild cried out, throwing his arm in front of his sister to protect her. His eyes widened as he took in the great golden beast with the ruby gem on its brow—and Serilda astride its back.

She smiled at him, though her whole body was shaking and her hands would not release the wyvern's scales. "We didn't get Solvilde or Hulda," she said, panting. "But we did free the god of war."

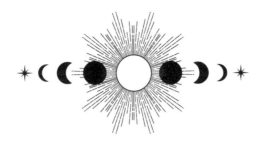

Chapter Forty-Five

The streets of Adalheid were dark, the window shutters latched, not a candle or torchlight to be seen beneath the cloud-covered sky. But Serilda was still afraid that one of the townsfolk might decide to peel back their curtains and peer out to see if the wild hunt was screaming by, and she didn't want them to see Tyrr. The dark ones were frightening enough. The people of Adalheid didn't need to start having nightmares of wyverns in their midst, too.

They retreated outside the gates, finding relative security in the graveyard that sprawled across the rolling hills north of the city.

"Stay alert," said Serilda, having finally caught her breath. "The veil is down and there can be vicious things in graveyards." She shivered, thinking of when her father's corpse had awoken as a nachzehrer.

In response, the princess started to laugh.

Gild and Serilda frowned at her and she cut off abruptly, as if surprised that they hadn't joined her. She returned their frowns in force. "*I* am a vicious thing," she said. "The graveyard should fear *me.*"

Serilda couldn't help the smile that crept across her mouth. Three hundred years old or not, it was impossible not to imagine this girl as a child playing make-believe.

She knew that wasn't fair to her, though. She had rallied countless monsters to her side and fought against Perchta and the dark ones. She had fought valiantly.

"I will keep guard," rumbled a throaty voice.

Serilda started and spun around to find that she was face-to-face, not with a wyvern, but a human. They were shorter than Serilda, but stout and muscular, with a braid of long auburn hair tossed over one shoulder, full lips, and piercing green eyes. Most striking of all was the cut ruby that gleamed from the center of their forehead, marking the division of their face and body—half of which was covered in lizard-like scales, the other half in shining amber skin.

Tyrr did not move while they gaped at them, as if they were used to humans being rendered speechless by their sudden appearance.

"Th-thank you," sputtered Serilda. "That would be appreciated."

With a slow incline of their head, Tyrr picked up a tree branch that had fallen from a nearby oak and cracked it over their knee before tossing away the less pointy end. They approached the side of a moss-covered tombstone and, with effortless grace, hauled themselves up on top. They crouched there, gripping their makeshift spear, still as a gargoyle.

Serilda cleared her throat. Of all the times she'd imagined meeting the gods since she and Gild had concocted their plan, she hadn't thought she would be quite so nervous around one.

"I cannot wear this," said the princess, picking at the nightgown she wore with disgust. "I want my armor back."

"Your armor is in Gravenstone," said Serilda. "For now, it will have to do, until we can find you something else."

"Here," said Gild, undoing the clasps down the front of his jerkin, the one he'd been wearing when he was cursed. Underneath was the same linen shirt he'd always worn, but much cleaner and newer looking. He handed the leather jerkin to the girl, who eyed it with distrust. "It'll be big on you, but it's the best we can do for now."

The girl huffed, but slipped it on over her nightgown. "It's a bit better," she admitted, her lip curled. "But what about my weapons? And my loom?"

"Loom?" asked Gild.

"For my tapestries," she said, as if it should have been obvious.

"Great gods," muttered Serilda. "We broke your curse! We freed you from Gravenstone, like we said we would. We're doing the best we can."

The girl lifted her chin, glaring at Serilda and then Gild. Finally, she said, "Yes, fine. I'm grateful." She did not sound grateful. "And I like that you brought a god with you. I'd never seen a wyvern before." She nodded up toward Tyrr approvingly.

Tyrr raised an eyebrow but said nothing.

"Perhaps we should introduce ourselves?" said Serilda, noting that Gild's eyes kept awkwardly alighting on the princess, then darting away, then back to her again.

"I know who you are," said the princess.

Gild's eyes widened. "You do?"

"Well enough. Your faces have been appearing in my tapestries for centuries." She gestured at Serilda. "Wyrdith-blessed and bride to the Erlking." To Gild. "Gold-spinner. Hulda-blessed, like me." Then to Tyrr. "God of war. Obviously."

Gild and Serilda exchanged looks.

"Yes, well," said Serilda, "it's a bit more complicated than that."

The girl gave Serilda a knowing look. "You do seem like the sort that likes to complicate things."

"No, that's not what I—" She huffed. "Gild, why don't you start?" She nudged him in the side.

"I . . . yes. I'm Gild." He scrunched his shoulders nervously toward his ears.

The princess stared, waiting.

He glanced once at Serilda, as if begging for help, but she just nodded, urging him to continue.

"And I'm . . . ," he started slowly, "the prince of Adalheid."

The princess's keen eyes did not leave his. "Should I *curtsy*?"

"No. No, no." He cleared his throat. "Do you know who *you* are?"

She stood taller, somehow making the oversize jerkin on top of her linen nightgown look almost respectable. "I am Erlenkönigin."

Serilda let out a startled laugh. "The Alder Queen?"

The princess smiled slightly. "You may call me Erlen for short."

"Erlen," repeated Gild. "I like it."

"I didn't ask your opinion."

His grin widened. "I like *you*."

The girl scoffed. "And I think *you* are a royal twit masquerading as a hero."

Above them, Tyrr chuckled.

Gild cast them an affronted look and Tyrr schooled their face into stone again and made a show of scanning the graveyard for potential threats.

Sighing, Gild reached for the chain around his neck. Months ago he had returned the locket to his mortal body, and now he lifted the chain over his head. "All right. But before you were the queen of Gravenstone, you were the princess of Adalheid." He opened the locket, revealing the girl's portrait inside.

Erlen took it from him, inspecting the painting, tilting it one way and then the other. "When was this painted?"

"Before you were taken by the Erlking," said Gild. "Before we were both cursed. My memories of my life before were stolen from me."

"It's a part of the curse placed on your family," explained Serilda. "The Erlking erased the whole world's memories of the royal family of Adalheid. Do *you* have any memories? From before you were in Gravenstone, I mean."

The princess stared at the portrait. "Not many. I remember a castle. Gardens. Learning to weave . . ." She looked up. "Should I remember you?"

"No one does. Turns out, I'm awfully forgettable," said Gild, trying to cover his sadness with a spark of humor.

No one laughed.

Gild cringed at himself, then reached forward to take the locket back from her. But she pulled back, hiding it in her fist. The gold ring on her finger glinted in the moonlight.

"That ring," said Gild. "It's our family seal."

Erlen tilted her hand, peering at the engraved symbol of the tatzelwurm wrapped around the capital *R*. "I've had this ring since I can remember. Lost it once. Took it off when I was weaving because it kept getting caught on the loom. That was years ago."

"Gerdrut found it in the hall with all the tapestries," said Serilda. "Gild has a ring just like it."

With a hard swallow, Gild held up his hand, showing his own royal seal.

Erlen's eyes narrowed. "Princess of Adalheid?"

He nodded. "And . . . also . . . my sister."

They stared at each other a long moment, Gild's eyes full of worry and hope, and Erlen's eyes full of . . . doubt, mostly.

But also a tinge of understanding.

Finally the girl tore her gaze away and dropped it back to the portrait. She snapped the locket shut. "This girl looks like a pretty clay doll. That isn't me. Not anymore."

She held the locket back for Gild, and he took it with a grin. "No. This girl never could have organized a bunch of monsters to set a trap for the Erlking."

She grunted. "Which you ruined."

"An honest mistake." He shook his head, his expression giving in to the wonder he must have been stifling since they'd first seen Erlen in the lunar rotunda. "I thought you were dead. I thought the Erlking killed you all those years ago."

"Please," said Erlen. "He just left me to rot away in that castle of his. The joke is on him, though, isn't it? He underestimated me. He left me a prisoner, but I became a queen. It took less than a year to earn the respect and loyalty of the monsters he'd left behind. Turns out, the dark ones weren't much nicer to them than they are to humans, so it was easy enough to claim them as my own." She smiled haughtily, but it was quick to fade. "Though, I suppose I'm queen of nothing now. These last months have been the worst of all my years of captivity. Having to keep hidden while the dark ones acted like the castle was theirs. And now I don't even have my dear monsters anymore. They were my family. My friends. But they fled after the battle and never came back and I . . . I failed them. They trusted me, and I failed them."

"You didn't fail anyone," said Serilda. "You were brave to stand against the dark ones. They are an impossible enemy."

"No. Not impossible," said Erlen. "I've seen them defeated. Tossed back into the pits of Verloren. I thought that we . . . that I could . . . I thought maybe I could be the one to do it. To save us all." She looked away, and for the first time, Serilda could see how she still had the heart of a little girl on the inside. A child doing her very best.

"What do you mean, you've *seen* it?" asked Gild.

She shot him a bewildered look. "In my tapestries, of course."

Gild's brow furrowed.

"He hasn't seen them," said Serilda. "He was locked in the dungeons the whole time we were at Gravenstone."

"No," said Gild, snapping his fingers. "I saw that one. In the great hall. The gross one, with the Erlking and Perchta being eaten alive in Verloren?"

Erlen brightened. "Easily my favorite. And you see? If the tapestry shows them in the land of the lost, then there is a future possible in which they are no longer in the mortal realm." Her shoulders drooped. "But the tapestries tell me only what's possible, not how to accomplish it."

Serilda sucked in a slow breath, understanding finally striking her. "You said that you're Hulda-blessed," she said. "This is your gift. You weave tapestries that tell the future."

"A possible future," Erlen clarified. "I make good use of them when I can. It's how I knew the dark ones were returning to Gravenstone, otherwise we never could have prepared like we did. Hiding away for weeks without being discovered wasn't just luck."

Serilda's legs felt suddenly weak and she slumped onto the step of a mausoleum. "The tapestry with the seven gods." Her gaze darted up toward Tyrr. "It shows that he will capture all seven. And . . ." Her lips quivered. "And the one that showed Perchta holding my child . . ."

"Perchta sometimes," said Erlen. "But sometimes you. You see? That future isn't decided yet. Once the future is permanent, the tapestry will be unchangeable, too." She frowned. "As for the one depicting the seven godly beasts . . . that one has never changed. I fear it's inevitable."

"No!" said Serilda. She swept her hand toward Tyrr. "We rescued Tyrr, and the Erlking doesn't have Wyrdith, yet."

Erlen shrugged. "We don't know when it's meant to happen. I wove that tapestry more than two hundred years ago, and I've never known when it would come to pass. But I am certain that it will."

Serilda studied the princess, amazed at her gift. "There's a tapestry in Adalheid. It shows a garden party, with the two of you and your parents—the king and queen. Except, the king and queen are dead. Depicted as skeletons." She cringed, wishing there were a gentler way to talk about this. "Do you think maybe it was one of yours?"

Erlen paled. "I . . . don't remember that." She picked at the lace cuff of her nightgown. "But it might have been, yes."

"That's awful," murmured Gild. "You must have been so young when you wove it. Do you think you knew what it meant? That it was . . . inevitable? That our parents would be killed and we would be . . . whatever we are."

Erlen shrugged. "I suppose we'll never know."

Serilda pursed her lips.

Had *Gild* known what it meant? Had their parents? Or had the young princess been so horrified she hadn't even shown it to them?

It did explain why the tapestry seemed to glow on the mortal side of the veil. Why it had not been destroyed by the basilisk's venom. It really was crafted of magic. A god-blessed tapestry.

Suddenly, Tyrr launched to their feet on top of the gravestone. "Nacht-krapp!"

Serilda gasped and stood, reaching for the sword at her hip only to remember it had been lost inside the castle.

A beat of wings was followed by a large black bird soaring toward them.

Tyrr lifted the broken stick over one shoulder, preparing to throw it. "Not as good as a bow," they muttered, "but it will do."

"Wait!" screamed Erlen. "Don't hurt it!"

Tyrr hesitated.

The nachtkrapp cawed shrilly and dropped straight into the princess's arms.

"Helgard!" cried the princess. "You're all right!" She tenderly stroked the bird's wings.

The bird cawed and pressed the top of its head affectionately against the princess's palm.

Then, suddenly, the foliage of the nearby oak tree began to tremble. More creatures emerged, squawking and hissing.

The princess released a cry of delight as the creatures surrounded her. "Udo! Tilly! Wendelina! You're here!" She set the nachtkrapp down on a tombstone and held out her arms to the nearest monster—a small, shaggy wood elf—then smoothed the fur of a feldgeist that would have looked like a plain orange cat if it weren't for the crackles of lightning that occasionally flickered along its tail. "Oh—Pim! You're hurt!" Erlen fell to her knees before a small drude with a broken wing. "Did this happen during the fight with the dark ones? You poor sausage. We're going to have to rebreak the bone to reset it properly."

The drude hissed and ducked away.

"I know, I know. We won't do it now. We'll need wrapping first, and something to use as a splint. But it will have to be done, and I expect you to be brave."

"Erlen," said Serilda, "how did they find you?"

"These are my subjects. We are connected by our very souls," said Erlen. "They will always find me."

Tyrr made a doubtful noise in their throat. "More likely, they were waiting in the woods, and they smelled her coming out of the castle."

Erlen stuck her tongue out at them.

"Which means the hunt will be able to find us pretty easily, too." Serilda glanced up at the sky, where clouds had partially covered the full Hunter's Moon. "They could be on their way to Adalheid now."

"Or," said Gild, "they're on the hunt for Wyrdith."

Serilda pressed her lips together. If Erlen was right, and it was inevitable that the Erlking would eventually capture all seven gods, then what was the point of trying to find Wyrdith first? It seemed the Erlking's wicked plan couldn't be stopped.

But there was still the matter of the wish. Of Wyrdith owing Serilda a favor, whether or not they knew it.

Her fate wasn't sealed. She could still reclaim her body and her child. But she would have to find Wyrdith first.

"Wait," said Serilda, tilting her head to one side. "Your tapestries. You said that the future in which the Erlking captures all seven gods is inevitable, but what about the future in which the Erlking and Perchta are sent back to Verloren?"

Erlen plopped down in the middle of the path, allowing the monsters to gather around her, not unlike how the five children had used to gather around Serilda when she told them tales. "I take it you didn't spend much time studying that tapestry?"

Serilda grimaced. "I found it rather disturbing. So, no. I guess not."

"Disturbing?" said the princess. "I always thought it was my best work. But if you had seen both depictions, then you would know that in certain lights it showed Erlkönig and Perchta in Verloren. In other lights . . . it showed them in Gravenstone. Not being tortured by monsters, but rather . . . being served and waited on." She sighed glumly. "By humans."

Serilda shut her eyes, discouraged.

"But that means there's still hope," said Gild, drawing her attention back to him. "There *is* a way to drive them back to the underworld. We just need to figure out how. Erlen, your tapestries don't show you what causes one future to occur over another?"

She shook her head. "No. I just weave, and the future is what it is."

Gild scratched behind his ear, deep in thought. "What if you wove the future that we wanted. What if you made a tapestry that showed us beating the Erlking?"

Erlen scoffed. "It doesn't work like that. I've tried a thousand times to weave the future I *want* onto the loom. To show my curse being broken. Myself being free of Gravenstone. To show the dark ones being buried under enormous piles of dragon dung. But it doesn't work. The threads weave what they want to weave."

"But the threads you use," said Gild. "They're just normal threads, aren't they?"

Her expression turned suspicious. "Sure. Whatever we could find in the castle. My monsters dismantled a lot of bed linens for me." She tenderly stroked the head of an alp at her side.

"Have you ever worked with spun gold before?"

Erlen's fingers stilled. "You mean . . . *your* gold?"

"Exactly. This might sound absurd, but . . . Hulda blessed us both with these gifts. What if . . . what if they're intended to work together?" Gild went on before she could answer. "What if . . . if you were to weave a tapestry using spun gold? It's supposed to be indestructible, so maybe that would make the future you weave with it indestructible, too? What if you could create an image that shows us how to win against the dark ones? We know it's possible, right? We just need to know *how*."

Erlen started to shake her head, but hesitated. "I suppose I could try. But do you have any gold for me to use?"

"Not here," said Gild. "I'll need a spinning wheel."

"And I'll need a loom."

"How long will this take?" boomed Tyrr's rough voice. "Weaving this tapestry."

"Days, if not weeks," said Erlen. "Depends on how big it's going to be. Bigger works tend to have more detail, and details give more information."

"But the wild hunt rides even now, hunting for Wyrdith," said the god. "Hunting for *me*, once Erlkönig knows I have escaped him."

"What else can we do?" said Gild. "We have no way to fight them. They're immortal."

"It would seem to me," said Tyrr, "you already fought Perchta once, and you won." They crossed their broad arms over their chest. "I do not remember *you*, young prince. But I remember the arrow that struck Perchta's heart, tethering her to the veil until Velos could claim her. It was a *very* good shot."

"Er, thanks," said Gild. "Did you have anything to do with it?"

Tyrr smirked. "I only gave a *little* help."

Gild sulked. "Thought maybe it was all me."

"It wasn't the precision of your aim that defeated the huntress," said Tyrr. "If any arrow could so easily entrap a dark one, they would not be nearly as formidable. So I wonder, what *was* that arrow?"

Serilda gasped. "Gold! It was a golden arrow!"

Gild blinked at her. "It was?"

"Yes. Or at least, a gold-tipped arrow. Just like the arrows the Erlking used to tether our spirits, and capture the gods. His arrows must be god-spun gold, too. I would bet anything that the arrows he uses were yours once. He probably stole them after he cursed you."

Gild started to pace. "So . . . if we had hundreds of golden arrows, we could shoot every dark one and send them all back to Verloren?"

"In theory, yes. If Velos was free to take them back."

"This is a lot of *ifs*," said Erlen.

"But it's not impossible, right?" said Serilda.

Gild heaved a long sigh. "Thread for a tapestry, gold for arrows . . . it will take time. Where do we find a spinning wheel?"

"Adalheid," said Serilda. "You're mortal now. The people there will welcome you with open arms—their own Vergoldetgeist. Plus, there's already so much god-spun gold in that city thanks to all the gifts you've given them over the years. Maybe you can use some of them."

"But if it's indestructible," mused Erlen, "how do you change it into arrowheads?"

"Gild can mold it into whatever he wants. Right, Gild?"

He nodded. "Easy enough. But . . . Serilda." His eyes darted toward the clouds, where a faint halo from the full moon was shining through. "When the veil falls . . ."

He didn't have to finish. As long as Serilda did not have a mortal body, they would be separated.

That is—unless the Erlking succeeded in having the gods destroy the veil, but that would cause far more problems that she didn't want to think about.

"I'm not staying with you," she said. "You and Erlen will go to Adalheid, and I will try to find Wyrdith."

"It's not the Endless Moon," said Gild. "What if Wyrdith can't grant your wish and put you back in your body?"

She shrugged. "The baby is due soon. If I wait until the winter solstice, it might be too late."

Gild dragged a frustrated hand through his hair. "You can't go alone. The wild hunt is probably searching for Wyrdith as we speak."

Serilda gulped and glanced at Tyrr. "Well," she said slowly, "I hoped I wouldn't be completely alone."

"Wyrdith lived a nomadic life," said Tyrr. "They might be difficult to find."

"I know," said Serilda. "But I know there was a time when they lived on the basalt cliffs in the north. I might be wrong, but I think they could be there still."

Tyrr regarded her for a long moment. "The cliffs are not far. We could be there before midnight."

Her insides warmed. "Really? You'll come with me?"

"I will take you to the cliffs," said Tyrr. They grinned hungrily, teeth flashing. "And should we encounter the wild hunt, I will relish the chance to return Erlkönig's favor and put an arrow into *his* flesh this time."

Chapter Forty-Six

Serilda did not know whether she was more terrified or euphoric. The wind in her face tasted of salt, so she knew the ocean was not far off. The crimson cloak billowed around her, whipping against her back, while far below, the world was painted in swaths of burgundy and ochre—the forest's final hurrah of brilliant colors before the onset of winter would cover everything in gray and white. Dappled moonlight lit the earth in patches of silver and she occasionally spotted the flickering torchlights of a village settled along a black, winding river.

She searched the ground below for signs of the hunt barreling across the land, but everything was serene and still.

She wished she felt comfort in that.

This was the final full moon before the winter solstice. This was the night the Erlking would be hunting Wyrdith.

They dove into a cloud, and she could see nothing but wispy gray. The cold gnawed at her fingers the farther north they flew, making it difficult to cling to the scales on Tyrr's back. She lowered her face as wind stung her cheeks and frost gathered on the tips of her braids.

Tyrr banked sharply to the west. They dipped beneath the cloud cover, and Serilda drew in a bewildered gasp to see a black abyss beneath her.

The ocean.

Churning waves speckled silver and white as they crashed against jagged rocks far, far below.

"Here!" she cried. "Land here!"

Faint moonlight defined a sharp line of the black basalt cliffs, giant columns plummeting toward the ocean. They were bigger than she'd imagined, and Serilda couldn't help the sense of foreboding, of helplessness. Could Wyrdith really be here, in this cold, inhospitable place? The cliffs stretched on for miles and miles. How would she ever find the god?

"There!" she said, pointing toward a narrow plateau. The god flattened their wings and soared down. Serilda's stomach swooped toward her throat and she clung tighter.

A whistle came from down below.

She felt a thud as something struck the wyvern. Tyrr hissed and bucked, leaning sideways so unexpectedly Serilda screamed and barely held on. As the wyvern regained control, she glimpsed the black fletching of an arrow jutting from behind one of the beast's shoulders.

Wide-eyed, she looked around, searching for the hunt below, but it was too dark.

Another whistle.

Another thud.

"Tyrr!" she screamed as the wyvern turned sharply again. Suddenly they were free-falling. The beast spun through the air—Serilda was upside down, then airborne—and her fingers at last lost their grip on the god's scaled back.

She screamed, arms flailing as her cloak whipped around her, and she dropped headlong through the air.

Then the wyvern was there. Claws in her cloak. Wings around her.

They slammed into the ground with such force, it knocked the air from Serilda's lungs. Their bodies rolled together across the rocks of the plateau, and she felt every scrape, every thump, every brutal strike of the unrelenting ground. When they stopped, she found herself sprawled beside Tyrr in their human form—not wings, but arms wrapped around her.

"Tyrr," she croaked, struggling to draw in breath as she pushed herself onto her knees. She saw the arrows. One had snapped in the fall, and only a broken shaft still stuck out from Tyrr's shoulder. The other arrow she found intact in their thigh. "Tyrr! Are you all right?"

"I will be," groaned the god, sitting up and looking around. "But the hunt is close."

"I'm sorry," she gasped. "I shouldn't have asked you to bring me here!"

"I made my choice," said Tyrr in their gruff tone. They grabbed the arrow in their leg and yanked it from their flesh. Not gold, she noticed, explaining why Tyrr was not already trapped in their wyvern form. Maybe the Erlking was finally running out of his magic arrows.

Serilda grimaced, covering her mouth with both hands as blood gushed across the rocky ground. "You're immortal. How can gods bleed when the dark ones do not?"

"We are made of flesh and bone," Tyrr said. "They are made of nothing but darkness."

Tyrr staggered to their feet and yanked Serilda up beside them. Folding their large hands over Serilda's shoulders, Tyrr stared into her eyes. "Find Wyrdith. Warn them the hunt is coming. I will lure the dark ones away and keep them preoccupied until the veil falls." Tyrr flashed a haughty grin. "Be careful, godchild of Wyrdith."

With a flourish of their arm, one broken arrow still jutting from their shoulder, Tyrr transformed back into the hulking form of the rubinrot wyvern. They raced for the plateau's edge and jumped, soaring out over the ocean waves. Moonlight glistened off their scales as they spiraled upward, *wanting* the hunt to take notice. The god of war spun back toward land and soared off, disappearing into the night sky.

Shivering, Serilda wrapped the cloak around her and looked around. For a long moment she couldn't move, paralyzed by fear and cold and the horrible sensation that the hunt would be upon her any moment. The Erlking must have been close to strike Tyrr, and yet, she heard no howling hounds or stampeding horses or the haunting bellow of the horn.

The night was eerily quiet, but for the crashing of waves far below.

Her legs shook from the flight and the fall, but she made her way to the cliffside anyway.

The edges looked like they'd been sheared away with a knife, plummeting straight down to the whitecaps below, only the occasional ledge breaking up the sheer cliff face. She felt like she was standing at the edge of the world.

"Wyrdith?" she called. But her voice was weak and the wind stole the name away as soon as it left her mouth.

Again she searched the horizon for signs of the hunt. The plateau was wide enough that she'd have some warning of their approach, but she was vulnerable here with nowhere to hide.

She looked over the ledge again, scanning the bluff. She saw nothing that suggested a shelter or a home. Nowhere a god might find sanctuary.

How did one find a god if that god did not wish to be found?

A cloud passed in front of the Hunter's Moon, casting the world in darkness.

Which was when she saw a glint of gold.

She squinted. Her eyes stung from the wind and she rubbed her palms into them, just as the moonlight spilled again across the cliffs.

She was peering at a long golden feather, trapped beneath a fallen rock on an outcrop, fluttering in the relentless wind.

Serilda got onto her hands and knees. It was a far drop, but there was a ledge wide enough to catch her, and a few craggy holds in the cliffside that she might use for purchase.

"Wyrdith?" she called again. "Can you hear me?"

Only the wind responded.

Checking the clasp on her cloak, she slid one leg off the ledge, turning awkwardly onto her stomach before sliding the other leg over, too. Her feet scrambled against the rocks until her toes found a ledge. Inhaling deeply, she scooted herself down until she was barely clinging to the clifftop. Already her arms were shaking from the effort, but she managed to find a small crevasse to wedge her left fingers into. She lowered herself down, foot by hand by foot, and managed to get halfway to the feather before the small foothold she'd found broke from her weight.

Serilda screamed and fell, hands scraping against the cliffside.

She landed in a heap.

With a moan, she held up her hands. Her palms were raw and bleeding, but she hadn't broken any bones.

She peered up to the plateau's ledge and realized with a sinking feeling that she had no way of climbing back up. Then she looked down toward the ocean and shuddered. The last thing she wanted to do was scale these cliffs, because even if she *could* make it to the bottom, the waves would just toss her against the rocks, with no shore in sight.

After picking bits of sharp rock from her palms, she scooted closer to the feather. How long could such a delicate thing last here, bombarded by the ocean winds? A day? A season? A decade?

She had no way of knowing, but she was sure of one thing as she grabbed the feather and yanked it free.

At one time, it had been Wyrdith's. The great golden raptor.

She twisted it in her fingers. A subtle haze of light bounced off the sheer black wall.

Serilda frowned. She twisted the feather again, watching its light glitter, almost imperceptibly reflecting along the surface.

Shimmer . . . sparkle . . . *nothing.*

There was a void, an opening, just a little farther along the ledge.

She climbed unsteadily to her feet, cringing as her ankle throbbed, but it wasn't so bad that she couldn't stumble forward. She made her way along the ledge until she came to the yawning mouth of a pitch-black cave.

Serilda stepped inside. The feather's glow did little to push back the shadows, and she could just feel along the rocky walls, slick and damp.

She bumped into something. It fell with a crash and Serilda cried out, startled.

"Sorry, I'm sorry," she murmured, dropping to her hands and knees and feeling around for what had fallen. Her fingers landed on a slender beeswax candle. She felt around some more, eventually finding a carved stone candlestick and—finally—flint and steel.

Hope surged through her veins as she lit the wick. It crackled and sputtered, the damp air not wanting to let the flame take hold. Finally, the candle burned steady enough for Serilda to lift it up and take in her surroundings.

This opening to the cave held nothing more than the small table she had knocked over, a box of candles, and two lanterns.

But just beyond stood a heavy black drape hung across a narrowing of the cave. To keep out the cold and, perhaps, to keep in the light, if someone did not wish to be found.

Holding her breath, Serilda pulled back the curtain.

Chapter Forty-Seven

The cave was just as dark and cold on the other side of the curtain. Serilda found a candelabra and lit its seven candles, illuminating the cavern in a reassuring light.

The space was smaller than the home she had shared with Papa beside the gristmill. A desk on one wall held golden quills and parchment and jars of ink in red and indigo, scattered alongside blown-glass paperweights and enormous seashells, a marble sculpture of a winged woman, a necklace of large wooden beads, a pocket atlas that seemed to be falling apart at the spine, a baby's cap knit from soft gray wool.

Behind the desk was a cot overflowing with fur blankets and thick quilts.

Along an opposite wall were rough-hewn bookshelves, their centers sloping from the weight of too many tomes. Some volumes were leather-bound with gilt-edged pages, others were little more than stacks of unkempt papers. There were bundles of yellowing scrolls. Journals and notebooks. She held the candle closer to the faded spines, reading the titles. Scholarly works on history appeared beside fables and fairy tales.

The walls were as eclectic as the shelves. An oil painting of a small cottage with a waterwheel hung beside a map of Ottelien. Two tapestries depicted animals of land and sea, while a series of charcoal sketches captured the same group of elderly fishermen throughout a day—preparing their nets, bringing home the day's haul, relaxing beside a fire with pints of ale.

Altogether, the space felt comfortable. Cozy, even.

But the air held a chill that seeped into Serilda's core, and there was a musky smell that suggested the room had not been aired out in some time.

It felt lived in, but not recently.

Wyrdith was not here.

Serilda thought of the last story she had told to the children, in which Wyrdith had ventured out to live among mortals.

And she knew that nearly nineteen years ago, on the Endless Moon, Wyrdith had been near Märchenfeld, for her father had found the raptor wounded and hiding behind the mill.

Her hopes crumbled. The god of stories was not here. They had left the cliffs long ago.

There was only one consolation. At least this time, her tale would not lead the wild hunt straight into the path of another god.

She dragged a finger over the assorted oddities on the writing desk. She hadn't realized until this moment how much she wanted to meet Wyrdith. The god who had blessed her. The god who had cursed her.

And what for? Her father had helped Wyrdith, and all he'd wished for in return was a healthy child. Why had she been given these wheeled eyes, this unfaithful tongue? Why had the god filled her head with stories—both true and false?

A piece of paper caught her eye, poking out from a stack of notes written in the tiniest, most meticulous handwriting. Serilda shifted the stacks aside and pulled out a small codex, hand-bound with black thread.

Hardworking Stiltskin and the Northern Prince.

She remembered this title from the collection of fairy tales Leyna had given her. Gild had liked this one, but she still hadn't read it herself.

She remembered Leyna telling her about the book's popularity in the library, having been written by some notable scholar from Verene. What had the introduction to the book said? Something about how the author had traveled the country, compiling folk stories that melded with local history ...

Serilda smoothed a wrinkle from the cover and opened the pages. This was not a finished, published copy. There were notes all over the pages. Words crossed out and changed, whole paragraphs marked to be reordered.

Her breath snagged. Could the scholar from Verene be *Wyrdith*?

"Of course," Serilda murmured. The god of stories . . . what *else* would they be doing?

She was a fool. Here she was, at the northernmost point of Tulvask, expecting to find a god hiding in a dark, cold cave, when in all likelihood, that god was probably in an apartment at the University of Verene, squandering their time in public houses and the parlors of nobility, collecting stories and spinning tales of their own.

She started to laugh, feeling like she'd once again been tricked by the trickster god.

"What has amused you so?" asked a lilting voice.

Serilda cried out and jumped back, knocking the candle to the floor. It extinguished instantly, but the candelabra in the corner lit up the strikingly tall figure holding back the curtain.

They stepped into the room, letting the curtain fall shut. Serilda gaped, speechless. They had pale pink skin and cropped black hair that shone almost purple when it caught the light. And . . . their eyes. Watchful and curious, with spoked golden wheels over dark irises.

"It is not that funny a story," said Wyrdith—for this *must* be Wyrdith. "More of a morality tale, really. With determination and a good work ethic, you *too* could inspire a kingdom." They snorted, almost derisively. "That's what happens when one prays to Hulda. They receive a legacy of hard work, and call themselves lucky for it." They took a candlestick off a shelf and lit the wick from the candelabra, then cocked their head toward Serilda. "Who are you? How did you come to be here?"

"I . . . Tyrr brought me," Serilda stammered. "I was looking for you. I didn't mean to . . ." She gestured at the papers on the desk, embarrassed to have been caught reading them.

"Tyrr?" said Wyrdith. "Truly? Are they still as cranky as ever?"

Serilda considered this. "I would say *stoic* more than *cranky*. They've had a rough time of late."

Wyrdith laughed. Not a mild, restrained chuckle, but a boisterous laugh, a *friendly* laugh. "Yes, well, it's hard to pity the god who once started a nine-year war over a game of cards. Now, why did Tyrr bring—"

Their words cut off abruptly as they raised the candle, throwing Serilda into the light.

Wyrdith's lips parted in surprise.

Serilda fidgeted. She hadn't meant to hide her eyes, exactly, but she found it difficult to hold eye contact with the god. "My father helped you," she said haltingly. "On the last Endless Moon. He found you, injured, and in return for his help you granted him a wish. He asked for—"

"A healthy child," whispered the god. "I remember."

Serilda swallowed. "I am that child."

"Yes," said Wyrdith, astonished. "Yes, you are." With a shake, the god looked away. They set to straightening papers on the desk, though the room was not overly tidy. "I was rather fond of that village. I'd passed through as a bard once and thought that perhaps I would go back and stay awhile. I'd been there for years, and not once had the hunt come through. So I became careless. I thought—what is the harm? Perhaps this Endless Moon, I will stay. Surely, the hunt cannot know to look for a . . . plain village maiden. Surely, when I am forced to take my beastly form, I can slip into the Aschen Wood, hide until the veil falls again." A faint smile touched their lips, then faded again. "But the hunt did find me. I won't make that mistake again. Now I come here on the full moons, where the hunt has never ventured."

Serilda stepped around the desk, gripping her hands together, though they still stung from the fall from the cliff. "Forgive me. I mean no intrusion, but we have to leave. The hunt is coming for you *now*. The Erlking is trying to capture all seven gods before the Endless Moon. I believe he means to wish for the destruction of the veil. He has five of you already, and might have Tyrr again by the end of the night. If he comes for you, too . . ." She trailed off.

Wyrdith's face was more contemplative than worried. "And where shall I go?" They gestured around at the cave. "You must have somewhere in mind that is safer than here?"

The question gave Serilda pause. "I . . . I just thought we would run. Keep running until the sun rises."

Wyrdith smiled softly. "Even on wings, I am not faster than the hunt." They peered up toward the ceiling. "The Erlking has searched the cliffs before, but he has not found me yet."

"I found you!" said Serilda. "And the Erlking *always* finds me." She grimaced, wondering if the god would think it a betrayal if Serilda's presence brought the hunt straight to them.

But the god's hesitant smile did not fade. "You surely did find me. How, exactly?"

"There was a feather, trapped beneath a rock, out on the ledge."

"A feather. My—how careless of me." Wyrdith scratched their ear, which struck Serilda as an oddly human gesture. "You brought it inside, I trust?"

"I did." Serilda gestured to where she had set the feather on a stack of books by the doorway.

"Perhaps fate and fortune intended us to meet this way all along. Regardless, I do think we are safer here than we would be braving the world beneath the Hunter's Moon."

Serilda gnawed on her lower lip. She felt anxious, her instincts telling her to run. But maybe Wyrdith was right. Maybe it was safer to hide.

She swallowed. "Wyrdith? There is . . . something else. Another reason I came."

Wyrdith met her eye. "Yes?"

Was it Serilda's imagination that they, too, seemed suddenly nervous? Did they know what she wanted to ask?

Serilda cleared her throat. "I want to claim a wish from you. It's a very long story, but you see . . . Perchta, the huntress, was given my body as a vessel for her spirit, and I want it back."

Wyrdith gawked at her, speechless.

"Can . . . can you help me?"

Slowly, the god exhaled. "It would seem you have a lot of stories to tell."

"That is a vast understatement," said Serilda.

A flicker of regret crossed the god's face, and they slowly shook their head. "I would very much like to help you, but—"

"Don't say no," Serilda interrupted. "You owe me. You cursed me for no reason, and my father *helped* you. Please."

Wyrdith lowered their eyes. They were silent a long moment, as if considering Serilda's words, before finally they said, simply, "Wishes can only be granted on the Endless Moon."

Serilda flinched. She had worried this would be the god's response. "But you're magic. You're a god. There must be something you can do."

Wyrdith gave a humorless laugh. Then they picked up the bound pages Serilda had been examining. "Do you enjoy fairy tales?"

The sudden change of topic was so disconcerting that Serilda wasn't sure how to answer. "I . . . yes, I do," she admitted. "I have this story in a book, actually. *Your* book, I think? A collection a friend gave to me, though I—I'm afraid I haven't had time to read the story, yet."

Wyrdith sat on the edge of the cot, flipping through the crackling pages. "It's an old story, though few know it. I've often found, when all is forgotten by history, a good story can still live on. A good story can live forever."

"I thought it was just a boring morality tale."

At this, Wyrdith grinned, meeting Serilda's gaze again. "Morality tale, yes. Boring? No." The god cocked their head, squinting at Serilda in the dim light. "Would you like to hear it?"

Serilda knew she should say no. The hunt was after them, even now. Surely there must be something they could do to prepare themselves for the inevitable fight once the Erlking found them.

But something had tugged at her when Wyrdith asked the question, a yearning in the pit of Serilda's stomach. Would she ever again have the chance to listen to a fairy tale told to her by the god of stories?

"Yes," she whispered. "I would."

In ages past, there lived a king who had thirteen children. Not wanting only his eldest child to inherit the kingdom, he determined that he would divide the land into thirteen equal portions, so that each prince and princess would be given a part of his kingdom and wealth. This led to a problem, however, for the thirteenth portion of the kingdom, that lay far to the north, was nothing but a dreary swampland, long overrun with vicious monsters, and none of the king's children wished to rule such a place. The king tried hard to persuade his youngest son, Prince Rumpel, to accept the gift, for he was the most pleasant of all the king's children and the least prone to complaint. But even the warmhearted Prince Rumpel did not want the northern lands, for he hoped to someday rule over a prosperous kingdom, and he did not wish to be saddled with a land in which nothing good could flourish.

Thus, the king planned a contest, which he believed would fairly determine who should inherit the northern parcel.

He made a decree to all his subjects throughout the kingdom that whosoever should bring him a golden acorn from the magical tree that grew in the center of an enchanted forest would be given their own kingdom to rule and the hand of whichever prince or princess they should choose. Thus, the chosen heir would inherit the lands of the north.

Now, there lived a peasant in the nearest village by the name of Stiltskin, and while he was very poor, he was also a diligent worker with many skills. All that he had, he had made for himself. His leather boots had been stitched by his own hand. His warm cloak made of wool he had spun and woven. He lived on the bread he baked and the vegetables he grew.

When Stiltskin heard of the king's contest, he thought this might be a chance to improve his lot in life, and he set off into the forest to find the tree with the golden acorns.

Stiltskin had not traveled far when he heard the pitiful squeaking of a mouse, who was shivering beneath a small leaf.

"Good day, little mouse," said Stiltskin. "Whatever troubles you?"

"The winter will soon be here," said the mouse, "and I have no shelter but this little leaf, which surely will not keep me warm or dry when the snows come."

Stiltskin thought hard on this, and then he slipped off one of the boots he had stitched himself and gave it to the mouse. "This will serve as a very good shelter for you to last until the spring."

The mouse was grateful. In return, he gave to Stiltskin a walnut shell filled with a single drop of morning dew. "Plant this in the ground, and it will become a great lake filled with clean, cool water," said the mouse.

Stiltskin thanked him and tucked the walnut shell carefully into his pocket, then set off on his way.

He had not traveled far when he heard the pitiful groaning of a great brown bear, who sat shivering outside his cave.

"Good day, great bear," said Stiltskin. "Whatever troubles you?"

"The winter will soon be here," said the bear, "and while my cave gives me shelter, it is so very cold. I have nothing to keep me warm when the snows come, and I am sure I will shiver the whole winter through."

Stiltskin thought hard on this, and then he took off the cloak he had woven himself and gave it to the bear. "This will keep you very warm until the spring."

The bear was grateful. In return, he gave Stiltskin a stone taken from the mouth of his cave. "Plant this in the ground, and it will become a great castle, with tall turrets and strong walls," said the bear.

Stiltskin thanked him and tucked the stone carefully into his pocket, then set off on his way.

He had not traveled far when he heard the pitiful mewing of a tiny deer, who sat crying in a meadow.

"Good day, tiny deer," said Stiltskin. "Whatever troubles you?"

"The winter will soon be here," said the deer, "and while my den will shelter me, and my brothers and sisters will give me warmth, we do not have enough food to last the winter through. Surely, my family will starve."

Stiltskin thought hard on this, and then he opened his pouch and took out the loaves of bread he had baked and the vegetables he had grown, and he gave them to the deer. "This will keep you very well-fed until the spring."

The deer was grateful. In return, she gave to Stiltskin a bouquet of wildflowers picked from the meadow. "Spread these seeds upon the ground," said the deer, "and any creature who eats of them will become your friend and servant."

Stiltskin thanked her and tucked the wildflowers carefully into his pocket, then set off on his way.

Soon, Stiltskin came to the great oak tree that grew in the center of the forest. Its branches hung with shimmering golden acorns, but the tree was protected by an enormous tatzelwurm.

Stiltskin greeted the tatzelwurm kindly and asked if he might have a golden acorn so as to win the king's contest.

The tatzelwurm studied the poor peasant. "No magic is given for free," said the beast. "What would you trade?"

Stiltskin considered. He did not want to give up the beautiful gifts he had been given during his journey, but he had nothing else to offer. He laid them out before the tatzelwurm—the walnut shell with the single drop of dew, the stone from the mouth of the bear's cave, the bouquet of wildflowers.

The tatzelwurm nodded, as if pleased with these offerings. But rather than take the gifts, the beast said, "I have been watching you as you journeyed through the forest, and I have seen that you are both hardworking and generous. I will not take these gifts. Instead, I ask that when this acorn is planted, you give to me whatever grows in that place."

Thinking this a very fair deal, Stiltskin agreed, and he was given the golden acorn.

He took the acorn to the king, who brought before him his thirteen children and offered Stiltskin his choice in marriage. But before Stiltskin could speak, all but the youngest turned their backs on him, proclaiming they would never be wed to a poor peasant so far beneath them.

Only young Prince Rumpel could see that Stiltskin was hardworking and generous, handsome and good, and he said that he would marry the one who had brought back the golden acorn. For their wedding, the king bestowed on the couple the golden acorn and two horses with which to make the trek to the northern lands of his kingdom, which now belonged to them.

Stiltskin and the prince traveled many weeks, for the terrain was difficult and the northern lands far. Winter came and snow covered the land. When they arrived at their new kingdom, Prince Rumpel looked forlornly upon the swamplands that greeted them, where nothing lived but monsters and beasts.

"What shall we do?" asked the prince. "There is no kingdom here over which to rule."

Stiltskin told the prince not to worry. He took the walnut shell with the single drop of dew and planted it in the soil. No sooner had he done so than the swamp waters ran as clear as crystal, and the land before them became a beautiful blue lake.

Then Stiltskin buried the stone from the mouth of the bear's cave, and in its place emerged a great castle.

Lastly, Stiltskin took the flowers and shook them, so that their seeds scattered across the ground. The monsters came and ate the seeds, and as they did, they transformed into humans—bakers and cobblers, spinners and weavers, farmers and millers and all manner of craftspeople. They were so hardworking and industrious, and ruled over by such generous kings, that the northern lands soon became very prosperous, just as Prince Rumpel had wished.

But as the years passed, there developed a sorrow in the hearts of Stiltskin and his prince, for they came to want for a child.

"We can take the golden acorn and give it as an offering to Eostrig, god of fertility," said Prince Rumpel, "and pray that they give us a child of our own."

But Stiltskin remembered the promise he had made to the tatzelwurm and told Rumpel that the bargain must be honored. "If fate wishes for us to have a child, we will find another way," he said. So he took the golden acorn into the castle gardens and planted it there.

From the acorn emerged a golden sapling. But when the leaves unfurled—inside lay a newborn child.

Stiltskin and Rumpel rejoiced, believing their prayers to be answered.

But in the next moment, Hulda, god of labor, appeared. "It was I, disguised as the tatzelwurm, who gave you that acorn," said the god, "and now I come to claim what is mine."

Stiltskin was heartbroken, but knowing that a deal is a deal, he offered the child to the god.

Hulda took the babe into their arms. "This child will bear my blessing," said the god, "as will all of your descendants. So long as they are as hardworking as their founding kings, their labors will be fruitful, their blessings abundant, their people prosperous. I give only one condition—that use of my magic never be given away without recompense, for all good work should be honored with proper payment. Honor my blessing, and your kingdom will thrive for generations to come."

With these words, Hulda gave the child back to the two kings, and was gone.

The child grew to be as hardworking as Stiltskin and as warmhearted as Rumpel, and the northern kingdom was joyful and prosperous forever after.

Chapter Forty-Eight

As Wyrdith spoke, Serilda had sunk down onto the foot of the cot, astounded by how comforting it felt to listen to the god's gentle voice, recounting this unfamiliar tale.

Though—not wholly unfamiliar.

"Like Gild," Serilda whispered once they had finished. "Given Hulda's blessing, but his magic can't be given away for free. There's always a price." She frowned. "Do you gods realize that your gifts often end up causing so much trouble?"

"Yes," mused Wyrdith. "Though we generally mean well."

Serilda smiled slightly, wanting to believe it. "Thank you for telling me that story. I feel like I've heard it before, but I can't place where."

The worn pages crinkled in Wyrdith's fingers. "Indeed. You have heard this story, many times, though I would not expect you to remember. You were so very young, but . . . but there was a time when it was one of your favorites."

Serilda frowned. "What do you mean?"

Tears sparkled in the god's eyes. "Serilda," they said, even though Serilda was certain she had not given her name. "I know you wouldn't recognize me, but . . . I would have known you anywhere."

They exhaled slowly and stood from the cot.

As Serilda stared, the god's hair grew longer, changing from purple-black to wavy brown locks. Their cheeks rounded, their figure became curvier, their lips fuller. In appearance, the woman before her was not much older than Serilda was now. When they opened their eyes, they no longer had the golden wheels on their irises. Their eyes, instead, were bluish green, and when they flashed an uncertain smile, Serilda saw a chipped front tooth.

She did not remember her, not beyond what her father had told her, but there was no mistaking that the woman before her—the *god* before her—was her mother.

Serilda shot to her feet and backed away. Wyrdith. The god. The—

The very being who had cursed her.

Blessed her?

Given *birth* to her?

"H-how?" she stammered, bumping into the corner of the desk.

Wyrdith lifted a calming hand, their expression worried. How was it that a fairy tale told long ago was more familiar to her than the face of her own mother? "Serilda . . ."

"No," she said, shaking her head. "You're a trickster god. A liar. This isn't—you can't be—"

"I don't wish to frighten you," said Wyrdith. "But, oh, my Serilda, if you knew how many times I dreamed of seeing you again. Planned what I would tell you. What I would say—"

"Did my father know?" she interrupted, surprised at the venom in her tone. There were so many emotions warring inside Serilda, she would not have expected anger to be at the forefront, but there it was. Anger, mixed with an odd sense of betrayal.

"That I was Wyrdith? No. No, of course not. He was so young when we met. And I was just . . . I was the poor orphan girl, come to Märchenfeld seeking work and a new beginning. He was so kind. So *good*. But I . . . I didn't realize how deep his feelings for me ran until the night he made his wish and I agreed to grant it."

"He loved you!" Serilda cried. "He loved you so much. How could you . . . ?"

"I loved him, too." Wyrdith stepped closer, hands held in supplication. "As I loved *you.*"

"Then why did you leave?" Serilda shouted, her emotions spilling out of her like a pot bubbling over. "We thought you were taken by the hunt! We thought you were *dead*! And all this time you were . . . you were *here*. Hiding in a cave, and . . . and writing books of fairy tales? Living in Verene?"

"I was trying to protect you. Both of you. I knew the Erlking would find me again. He had come so close before, and I knew he would not give up. If he ever found out about you or Hugo, he would use you against me. I couldn't let that happen."

Clutching the sides of her head, Serilda paced between the desk and the bookshelves. Her thoughts were spinning. Her entire world was spinning.

Wyrdith. God of stories. God of fortune. Her own patron deity.

Wyrdith was her mother.

Her mother was alive.

Her mother was not mortal.

"Great gods," whispered Serilda. "Am I . . . ? What does that make me? Am I . . . *part god*?"

Wyrdith burst into chiming laughter. "There are no half gods. That isn't how it works."

"But my eyes! And my stories! I can . . . I can tell stories that often end up coming true, somehow."

Wyrdith nodded. "You have some of my magic. I knew it from the moment you were born. Of course, your father blamed the wish." Wyrdith's eyes crinkled at the corner. "Is he . . . did Hugo ever . . . find happiness? After I left?"

Serilda could feel the hope coupled with dread at this question. Was it possible that the god of lies had truly loved her father? Simple, compassionate, hardworking Hugo Moller?

Serilda sank against the bookshelf. "He's dead."

Wyrdith gasped and pressed a hand to their chest. "No. Oh, Hugo. How did it happen?"

A mist of tears gathered in Serilda's eyes. Then, without warning, a great, wrenching sob.

She slid down the bookcase and buried her face into her knees.

"Serilda!" Wyrdith was at her side, arms around her. It was all too much. The affection, the comfort, the arms of her own mother, the truth of who that mother was . . .

Between her sobs, Serilda told Wyrdith everything. From the night she had hidden two moss maidens in her onion cellar to protect them from the wild hunt, to the lie of gold-spinning she had told the Erlking, to being taken away to his castle. She told her about Gild and the children and how Papa had become a nachzehrer. About the curse and Gravenstone and Perchta and—

Her own child.

Her own baby.

Who was due to be born in four short weeks. Who she had not even had the pleasure of feeling grow inside her belly. And yet, the love she felt for that unborn child was so strong it made it hard to breathe when she let herself think about it. Think about how much she wanted that child. How much she wanted them to be all right.

How much she knew that child would never be all right, because Perchta had her body and everything was wrong, everything was terrible, and she didn't know how to fix any of it.

Wyrdith held her and let her cry and didn't interrupt the tale, not once.

By the time Serilda finished, they had both settled with their backs against the bookshelf, Wyrdith's hand rubbing soft circles between Serilda's shoulder blades.

"What am I going to do?" Serilda said, using the red cloak to wipe away her tears. "He's taken everything from me. I can't win against him."

"He is a dreadful opponent," said Wyrdith. "One we have been fighting against for longer than I can remember."

Serilda groaned and pressed her forehead to her knees. "And you're *gods*. I'm just me. A miller's daughter."

Wyrdith hummed. "You're my daughter, too."

The words sent a chill racing along Serilda's spine.

"That is one of the great things about being a storyteller." Wyrdith nudged Serilda gently. "We get to write our own story, too."

Serilda cast them a dismayed look. "My stories tend to cause more harm than good."

"Do they? Or have your stories allowed an entire castle's worth of imprisoned ghosts to finally rest in peace? Have they reunited a prince with his long-lost sister? Have they reunited *us*?"

"You don't understand. The gods he's captured? It was because of me. I didn't realize I was doing it, but my stories were telling him exactly where to go. It's my fault!"

"I *do* understand," said Wyrdith. "Stories are powerful." They threaded their fingers through Serilda's. "What *you* don't understand is that you have not yet written the ending."

Serilda started to shake her head, when a loud thump startled them both.

Wyrdith tensed and rose as the curtain shifted. Pale fingers appeared at its edge and peeled the curtain back, revealing the Erlking in the halo of candlelight. Crossbow strung at his side and golden chains at his hip.

"No!" Serilda launched to her feet and threw herself in front of Wyrdith, arms outspread. "You can't! I won't let you!"

"If it isn't my mortal bride," he mused, grinning wolfishly. "I heard rumors you were still about, ever causing trouble." He strolled into the cavern, as if he'd been invited in for a pint of ale. "Your spirit was untethered. How are you still here?"

Serilda felt the press of the broken arrow, the shaft of ash, against her sternum. "Vengeance," she spat. "I will not rest so long as that demon huntress of yours carries *my* child."

He chuckled. "I doubt she'll be carrying it much longer, given the state of things." He glanced past Serilda, his gaze sliding over Wyrdith from head to foot. "Wyrdith. Why are you wearing the guise of a common peasant? Seems beneath you."

"Then you have not met many common peasants," said Wyrdith. They squeezed Serilda's shoulder and stepped past her. "I know why you are here, Erlkönig. There is no need to bluster about with your weapons and gadgets. I will come with you willingly."

"What?" Serilda gasped. "No! Haven't you heard anything I've said? What he plans to do?"

Wyrdith flashed her that broken-toothed smile. "It has to be this way. I would not have written it differently myself." Emotion clouded over the flippant grin and they cupped Serilda's face. "The question is, where does the story go from here?"

"I don't understand," said Serilda. "What do I do?"

Wyrdith shrugged. "Run?" they said, smoothing back Serilda's hair. "Hide? Give up?" Their cheeks dimpled and they kissed Serilda's brow. "But what sort of story would that be, my beautiful, strong-willed child?"

The Erlking grunted. "I have not known you gods to care so much for your godchildren."

Wyrdith turned away. "You have not known us at all."

Again, the god shifted. From the mother Serilda could not remember to, suddenly, an enormous golden bird. Its wings outspread reached from wall to wall.

The Erlking was almost tender as he draped a loop of chain around Wyrdith's neck and cinched it tight. "Not quite as enjoyable doing it this way, but I do appreciate your cooperation." He met Serilda's gaze, pinning her in place with his icy stare. "Do you know what becomes of wandering spirits when they cannot find their way to Verloren?"

Serilda glowered at him, searching for the threat in his words. "I plan to haunt you until the end of time."

He smirked, then leaned closer. "They become *monsters*." He reached for her, running one cold knuckle along her cheek. "Whatever is keeping you here, dearest Serilda, I suggest you let it go, before it is too late."

She shuddered, hatred pooling inside her. She wanted to scream at him. To wrap her hands around his neck and squeeze. To stab him with his own stupid arrows. To gouge out those hideously beautiful eyes of his.

She wanted to hurt him. As he had hurt Gild and Erlen and the children and her father and the seven gods.

She wanted to *destroy* him.

"And oh yes, in case you were wondering," he said, stepping back, "we did find Tyrr again. Easy to track, once the beast is wounded. Put up quite a fight, but that temper always did make them careless. Now, if I'm not mistaken"—he glanced upward, pretending to count—"why, I do believe that makes seven. I couldn't have done it without you, miller's daughter."

Serilda said nothing. She did nothing. Just glared at him, emotions roiling.

And when the Alder King turned away from her and took the golden raptor—god of fate and fortune, god of stories and lies—away, Serilda stood there and watched them go.

Chapter Forty-Nine

Serilda sat on the ledge, feet dangling over, staring out at the endless ocean as the sun set fire to the horizon. She thought of merchant ships caught in storms, being thrown upon the unforgiving rocks below. She thought of sea serpents slithering through the inky depths. She wondered how many fishermen had sailed off one day, never to return.

Solvilde was the patron god of sea merchants and sailors, and they should have been watching over the oceans and the men and women who braved these waters. She knew that many still prayed to Solvilde, asking for safe passage, a safe return.

Those sailors did not know that the god they were praying to had stopped listening to prayers long ago. They did not know Solvilde was, even now, trapped in Adalheid Castle, powerless to help anyone.

Serilda groaned and bent her head. She had tried to climb back up to the top of the cliff. Her hands, still raw from the fall, were not strong enough to pull her upward. The columns of the cliff were too slick, too sheer. She was too weak.

What would happen if she fell?

The water was so far below, and she knew she would be thrown back against the rocks, sharp as teeth. It would hurt terribly. She could not even guess how much it would hurt.

But she would not die.

She *couldn't* die.

She was merely a soul, untethered to a human body.

A wandering spirit, the Erlking had called her.

What would happen if she jumped?

Would she be battered against the rocks, trapped in those cold waters until the end of time?

Could she swim toward the harbor cities in the west, searching for a place to come ashore?

Or—was there another way?

An easier way?

She reached for the thread at her throat and pulled out the broken arrow shaft. She twisted the arrow in her fingers. The feathers were silken black. The ash wood flexible but strong.

This was all that was keeping her here. All she had to do was release it. Drop it down into the water, and she would be free. Her spirit would float away, and in time, even without Velos's lantern to guide her, she trusted that she would find her way to Verloren.

To her father.

To the children.

The Erlking would no longer be her problem to solve.

It was tempting. So very tempting. But every time she thought she could do it—just throw the arrow away and seal her fate—she thought of Gild. The way he looked at her, like she was the most amazing being to ever come from the mortal realm. The way he kissed her, like every touch was a gift. Like she was a treasure so much more valuable than gold.

And what they had created together . . . unwittingly, through some ironic twist of magic and fate. A baby.

If she did this, if she gave up, she would never meet her child. She would never have a chance to save them.

What sort of story would that be, my beautiful, strong-willed child?

Maybe her child would be all right, she reasoned. Maybe they would be stronger than Serilda, braver than her. Maybe they had to be the one to finish this story.

"How much longer are you planning to stay down there?"

Serilda screamed and dropped the arrow. It fell, plummeting over the side of the cliff. She cried out again and stuck out her foot—barely catching the loop of thread on the toe of her boot.

Her phantom heart galloped against her chest as she carefully, with trembling fingers, took hold of the cord and pulled it back over her head, before finally looking up.

Two figures stood on the plateau above her, glowing golden beneath the rising sun. Each with tall, foxlike ears and small, fuzzy antlers and black doelike eyes.

Serilda squinted. "Parsley? Meadowsweet?"

She almost couldn't believe it, but yes, it was them. The very moss maidens that Serilda had once hidden in her father's root cellar. The moss maidens who had given her Gild's ring and locket. "How did you . . . What are you doing here?"

"After waiting months for the wild hunt to emerge from Gravenstone," said Parsley, hands on her hips, "we tracked them here. Saw them shoot down the wyvern. Saw *you* climb down this cliff, and the Erlking follow, and a big giant bird come back up with him. Figured you'd have come back up hours ago. What are you waiting for? Another wyvern to swoop in and carry you off?"

"I . . . I can't," said Serilda. "I hurt my hands, and I wasn't good at climbing to begin with."

"Told you so," said Meadowsweet, grinning at her sister. "Remember how clumsy she was in the forest?"

Parsley sighed. "Humans." She grabbed a rope of vines from her back and tossed one end down to Serilda. "Wrap this around yourself. We'll pull you up."

☾

"They killed more than half of our sisters when they attacked Asyltal," said Parsley. Despite the tragedy in her words, her voice was hard and factual.

"But enough of us got away that we were able to scout a perimeter around Gravenstone. We knew that eventually the hunt would go riding again, and we planned to use that opportunity to lay siege to the castle. To find Pusch-Grohla and free her. But it didn't turn out that way."

"What happened?" asked Serilda.

"It wasn't just the hunt that rode when the veil fell last night. An entire caravan of dark ones left the castle, traveling into the forest, just as when they came to Asyltal. Not as many as before. No ghosts this time. We sent a contingent to follow them and realized they had Pusch-Grohla, along with a gryphon and a giant black wolf, kept in cages and heavily guarded. The hunt came out after. A group of us followed the Erlking. The rest stayed behind to keep watch on the caravan."

"We believe they were going back to Adalheid," said Meadowsweet.

Serilda nodded. "Then they will have all seven gods together on the Endless Moon."

She had expected the moss maidens to be stunned when she told them their Shrub Grandmother was none other than Eostrig, god of fertility and springtide. But as it turned out, they had known this all along, and they thought *she* was dense for not having realized it a long time ago. This sparked a few offhand comments about how clueless mortals were before they let her explain all she knew about the Erlking's plans to capture the seven gods and—she believed—wish for the destruction of the veil.

The only thing that *did* seem to surprise the moss maidens was when she told them about the return of Perchta, who had not been among the hunters who had set out to capture Wyrdith.

"What was most unusual," said Meadowsweet, "was that after the caravan went past, there came earthquakes, rumbling through the forest. Creating huge cracks in the ground, as if they were fanning out from Gravenstone."

"As if they were chasing after the dark ones," added Parsley in a somber tone.

Serilda shuddered, remembering the destruction that had happened in the chamber deep beneath the castle. What did it mean?

The basalt cliffs gave way to a rocky moor and a long stretch of scattered grasslands. Serilda felt they had already been walking for miles, the sun making its slow climb overhead, when they finally reached the northernmost edge of the woods.

Serilda heard a low keening sound that made her pause, gooseflesh blanketing her skin.

Parsley groaned. "Don't mind her. Just keep walking."

"What was that?"

"A salige," said Meadowsweet, gesturing off into the woods. "We think she made her way up here from one of the fishing villages, maybe killed herself on the bluffs. We saw her wandering through the forest last night. They are drawn to bodies of water, so maybe she's trying to get to the ocean."

Another heartbreaking wail echoed around them, startling a flock of black-winged gannets that had been nesting on the cliffs. They screeched and flurried through the air before gradually settling back down.

Serilda spotted her then, the salige. A woman in a flowing white gown, moving slowly through the forest. She was walking away from Serilda and the moss maidens, sobbing to herself.

Serilda had met a salige once before, deep in the Aschen Wood. Beautiful but miserable, she had begged Serilda to dance with her atop a bridge of bones—the bones of all those who had come before. Enchanted to dance until they fell down dead, all in an effort to break some unknown curse. *You alone can break this curse. All it takes is a dance . . .*

A hand fell on Serilda's shoulder and she jumped. Meadowsweet was watching the salige, the tiniest hint of sympathy in her lovely face. "You cannot help her. Trying will only get you killed."

"But they're cursed, aren't they?" said Serilda. "Can't all curses be broken?"

Parsley crossed her arms impatiently over her chest. "Salige are cursed to kill anyone who attempts to break their curse. So, no. Not all curses can be broken."

The salige's cries drifted away as she moved toward the plateau. She sounded so devastated. So . . . lost.

The Erlking's words struck Serilda then, taking the breath from her lips.

"They become monsters," she whispered. "Salige were once wandering spirits. Women mourning for lost children or trying to find their way back home—but they wandered too long. This is what they become when they refuse to cross over to Verloren. They turn into monsters."

Her hand wrapped around the arrow at her neck.

This is what would become of *her*, if she didn't find some way to get her body back. A feat she wasn't sure was possible.

They stood in silence until they could no longer hear the woman's mournful, bitter cries.

Parsley was the first to turn away and head into the woods. "If we waste any more time out here, we're all going to turn into wandering spirits."

They had not gone much farther before they were met by six other moss maidens who had set up a small camp among the trees. They served Serilda a meal of not-particularly-satisfying nuts and dried fruits while Meadowsweet and Parsley told them all they had learned.

"Perchta," growled one of the moss maidens, lip curling. "No forest creature will be safe with her return."

"Oh—there is one more thing I forgot to mention," said Serilda, fidgeting with the hem of her cloak, which was fast becoming as filthy and tattered as the reliable wool cloak she so missed. "Perchta is . . . not trapped on the dark side of the veil."

They all frowned at her.

"But she is a demon," said Meadowsweet.

"Yes," said Serilda. "But—"

"But she is a demon inside a mortal body," said Parsley, baring her teeth at Serilda as if that were *her* fault.

Which was fair, all things considered.

One of the maidens spat at the ground. "The great huntress, unleashed in the mortal realm. Grandmother captured. Asyltal destroyed. What does this mean for the creatures of the forest?"

"Nothing good," murmured Meadowsweet.

"Wait," said Serilda. "The veil is down *now*." She put a hand to her chest. "I am trapped on the dark side of the veil, but you're not. How can you see me?"

Parsley cocked her head in an oddly deerlike manner. "Forest folk are magic. Just like the drudes and the nachtkrapp. The veil was never meant to be a boundary to *us* when it was created, so we can slip in and out of the realms as it pleases us. We just don't usually choose to be on the side with the dark ones."

"Ah—I see," said Serilda. "Thank you, then. For staying with me on this side of the veil. And for coming for me on the cliffs."

"It isn't charity," said Parsley. "You have information about the Erlking and the hunt. Information that might help us rescue Pusch-Grohla."

Serilda straightened her spine, surprised at the hope this stirred inside her. Taken by surprise in Asyltal, the moss maidens might not have been a match against the dark ones. But they were fierce allies all the same, and they were determined to free at least one of the gods.

It was more than she'd had this morning.

Serilda's gaze fell on a longbow leaning against a tree trunk where one of the maidens was sitting, and the first stirrings of a plan came to her, unbidden.

"Golden arrows," she whispered.

"What?" said Parsley.

"Golden arrows," she repeated, eyes widening. "That's how Gild defeated Perchta the first time. An arrow of god-blessed gold shot straight into her heart." She looked around at their small group. "How many moss maidens are left? And how good are they at archery?"

Parsley shot her a look that was as cold as any the Erlking had ever given her.

"Only a mortal," she said, "would ask such a stupid question."

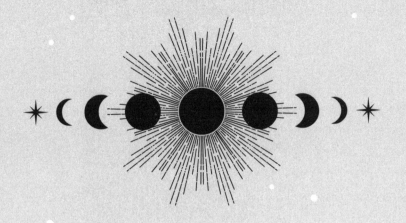

THE
WINTER
SOLSTICE

The Endless Moon

Chapter Fifty

S now had been falling for more than a week.

The moss maidens had made a hastily constructed camp in the Aschen Wood, with camouflaged shelters that blended into the trees. It was comfortable enough, but Serilda longed for a fire in the hearth of the Wild Swan and a cup of mulled cider. She longed for heavy blankets and Gild's arms around her.

She grew more anxious with each passing night. For weeks she had watched the moon wane into nothing, then slowly wax its way back to fullness. Every day, the ground rumbled beneath their feet, as if the earth was stirring far below them. Every day, new cracks appeared across the forest floor. Small fissures at first, but slowly growing wider, until there was a series of crevasses as wide as fists cutting through their camp. Always in the direction of Adalheid and the lake. The moss maidens seemed as concerned about the earth's instability as they were about recovering Pusch-Grohla, but Serilda's mind was often preoccupied with other concerns.

Somewhere in the world, Perchta's belly was swelling more with every passing day.

The baby would be coming soon.

She tried to stay out of the way while the moss maidens crafted weapons and sent scouts to spy on Adalheid and the castle, where the Erlking and his court had once again taken up residence.

Serilda had begged to go with them, if only so she could sit in a corner of the public house and watch over her friends from the shadows of the veil. They wouldn't know she was there, but it would bring her so much comfort to see them.

To see Gild.

To know he was all right.

But the moss maidens refused. She was too clumsy, too brash, and they could not risk the dark ones seeing her.

At least they had brought word that Gild and Erlen were alive and were staying at the Wild Swan. It was all that anyone had been talking about in town, it seemed. Vergoldetgeist in their midst, toiling away on some secret project. The townsfolk, at Lorraine's urging, had supplied a spinning wheel and a loom and were bringing in cartloads of everything from sheep's wool to winter-wilted straw for the gold-spinner to work with.

Making gold and, Serilda hoped, crafting it into weapons and arrows like they'd talked about. Using it for Erlen's tapestries, to secure a victorious future.

Serilda had asked if they couldn't just take the weapons Gild was constructing and storm the castle, take the dark ones by surprise before the Endless Moon ever rose. But Meadowsweet had explained that so long as Gild was in the mortal realm, his spun gold could not be used against the dark ones until the veil fell.

No—they would have to wait.

(

Finally, the day of the Endless Moon arrived, bringing with it a powdery snow that fell dreamily from the sky, filling up the tracks left by scavenging deer and rabbits the night before.

Serilda's hands were shaking as she affixed the clasp on her bloodred cloak. With fear and nerves, but also excitement to finally be doing something. The solstice was here. They would save the gods and reclaim her body. They would defeat the dark ones.

Or they would fail. The veil would fall and the mortal world would never be the same again.

"I trust we do not need to remind you of your role in all this," said Parsley, handing Serilda the small reed whistle that would summon the moss maidens when the time came.

"I know what I need to do," she said. The whistle was attached to a strap that she slipped over her head, tucking it beside the broken arrow. "I know what's at stake, as much as anyone."

"Then go, and make sure no one sees you leaving the woods."

"Of course." The last thing Serilda wanted to do was to lead their enemy into the camp mere hours before they were set to invade Adalheid Castle. She expected and hoped the Erlking's court would be busy preparing for the Endless Moon, and would not concern themselves with a pack of forest folk loitering about in the forest.

"We will be ready."

Serilda bounced nervously on her toes. Once she had offered a friendly embrace to Parsley and Meadowsweet, after she had protected them from the wild hunt. She was tempted to extend her arms to them again now, after all they'd been through.

But Parsley's look darkened, as if she could tell what Serilda was thinking. Prickly as ever.

Serilda shrank back. "Tonight, then."

"Serilda?" said Meadowsweet.

Serilda faced her, hope rising in her chest.

With an exaggerated sigh, Meadowsweet held out her arms to Serilda.

Serilda beamed and accepted the hug.

"Don't try to be clever," said Meadowsweet. "Just follow the plan."

"I will. I mean—I won't. I mean—" Serilda stepped back and clapped a hand to her empty chest. "I'll do my best."

"How promising," muttered Parsley.

She bid farewell to the rest of the moss maidens, who, despite having spent the last month with her, still watched her go like a bunch of suspicious foxes. Serilda left the camp alone.

She would go to Adalheid and slip into the public house, so that as soon as the veil fell, she would be ready to explain everything to Gild and Erlen. She would ensure that the weapons Gild had been making were delivered to the moss maidens. Then she would enter the castle and do whatever she needed to do—cause a distraction or stall the Erlking, keep him from making his wish—giving the moss maidens time to get into position. When the time was right, she'd blow the whistle and the maidens would descend and slaughter the dark ones, one by one, using the same spun-gold arrows that had once killed Perchta.

The plan was a good one, she told herself, as she made her way through the forest.

It will work, it will work, it has to work.

As soon as she reached the edge of the Aschen Wood and saw the city wall rise up in front of her, she felt a tug deep within her chest. Somehow, this place had started to feel like more of a home to her than Märchenfeld ever had. All she had loved in her old life was gone, snatched away from her.

All she loved now was here, within these walls.

If the veil fell forever, this city would fall. The first victim to the demons. She could not let that happen.

Serilda made her way down the quiet streets. Though wagon and carriage wheels had cut grooves through the snow, they were quickly filling up again. All was quiet and still, most of the people bundled up inside their homes, smoke rising from every chimney. She passed a young boy throwing seeds out for a brood of chickens, and a man shoveling snow from his front step, and an old woman bustling by with her hood pulled over her head and a basket smelling of warm yeast buns on her elbow.

No one saw Serilda, right beside them but hidden behind the veil. The spirit who did not even leave footsteps in the blanketing snow.

She made her way to the public house and slipped into the front door right as Frieda was slipping out, humming to herself and carrying an armful of books. She paused briefly as she passed Serilda, a shiver overtaking her. She glanced around with a curious expression, before she shook it off and continued her humming, heading toward the library.

The main room was empty—the townsfolk kept away by either the snow or the ominous Endless Moon. Serilda headed up to the second floor. A door stood open at the end of the hall, where she could hear the telltale sound of a spinning wheel whirring diligently, matched with Leyna's chipper voice.

Serilda glided down the hall, already beaming when she came to the doorway.

The room was cold, due to the single window left open, where snow was dusting the sill. Despite the chill, heat flooded Serilda as she stepped inside.

Bundled in a jacket and scarf, Gild sat at the spinning wheel, feeding strands of wool into the maiden hole, his foot tapping against the treadle, strands of glistening gold winding around the bobbin as if it were the most natural thing in the world. A tray of meats and cheeses sat on a table beside him.

Leyna sat cross-legged on the rug beside him, using a comb to pick through raw wool fibers, preparing them for Gild to spin. She was prattling on about some prank one of her friends had pulled on the superstitious old man that lived up the hill, and Gild was beaming, perhaps a bit too encouragingly.

The sight of them both made Serilda's nerves sing with inexpressible joy.

They were safe. Gild was *alive*—not cursed, not trapped—no longer the poltergeist forever haunting Adalheid Castle.

What's more, as she took in the room, she saw that he had been very busy.

Bundles of golden thread were stacked against the walls. Some had been braided into thick chains, like those the hunt used. But much more had been twisted and forged into arrowheads, swords, daggers, and spears. She wondered if Gild had even slept, to have been so prolific.

It was more than she could have hoped.

The moss maidens would be thrilled. As thrilled as they ever were, at least.

Biting her lower lip, Serilda stepped across the room and knelt beside the spinning wheel.

"Gild?"

Did she imagine the way his fingers hesitated?

But then Leyna handed him another bunch of wool and he returned to his work.

Serilda reached forward, wishing she could push back the lock of hair falling into his eyes, but her fingers slipped right through.

Gild's brow furrowed and he reached up to scratch his forehead.

With a sigh, Serilda glanced out the window. There were still hours until sunset.

A loud caw made her jump.

A nachtkrapp landed on the windowsill and shook snowflakes off its bedraggled feathers. Serilda's instinct was to launch herself forward, shove it back outside, and slam the window shut.

But Leyna cooed at the bird. "Welcome back, Helgard. Erlen is in the other room, working on her tapestry."

Helgard seemed to stare at Leyna through its empty eye sockets. Then it cocked its head, and Serilda was sure, even if it could not *see* her, it could sense her.

She stood. "Do you remember me?"

The bird fluffed its feathers, then hopped off the sill and flew into the hallway.

Gild stopped spinning to frown after the bird before glancing in Serilda's direction, suspicious. "Did you hear something?"

Leyna stopped picking at the wool. "Was my mother calling me?"

Gild didn't respond. After a moment, he shook his head and popped a cube of cheese into his mouth. "You know, being able to accept food in payment for spinning is one of the greatest things that's ever happened to me. I love it here. I never want to leave.""

Leyna giggled. "Cheese for gold? Any town in the world would take that deal."

Erlen appeared in the doorway, Helgard perched on her shoulder, a troubled look on her face.

"What is it?" said Gild.

She stared at him, wide-eyed, chewing the inside of her cheek. She opened her mouth to speak, but hesitated and shut it again.

"What?" Gild pressed.

"Are you almost finished?" she asked.

"Just about." Gild gestured to the last remaining bits of wool. "I should get another half dozen arrows or so out of this. We'll be done by nightfall."

Erlen nodded.

"How is the tapestry?" asked Leyna. "Can we see it yet?"

"No," said Erlen, a little too sharply. Then she flushed and scrunched her shoulders up by her ears. "It isn't done. But . . . it will be. By nightfall. I just thought I'd take a break. See how things are coming."

"You look nervous," said Gild.

Erlen's expression darkened and she lifted her chin. "I am not nervous," she snapped, before marching back out of the room.

Leyna and Gild exchanged looks.

"I thought she seemed nervous, too," said Leyna.

"Very," Gild and Serilda agreed—though no one heard *her*.

No matter—she had gathered the information she needed, and one of the moss maidens' carrier pigeons would be waiting outside the inn to take word back to their camp. Serilda fished out the birch paper and charcoal the moss maidens had given her and took inventory of how many weapons were available.

When she was finished, she paused just long enough to bend over Gild and press a kiss to his cheek.

He jerked upward, and lifted a hand to his face. His eyes shifted around the room.

Serilda laughed. "See you soon," she whispered, and darted out the hallway and back down the stairs.

"Ah—good day, Lorraine!" she chirped, seeing the mayor behind the counter. "Lovely night to storm the castle, don't you think?"

She was halfway across the room when the front door was suddenly thrown open with a loud crash.

Serilda froze, startled, as a gust of wind and snow flurried inside and a figure appeared, silhouetted in the gray afternoon.

A figure with long brown hair and a crimson cloak.

Serilda's veins ran cold as the woman pulled back her hood, revealing sharp black eyes inlaid with golden spokes. She kicked the door shut with her boot, then stumbled forward a step, supporting her rounded belly.

Lorraine gasped. "Serilda! Is that . . . Is it you?" She dashed around the counter, passing right through Serilda's invisible form as she approached the woman, who had leaned against the back of a chair for support.

Perchta met Lorraine's eyes and drew in a hiss through her teeth.

"I need a room," she said brusquely. "And a midwife."

Chapter Fifty-One

Well, I'll eat a broom," murmured Lorraine, clapping a hand to her mouth. "Serilda . . . When did . . . How . . . ?"

Perchta's knuckles whitened as she squeezed the back of the chair. She bared her teeth at Lorraine. "There isn't time. Help me!"

It was more an order than a request, and Lorraine stiffened in surprise. "I . . . Yes, of course. Come, let's get you up into one of the rooms." She let Perchta lean on her for support, while Serilda bolted back up the stairs, taking them two at a time. As soon as she had reached the upper landing, she heard Lorraine shouting for Leyna.

Serilda ran down the hall and caught herself on the doorway, just as Leyna was standing up. "Yes, Mama?" she called.

"Come quick!" Lorraine shouted. "And bring some towels!"

"Towels?" Leyna frowned at Gild, who only shrugged and started to stand himself.

"No," said Serilda, holding out her arms. "Don't go!"

"It's Serilda!" Lorraine's shout was coupled with the creaking of the lower steps. "She's back! Hurry!"

"Serilda?" breathed Gild. His eyes widened and he strode toward the door.

"No!" Serilda shouted, reaching for him. Her hand went through his shoulder, his arm, grasping at nothing. "Gild, don't!"

Gild hesitated and rubbed at his elbow, suddenly covered in gooseflesh.

The stairs creaked, followed by a low, pained groan.

Gild peered toward the hall, hope shining on his face. He took another step.

Serilda tried one more time, this time grabbing for the locket at his throat.

Her fingers met with cool metal. Gritting her teeth, she tugged, managing to pull the necklace taut against his neck for just a moment before her strength left her and the chain slipped from her grasp.

But it was enough. Gild halted, reaching for his throat. He spun around, eyes searching the room.

When Leyna tried to dart past him, he grabbed her shoulder. "Wait."

She gaped up at him. "But, Serilda—"

"It isn't her," he said, going pale. "It's Perchta."

Horror crept over Leyna's face. "What? How . . . how can you know?"

Gild shut the door as the hallway floorboards groaned. "Remember what we told you?" he said, lowering his voice. "About what happened in Gravenstone?"

Leyna's breaths became halting. "M-Mama! Mama's out there! She doesn't know!"

She tried to push past Gild, but he stopped her. "You can't let Perchta know that you know the truth. You have to pretend that she really is Serilda."

Leyna's lips hung open.

Down the hall they heard a bellow of pain, followed by Lorraine's voice, growing sharper. "Leyna! Now!"

"Is Perchta having a *baby*?"

"I . . . think so. Yes."

"What do I do?"

"Go," said Gild. "Do as your mother says, and just . . . don't let Perchta know that Erlen and I are here. Can you do that?"

Leyna swallowed hard, then gave a sharp nod.

Gild released her. "It will be all right."

Leyna approached the door hesitantly, then squared her shoulders and went out into the hall. As soon as she was gone, Gild scanned the room again. "Serilda? Are you here?"

Spotting the open windowsill, Serilda used all her will to shove a drift of snow onto the carpet.

Gild drew in a shaky breath. "I've missed you," he said. "I wish I could talk to you." Emotion flooded his face, but he was quick to shake it off. "I have to warn Erlen."

"Of course. Go," said Serilda.

He had just started for the door when Erlen popped in, eyes wide.

"What is going on?" she whispered. "Lorraine just sent for a midwife!"

As Gild explained, Serilda headed down the hall toward the sound of Perchta's moans.

Lorraine had taken her into one of the guest rooms and stripped the bed down to sheets. Perchta lay against a mountain of pillows, her eyes wild and teeth clenched while Lorraine poured a pitcher of water into a bowl on the washstand. Leyna was nowhere to be seen.

"It will be all right, dear heart," said Lorraine soothingly. "The midwife is on her way."

"Don't call me that," snapped Perchta.

Lorraine tittered nervously. "Pain really does change a person, doesn't it?" She dipped a cloth into the water and wrung it out. "Just try to take deep breaths." She went to place the cloth on Perchta's brow, already beaded with sweat, but Perchta snatched it away with a growl.

Lorraine jumped back.

With a huff, Perchta slapped the cloth onto her brow herself, then slumped back into the pillows. "Awful timing," she said. "Better be worth it."

"Here, Mama," said Leyna, bustling in with an armful of clean towels.

"Good, good, set them here," said Lorraine. "I've been waiting to tell Serilda the wonderful news. Thought you might like to do it. Maybe it will help take her mind off the pain."

Leyna's eyes were round as the coming full moon. "Uh...yes." She beamed at Perchta, then immediately shriveled beneath the huntress's scowl. She cleared her throat. "Mama and Frieda were married last month!"

Lorraine laughed. "Not *that* news, silly girl," she said, then gestured at Perchta. "The news about our special guests. That Serilda will be *delighted* to see?"

Leyna gave an unsubtle shake to her head, which Perchta missed only because she had squeezed her eyes shut as another wave of pain struck her.

Lorraine frowned. "What—?"

"It's a surprise!" said Leyna. "Let's . . . let's leave it as a surprise. Let her focus on . . . that." She gestured toward the bed. "It's enough excitement for now, don't you think?"

Lorraine's lips bunched to one side. "Perhaps you're right. I just thought she'd be so happy . . ."

Leyna cleared her throat. "Let's not say anything yet. What can I do, Mama?"

"Oh! Uh . . . if you could put a pot of water on to boil."

"Of course!" Leyna started to leave, but paused in the doorway and held a finger to her mouth. "Don't tell her!" she whispered, then ran from the room.

Perchta snarled. "Tell me what?"

Lorraine tittered. "Nothing at all. I think I just heard carriage wheels outside. That must be the midwife."

It was the midwife, who bustled into the room a moment later with her hair pulled tightly back and a no-nonsense expression on her face. Her appearance brought a sense of calm to the room, and though Lorraine was one of the most capable women Serilda had ever known, she could tell that the innkeeper was relieved to pass some responsibility to a professional.

Serilda was relieved, too. She might loathe Perchta with all her soul, but the child . . . She wanted so much for the child to be born healthy and strong.

She lingered in the corner, chewing on her envy that Perchta was experiencing something so precious, so *miraculous*, hating that this moment had been stolen from her. And yet, when the screams started in earnest, she found herself feeling a little less disappointed.

Lorraine and the midwife bustled around. Leyna came and went, hurrying to bring whatever was needed. Perchta gripped the bedsheets and loudly cursed *this fragile, pathetic, mortal body* and ignored the baffled looks exchanged around her. Serilda watched, holding her breath, feeling disconnected from it all. This moment that should have been everything to her.

Then—suddenly—there was a new scream.

Shrill and bewildered, a cry that tore at Serilda's insides.

She stepped forward, trying to peer around the midwife who stood at the foot of the bed.

"Here we are," said the woman, cutting the umbilical cord and taking the newborn into her arms. "A baby girl."

Tears sprang into Serilda's eyes as she took her in, all wrinkled and pink, with a pinched, furious face and a wisp of red-gold hair. She tried to reach for her daughter, but her arms met only air. She stayed close, tears on her cheeks as Lorraine took the baby and washed her.

"Hello," Serilda cooed, desperately wishing the child could hear her voice and know it was her mother speaking to her. Her mother, overflowing with a love so powerful it nearly drove her to her knees. Her mother, who would do anything for her, *anything.*

Lorraine swaddled the child in a clean blanket while Serilda hovered close, her arms aching to hold the baby. She wasn't sure when she had begun to cry in earnest, but she could not bite back the sob when Lorraine settled the child into Perchta's arms.

"Talk to her," encouraged the midwife. "She'll want to hear her mother's voice."

Perchta leaned up against the pillows, flushed skin and sweat-dampened hair, and peered into the child's face. The baby's crying had stopped, replaced with curious squirming. Then she scrunched up her face and slowly opened her eyes.

Serilda gasped.

The baby had her eyes. Wyrdith's eyes. Black irises overlaid with two perfect golden wheels.

"Wyrdith's godchild," muttered Perchta, tracing a finger in circles around the baby's cheeks. "How sweet."

"What will you name her?" asked the midwife.

Serilda bit her lip, considering. She had been too afraid to try to choose a name for her child, worried that to do so too early would bring bad luck. Superstitious nonsense, the Erlking would have said.

As for Perchta, she just smirked. "Names have too much power to be given easily."

Leyna burst back into the room. "I heard . . . is it . . . ?" Her gaze landed on the bundle in Perchta's arms.

"A baby girl," said Lorraine. "Healthy as can be." She settled a hand on Perchta's shoulder. "We'll have a room prepared with fresh linens. You can stay and rest as long as you need."

Perchta scoffed and pulled away from the touch. "I do not need rest, not on the Endless Moon. What I need is a wet nurse."

The midwife let out a bewildered laugh. "A wet nurse! What are you, the queen?"

Perchta sent her a murderous look that cut her laughter short.

"There aren't any wet nurses in Adalheid," she said, more sober now. "You will have to feed the child yourself. You . . . are her mother."

Perchta sighed. "Fine. Then I will require a governess, at least for the night." She glanced at Leyna. "You will do. Here, come take her."

"Wh-what? Me?" said Leyna, accepting the baby into her arms.

Perchta swung her legs over the side of the bed. Lorraine and the midwife both cried out and rushed to stop her.

"You have to rest!" said the midwife. "You just gave birth!"

"I will not rest. I am needed in the castle."

"The castle!" said Lorraine. "Serilda, be sensible. I understand you and that prince have been plotting to gallivant off to—"

"Prince?" said Perchta, eyes blazing. "What prince?"

Lorraine drew back, surprised, then gestured toward the wall and, far down the hallway, the room where Gild had been toiling away all month. "That's what we were going to tell you before. Your prince has told us everything and he's—"

"In the castle!" blurted Leyna.

Lorraine started. "What?"

"He's waiting for you in the castle," said Leyna, bouncing the baby nervously in her arms. "He wanted me to tell you that he was going early. To wait for the moon to rise, so he could set a trap. For the hunt."

Perchta raised an eyebrow and said nothing for a long moment. Then a slow, cruel smile came over her face. "I see. Well. As the Endless Moon is upon us, I shall not keep him waiting."

Serilda blinked. At some point, Leyna had lit the candles around the room. At some point, the snow had stopped falling and the sky had dimmed.

The sun was setting.

The veil was about to fall.

Serilda gasped and rushed from the room. Behind her, she heard Lorraine pleading with the huntress to lie back down.

Then she felt it. That tingle that swept across her skin. The way a flush of new color spread over the world, always a surprise after seeing so muted a palette for so long.

The veil was down.

"Stop whimpering and bring me my boots," Perchta demanded. "And you—can't you keep the child from crying?"

The baby was not crying, not really, though her little snuffle sounds were becoming increasingly agitated.

"She might be hungry?" Leyna said hesitantly.

"She will have to wait."

"Serilda!" said Lorraine. "What has gotten into you?"

Serilda ducked into an empty guest room, leaving the door open a small crack. Seconds later, Perchta emerged and came storming down the hall, Leyna on her heels, clutching the swaddled baby.

"I am fine," said Perchta. "I've never rested on a full moon before, why should I start now?"

"Lorraine? Leyna?" called a voice from downstairs—Frieda. "I thought I heard . . . oh! Serilda!"

"Move!" shouted Perchta.

As the hall fell quiet again, Serilda crept out from the room and peeked around the stairwell, watching as Perchta grabbed her cloak, left behind on the counter, and tossed it around her shoulders.

"She thinks she's going to the castle!" said Lorraine. "Not *minutes* after having a baby. And she wants Leyna to come with her. Serilda, you're being absurd. You cannot possibly—"

A ring of steel silenced her.

Serilda gasped, throwing a hand up to her mouth.

Perchta had drawn a hunting knife from somewhere within the cloak and now held it to Lorraine's chest, right over her heart.

Leyna and Frieda stood frozen, terrified.

"I will do as I please," said Perchta. "Thank you ever so much for your assistance, but your services are no longer required. Come, girl. Stay close." With a flick, she tucked the knife away and gave Leyna a shove toward the door.

Leyna stumbled but managed to catch herself. The baby began to cry.

"L-Leyna!" cried Lorraine. "What is this? Leyna!"

Clutching the crying newborn to her chest, Leyna glanced back once at her mother. Then past her shoulder—to the stairs.

Her eyes met Serilda's. She gasped.

Then Perchta shoved her out the door and they were gone.

Chapter Fifty-Two

Serilda rushed up the staircase and barged through the door at the end of the hall, into the room where she'd seen Gild spinning. The moment the door slammed shut behind her, she felt the cold press of metal against her throat.

Serilda drew up short with a squeak.

"Halt right there, Huntress!" cried Erlen, gripping her sword in both hands. She was standing on Gild's spinning stool just inside the door, so that she would be tall enough to hold the sword at Serilda's throat.

Gild stood on the other side of the room, an arrow nocked into a bow, aimed for her heart.

"It's me," said Serilda, lifting both palms. "It's Serilda. I swear it."

"Prove it," snapped Erlen.

"The veil just fell!" She took in a shaky breath. "Prove it? I don't know! Listen, Perchta had her baby. A baby girl, she's *beautiful*, but Perchta said she had to get back to the castle and she took Leyna with her, to care for the child while she . . . while the dark ones . . . They must be planning to make the wish any moment now and we don't have time for this! We have to help Leyna, and get the baby and—"

Gild lowered the bow. "Serilda! It is you!"

"Oh please," said Erlen. "She didn't say anything convincing at all!"

"Let her go, Erlen!"

With a huff, the princess lowered the sword. "If she kills you, don't complain to me about it."

Serilda sobbed and threw herself across the room, into Gild's arms. He was quick to hold her, dropping the arrow and bow so he could pull her close.

The moment didn't last. She caught her breath and pulled back, digging her fingers into his shoulders. "She took Leyna!"

"What of the gods?" he asked.

She cringed. She'd forgotten that he and Erlen didn't know. "I found Wyrdith, but . . . the hunt came, and took both Wyrdith and Tyrr again. They have them. All seven."

Erlen cursed beneath her breath.

"Then we really are out of time," said Gild. "Erlen—pack up the weapons." Pulling away from Serilda, he strapped a scabbard to his belt and threw a quiver of arrows over his back.

"I do have some good news," said Serilda, and told them about the moss maidens and their plan.

Gild nodded. "The townsfolk agreed to help us, the ones with some skill in archery, but they aren't warriors like the moss maidens. Erlen, can we send some of your monsters to meet with them and begin arranging the transfer of weapons?" His eyes were intense and focused in a way Serilda had rarely seen him. "We'll enter the castle and stall for as long as we can."

"No—wait! You can't," said Erlen, looking up from the bundle of arrows she'd been hastily tossing into a quiver. She stood suddenly, eyes wide. "Gild, you have to stay here."

He blinked. "What? We decided I would lead the attack."

She gave a furious shake to her head. "You can't. I meant to tell you earlier, but I didn't know how, and then, with Perchta—" She swallowed roughly. "I finished the tapestry. And—and you just can't go!"

Gild's hand tightened on the hilt of his sword. "What are you talking about? What did it show you?"

Erlen waved her arm, beckoning them to follow, and darted across the hall.

"We don't have time for this!" Gild said, even as he stormed after her.

But as soon as he stepped into the other room, he froze.

Serilda crept in close behind him, eyeing the tapestry on the enormous loom. The workmanship was as impeccable as Serilda expected from Erlen, the colors stunning and vibrant, now run through with the occasional fleck of golden thread.

But the depiction was horrific.

The tapestry showed Gild, kneeling and hunched over on the ground, a sword through his back.

It was so awful that, for a long time, Serilda could hardly breathe.

"I finished it this afternoon," said Erlen. She sounded on the verge of tears. "I mean, this part of the tapestry was finished days ago, but I kept hoping . . . I had to believe there was more to it. And there is, obviously, but it isn't what I hoped . . ."

"Please, explain it," said Gild, his voice hoarse.

Erlen ran shaking fingers over the image. "Up here, we see the seven gods, in beast form," she said, gesturing to the seven beasts Serilda had become so familiar with. "And here, you—dying—obviously. But over here, you see, the gods are free." To the left and right of Gild's form stood seven figures in colorful cloaks. Serilda recognized Wyrdith by the golden plume in their hand. "And here"—Erlen gestured half-heartedly to the bottom of the tapestry, where a series of shadowy figures had fallen into a broken gash in the ground—"the dark ones, in Verloren. I think . . . I don't know!" Erlen stomped her feet, petulant. "I don't know what to think! They aren't always clear, the messages in the tapestries."

"That isn't true," said Gild, sounding oddly distant as he took in this tragic image. "You were trying to weave a tapestry that would show us how to defeat the dark ones. So . . . maybe this is it."

"No," said Serilda. "Gild, you can't think—"

"I don't understand it fully," he said, "or why or how, but maybe . . . maybe my death brings about their freedom. Look." He pointed to the golden chains, woven from golden thread, that bound the seven beasts. Down below, the chains lay broken at their feet.

"We are mortal now," whispered Erlen. "If you die, it will be forever."

"But why?" said Serilda. "Why would you have to die for this to happen?"

He shook his head. "I don't know. But Erlen used my threads in her weaving, and I do think that makes this future unchangeable. That was the whole point, wasn't it?" He looked at his sister. "We free the gods, we defeat the dark ones. This is . . . this is a good thing. This is what we hoped for."

"That you would *die*?" Serilda cried, at the same time Erlen yelled, "This is *not* what we hoped for!"

Gild grimaced. "We don't have time to debate this. If I have to die so the Erlking doesn't get what he wants, I will. To protect you . . . both of you. And"—he gazed at Serilda, his eyes shining—"and our child. Our daughter."

"No," Serilda said. "Our daughter needs you. This can't be the only way."

"Serilda—"

"Promise me." She grabbed his hands. "Promise me you won't go into that castle. At least give me and the moss maidens a chance. Maybe we don't need you. Maybe we can do this on our own."

"But the tapestry—"

"Is wrong! It has to be wrong." She gestured at Erlen. "She's never woven anything with god-blessed gold before. We're just guessing at everything! The future can't predetermined. Isn't that what you said?"

Erlen looked pained as she took in a shuddering breath. "When there are two possible futures, the tapestry shows them both. But this . . . there's only one image here. This one."

"No. This isn't right. Your gift must work differently with the golden threads."

"Yeah," said Gild. "It makes the tapestry indestructible. Like we thought."

"Let's not argue over the king's beard," said Erlen. "The point is, if you go to the castle tonight, you're going to die."

Serilda pressed her hands to either side of Gild's face. "I can't lose you, too."

His expression shuttered. He gave a long sigh, then pulled her close and pressed his lips to hers, his fingers digging into the back of her cloak.

When he pulled away, tears were on his cheeks. "All right," he whispered. "I won't come with you. Please—please be careful."

Serilda nodded. "I will bring our daughter back. I won't fail." She turned to Erlen and quickly went over the plan, deciding where and how she and the monsters could get as many gold-tipped arrows to the moss maidens as possible.

"I need to hurry," said Serilda. "Planning will do us no good if I'm too late to keep the Erlking from making his wish."

She gave Erlen a quick embrace and kissed Gild one more time before rushing down the stairs.

Lorraine was sobbing at one of the tables. Frieda stood beside her, trying her best to give comfort, but she, too, was crying. And, in the moments since Serilda had gone upstairs, it seemed half the townsfolk had arrived.

When Lorraine saw Serilda, she let out a shriek and stood up so fast the chair toppled over behind her. "Serilda! You—how—"

"I don't have time to explain, but Gild can tell you everything." Serilda took Lorraine's hand into hers. "I am so sorry for all the hurt and trouble I've brought you. I promise I will do everything I can to bring Leyna back."

"What . . . what are you going to do?"

Serilda didn't answer, in part because she wasn't entirely sure.

She was going to march into the Erlking's castle. She was going to save the seven gods. Rescue her child and Lorraine's. Keep the Erlking from destroying the veil that protected the mortal realm. She was going to summon the forest folk and send the demons back to the land of the lost.

It all seemed impossible.

Nothing but a fairy tale.

But she was Wyrdith's daughter. Stories and lies. Fortune and fate.

That had to mean something.

She strode determinedly into the night, where silver clouds wisped in front of the Endless Moon and snow crunched beneath her boots. Adalheid Castle loomed over the lake, its windows glowing with firelight. Torches lined either side of the cobblestone bridge. Though the night was eerily silent, there was also a serenity to it, everything touched by the glistening snow. Her breath danced in the air. Quiet waves lapped against the shore.

She did not see the moss maidens. She did not see Erlen's monsters.

But she knew they were near. Camouflaged by the night. Stealthy as spiders, they would be gathering their weapons and supplies even now.

Serilda was not alone.

She would have gone anyway, even if she were.

Beyond those castle gates, Perchta and the Erlking had her child. They had Leyna. They had the seven gods . . . including her mother. The gatehouse yawned open, beckoning to her. The courtyard beyond was like a painting, the gray stone walls lit by moonlight, the new-fallen snow pristine but for two sets of footprints: Perchta's and Leyna's.

Squeezing her hands into fists, she marched over the drawbridge. The keep loomed before her, every ledge dusted in snow. The courtyard glistened like a dream. She could hear the quiet snuffling of horses in the stables. The crackle of the torches set into the walls.

She did not care to be stealthy. She wanted to bring attention to herself. Tonight, she was the distraction.

But so far, there was no one to distract.

She was halfway to the keep when she heard a baby's keening cry, distant, but distressed enough that it made Serilda's chest ache.

She ran toward the sound, certain that it had not come from inside the keep, but rather around toward the gardens. So many times she had run from those gardens. Run from this castle, with its monsters and haunts. She would not run anymore.

This time, she wanted the Erlking to know that she was coming for him.

Chapter Fifty-Three

The dark ones were gathered in the menagerie, along with countless monsters, their torches casting shadows of giant cages against the castle walls. No one had spotted Serilda yet as she made her way through the gardens, with their snow-covered trees and hedges. They were all too focused on dragging seven beasts from their captivity, each one held with golden chains.

Leyna stood off to the side, bouncing and shushing the newborn baby, but the child refused to be mollified.

"Would you quiet her down?" snapped Perchta, connecting the chains between the gryphon and the tatzelwurm. Freydon and Hulda.

"I'm trying," said Leyna, sounding desperate. "She's hungry. You haven't fed her yet!"

"It is all right, my love," said the Erlking, taking the chains from the huntress. "Tend to our child. She will not keep forever, and there is no shame in enjoying your first night with her."

"I am not *ashamed*," muttered Perchta. "I just hadn't expected a newborn to be such a nuisance. The others you gave me were far more self-reliant."

Despite her griping, she did take the child from Leyna. Perchta's expression softened as she peered into the baby's wailing face, and the bite was gone from her voice when she spoke again. "They are odd, these little mortals. So helpless."

Leyna watched apprehensively, looking like she wanted to snatch the child back. As if she expected Perchta to march over to the cages and feed the infant to the wyvern.

She only relaxed when Perchta lowered her bodice for the baby to suckle at her breast.

Watching from behind a hedge, Serilda's jaw tightened. *She* was that little girl's mother. She should have been feeding her, caring for her, rocking her in protective arms.

Everything about this was wrong, wrong, wrong.

She steeled herself and was about to march into the menagerie when something sharp pressed against her back.

She gasped and froze.

"Hello, little spirit," cooed a voice. "What are you doing, loitering about?"

Serilda turned her head just enough to see the dark one. A hunter, with golden brown skin and a face like poetry. But Serilda had grown accustomed to the demons' unnatural beauty, and now she saw only what lay beneath. Cruelty and selfishness and greed.

"I heard the Erlking was throwing a ball," said Serilda. "Thought my invitation got lost. Those nachtkrapp are so unreliable."

"Always with the clever stories. Go on." The hunter grabbed Serilda's arm but kept his dagger at Serilda's back as he shoved her forward onto the menagerie's lawn. "Your Grim, that annoying mortal has graced us with her presence yet again."

The gathered dark ones glanced their way. Curious. Amused. Annoyed. Serilda didn't care. She glowered at the Erlking, chin lifted.

"Somehow, I am not surprised," he said. "Always so stubborn, miller's daughter."

"I have unfinished business," said Serilda. She pointed at Perchta. "That child belongs to me."

Perchta laughed. "What a brave little spirit. I can almost see what you liked about her."

"She does have her charms," muttered the Erlking.

The baby had fallen asleep in Perchta's arms, eyes closed and small mouth hanging open. The sight made everything in Serilda cry out with wanting.

Perchta crooked a finger to Leyna, who scurried forward, her eyes darting between the child and Serilda. But just as Perchta shifted the infant to pass her to Leyna, the baby coughed—twice—and a glob of milky spittle sprayed onto the front of Perchta's cloak.

Leyna froze, her hands outstretched to receive the child, her expression too terrified to laugh, though Serilda suspected she wanted to, deep down.

With a snarl, Perchta heaved the infant into Leyna's waiting arms, her face flushed. "Insolent child," she growled, and Serilda didn't know if she was talking about Leyna or the baby.

"Your Grim," said the hunter, still holding Serilda by the arm, "what shall I do with the mortal?"

"Let her stay," said the Erlking. "If it weren't for her, we might not have procured all seven gods. She deserves to be a part of this, does she not?"

Serilda frowned. She had expected the Erlking to do *something* at her presence. Throw her in a dungeon or bind her in chains, or something, anything, that would have taken up a bit of his precious time. She had not expected him to turn away so dismissively and strut into the center of the lawn, surrounded by the beastly gods.

It was a striking sight to see. The dark ones in all their glory. The Erlking in his black leather armor, his abundance of weapons. Perchta in her majestic red cloak, looking every bit the Alder Queen, despite having been spat upon. And all around them, seven mythical beasts. The wyvern. The basilisk. The tatzelwurm. The unicorn. The gryphon. The great black wolf. The golden raptor. Together, they seemed too glorious to be real.

"The Endless Moon has risen, O ye old gods," he said in a sardonic voice. "You are captured and chained, and should you want your freedom, I will give it in exchange for my promised wish."

"Wait—no!" said Serilda, her thoughts racing. The hunter's grip tightened when she tried to stumble forward. "You can't . . . not yet!"

The Erlking quirked a smile at her, then lifted a hand toward Perchta. "Beloved, will you join me?"

The gods watched with piercing eyes as Perchta went to stand beside the Erlking.

"For my wish," the Erlking declared, "I would have the veil between our world and the mortal realm destroyed."

"No!" cried Serilda. This could not be happening already, so soon. Didn't there need to be a ritual of some sort? A casting of black magic? Runes drawn in blood and black wine drunk from crystal goblets and chants muttered to the gray sky?

Seven beasts. Seven gods. A solstice moon and a wish.

Was that all it would take?

Her eyes darted toward the castle walls. Were the moss maidens there yet? Had they had enough time? It was too early, too soon, and with the dark one pinning her arms, she could not reach the reed whistle.

In the wake of the Erlking's wish, a silence draped itself thicker than the blanket of snow at their feet. The gods did not move, but for the occasional blink of narrowed eyes.

The Erlking cocked his head, and when he spoke again, his voice carried a new current of brutality. "Would you dare to deny me?"

The tatzelwurm rose up, pushing back on its two clawed forelegs, one still bent at an unnatural angle. Its feline ears twitched, turning inward toward the Erlking. A gash in its side was dripping emerald blood, and Serilda realized that the arrow had been removed. The one that had long kept Hulda trapped in the body of the tatzelwurm.

With an annoyed huff, the Erlking strode toward the beast. He reached for the golden chains around the tatzelwurm's throat and unraveled them, throwing them to the ground. With so many hunters gathered, he must have been confident that the gods would not attempt to escape, even with their chains undone.

"Go on," said the Erlking. "If you wish to speak to me, speak."

The tatzelwurm held his gaze, looking very much like it wanted to devour him whole.

Instead, the beast curled its long serpentine tail around its body. The transformation was quick. A blink and Serilda would have missed it, for the creature shed its beastly form and emerged a human as quickly as Serilda would peel off her cloak.

Hulda was not as tall as Wyrdith or Velos, but they were still an imposing figure, with honey-colored skin and pointed, catlike ears surrounded by tufts of speckled fur. Their eyes remained catlike, too, piercing yellow with diamond-shaped pupils. Their hands were enormous and powerful, made for labor.

"We cannot fulfill your wish as you've made it," said Hulda, as if this should have been obvious.

"I have made my wish beneath this Endless Moon," growled the Erlking. "By the laws of your own magic, you must fulfill it."

"What you have asked for," Hulda said, "is no small trifle."

The king's fingers flexed, as if he were tempted to reach for one of the swords at his hip and impale the god for nothing more than the pure enjoyment of it.

"You created the veil. I know you can undo it."

Hulda pressed their lips into a thin line. After a long moment, they responded, "The creation of the veil required a sacrifice from each of us. To destroy it will require a sacrifice as well."

"Fine," said the Erlking. "Sacrifice whatever suits you. It matters not to me."

"Not from us, Erlkönig. This wish belongs to you and your demons. The sacrifice must be yours as well."

Perchta let out a guttural laugh. "That is the problem with you gods. Always demanding a payment."

"All magic comes with a price," said Hulda. "And this is very powerful magic you are asking for."

"If you insist." Perchta gestured to the shadows. "You, human girl. Come here."

Leyna's expression flushed with horror.

Again Serilda tried to pull away from the dark one, but his grip was iron.

Slowly, uncertainly, Leyna ducked beneath the chains that connected the gryphon and the wolf, still clutching the sleeping baby in her arms.

"Give me the child," said Perchta, taking the baby from her without ceremony. She hefted the newborn in one arm, then grabbed Leyna's arm and tossed her down to her knees in the middle of the ring of gods. "There. A perfectly healthy mortal girl. Darling thing. Quite responsible. Will be terribly missed by whoever that woman was at the inn. What better sacrifice could you ask for? I'll even do the honors myself. My star, would you hold the baby?"

"No!" Serilda screamed, struggling against her captor. "You can't!"

"That will not do," said Hulda, before Perchta could pass the infant over to the Erlking. "You have no love for this mortal child, so the sacrifice would mean nothing. It must be something valuable to you. Something precious. We each gave up a bit of our magic, a piece of *ourselves* in creating the veil. If you have nothing of yourself that you would part with, then this charade is at its end. You will free us, Erlkönig."

The Erlking snarled. "But I so enjoy having you as *pets*." Nostrils flared, he faced Perchta. She looked equally frustrated by Hulda's words, but it took her a long moment to comprehend the king's unflinching expression.

The huntress straightened, her arms tightening around the baby. "*No.* I just got her! Do you know what I had to go through?"

The Erlking raised an eyebrow. "She was not easy for me to procure either, my love."

Perchta cackled. "Oh yes, how awful being wed to the little mortal. Must have been torture."

The king's lips quirked upward as he glanced at Serilda. "It had its moments."

"I don't want to give up the child. *My* child! She came from me!"

Serilda's jaw hung. Her relief at knowing that Leyna was safe, at least for the time being, was fast eclipsed by this awful, impossible conversation. "You can't. *Please.*"

The Erlking ignored her as he slid his long fingers along Perchta's arms and lightly grasped her elbows. "I hate to ask this of you, and certainly I did not think it would come to this. But if this is what the magic demands . . ."

Perchta growled and held the baby tighter, pressing her cheek against the tuft of strawberry hair. "She was meant to be a gift. From you to *me.*"

"She *is* a gift." The Erlking stroked his thumb across Perchta's cheek. "The most precious I have ever given. But, my love, you are mortal now. You wear a mortal's skin." His voice lowered. "We can make another."

A shudder overtook Serilda at the very idea of it. How could they even consider this? If Perchta had the slightest bit of motherly love, any hint of maternal instincts, this conversation would have ended before it began.

But Perchta didn't pull away.

She didn't scream at the Erlking, tell him how preposterous this was. She didn't tell the gods that they could keep their veil, so long as she could keep her child.

No. She bowed her head so that her lips flitted against the baby's brow, so unconcerned in her slumber.

Then, hardening her expression, Perchta regarded the god of labor. "Would sacrificing this child fulfill the requirement?"

"*No!*" Serilda cried. "You can't! *You can't!* Please, take me instead. Just don't hurt her, *please.*"

Hulda briefly closed their eyes, a shadow of disgust on their face. When they opened their eyes again, it was to peer at Serilda with visible regret.

"It would," said Hulda.

Serilda screamed, the sound agony and rage. She yanked her arms from the dark one's hold, his nails leaving red welts on her skin. But two more demons were upon her in an instant, holding her back. Tears clouded her vision. "No! Please—Wyrdith! She's your grandchild. You can't let them do this!"

A cry—a baby's cry—struck her like a thousand arrows. Her screaming had awoken her daughter, but everyone else was ignoring her.

Everyone but Wyrdith, the giant raptor, rattling the chains that kept it bound. Helpless.

"Don't do this," Serilda pleaded through her sobs. "Please don't do this."

"Perchta! Erlkönig!" A voice rang out across the menagerie, sharp and angry.

Serilda's ragged sobs caught in her throat.

The Erlking and the huntress turned toward the newcomer.

Gild strode purposefully through the garden gates. He did not look afraid. He looked furious, his gold-tinged eyes sparking in the torchlight.

Perchta gave a delighted laugh. "The prodigal prince returns," she said. "What a fool."

Gild did not glance at Serilda as he strode into the circle of god beasts. He kept his focus on the two dark ones before him, and the tiny infant clutched in Perchta's arms.

Leyna used the distraction to scurry backward toward the circle of gods. No one paid her any heed.

"I will be taking that child," said Gild, nodding toward the baby crying in Perchta's arms. "By the terms of a bargain struck with magic, in exchange for spinning straw into gold, Serilda's firstborn child rightfully belongs to me." He took another step forward. "I am here to claim her. You *will* give her to me."

Color flooded Perchta's cheeks. She snarled and drew back. "In exchange for spinning straw into gold?" she said mockingly, then cast a hateful snarl at Serilda. "What sort of woman would strike such a bargain?"

Serilda wanted to claw out the huntress's throat. "What sort of woman would sacrifice her baby for a god-wish?"

Perchta shook her head, as if the two were not at all comparable, then turned her attention back to Gild, eyes narrowing. "I will give you your castle back."

Gild's brow twitched. "What?"

"Your castle. Returned to its full glory on the mortal side of the veil. It shall be yours. In exchange for the child."

He blinked, speechless.

"It is your ancestral home, is it not?"

A breath of laughter escaped him. "I wouldn't know. My ancestry was stolen from me."

"Even better. Here, you can have something returned to you. All of this, for a child. More than fair."

Gild snarled. "That child is worth more than all the castles and all the treasures and all the gold in the world." He held out his arms. "Give her to me."

Magic sparked between them. Serilda could feel it, a tug in the air, a magic bargain demanding to be fulfilled. She could see Perchta fighting against it. Clutching the baby tighter, trying to back away.

But the magic was too strong. The bargain had been struck and it was unbreakable. Serilda's firstborn child *did* belong to Gild, and there was nothing Perchta could do about it.

With a furious hiss, she all but dropped the infant into Gild's arms. He stumbled in surprise, before scooping the baby against his chest, cradling her head. The baby's cries grew louder.

Gild looked shocked, as if he couldn't quite believe it had worked.

Serilda could hardly believe it herself. Desperate hope fluttered inside her, met with tenuous, wary relief.

Gild took a step back. Then another. He swallowed. "Also, the mortal girl," he said, tipping his chin toward a trembling Leyna. "She will come with me as well."

The Erlking, who had been silent through this exchange, lifted a warning eyebrow. Perchta gnashed her teeth.

"You have no more need of a governess, do you?" added Gild.

Leyna did not wait for the dark ones to answer him. With a frightened squeak, she peeled herself from the snow and ran to Gild, hiding behind him as he took another nervous step away.

A group of dark ones had clustered by the gate, hands on their weapons. Ready to stop Gild if their king demanded it.

Gild glanced at Serilda, and she could tell he was trying to retain his air of confidence, even if he wasn't entirely sure what to do now that he'd actually gotten the child.

"Go, then," spat Perchta. "You have what you came for. And we have a sacrifice to consider."

Gild did not tear his gaze from Serilda. She knew what he was wondering—could he really leave without her?

Yes, of course. He had to.

"Go," she pleaded. "Take care of her."

Gripping their daughter, he took in the Erlking. The huntress. The villains who had taken so much from him.

Adjusting the swaddling blanket around the baby, Gild slowly turned away.

He had taken a mere two steps toward the gate when Perchta let out a roar. Quick as a snake, she reached for the sword that hung at the Erlking's hip, pulled it from its scabbard, and drove it into Gild's back.

Chapter Fifty-Four

A stillness cascaded over the world.

Gild dropped to his knees, hunched over the baby. The baby who had stopped crying. Whose sudden silence was as abrupt as a lightning strike.

A muffled scream thundered inside Serilda's head.

Her body went limp. The dark ones released her and she collapsed hard to the ground. She couldn't breathe. Couldn't feel anything but a great, cavernous void opening inside her, tearing her in half.

It was Erlen's tapestry. Gild. Dying. A sword jutting from between his shoulder blades.

But the tapestry had not shown the baby in his arms, also pierced by Perchta's blade.

Also dying.

"Satisfied?" crowed Perchta, spinning around to glare at the circle of gods. "Is this enough of a sacrifice for you? Or will you dare tell me that I did not cherish this child, the first I ever birthed, the first I could ever claim as my own, when you bless mortal women every day with such a gift!" She turned furious eyes on Eostrig, the unicorn, her nostrils flared. "Finally, a child that should have belonged to me. Is *that* the sacrifice you wanted?"

"No," said Hulda, their voice strained. "This was never what we wanted."

Perchta flushed almost purple.

"But," Hulda went on, "it will serve."

The Erlking put his arm around Perchta, holding her to his side. "Then you will grant our wish," he said. "You will destroy the veil."

Serilda's thoughts churned. She couldn't understand. Why would the gods demand such a price? Why would *magic* demand such a price?

And Perchta . . .

Perchta had not loved this child. Had not cherished her baby girl. She had thrown that love away like it was nothing.

Hulda shut their eyes with a shudder. "Allow us our human forms."

A muscle twitched in the Erlking's jaw, but he nodded and six dark ones stepped forward to remove the chains from the remaining beasts. As soon as the gods were freed, they took their human forms—and the dark ones immediately threw the chains around them again, securing their wrists like shackles. The gods roared with betrayal, but the Erlking merely snorted with contempt.

"You have been allowed your human forms so you may grant my wish," he said coolly. "But you will not be given your freedom until I have what I want."

Serilda heard a voice calling her. A compassionate voice, thick with sorrow.

Wyrdith.

But Serilda could not tear her gaze away from Gild and the blood soaking into his shirt.

"Beneath the Endless Moon," said Freydon, anger lacing their voice, "by the laws of magic that bind us to this world, we grant your wish, Erlkönig."

Serilda felt a change in the air. An invisible force was pushing against her, as the heavens shimmered with powerful magic. She felt as if she were in the eye of a storm, pressure from every side threatening to suffocate her.

With no one paying attention to her, Serilda fought against the discomfort of her crushing lungs and forced herself forward, crawling on hands and knees.

"Gild," she gasped, reaching out to touch him. "Gild?"

A groan, so faint she barely heard it.

"Hold still. The sword. I'm going to . . ."

Her arms were so weak, her fingers trembling as they wrapped around the hilt.

"I'm so sorry," she said, sobbing, and pulled.

Gild gasped, but did not cry out. As soon as the sword was removed, he collapsed onto his side, still holding the bundled baby in his arms, the blanket soaked in crimson. Serilda fell over them both. She dissolved. Her child. Her baby. Dying. Or dead. Or—

A hand found her, sticky and weak. She stared at Gild, her vision bleary.

"Take . . . the ring," he croaked.

She didn't know if it was her heartbreak or the strangling magic all around her that was making her light-headed, but it took her a long time to make sense of his words. Finally, she looked down at the golden ring with his family's crest. Bloody, like everything else.

"Don't forget me," he said. "At least someone . . . won't forget me."

"Never, Gild. I could never . . ."

The light was fading from his eyes, as if he'd been clinging desperately to these last moments of life so he could speak to her one last time.

"I'm so happy . . . I met you," he said, trying to smile. "I love you. I wanted . . . to protect . . . both of you. I'm sorry."

"No, I'm sorry. I'm the one who's sorry. Gild. *Gild.*"

His eyes became unfocused. His hand fell onto the blanket.

Then, as quick as it had begun, it was over.

The magic's pressure released. Air poured back into Serilda's lungs. The sky no longer shimmered. Clouds drifted across the full moon as if nothing had happened.

And Gild and their baby were not breathing.

"It is done," gasped Freydon. Each of the seven gods groaned and collapsed to their knees.

Ignoring the weakened gods, the dark ones looked around, as if inspecting the world anew. Since the veil was already down for the Endless Moon, they would not know until sunrise if the magic had worked.

Serilda screamed. A torrent of a wail as she curled against Gild's body, her hand pressed to the back of her daughter's head. Impossibly delicate, impossibly soft, with those faint reddish curls. Serilda sobbed into the swaddling blanket, cursing demons and gods and fortune and fate.

And there she might have stayed, if the ground all around her hadn't begun to tremble.

The Erlking frowned at the shuddering castle walls. The drifts of snow flurrying from the parapets. "What is happening?"

"Verloren has been calling out to me," muttered Velos, peering up at the Erlking through weary eyes, "ever since you took me from the gates. With the use of my magic, Verloren has found me."

A crack shot across the gardens, quick and jagged, creating a tear in the earth from the base of the keep through the menagerie and out to the far wall.

"Free us," said Velos. "Let me return to my home."

The Erlking snarled. "Not until I know for sure the wish was fulfilled."

Velos shook their head. "Your distrust will end us all, Erlkönig."

The Erlking let out a pent-up roar. "When have you ever given me cause to trust you?"

"Serilda!" Hands were on her. Shaking her. Leyna? "We need to get out of here! Look!"

Serilda looked, but she didn't understand.

Beneath her, the earth groaned and started to split apart. She gasped, her fingers digging into Gild's shirt. A jagged cut tore through the snow, opening to the size of a fist beneath them. Serilda screamed, instinctively pulling Gild and the baby across the snowy ground, just as snow flurries fell into the crevasse where they had lain seconds before.

Gild did not move. Their baby did not cry.

The gash in the ground widened farther. The dark ones were tense, hands on their weapons. The gods were desperate, pleading with the demons to release them.

"Silence!" screamed the king. But there was no silence to be had. Stones were tumbling loose from the walls. The ground screeched as clay and rock and ice rubbed together and pulled apart. The Erlking looked at Perchta, who met his gaze with a fierce nod.

The king's expression hardened and he faced their court. "Let Verloren take the castle! Let it take the old gods. With the veil down, all of the mortal realm will be our kingdom!"

The dark ones cheered.

"No!" screamed Eostrig, who looked like Pusch-Grohla once more. "Erlkönig, you will not leave us like this!"

The king ignored the god, ignored them all.

"To the gates!" he declared, and the dark ones rallied at his side. The castle's monsters, those that could fly, soared into the night. The imps and hobgoblins hurried ahead of their masters, eager to escape the gash that had grown to the width of a carriage. The first outer wall of the castle gave way with a roar, tumbling across the eastern edge of the gardens.

Only then did Serilda remember, as the hunters and their court fled across the gardens.

Hand trembling, she reached for the collar of her dress and pulled out the two necklaces at her throat. One—the broken arrow that kept her tethered to this world.

The other—the whistle.

Loathing bubbled up inside of her as she pressed it to her lips and blew. The sound was piercing, louder than the splitting earth, louder than the stampeding footsteps, louder than the angry yells of the abandoned gods.

She blew and blew and let the whistle ring out like a war cry.

They came, just as they'd promised.

Dozens of warrior maidens leaped atop the crumbling castle walls or rushed in from the gates. The whistle was still echoing when the first volley of golden arrows rained down upon the escaping dark ones.

Not just moss maidens. Erlen and her monsters, too. Surging forward. Cutting through the demons with merciless brutality, golden swords and knives glinting in the moonlight.

Surprised by the ambush, the dark ones fell back in confusion. The first demon fell, tumbling into the abyss, where Verloren waited far below to claim him. His cries echoed from the darkness for ages, before finally, finally vanishing.

Parsley shouted an order, and like a well-trained army, the maidens' tactics changed. They herded the dark ones toward the ever-widening crevasse. The castle keep began to collapse inward on its compromised foundations.

Where was the Erlking? Where was Perchta?

Hatred surged through Serilda. She wanted them returned to Verloren, where they belonged. She wanted to see them fall.

There.

Perchta and the Alder King stood in the midst of the battle. His crossbow firing into the swarm of moss maidens, while Perchta drove them back with a barrage of thrown knives.

"Serilda!" screamed Leyna. "Help us!"

She started. Leyna and Erlen were working to undo the golden chains still holding the gods. Not just binding the gods together, but also keeping them leashed to a series of stakes around the menagerie, like animals around a feeding post.

Serilda forced herself to her feet, but her attention returned to the battle. The horrific screams as dozens—no, *hundreds*—of demons were sent tumbling over the jagged precipice.

But no one could get near the Erlking and the huntress.

"Serilda!" cried Wyrdith.

Serilda stumbled toward the god of stories, whose devastated eyes made Serilda want to scream. She bit back the sound and reached for the chains on Wyrdith's wrists.

"Daughter—"

"Don't," Serilda snapped. "Is this the ending you wanted? Is this what your wheel of fortune decided for me?"

Wyrdith's face crumpled. "Serilda, I—"

"I don't want to hear it. I can't . . . I can't." She bit back a sob as she managed to undo the chains. They fell to the snow with a thud, just as another wall fell, crashing into the lake.

"Go!" cried Erlen, pointing toward the courtyard. "We have to get out of here before the entire castle falls!"

Though the gods were still weak from bringing down the veil, they leaned on one another as Erlen and Leyna ushered them toward the gatehouse, toward the safety beyond the drawbridge. Only Velos and Wyrdith lingered behind.

"Serilda, come with me," said Wyrdith, reaching for Serilda's hands, but she yanked them away.

Serilda had eyes only for the Erlking and the huntress. Having used up his bolts, the Erlking switched to two long, slender swords, and Perchta now held a mace—but the moss maidens were dancing around them, just out of reach.

And the rest of the demons, the hunters and the court . . .

They were gone. The ambush had worked. Caught off guard against the moss maidens and Erlen's monsters, they had fallen easily to Gild's golden arrows. The demons had been forced back into the gash in the earth, back to the depths of Verloren.

All but two.

"Serilda, *please*," said Wyrdith.

"I'm not leaving until Perchta and the Erlking are gone."

"We will all end up in Verloren if we don't go now!" Wyrdith turned to Velos. "Can't you stop this?"

Velos's voice rumbled regretfully. "The ground is too weak, and the land of the lost has grown unstable in my absence. This castle will fall."

Serilda looked down at the bodies of Gild and their child. Crouching before them, she took the ring off Gild's finger and slipped it onto her own, as he'd asked, then scooped her baby into her arms.

Holding her for the first time.

Tears threatened to smother her again, but she fought them back as she turned to Wyrdith. "Take her, please."

Wyrdith's face crumpled as they took the still form of their grandchild into their arms.

"I will take the gold-spinner," said Velos.

Serilda rounded on the god, teeth bared. "No! You can't have him, not yet!"

But Velos gave her a kind smile and settled a hand onto her shoulder. "Their spirits are already gone. You cannot keep them here."

Horror tightened around her throat. "No, no, they can't . . ."

"I will carry his body," the god said. "So you might give him a proper burial."

Tears streamed down her cheeks as the god lifted Gild's body into their arms.

Wyrdith and Velos started after the others.

"Serilda!"

Parsley was running across the parapets, which swayed dangerously beneath her. With a grunt, she jumped, launching herself into the gardens. She struck the ground with a graceful roll and looked up, panting. "We are out of golden arrows. They are getting away—the Erlking, the huntress! What else can we use to fight them?"

Serilda spun around in time to see the Erlking and Perchta cutting their way through the forest folk that were still desperately trying to hold them back. But it was a losing fight. Without the golden arrows, they were no match for these final two demons.

Serilda scanned the menagerie, the gardens, the wide-open gates that led to the courtyard. A ferocity like she'd never felt before surged inside her. "I have an idea."

Chapter Fifty-Five

ive me two minutes," said Serilda. "Meet me at the drawbridge, and tell the rest of the moss maidens to retreat!"

"Retreat?" bellowed Parsley.

"Trust me!"

Doubt flashed over Parsley's face. Then she steeled herself and gave a firm nod. Without another word, she was gone, rushing back into battle.

Serilda hardened her resolve, made it as unbreakable as god-spun gold. Then she started to gather armfuls of the golden chains that had been used to bind the gods.

The courtyard was in turmoil when she reached it.

Pillars and walls were toppled, the cobblestone ground undulating like ocean waves. Spiderweb cracks spread through the stonework like black streaks of lightning through the powdery snow. And in the middle, running straight from the gatehouse down the center of the courtyard and underneath the crumbling keep, was a gash as wide as the drawbridge itself. Glass had shattered from the castle windows and lay in sparkling shards across the steps. The stables had collapsed in on themselves, but judging from the mass of hoofprints in the snow, someone had thought to release the animals in their rush to escape.

All except the hounds, who could be heard howling from the kennels.

Serilda reached the gatehouse, edging around the widening fault line, aware of the ice-covered stones beneath the fresh snow that would send her slipping over the edge in a blink if she wasn't careful.

She had just started to unspool the chains when she heard Parsley and Meadowsweet darting across the uneven ground.

"They're coming!" Parsley cried. "The other maidens have escaped to the lake and will swim for shore. The Erlking and Perchta are coming!"

Serilda thrust the ends of the chains at them, tripping over her words to explain her plan.

They weren't ready by the time Perchta's mad laughter reverberated off the courtyard walls, a gleeful cackle as she and the Erlking came racing in from the garden gates, practically waltzing over the stones as they dodged the crashing walls.

They weren't ready.

They had to be ready.

"Your Grim!" Serilda screamed from her place half-hidden behind the blacksmith's forge.

The Erlking glanced toward her, startled.

Serilda bared her teeth at him. "Have I told you the story of when the earth opened up and swallowed the demon king whole?"

The Erlking started to grin. He opened his mouth to speak.

Parsley and Meadowsweet emerged from their places behind the gatehouse. Each maiden holding the end of two golden chains, they wrapped them around the Erlking and Perchta, quick as foxes, and immediately started hauling them toward the crevasse.

Perchta screamed. Not in pain, not in fear, but in gleeful delight.

Serilda ran to help. She gripped the chains and heaved, feet skidding on the icy stones.

They had managed to pin one of Perchta's arms to the side, but not the other. No time. They yanked harder.

In her thrashing, Perchta managed to get hold of a dagger. She lifted it over her shoulder. Serilda's eyes widened.

As the huntress threw the knife, Serilda released the chain and lunged for Parsley, knocking her to the ground. The knife sailed over them, striking the edge of the rift and clattering down into its depths.

Meadowsweet could not hold them on her own. She cried out as the chains were ripped from her hands. In seconds, the dark ones had shoved the chains off themselves.

Something inside the keep gave a deafening crash. The rift in the earth was pulling the structure apart. The entry doors bent forward on their hinges. One wall collapsed inward. The gash in the earth grew ever wider.

The Erlking stormed toward Serilda. At her side, Parsley tried to stand and face him, but she grunted and fell back to one knee.

Perchta grabbed Meadowsweet by one of her antlers and dragged her through the snow, throwing the maiden to Serilda's other side.

They were ice and fire, the Erlking and his huntress. And they were murderous, standing over Serilda and the two moss maidens.

The Erlking's lips curled into a bruise-purple smile. "You should have gone on to Verloren long ago, miller's daughter." He pulled one of his thin swords from its scabbard. "This is the last kindness I will grant you."

"Wait!" Serilda cried, holding up her hands as he prepared to thrust the sword into her chest. "Not like this. Please. I'll . . . I'll release the arrow that keeps me tethered. I'll go willingly to Verloren. Please . . . don't throw me down there." She cast a terrified look at the hole stretching out behind her. The abyss that led to nothingness.

The Erlking snarled.

"You told me once that you aren't a villain," she said. "Have mercy."

When he hesitated, Serilda peeled back the side of the cloak. Red and fur-lined and stained with blood. She reached for the pocket on the inside lining and showed him the fletching of the arrow.

"I will let it go," she said, voice quivering. "I won't try to stop you anymore. Please . . . just let me go in peace."

"Pathetic mortal," Perchta growled. She reached for the Erlking's sword, but he lifted a hand, stopping her.

Perchta drew back in surprise.

"It is a small request," he said, "for the mortal who *was* my wife."

"Thank you," Serilda whispered. "Thank you."

Then she pulled out—not one, but two broken arrows. The same shards of gold-tipped arrows that she had once pulled from the flesh of a prince and a princess who had been cursed to suffer in their haunted castles for all eternity. Identical to the arrow that had once cursed her.

With a fierce cry, Serilda drove the arrows into the dark ones' wrists— one for the king and one for his huntress.

In the same moment, Meadowsweet lurched upward and snatched away the sword. Parsley grabbed the remaining daggers from Perchta's belt.

"Those arrows now tether you to this castle!" Serilda shouted over the roar of falling stones and yawning earth. "Your spirits no longer belong to the confines of your immortal bodies, but will be forever trapped within these walls. From this day into eternity, your souls belong to Velos, god of death!"

As the words of the curse echoed off the castle walls, their spirits separated. Their bodies—the Erlking's body, *Serilda's* body—split from their inhabiting souls and fell back onto the frozen cobblestones.

Perchta, looking again like the great huntress, with shocking white hair and skin tinged faintly blue. She screeched and lunged for Serilda.

But in the next moment, Serilda was no longer there. When she opened her eyes, she was on her back, staring up at a cloud-filled sky, a glow above where the moon refused to show its face.

She was in her body again. *Her* body.

She was mortal.

She was *alive*.

And she hurt. Everywhere, she hurt. Her legs, her thighs, her womb. Serilda groaned, placing a hand to the base of her stomach. Her flesh felt distended and unfamiliar, her muscles weak. Perchta had given birth and immediately gone into battle, treating her mortal body like it was disposable. She'd had no time to rest, and Serilda felt like her flesh had been stretched too long on a loom and was now left fragile and tired and sore, so incredibly sore.

Serilda rolled onto her side and tried to push herself up. If Perchta could be a warrior in this skin, then so could she. But before she could even grasp that this was real, and she was back in her body, and she was whole again—the ground split open beneath her. A jagged offshoot from the crevasse, burrowing across the courtyard toward the collapsed stables. Hounds were howling, Perchta was screaming, and suddenly—Serilda was falling.

She cried out, arms flailing, trying to find purchase, but there was only snow and ice and weakened stone, her legs kicking at nothing, a black emptiness reaching up to claim her.

Then hands on her arms.

Parsley on one side, Meadowsweet on the other. Their fingers crushingly tight as they hauled Serilda out of the abyss. They all fell into the snow.

Perchta and the Erlking ran for them.

"Get up! Get up!" Meadowsweet shouted, as they scrambled on the slippery stones. Serilda felt awkward in her body, with its soft belly and delicate limbs, like it was a dress that no longer fit her. But she made it to her feet. The Erlking and the huntress gave chase.

Long fingers clutched at the back of the cloak, but Serilda reached for the clasp and let it go. The Erlking stumbled back and she continued, racing for the gatehouse. The moss maidens ran ahead of her. Her feet felt leaden as they pounded against the boards of the drawbridge—until she slipped on the ice and fell.

Serilda screamed, instinctively rolling onto her back, preparing to fight.

Perchta had gathered up a handful of golden chains. She grinned at Serilda, pulling the chains taut, and Serilda could see the bloodthirsty vengeance in her eyes. She could imagine how the huntress would wrap those chains around her throat and pull tighter—tighter—

Perchta stepped over the threshold of the gatehouse, out from its shadows.

And vanished.

Serilda drew in a breath of icy-sharp air as the huntress reappeared, bewildered, back in the center of the courtyard.

Mere steps away from the crevasse.

The gatehouse gave one final groan. The wooden support beams splintered. The stones began to fall, crashing down across the drawbridge.

Serilda pushed herself up and lurched away. Parsley and Meadowsweet reached for her and they dashed over the wooden planks and onto the land bridge with its rows of shuddering torches.

A crowd waited on the shore. The townsfolk were gathered on the docks, watching, horrified. The moss maidens that had survived the battle, soaked from the icy lake water, clutched wool blankets to their shoulders. Serilda saw Leyna, gathered up in her mother's arms, Frieda at their side. She saw the seven gods. She saw Wyrdith, her mother.

And on the ground—lying side by side—she saw Gild and their daughter.

Serilda staggered off the bridge and fell to her knees. Her strength drained away from her as if a plug had been pulled from the pit of her stomach. Her heart, an erratic, strangled heartbeat, was finally back. Thumping, thumping, thumping inside her chest.

She turned back in time to see the castle fall. The keep, the towers, the walls. Swallowed up not just by the gash in the earth, but by the entire lake. Water surged into the vacuum it created. A whirlpool churning, pulling the castle into its depths. Waves crashing against what remained of the bridge.

The castle collapsed down into Verloren, taking the Erlking and his huntress with it.

Serilda watched until the destruction was over and the lake water gradually returned to a calm, steady surface.

The castle was gone.

Chapter Fifty-Six

Serilda hunched forward, sobbing. She shut her eyes. Dug her fingers into the snow until she could no longer feel them. For a long time she didn't move. Too afraid to face the reality that would tear her apart.

For a long time the wind whistled past her ears and no one spoke.

The story was over. She had won. And she had lost.

The wheel of fortune, mocking her again.

With a shudder, Serilda swiped a sleeve across her eyes and forced herself to turn around. To look at them. To see them.

Someone had thought to put a new blanket around her daughter, one that wasn't covered in blood. But that wouldn't bring color back to her lips and cheeks. That wouldn't bring life back to her perfect little face.

Erlen was crouched at Gild's side, her cadre of monsters spread around them, looking as mournful as any of the humans. Someone—perhaps Erlen—had untied the laces on Gild's tunic and pressed a clean cloth around his wound to stop the bleeding, though Serilda knew it was useless.

He was gone.

They were both already gone.

Serilda crawled toward them, ignoring the aching tenderness of her body and the icy snow that soaked through her skirts. She took the infant into her arms, held her close to her chest. The body felt cold. Too cold. Too still.

Dragging in a sorrowful breath, she looked up at the assembled gods. The seven old gods, who had stopped answering prayers a long time ago.

"I want to make a wish," she declared, in a voice as strong as she could make it. "I wish for you to bring them back. Bring Gild and my child back!"

The gods watched her, and there was pain and sympathy in their faces, but no one stirred. No one moved to answer her.

It was Wyrdith who finally knelt in front of Serilda. Before they had spoken, Serilda could feel the regret. The refusal perched on their tongue.

"No!" Serilda yelled. "Don't tell me you can't do it! It's still the Endless Moon! You have to do this!"

"My girl," murmured Wyrdith, eyes shimmering. "The wish promised on the Endless Moon was already used by the Erlking. Destroying the veil took too much of our magic. We cannot grant another wish."

Serilda screamed. A soul-searing scream that clawed at her insides. She bent over Gild, burying her face in his chest, holding their child between them. She screamed and screamed until those screams dissolved into agonized sobs.

Only then did she hear Wyrdith's words, so faint she almost missed them.

"But . . . perhaps . . . ," started the god of lies, "there might be something that Velos can do."

Hope surged through her. Serilda lifted her gaze again.

Velos's expression darkened toward Wyrdith, and they gave a strict shake of their head.

"Please," gasped Serilda. "Please don't take them from me."

Velos stepped forward. "Their spirits have already passed on. There was nothing to tether the boy to the mortal realm, and I cannot break the bond between the boy and the child that was forged through the bargain you struck. The child is his, in death . . . as in life. I am sorry."

"I won't accept that! You brought back Perchta, why can't you bring him back, too? There is a vessel here, right here." She placed a hand on Gild's chest. "So bring him back!"

"A vessel, yes, but . . . in order to summon a spirit to the mortal realm, one must speak their true name." Velos sighed. "I wish I could help you, after all you have done for us. But I cannot. Without a name, he will not even be able to pass through the gates on the Mourning Moon, as most spirits can. I am sorry. But he can never leave."

Serilda gaped at Velos. At Wyrdith. At the gathered gods and the townsfolk, Erlen and the monsters, Leyna and her friends. No one could help her.

The horrible truth of the Erlking's curse struck her in a way she'd never understood before. It wasn't just about erasing Gild and his family from history. It wasn't just about taking away his memories so he would never know who he had been or the love he'd had.

It was a cruelty that would last forever. Even if the prince did manage to untether himself from the castle, to become mortal, to eventually die and pass into the land of the lost . . . his spirit could never return. He would be in Verloren forever. Unremembered, unloved.

She gazed at Erlen, and realized that the curse would affect her in the same way. Three hundred years old, and still so young and fearless. Trapped in an unjust destiny, all for the Erlking's vengeance.

"His name is Gild," Serilda said weakly, returning her attention to Velos. "The prince of Adalheid. Vergoldetgeist—the Gilded Ghost. How many names do you need?"

Velos shook their head. "None of those are his true name."

"But this isn't fair. He was cursed. The Erlking stole his name! No one knows what it was . . . not even you!"

"That is true," said Velos, "but the magic would answer if you spoke true."

Serilda sagged. She studied Gild's face, too pale beneath his wash of freckles. His hair and skin smeared in blood. Would she really never see his mischievous smile again? Never know that impish laugh or witness that particular glint in his eye when he was about to do something he knew she wouldn't approve of?

"I love him," she whispered. "And I never told him."

"I am sorry," said Velos, "but there is nothing you can do. Let them be at peace now."

She smoothed a lock of hair back from Gild's brow, then peered into the face of her child. Who she had never had a chance to know. Who she hadn't even given a name to.

The baby was tied to Gild. If she could save Gild, she could save them both.

But she couldn't.

She didn't know his true name.

"Hulda?" she said, her voice breaking. "You blessed him. You blessed his whole family. Surely, of anyone, you must know his name?"

But Hulda shook their head. "The Erlking's curse was complete. The name was erased even from the memories of the gods."

"But it can't be gone. Something always lives on, doesn't it? A legend, a myth . . . a truth, buried in the past." She looked at Wyrdith. "That's what you said. When all is forgotten by history, a good story can still live on, can live forever. Well, this *is* a great story. A prince who fought against the dark ones and the great huntress, who bound himself to an unborn child, who saved a miller's daughter, who . . . who . . ." She sobbed again. "Who was blessed by Hulda."

As tears overtook her again, those words echoed in her thoughts.

Blessed by Hulda.

A gasp escaped her. Serilda went still. "A prince blessed by Hulda. A family who ruled over a prosperous land, who lived in a castle by a lake, in the northern lands, who . . ."

Her heart beat faster, becoming erratic. "'Hardworking Stiltskin and the Northern Prince,'" she murmured. "The story was inspired by his ancestors. This was the kingdom they founded. That's why Hulda was his patron deity, and the tatzelwurm their symbol, and"—she took in the ring on her finger—"the letter *R*. For Rumpel and . . ." Clutching her child in her arms, Serilda climbed to her feet. "Rumpelstiltskin," she said. "The family name was Rumpelstiltskin."

She felt it then—that tug of magic. Wind whistling past her ears. The air sparking against her skin. The pressure, like her breath was being dragged from her lungs. A panicky moment in which she couldn't breathe.

Then it was over, and she could see it in the eyes around her.

"I remember," whispered Hulda. "I remember giving my blessing. And the redheaded boy, a precocious, troublemaking thing. I gave him the gift of spinning, because I hoped it would imbue him with a stronger work ethic. And the little girl . . . given the gift of weaving. I remember them both, and all their ancestors before."

A startled, hopeful cry fell from Serilda as she faced Velos. "That's it, then. Rumpelstiltskin! Now please—*please*—"

But she didn't finish. Already, she could see the refusal etched into the god's face.

"What? *Why?*"

"You have given his family name," said the god. "What is *his* name?"

She let out a frustrated growl. "I don't know! That story told the start of his lineage, *hundreds* of years before he was even born! How should I know his full name?"

"Wait!" It was Frieda who called out. The librarian was gripping Leyna's hand, and pressing her other palm to her forehead. "Wait," she said again. "I've read about this family. In those books I showed you, remember? When you came to the library?"

Serilda shook her head. "They were blank. Everything was . . ." She trailed off. *No.* They wouldn't be blank. Not anymore. They would be full. Full of history. Full of a powerful and respected dynasty—the family who had ruled over this city and the northern lands for centuries.

"It's baffled scholars for ages," said Frieda. "How the family died out suddenly three hundred years—"

"The prince," said Serilda, hardly daring to hope again. "Do you remember the name of the prince?"

Frieda considered the question. "They call him the lost heir," she finally said. "Ermengild? I . . . I think his name was Ermengild."

Serilda turned back to Velos.

The god of death gave her a slow nod. "Who would you summon?"

She licked her lips and steeled herself, afraid that it wouldn't work if her voice trembled. "I would have you bring back Ermengild Rumpelstiltskin, prince of Adalheid. Gold-spinner. Hulda-blessed." She hesitated, before adding, "Poltergeist."

Velos gave her a look that was almost proud. "You have spoken true."

The god of death raised their lantern. The flame inside glowed brighter.

Serilda held her breath. Too scared to hope. Feeling like she would shatter into a thousand brittle pieces if she dared.

And then—a baby's cry.

She gasped and looked down at the tiny bundle in her arms.

Her child was wailing. All pink cheeks and flailing hands.

Serilda was so surprised she nearly dropped her, and every person in the crowd jumped forward as if they could catch the child themselves.

She started to laugh. Then every emotion poured out of her as she squeezed her daughter against her chest, sobbing and shaking and afraid to believe, to trust this was real—

"Serilda?"

She spun around. Gild was sitting up, staring at her. He looked half dead still. Pale and wounded, one hand pressed to his chest, his face pinched, even as he tried to smile.

"After all that . . . please don't drop our child."

Her laughter continued, uncontrollable, as she fell to her knees. "I'm sorry," she said. "I'll be more careful. I'll be—Gild. You're alive! And you aren't cursed and I'm not cursed and our baby—and the Erlking and—"

"Too much," he groaned. "Slow down."

She couldn't stop crying. Couldn't stop laughing. The child wouldn't stop wailing. Serilda knew she would need to be fed soon, and bathed, and loved—loved so very much.

But first . . .

"I love you, Gild," she said, pressing a hand to his face. "I love you."

Though still weary, his grin was brilliant. "I love you, too, storyteller." His gaze found Erlen, seconds before she joined their embrace. "I even love you, Alder Queen."

"You have your moments," said Erlen, not trying to hide the fact that she was crying, too. "Do you think we can figure out *my* name?"

"I'm sure we can," said Serilda. "We'll have Frieda check the books in the library."

"And what about this little girl?" said Gild, rubbing a thumb across the baby's wrinkled, blotchy face. "I love her, too. I can't even believe it's possible. The noise she's making right now is the worst thing I've ever heard, and I lived in a castle with a screaming bazaloshtsh. But still . . . I love her so much."

The sun surpassed the horizon, chasing away the midwinter chill. Serilda kissed Gild, and she kissed her daughter, and she kissed Leyna and Erlen and then laughed when Erlen made a face and swiped it away. Serilda could have gone on kissing every single person in Adalheid, except Lorraine chose that moment to suggest they all go to the inn and warm their toes by the fire—even the gods were welcome.

Serilda helped Gild to his feet, beaming. "What should we name her?"

"No idea. I've never gotten to name anyone before. Seems like a big responsibility, especially now that we know how powerful a name can be."

Their daughter's cries quieted as Serilda rocked her. "We'll think of something," she said, in awe at the tender way Gild rubbed one knuckle along the baby's flushed cheek.

Then he grinned and pulled Serilda close, their brows pressed together, their child cradled between them. "Whatever name we choose," he said, "I guarantee it will never be forgotten."

There is the end of my tale, how it happened in truth.

But I see you are unsatisfied. That is the plight for us storytellers, to know that the story is never finished, our listeners never content.

Hush, now. I wish to tell you a different story, and perhaps if you listen closely, you will hear the answers to your questions.

I trust you have heard of the great tapestry maker, famous throughout Tulvask? Her most acclaimed work hangs even now in a Verenese university. People travel from all over the world to admire it, for it is a great work of art—the pinnacle of craftsmanship and skill. Its subject was considered most unique when it was first revealed, though many artisans have attempted to replicate it since.

You have not seen the tapestry? Allow me to paint you a picture.

Imagine a flourishing city beside a crystalline lake. The townsfolk are enjoying a celebration—New Year's Day, perhaps. There are streamers hung over the streets and baskets overflowing with spring flowers, despite the snow still on the ground. There are the mayor and her wife leading a waltz across the docks. And not far away, a giddy child dancing with—of all things—a hobgoblin.

Ah yes. You are surprised. So is everyone when they finally look. When they finally see. You thought it was only half-timbered buildings and vibrantly painted doors, merry townsfolk and their simple lives. But now you notice the drude peering around a chimney. The nachtkrapp hidden among the ravens. Through the public house window, two moss maidens drinking ale.

Look closer still and you might find yourself making some unusual interpretations as to who these simple townsfolk are. Certainly, the scholars have had their say, but what of you?

Could that be Hulda sitting at the spinning wheel in the background? Could the farmer with a sickle over one shoulder be none other than Freydon? Could the archer with the quiver of arrows be Tyrr? The cloaked figure holding the lantern must be

Velos, and the out-of-place sailor could be Solvilde, and yes, there is Eostrig in that little garden, looking strangely similar to the mythical Pusch-Grobla. The bard with the golden quill? Wyrdith, naturally.

Remarkable, really. You see now why the tapestry was heralded as such a treasure when it was first revealed, how it ushered in an entirely new era in artistry and iconography. Why, to show the seven gods not only among the mortal realm, but interacting with humans? To show the townsfolk no longer afraid of monsters, but welcoming them, befriending them?

It was a novelty in its time, one that is sure to be studied for generations to come.

Yes—you might ask—but what of these four figures, the ones standing in the midst of the revelry? The ones lit by a radiant sunbeam? Surely they must be important, to be given such a place of prominence. But who are they?

Ah, my young scholar. You see now why the tapestry continues to bewilder. There are too many theories to count, and this mystery has yet to be solved.

A man. A woman. A child. A baby.

The most obvious assumption is that these are the lord and the lady of the village, along with their two children, presiding over the festival.

But of the four, only one—the child, a little girl with golden hair—wears a crown atop her head.

The man and the woman wear simpler garb. A pale tunic, a gray traveling cloak.

And her strange eyes—we mustn't forget that. It is easy to miss at first, the detail is so small. But do you see it now? The touch of gold? Do they look like wheels to you? I've always thought so myself, but what can it mean?

Look closer still.

The baby has those golden eyes, too.

Strangely enough, so does the god of stories.

Maybe that is the message the artist wished to convey. Human, god, monster— we are all the victims of fate and fortune. Whether or not the great wheel will land in our favor, only time will tell.

Or maybe that is not the message at all.

Maybe we are asking the wrong questions.

Ask instead, why does everyone look so peaceful, so cheerful, so content?

Why do the man and woman gaze at each other with such affection?

Why did the artist, after creating such a masterpiece, sign the piece only with an R entwined with a tatzelwurm? An artist's seal that has not been seen before nor since.

I do not have these answers. Perhaps they will never be known.

Perhaps you think this tale is false, and I will not try to persuade you otherwise. For every great story has a little bit of truth in it, and a little bit of make-believe.

I leave you with one final truth . . . or one final lie . . . and you shall decide which is which.

That family? That town? Those monsters and gods?

They all lived happily to the end of their days.

Acknowledgments

Oh, my heart! I have so much gratitude for everyone who has helped bring this book and story to life. Among them:

The all-stars at Jill Grinberg Literary Management: Jill Grinberg, Katelyn Detweiler, Sam Farkas, Denise Page, and Sophia Seidner.

The phenomenal team at Macmillan Children's Publishing Group—Liz Szabla, Johanna Allen, Robby Brown, Mariel Dawson, Rich Deas, Sara Elroubi, Jean Feiwel, Carlee Maurier, Megan McDonald, Katie Quinn, Morgan Rath, Dawn Ryan, Helen Seachrist, Naheid Shahsamand, Jordin Streeter, Mary Van Akin, Kim Waymer, and the sales reps and production team who help bring books to readers everywhere.

My incredible copyeditor Anne Heausler.

My immensely talented audiobook narrator Rebecca Soler.

My German cultural guru Regina Louis.

My German pronunciation expert Ezra Hughes.

My brilliant critique partner Tamara Moss.

My assistant and podcasting accomplice Joanne Levy.

My local writing group: Kendare Blake, Martha Brockenbrough, Arnée Flores, Tara Goedjen, Corry L. Lee, Nova McBee, Lish McBride, Margaret Owen, Sajni Patel (we miss you!), and Rori Shay.

Jesse, Delaney, Sloane, and all my family and loved ones. Thank you for years of support, laughter, adventures, and joy.

And you, Reader. Thank you for joining me on this journey and letting me share my stories with you. It is an honor that I hope never to take for granted.